Increm

Paperback \

© 2018 by Ge
ISBN: 978-0-9

Published in the USA by LL-Publications 2018
www.ll-publications.com
PO Box 542
Bedford
Texas 76095

Edited by Billye Johnson
Book layout and typesetting by jimandzetta.com
Cover design by jimandzetta.com

ARIA: Left Luggage is a work of fiction. The names, characters, and incidents are entirely the work of the author's imagination. Any resemblance to actual persons, living or dead, or events, is entirely coincidental.

Feb 2019

Praise for Geoff Nelder's Books

Nelder's dialogue is witty, snarky and fun.
– Paul Goodspeed

The plot thickens, of course. This is expected from an excellent author like Geoff Nelder. "Humor delightful, and drama suspenseful."
– Martin Lamberti (International circus entertainer)

"Nelder's ingeniously crafted stories have the feel of MR James between their luscious lines."
– M. Kenyon Charboneaux –
Horror tutor and author of BLOOD KISS

"I've always found Geoff's work both inspirational and brilliant. I know that whenever I pick up one of his works I'm in for a damned good read. When I learned that I'd be sharing a place with him in the 'ESCAPE VELOCITY ANTHOLOGY', I knew I was in very good company indeed. For those who've never read any of his works before, welcome to the Geoff Nelder club."
—Mark Iles, author of
THE DARKENING STARS series.

"Interesting characters combined with a skilfully fed-in hint of weirdness."
– Jaine Fenn - the HIDDEN EMPIRE series.

"Geoff Nelder inhabits science fiction just as other people inhabit their clothes."
– Jon Courtenay Grimwood
- FELAHEEN, PASHAZADE AND
END OF THE WORLD BLUES

CONTENTS

Introduction

These twenty-five tales from Geoff Nelder have increment as a theme.

INCREMENT:

Noun–an increase or addition, especially one of a series on a fixed scale.

Synonyms: increase, addition, gain, augmentation, step up, supplement, addendum, adjunct, accretion, boost, enhancement.

Verb–cause a discrete increase in.

Mathematically the difference can be negative–decremental.

For example a pothole doubles in size every day, a meteorite hits the same house daily at the same time, or a heavy leather-bound book on the top shelf teeters closer to toppling at each library visit. A sound is heard all over the Earth, but more worrying, it gets louder each day. A couple of astronauts crash land on an ocean planet (apparently) and incrementally sink.

A few stories are more mental than incremental, you'll see.

Some of the stories have won awards and have been published before, but most of the wordage is new and drawn together for a common theme. I do not apologise for the mix of genres in this collection. I write as the muse takes me and only afterwards am I asked, is it hard SF, bizarre, horror? You have a smorgasbord of fantasy, science fiction and speculative in your hands.

Notes about the stories are at the back along with copyright information.

POTHOLE

DAY 1

Bikekid Madrid@mateo: Hey, Zoe, I bunny-hopped a pothole today. Only the size of a plate but it could've thrown me

Poetess1987@Zoe: Hi, Mateo. Where?

@mateo: Ave Albufeira on Madrid outskirts

@Zoe: Report on that app Fillthatpothole

@mateo: *Si. Reparar el bache* I'll go tomorrow and take a photo. Measure it, too

DAY 2

@mateo: Hola, Zoe. See photo. This hole is twice the size it was before. It's 40 cm. I've sent it off. See what they say. Meet tonight at Ocho y Medio

@Zoe: Right but if I'm gonna go all Goth for it so are you. BTW how deep is that hole?

@mateo: I cannot tell, it's black

DAY 3

@mateo: great night. Hope your landlady wasn't mad

@Zoe: She's threatening to phone dad all the way in New Jersey. How's your hole?

@mateo: Escape your lecture. Come see it with me now

Zoe saw Mateo's red mountain bike leaning against an ancient, gnarled tree. She parked her own cycle on its kickstand and admired the view. A stark blue sky contrasted with the maquis vegetation of dotted scrub in ochre soil. The landscape appeared flat although on closer scrutiny the horizon undulated. Looking back at Madrid, the modern spaceship-puncturing of the atmosphere by the Quattro Torres was balanced by the traditional curved roof and bell towers of the Almudena Cathedral. She'd better pay attention to Mateo's discovery even though it was not likely to be signi—what on Earth?

She shook her head sending black curls into a dance. She crouched down to finger the edge of the perfect circle. "It's nearly a metre across, and you're right about it being black." She snatched back her hand when tingling tickled her fingers. She frowned, but pressed on. "I'm dropping this stone in."

Mateo, nineteen-years of tall and lanky, leaned over the abyss. "Just a minute while I set my stopwatch app. What's the formula? A metre a second?"

"About five metres in the first second. Twenty after two seconds. Roughly five times the square of the seconds."

"Always the clever one with physics, Zoe."

She flashed a grin at him. "That's why you want me, isn't it?"

His teeth revealed a gap between his front teeth through which he worked chewing gum. "What are you going to drop?"

"It's just a fragment of road. This lane is a disgrace, good job no one uses it, except—"

"Fearless cyclists like me?"

She stood and held out her arm, noting the absence of static, or whatever at that height. "Three, two, one, go!"

They both stared at the stopwatch app on his phone, their mouths opening wider with every ten seconds without hearing the stone land. She dared not speak in case they missed the telltale sound.

Zoe spoke first. "That's a minute. It's now over fifteen kilometres down. We'd not hear it anyway."

Mateo laughed at her. "*Si*? Not that it's just a sink hole and it's fallen into soft sand a few metres down?"

She smiled, her plump lips curling as she collected more sensible answers. "Maybe there are old mineral workings in the area, or there could be subsidence from a broken sewer or even a geological fault line."

Mateo agreed. "You could check out the latest tremor on that Did-the-earth-move-for-you site."

She tapped at her phone like a bird pecking at crumbs. "Did you know this road was lottery-funded to lead to an observatory up there?"

"Earthquake?"

"They didn't finish it. Shame. Okay, okay...maybe a tremor a few days ago. Hey, I felt one then!"

Withered brown leaves drifted down from the tree. A green lizard scampered between Mateo's feet. He'd never seen a reptile's legs blur like an egg-beater before. He knelt down at the hole. The edge was remarkably smooth and..."Yes, the hole is widening. I can feel it, tremoring? Is that a word in English?"

She flicked the metal tape measure across the hole. "Trembling. Eighty-five centimetres. Better find a board to put over it to stop other cyclists falling into it."

He scrabbled around in the road edge and pulled out a battered No-Entry sign. "That's double yesterday's size."

He placed the circular metal over the hole. "Should we be putting a no-entry notice into this entrance? Oops, too small, hey look at it go!"

The sign must have been just a millimetre smaller than the circular hole and vibrated as it slowly dropped down. "Look, Zoe, it's hovering. No, it's disintegrating."

She leaned over watching the crumbling sign rock a dance as it tried to resist falling. She daringly put her hand to the edge. "Air pressure, you can feel the displaced air coming up as the sign goes down. We should've stuck a LED light on it. Ow!" She snatched her hand back examining it for burn marks., finding none.

Mateo leapt up, ran to his bike and rushed back. He turned on a thumb-sized bike light and used his chewing gum as an adhesive. Before Zoe could stop him he reached over and dropped the light in the middle of the no-go sign. "No, don't tilt! Ah, it's all right, down it goes."

His fingers probed the edge as he watched his experiment oscillate downwards. He jumped back and shook himself. They exchanged knowing glances.

"I'm surprised at you, Mateo," Zoe said, stroking his back as if her were her cat. "You've sacrificed your only front light in the cause of science. Is it speeding up its descent?"

"Think so. I should've put your phone on it instead with the line-of-sight app running with mine."

Zoe checked her fluorescent green watch. "Ten seconds and we can still see not only the light but the circular hole. It's like a well."

"Maybe it *is* a well."

"As in maybe it was a well and this road just happened to be built across it? Possible I sup—hey, the edge is vibrating, moving. I've never heard of wells that expand. Mateo, you *did* report this?"

They cycled two kilometres before finding a board big enough to cover the hole. It was white with the blue square and ring of European Union stars, declaring the funding for the observatory and road. It took Mateo three bangs with a rock to de-nail the board from its wooden posts. He muttered about "greater need" as they carried the board back up the lane to the hole.

They threw it over the hole, which took a big chunk out of it as if it was a giant worm eating a biscuit.

Zoe rubbed grit off her hands. "Should have realized it'd do that. Well, I really must go to uni tomorrow, Spanish and Probability Theory then work at the Bistro at the weekend. I can't get back here for three days."

"Same here, re-sitting Construction and Italian."

"Just what we need, more Roman aqueducts. Here, Monday?"

DAY 6 (3 DAYS LATER)

"It's gone!" croaked Mateo, when shock abated for any kind of speech.

Zoe played with the metal tape measure, pulling it out and letting it snap back in. "It's now the width of the road. Um, I want to be exact, take the end of the measure."

He sidestepped off the hot tarmac onto the baked soil sprinkled with a living salad of herbs and chickweeds. Zoe saw him stretching up and over to peer into the hole.

She called out, "Three metres twenty. You said it was ten centimetres six days ago, right?"

"Right, so..."

"It's doubled in diameter every day. Hey the hole is eating the tape."

Mateo let go the tape, which started its rapid journey back into Zoe's hand. An experience that caused pain the first time so she threw it away from the hole so the retraction caused the metal holder to spin. She watched it while Mateo snorted a laugh in embarrassment.

"Sorry, Zoe, just fooling and we don't know it actually doubled daily, the road might have subsided two metres just before we arrived today."

She looked up to the nearest lamppost, intending to glue a camera in place. Dismissed it because if she was right, that post would be gone by tomorrow. As her brain rattled through possibilities, a gust of wind blew sand across the tarmac and vanished into the hole.

As if he'd read her mind, Mateo strode to the next nearest pole. "I brought a spare cam-phone, if I give you a leg up, tape it, will you?"

"Okay, but afterwards, I'm phoning the Guardia Civil. It's dangerous and if I'm right about the doubling, we'll have to move house soon."

Mateo's eyebrows danced in disbelief. "I live five kilometres away! The Guardia won't even come out here until someone falls down the hole. Ah, that's what you're going to tell them. Sneaky. I like it."

She shook her head sending a forgotten hairgrip in a parabolic flight up then into the hole, never to be seen again. "I don't like having to say that, but this is too darn dangerous to be left up to us. Just suppose it doesn't stop doubling in diameter every day?"

Mateo looked up in the air as if looking for evidence of the vertical extension of the hole into the blue. A passing cloud could be eaten. Meanwhile, Zoe used a spreadsheet on her phone to calculate.

"Right, the hole would swallow both our Madrid homes by Friday after next, seventeen days after you first saw it. Six kilometres. The whole of Madrid the day after."

"What?" He kicked a stone in the hole as if to slow it down.

"Exponential growth, Mateo, like population growth was thought to be by Malthus in 1798, although—"

"What about the whole of Spain? We are in the centre, *Si*?"

"Oh, the borders of Spain will be fine until another week

passes. Day twenty-four, give or take twelve hours. Two weeks and five days from now."

Mateo pulled at his own black hair. "You're assuming it grows at a constant rate."

"No, doubling daily. Yes, that's an assumption. It could slow down, stop—"

"Or, speed up?"

Mateo picked up a discarded coke can, probably one of his, peered into it then jerked his head back as a scorpion escaped. Both can and insect fell onto the hot, tacky tarmac. "It's all right for you, Zoe, your relatives are in America, whereas mine..." He waved his arms in the northerly direction of Madrid. Heat haze befuddled details but life went on as if a hole wasn't creeping towards them.

She peered at the city too. "Mateo, how much flight money can you get your hands on? Hopefully, the hole will wear itself out or some clever scientist will figure and plug it before—let's see—twenty-two days from now, when the whole planet will be gone."

"It's just a sinkhole that hasn't finished sinking. I can afford only a bus to Barcelona. What, if there are more holes? Won't that make a paella out of your calculations?"

"Yes." She frowned at her phone with her thumbs a blur. "Checking news. Ah, must look at our antipodal. Meantime Mateo, book a trip quick. Use your phone to book a flight to JFK. I'll do mine. We'll go tomorrow in case there's panic. I shouldn't have told the Guardia Civil to come straight away. I can't hear them, can you?"

They both looked up from their phones, shook heads and continued.

Mateo laughed like a horse. "Seven hundred euros! Impossible for me."

"I'll pay, you dolt. Or my dad will—eventually. There's an Iberia flight at 0905. Tell you what, I'll buy two seats now, fill in the details tonight for online check-in. Just carry-on luggage. Meanwhile..."

"What details and what's antipedalling?" He was bent over, phone in one hand and a stick in the other, upturning stones in front of the scorpion. "I can't take your money, though I'd pay it back...assuming the hole doesn't get me first."

"Yes, there is something going on at the antipodal point from us!" She showed him her phone—Google map of New Zealand. "Not sure what's happening there. No big city, just a village called Weber."

He pointed at her phone. "Is there a tall thin hill down there, the opposite of this hole?"

"It's the local sheep farmer who sent a photo of their hole to the online newspaper. She's worried the sinkhole will take her barn. By now it's probably gone. Picture's poor, too pixellated." She took the phone back and looked at her own snaps of their hole. They too were fuzzy, as if while their eyes and brain interpolated missing detail the camera couldn't.

A tremor sent them to the ground. Zoe grazed her knees, but at least her yellow Lycra cycling shorts hadn't torn. She looked through a haze of dancing motes at the city. Still there, for now.

Mateo was the first to leap to his feet. "*Quizás* we should get farther from the hole." He kicked the scorpion's can at the hole. Instead of falling in like the stones and road sign, it disappeared in a puff of dust. "Whoa, that tremor's changed the hole."

They both threw stones, which all vanished when passing the edge. "It's a kind of event horizon," Zoe said, "It's a hole that's black, but not a black hole. If this was a real event horizon and that a real black hole, its gravity would pull us, our bikes and Madrid into it, and our time would be really slow."

"Suppose it is slow for someone else looking at us, but it can't be because our phones still work at the right speed. By the way, I can't go to America."

Zoe threw a stone in the air over the hole. It didn't fall down, it vanished. If only the rain in Spain really did fall on the plain, then they'd have clouds to look for the hole extension. "Can I see a black spot in the blue up there? Looking straight across the hole we can see the landscape clearly–it's not like a black column going up, so photons can pass through it. Odd. She took several steps back, crushing and releasing wild Thyme aromas and threw another stone making sure it went higher than three metres. It landed in the field on the other side, sending up dust. Hey, the hole is growing upwards at the same height as it is wide. Why not to the States? You have a crime record?"

He reached for his bike. "No passport. My identity card is enough for anywhere in mainland Europe."

Zoe checked her bike over and pulled leaves out of the spokes. "You watched me pay for both our tickets!" She stamped a foot and glared at him.

"*Lo siento.* I'll pay you back, eventually. You go home. I should tell my family and friends to get away too."

"We're in this together, Mateo. Where's Europe's farthest east airport?"

"Could be Estonia, Latvia, but if we go to Romania and have lots of money, we could speed across the Black Sea to Georgia."

Both cycling but slowly, meandering on the road to Madrid, Zoe used her phone one-handed. "I've cancelled JFK, got some back. If we get to Georgia, the hole will catch us in twenty days, whereas if we'd gone to Japan it would have given us another day."

"Assuming the world would still be in one piece, though a ring doughnut." He laughed, this time more like a dog. He did a wheelie to lighten his mood. "It's all a joke though, isn't it? Just a mine or sewer collapse. A sinkhole."

"Yes, a torus. Ring doughnut is a good description. With an equal hole growing at its antipodal point? And the puffing into nothing of anything over... hey, we'd better tell the airport. Suppose an airplane—"

His brakes screamed as he stopped. "*Si!* We should warn them, if they'll take notice, but shouldn't we fly to Bucharest first?"

"Today. I'll book flights for both of us. Flying to America might have taken us over the hole, or at least one wing." She tapped for a minute or so. "Tomorrow evening, seven o'clock flight via Blue Air. See you at check-in at five thirty. Bring chargers, money, ID, et cetera. I suppose you'll need to tell your folks something?"

"They might try and stop me. I'll phone them from Georgia, if we find somewhere to land with no passport for me."

DAY 7

"Mateo, I thought you'd be packing this morning."

He grinned, was about to lean his bike against the olive tree, but the hole was frighteningly close. The hole was twice as wide, eating into sandy dirt. "Packed my bag last night and like you I needed to see if it really was expanding."

"Obvs it is, but tricky to measure now the hole is spreading upwards. Can you smell ozone?"

"Ah, I've brought Papá's laser measure. I aim it from the edge here to over there. Six thirty, no, six twenty-eight. No, six thirty-five, four, six. About that."

"Yeah, good to have precision. Whatever, it's doubled from yesterday. We do right to escape this evening."

Mateo continued pointing his measurer at the hole. "*Si*, but it's hard with family. I told my mother but she assumes I'm in dreamland."

She hugged him. "All we're doing is buying a few days—two at most, in the hope it either stops or some genius saves the planet. I know it's selfish but best not to tell too many people in case they can't handle it."

"You've told the Guardia Civil, or did you retract your statement?"

They both looked down the lane towards Madrid. "I guess they were just too busy and waiting for another report before doing anything. Did you bring your webcam?"

He grinned. "I installed it at my aunt's top-floor apartment. It's five kilometres away. I could see the end of the lane and it should pick up the hole in time."

"Is it good enough?"

"Seven twenty p HD. Got it for my birthday last month. Latest. I can zoom with an app on my phone." They put a pole across the road and leant a different red stop sign against it at the town outskirts.

Day 8

Their holiday apartment in the ancient port town of Kamakura smelled of lemons, a pleasant change to the musty taxi that brought them there from the station after the twenty-hour flight to Tokyo. Zoe had to pay for a three-day minimum stay, but at three-hundred euros it was a bargain as they basked on a setting sun balcony.

"I can't believe you kidnapped me," moaned Mateo, sipping his bottle of Kirin beer. "Making me a fugitive, criminal."

Zoe was on her second bottle. "It was the logical thing to do." She had made contact with an acquaintance of a cousin of a friend. Only three degrees of separation to the underworld. Tricky job was to persuade him to accept her American Express card and find an acceptable photograph of Mateo online. She suspected his Spanish ID card might not dunk the doughnut at the Japan Airlines check-in.

Gradually, the yeasty aroma of the local ale swamped the limonene of the apartment. "I've checked my webcam and even with zooming in the edge of the hole isn't showing, yet."

"Well, no, it will only be fifty or so metres. It will take another week of doubling before it is over three kilometres and visible in that lane view."

Mateo looked at her as if she'd trumped. "Then why have we rushed away so quick? Ah, in case the authorities finally take notice, or an airplane has a wing sliced off—over Madrid or New Zealand. I'll send Marcello to have a look for it. I've already told him and while he's not seen it he's convinced it will be a collapsed Roman sewer. He read about one such in Kyushu."

Zoe had tilted her white plastic chair dangerously far back. "Didn't know the Romans were in Japan."

"Over twenty metres in diameter, that one, so ours could still be—"

"If that's what it is and the New Zealand one is a coincidence, then we can enjoy a holiday while we're here. Did you pick up that card for take away veggie soba?"

DAY 11 (THREE DAYS LATER)

The sun startled Zoe into waking, not being sure where she was. Ah, not far from Tokyo. She looked over at Mateo's bed. He'd graciously insisted she luxuriated in the king size, while he occupied the single. He won out because the sun couldn't find him.

She brewed cups of tea while checking the webcam. Nope. News sites. Nope.

At the table, Mateo thumbed through his fake passport. "I am astonished," Mateo spluttered as jam and pastry flakes decorated his face. "Little Senorita Perfect dips under the legal horizon. Cool, in a nefarious way."

"We gain a day, don't we?"

Three baking-sun hours later they found a local taxi and guide to take them to find another accommodation partway up Mount Fuji. They wanted a vantage point for the end. The driver's mass of grey hair held up a too-small worn baseball cap that announced the wearer's ardour for NYC. His olive-coloured face had more furrows than a ploughed field and the ends of his white moustache could have been tied in a bow under his chin if he needed to be tidy. His eyes were the more salient feature. Typical epicanthic fold but unusually green and laughing. Probably amused at these two probable teenage runaways.

Zoe leaned towards Mateo. To their surprise their fingers touched by accident but they didn't let go. "Is he smiling, imagining how much dough he's going to make when he dumps our bodies in a ravine?"

Mateo squeezed her hand. "No, he's laughing at the ransom note he's composing in his head."

"He doesn't need us alive for that. Ah, look, his interpreter."

A teen girl with a Taylor Swift T-shirt disembarked from the ancient Toyota taxi. She looked innocent enough. Slim and smiley. She pointed at the opened boot.

"Rucksacks?"

The Sea of Japan shimmered turquoise on their left as they meandered up through foothills of terraced fertile volcanic soil growing soybean and almonds. Bright-red berries on roadside bushes exuded wafts of nearly-burnt cinnamon. They might have been on another planet, it was so different from her native America or Europe. Yet it was part of patchwork Earth that continued to rotate in defiance or ignorance.

Zoe leaned forward to speak to the driver. "It's so serene, beautiful, Mister erm Katsuro."

He grunted agreement then, "I am Cap."

Zoe's eyebrows arched as she turned to the girl, who had opened a cool box and handed out opened bottles of something beer-like. No labels. Her winsome smile belied her words. "Don't trust him, you Americans, he's called Cap because your souls will go under his hat." She laughed at Zoe's frown then she leered at Mateo, who'd raised a protesting finger.

"Spanish. I'm from Madrid."

Cap roared with laughter yet threaded with a shout of disapproval at the girl. "Granddaughter—Yasu. No respect for elders."

Zoe didn't want Mateo to be lured by the girl, so held his hand, warm and firm.

He asked Yasu, "Will we be there for lunch?"

Zoe dug him in the ribs as the two Japanese laughed. She whispered to him about the hundred kilometres to go.

His Spanish natural tanned face, reddened as their lips inadvertently brushed. She liked it.

"Well, that's only two hours at fifty kilometres per hour. *Si, si,* winding road, dangers. Ah, I have a text from Marcello. 'Mat, hole is bigger. I might start believing you.' He doesn't say how big."

"It should be over a hundred metres. Still won't see it on your webcam. Check it though in case there's activity from police."

Zoe expected to be deposited at a Holiday Inn, Japanese style. She must have nodded off because she awoke to sunlight strobing her face through the taxi's quirky venetian blinds, followed by a lurch that tested her seatbelt.

Mateo stirred. "Zoe, I hear people, laughing. Has he sold us out?"

She checked her watch—two PM—fingered apart the blinds and saw they'd stopped in a hill village.

Curious, she stepped out keeping a lookout for CCTV. She couldn't see Cap, but Yasu's face was lit by the glow of a smartphone.

"Hi, Yasu, are we here?"

"Hey, Zoe. This is destination. Get your bags. Cap finds you a place."

Zoe straightened up a little. "The mountain is kilometres away. I suppose this is the nearest hotel. Right?"

"He do you good deal...you know?" She winked though it

could've been a trick of the varying light as the sun flickered through clouds.

She urged Mateo to grab his rucksack. He'd grown a three-day beard, which could have looked fashionable except it was more like a moth-eaten carpet.

Ten minutes and a steep lane later, they shook hands with Whistler's Mother, right down to the floor-length black dress, white bonnet and fragrance of lavender, though the aroma existed only in Zoe's mind when she saw that portrait. The woman, Maria Desestret, recoiled in horror at dollars, but bizarrely smiled at Mateo's euros.

"Yasu," Zoe whispered, "She's European."

"You not have Europe people in America?"

Mateo coughed. "Spain."

The top floor room surprised Zoe with its light spaciousness, decorated neatly in Wedgewood blue, a long navy sofa and such a heap of pillows and red cushions she couldn't see the bed resting beneath. A whiff of cabbage, rice and mustard escaped a bead-curtained kitchen area.

She dove on top of the cushions, trusting to logic the existence of a bed beneath. "What news of our hole?"

Mateo thumbed his phone with one hand while pushing buttons on the side of the aging flat-screen TV. "No sign of it on the webcam."

"What about your local—"

"*Si! El Pais* reports the hole. Sinkhole, keep away–that kind of thing. Oh, a report of a small plane crash. Cause unknown."

She used her own phone to find New Zealand news. "The NZ Herald reports the disappearance of the farm buildings near Weber, North Island. They're assuming it's volcanic, maybe a collapsed lava tunnel. Grief, they're hoping it will attract tourists!"

"Nothing from Marcello. You don't suppose they're right? Perhaps the hole—all right, holes—have stopped growing?"

"Well then, let's enjoy our holiday. There must be a café for meals. Let's go explore."

She guessed that in spite of the probable apocalypse to come, and ensuing angst being away from family, this was the most exuberant time of her life. Plus a feller to explore. She wondered if he saw her in that way. The butterflies rampaging in her stomach came from the need for a late lunch, the incipient danger and relatively inexperienced romance.

DAY 16 (FIVE DAYS LATER)

"Well," Zoe said, "That woke them up."

Finally, Mateo's webcam showed the arc of a black shape creeping towards his Aunt's building.

He became excited and reached for a beer from a crate under the kitchen table. "I'm sure I can see it moving. I saw a few days ago a no-fly zone alert in the area, but no reason given."

Zoe had been working her phone's calculator. "It should be spreading at four centimetres a second, increasing all the time.

They'd both emerged from their bed, which had been tested as had their bodies during the last five days. Jokes about being with the last person in the world went through various flavours even though the global population had continued increasing. So far.

Mateo pulled on a new T-shirt all black and red with the Ukrainian girl pop-singer, Elka, blazoned on the front followed by two fingers up the back. "Shall we then?"

She frowned. "I'm sore—ah, YouTube. Yes, upload the doc we made with the latest. Links to all those sites we found. Oddity Central, etc. Reuters, AP, Xinhua and New Zealand."

Her T-shirt, one she'd brought from Texas declared, 'Gustav Mahler lives' with only grass stains on the back.

She fetched up her spreadsheet. "Three kilometres three hundred metres by the middle of today. Finally, it's in the suburbs. We'll lose your Aunt's building and the cam by early morning. Have you spoken to her?"

"*Si*, but she's only going to my parents in the east of the city. I can't get an answer on their phones. I left messages to fly to the far east or west. I'm really worried, Zoe."

She hugged him. "They might not be able to escape. Roads, trains and airports will be so congested."

They sat in silence, silent tears rolling.

Zoe was the first to snap. "Hell, come on. It will still be over a week before the hole reaches here. Maybe it will stop. Or whoever's doing it will get bored."

Mateo wiped his eyes with Elka. "Who? You mean God?"

"Worse, a kid."

"No, this isn't a computer game. It'd have to be running for over four billion years."

"Only in our perception. Really, I've no idea what it could be. I'm still in awe that a bigger fuss isn't being made anywhere."

"I'm not," Mateo said, while he pulled on jeans and sneakers before they go for a walk before supper. "There hasn't been a whole town eaten up, nothing affecting America, or any other large country. Planes have already been diverted and perhaps none flew over that bit of New Zealand anyway."

The simmering summer heat of the day rapidly passed into the cool of the early evening. The distant sea was truly black except for the odd twinkle of fishing boats, and the mirrored brilliance of a sedate cruise ship.

Zoe shrugged-on a newly acquired second-hand knitted coat. She'd have bought a new one but there were no clothes shops in the village. Locals bought online, but the hole would reach them before a new coat.

"Where shall we dine?" she asked.

He pretended to think. "Let's see, how about the Setsunai, same as all our meals every day. Chicken rice for me and tofu for you."

DAY 17

Zoe woke Mateo up. "Madrid is being evacuated now a third of it has gone. Two million people homeless and another four million on the move. No reports of deaths though there are hundreds of persons classified as missing."

Mateo, still in bed, angrily waved his phone. "Our YouTube files!"

"Gone viral?"

"Gone."

"What?" Zoe flicked at her own phone. "Not only have our vids gone, but we only know about Madrid's evacuation from our own contacts. Surely, Madrid's too big. There must be loads of people on buses now texting their departures to people all over the planet."

Mateo's eyes welled up. "I've not heard anything from my family nor Marcello since last night. It's a cover up, but how? I can't imagine they've confiscated all the phones in Madrid."

"Sorry to say this but the police are able to shut down land and cell phones. They could jam them like the Boston police were accused of in 2013, with or without the connivance of the phone companies. The question is why? Is it just to stop wide-scale panic? Or, they jam the public comms so they can use their own. Oh no. Mateo, we might be on the FBI's most wanted list. Our photos might be on television and newspapers."

"Why? Ah, we were the first to see it and put the video up."

"Exactly. Good thing we're in a remote place. Keep growing your beard, Mateo."

He rubbed his scraggy growth. "What reason then for the hole, Zoe? Maybe the hole is of human design, or error. Is there a collider we don't know about in Madrid?"

She paced their room, thinking it was about time they disposed of the boxes of bottles. At least there were no pizza boxes. No junk food in their village. "I've been thinking that maybe a maverick physicist pressed the wrong button somewhere, or a mathematician has solved the mass gap problem with this as a consequence. Or..."

"Mass gap? And how could a mathematician thinking of a solution to one problem create a physical effect like this?"

"Like what? Interesting in that is it easier to create an absence of mass than a presence of more mass? Mass gap is part of a yet unsolved Math problem. As for thought creating a physical effect. Some say in quantum mechanics it's possible for a physical effect to be changed by a set of theoretical situations such as entanglement, but admittedly on a microscopic scale."

Mateo, now dressed, rubbed his stomach to stop it grumbling for breakfast. He was beginning to enjoy the spiced poached eggs dropped in rice the village café offered. "Zoe, the hole could have started as a point."

"True. You know about neutrinos, right?"

"Microscopic things that zap through the Earth and us? Harmless."

"Subatomic particles with hardly any mass, but suppose an antineutrino met with a neutrino just as it was passing your road and it went rogue. Starting as a point, like you said, but all the way through the planet."

He was holding the door open when Zoe realized she was still dressed only in a Madonna T-shirt for bed. "Wonder if it was coincidental it happened near a site of an observatory? Have you been up to the top?"

He pointed at his mouth. "*Rapido*, Zoe, *comida*. I have been to the top a few years ago. A partly completed building. You know how we do it in the Mediterranean. Floor, ceilings, walls then wait. Ah, you're thinking perhaps they finished it after all and something happened."

"The mathematical mass gap button was pressed."

DAY 20 (3 DAYS LATER)

Whistler's Mother might as well had been their mother the way she brought them home-baked treats, did their washing and recently, tidied their room although maybe she didn't want vermin invading.

The authorities might have been able to jam Madrid's networks, tamper with social media and more but at fifty-two kilometres wide, the hole had been seen by weather satellites and airplanes not under the displaced Spanish government's jurisdiction, or the UN or whoever.

"Zoe, I uploaded our original videos yesterday and they've stayed up this time, but just look at this amazing sight from North Island. A third of it has gone but unlike Spain, half the hole is in the ocean."

Both of them watched with mouths open at the semicircular cliff of water. Not like Niagara's Horseshoe Falls because the water didn't fall. The water molecules must have vaporised on contact with the hole.

"Have you heard from your family, yet, Mateo?"

"The authorities' jamming has ended. Just received a text from Marcello who says they were bussed to Toledo because the authorities didn't believe the doubling every day bit. So, they're being moved again to Valencia. How long will they have?"

"Four days at the most. The whole of Spain in four days. Us here, three days after that."

They sat on the recently-made bed, thinking, while Whistler's Mother, who didn't admit to knowing English, continued disturbing spiders with a fluffy tickle stick.

Mateo's phone buzzed. "It's Marcello. He says check CNN. A link. It's us! Terrorists on the run."

She didn't know whether to be seriously worried. By the time anyone local recognised them, the future would be here before the law. She hoped. "You'd better grow your beard even faster."

Mateo stood. "Let's walk up the hill. Take some bottles. Cheated it's not Fuji proper but still high up for views."

Zoe nodded at their landlady and said to Mateo, "What about her and the other local friends we've made? Do we tell them their world will end within a week?"

"What good would it do? Although it is not for us to make those judgements so—"

Zoe's phone took a turn to ring, a rarity. "Hi, dad. Yes, I'm fine. How are—well yes it was us who first—yes, we left Spain some time ago... Fuji, not the deli near— Yes, there is an airport, but no we're not coming to you, much as I'd love to be with you and mom. What? Yes, I have a 'young man'. Yes, of course we take prec—" She winked at Mateo as if to say, 'what's the point? The world is gone in a week.' "Dad, stop going to the office. Take mom to the lake. Yes, quality time. Nothing too rash in case it stops. Hoarding? Dad, here there are no stores as such. No panic buying. What? Oh, you be careful. Guns, no we don't...you be very careful. Sun tan lotion? We'll get some from the nearest town. Hello? Line dead. Strange he didn't mention our photos and names on the television. More control freakery by the CIA. Could be the hole has wiped out their satellite television."

Mateo grinned though while shuffling his feet. "Young man. Haha."

She knew his humour was to hide anxiety about his own folks. "Suntan lotion, eh? Actually, he has a point."

"Ours ran out. We're really going down to panic-buy suntan lotion among other things?"

"No, but everyone needs more. The weather will change, might already be."

"The hole is sucking in air? But I thought it didn't suck anything just make it vanish on contact."

"Yes, Mateo, but we know the hole goes all the way through the planet, and so it has gone through the inner core, removing it. Another day and the inner solid core will have gone along with a column of nothing above and below it. The magnetic field is generated by the dynamo effect of the liquid outer core rotating around the inner. No inner, no magnetism, so no protective magnetosphere in the outer atmosphere. Eventually, if the world ring doughnut survived, solar winds would strip our air. Other things would happen too, such as gravity would be significantly less."

"Theoretical, of course since the hole will wipe all away. Let's go for that walk up the hill."

DAY 25 (5 DAYS LATER)

"Spain's gone, Mateo, so sorry." They sat at a rustic table in Café Setsunai. Apparently, it used to sport modern plastic furniture but locals were so upset, they made and donated tables and chairs hewn from local pine.

Mateo had not heard from his family for days. Sometimes he braved it out with humour but it would always hurt. "So you think it might be the satellites being disappeared when they pass through the hole?"

Zoe looked up as if she could see a moving spot. "If the height of the hole is the same as its width, most of the polar orbiting satellites are within the hole's reach."

"When again for the hole to reach us? Assuming blah blah."

"Three days. We'll be able to see it approach if we go up the hill for the last Sunday, last day..." They let the thought hover between them before she continued. "By then the edge will be travelling at around four hundred kilometres per hour. The Earth will have gone by the end of the twenty-seventh day after you bunny hopped over that hole."

Mateo coughed a laugh as if it was all his fault.

She sobbed more at the thought of her family's imminent demise than at her own.

"Ah, sorry, Zoe."

"Don't be. It'll be interesting, won't it?"

"And all from a meddling quantum error with the solving of a mass gap problem."

"Maybe."

DAY 26 AND A HALF

On the summit of a crag near Mount Fuji. They sat on a thick rug, quilted with all the colours of the rainbow and some. They ate sandwiches made from the local black bread, which they'd just about got used to with lashings of pickle washed down with local sake.

Zoe stabbed at her phone after last night's tearful round of goodbyes to her parents. "The horizon is seventy kilometres away. We should see the black hole coming in an hour but look to the west and the sky already looks darker."

"And to the east. The sea's farther away in that direction but we could hardly have found a better spot to see the hole coming in both directions."

In spite of the world in turmoil and the mighty angst of its people, the planet, or its remnant ring, kept on rotating as if nothing unusual was happening.

Zoe stood and found herself more buoyant because of the reduced gravity. "I can see stars in the darker sky above the horizon. The atmosphere has disappeared over the holes and must be thinning here." She sat again to be with Mateo, holding each other. She'd hardly slept the night before, their last night. She couldn't remember falling asleep, just the many awakenings.

"You know, Mateo, even if the holes stopped spreading this instant, we'd have no atmosphere pretty soon, and freezing. It would be a ringworld like in the scifi books." They gulped back tears, trying to think of the amazing experience rather than the lost lives and absence of future.

A noise made them turn to see a grey dog watching them. It pawed the ground. Mateo looked around for a stone, but chose the half-empty wine bottle as a weapon.

"No," Zoe said, "Japan's wolves are extinct. Must be a stray mutt. She's hungry. I'll give her my bread."

She gently tossed one of her sandwiches to a halfway point. Slowly, the wolf-dog walked forward then ate the meal in two gulps. She sat down, resting her head on her paws as if to wait the end.

"Ironic, Mateo, that some say the word Fuji means never-ending."

They saw the ink on the ocean horizon on both sides.

Zoe laughed—an emotional noise like a duckling. "Mateo, your bunny jump? That's some hell of a hole."

Just before it reached them they stood and held hands. The wolf whimpered.

DAY 43

Poetess1987@Zoe: Hi Mateo. Is that you?

Bikekid Madrid@Mateo: *Hola* Zoe. Are we alive?

@Zoe: Don't know

@Mateo: Where are we?

@Zoe: Don't know

@Mateo: How are we doing this?

@Zoe: Don't know. What can you see?

@Mateo: Nothing. Some motes perhaps like when you squeeze your eyes shut. Could be stars but without the twinkling

@Zoe: Okay, but how are you reading this?

@Mateo: Don't know

@Zoe: Can you actually see this?

@Mateo: Don't know. It's kind of in my head

@Zoe: Ditto. Have you tried talking to anyone else like Marcello?

@Mateo: I dare not try in case I lose you

@Zoe: Me too

@Mateo: Are we the only ones left?

@Zoe: Don't know. Maybe we are because we were the first with the hole? Don't laugh but maybe it has an affinity with us

@Mateo: I don't know how to laugh. Still think we're in a game?

@Zoe: Don't know

@Mateo: why have we found awareness now?

@Zoe: It's day 43. Sun's gone out. Must be significant

@Mateo: That's why it's dark. What's next?

@Zoe: Hole will reach the nearest planetary system, Proxima Centauri, by day 61

@Mateo: We'll be all right, right?

@Zoe: Don't know. You know the universe is finite even if expanding, right?

@Mateo: The hole won't... will it?

@Zoe: Day 95 it will be gone. Maybe see you in the next one?

@Mateo: Don't know. Hope so.

VIEW FROM

I REFUSE TO OPEN MY EYES.

Monday morning waking up is never welcome; it presages the need to face another teaching workday. Wild animal management wasn't my career ambition when I trained as a teacher but that's what it's like.

The six-thirty alarm bleats. My arm flails in the air, but misses. My eyes refuse to open so I close my ears to the alarm.

The sound comes from the wrong direction. Perhaps it isn't my wake-up, but Alan's in the apartment above.

As long as I don't open my eyes I won't worry. I shuffle in preparation to roll onto my right side. Whoa, I can't. My back muscles won't cooperate.

At last I open my eyes... and I discover that *I am on the ceiling.*

...

I LAUGH. NERVES. Then my stomach knots. I *am* on the ceiling, looking down. Aren't I? Has Alan re-arranged my room during sleeptime in order to make it appear inverted? The only thing worse than a science teacher is one with a warped sense of humour. I squeeze my eyelids shut then slowly re-open them. Below, covered with an untidy red quilt, is my bed. The bedside cabinet is next to it, supporting the alarm clock, which periodically bursts into indignation at being ignored.

I send my impending terror into an unused lump of brain, a trick learnt when teaching difficult classes.

How can I verify whether the room has turned upside down or it's me? Has a trickster stuck my furniture down? My right arm that had swung into action has returned up to the ceiling. Turning my head, I see the white plaster ceiling-rose. I've not seen my Georgian ceiling this close up. Cracks in the paintwork and plaster missing near the rose remind the few functioning brain cells that I should get workmen in. Banality subjugates fear.

I seek evidence of gravity. Before my mind boils in terror I allow a drop of spittle to go where it will. It accelerates away to the quilt below. A dark red splodge grows like a bloodstain.

Forcing my mind into more experiments, denying the inevitable panic, I turn my head to the left. As I thought from its soft undulations, the pillow remains under, or rather above–all right, behind–my head. Good loyal pillow.

This is absurd. I must be in a nightmare. Nevertheless, perhaps I should exercise caution in any effort to break free from the ceiling's suction force. What if normality returns? I'd fall at an acceleration of ten metres per second each second. Well, it's no more than three metres so a quick calculation tells me I'd land at seventeen miles an hour. Is that fast enough to hurt? My blob of spit must have landed at that speed too. The fall was languorous to me; yet look at what happened to it.

Hopefully, the bed will be kind to my eventual return. The mattress is one of those with memory. It's probably wondering where I am.

I wriggle again. Has Alan velcroed my pyjamas to the ceiling? Even if he had, how did he get a stepladder and manhandle a sleeping adult up to a tall ceiling?

It couldn't be Velcro holding me up. My arms are free but kind of floating. It's like when I go snorkelling: face-down looking at the seabed. It's a strange but pleasant experience in the water, but weird and worrying now. Perhaps my room is full of water.

I look for contrary evidence. On the green carpet, there's a bedtime book, *Orbital Geometry*. It isn't floating: too heavy. If I'm in water my spittle shouldn't have fallen–unless it isn't normal water.

A worry headache is brewing.

I scan for objects that should float. What is there in a bedroom that should float, besides a person? I assume I'm breathing, aren't I? And the usual air. Now I'm holding my breath wondering if somehow I'm immersed in a highly oxygenated liquid, or perhaps I've not been breathing.

"Am I dead?" I yell, realizing instantly that I'd breathed to make the shout.

"No!" A female voice far down the corridor. It sounded like Suzette.

"In here, Suzy, but keep hold of the door frame." I want to tell her to rush around to the garden, fetch the washing line, tie it to her waist and then to the radiator before opening the door, but it would sound too bizarre.

"What did you say?" Her voice becomes louder as she walks down the corridor to the door of my bedroom. As I watch the mock-crystal handle rotate I wouldn't be surprised to find her walking on the ceiling. But no, there's her mass of hazelnut brown hair, far below. She hasn't removed her beige raincoat. Her naked foot steps into the room.

"John, where are you?"

Why hadn't she seen this ceiling person immediately and scream? My panic turns from defiantly off to simmer. How to mention my predicament without freaking her out? I absently cough.

Her face is a picture. The Scream by Edvard Munch comes to mind. I see she's had her teeth whitened recently. I hadn't noticed before.

"What the heck are you doing up there?"

I struggle to answer, but remain silent.

Suzy wags a finger at me. "Get down, you goon."

"Nothing I'd like better. Any suggestions?"

She stands hands on hips, her raincoat unbuttoned at the neck with no visible clothing beneath, the thought wheedles into my head that she may have planned an interesting morning. Damn.

"Why did you go up there?"

Not how?

"I woke up like this." It sounds stupid but then it only confirms the perception she possesses of my propensity for finding myself in odd situations.

"Maybe I can lure you down." She undoes a couple of buttons revealing her cleavage, which translates to part of my anatomy that finally points towards the floor.

"I am lured, but... hey, Suzy, don't climb on the bed. This isn't like the leaping-off-the-wardrobe scenario."

"Idiot, I was seeing if I could reach you."

"You know these old buildings have really high ceilings. And what if you could reach? You could have been seriously injured."

"John, stop all this now."

"It's not much fun for me. Go tell Alan to turn off whatever he's done upstairs."

"What, you think Einstein has invented a man attractor in his apartment and it's sucked you up? How do you know it's not Freya?"

I'd forgotten about Alan's latest oddball woman. "Be careful if you go upstairs and see her, she's quite unpredictable."

"We've met. Freya gave me a bangle at Alan's birthday party last week. It turned my veins green, from my wrist up my arm and down the other one–remember? I'll give Alan a call."

Only when she leaves the room does my nose detect the heady aroma of Freesia. She only wore it for our romantic interludes. In spite of my increasing concern I smile ruefully then frown. It is Monday mid-morning. I should, by now, be edutaining the masses, so why is Suzette here and dressed for action? Who was she expecting, and in *my* room. Alan? Freya? Both?

I wriggle, but it is as if my lungs are made of iron and a powerful electro-magnet is above the ceiling. Even with both hands pushing, trying to make fists, my back presses firmly upwards. In frustration, I bang the ceiling. Mistake. White flakes of plaster wander down messing up my bed. My nose pinches with the musty aroma.

I hear dragging noises. Someone must be moving furniture, a large machine, or is intent on driving me insane. I try to think if I've annoyed Alan recently, or at all. Perhaps someone else. Plenty of parents would be aggrieved at my honest grading of their kid's work. The Wagners, from the time I wrote 'the dawn of legibility in Kevin's handwriting revealed his utter incapacity to spell'? Surely not enough. It must be that mad bitch, Freya.

Then there's Suzy. The teasing raincoat and perfume for someone else.

The front door slams. Suzy must have gone outside to make that call to Alan, but she has a mobile. She must have left it in her car in spite of all my warnings.

Footsteps in the corridor.

"Is that you, Suzette? ... Suzy? ... Freya?"

The door handle moves, and the door cracks open, but then a scuffling noise followed by Suzy's scream.

"What's happened, Suzy?"

I strain harder, trying to arch my back even though it's agony now.

A feeble voice reaches me from the corridor. "John, whatever it is holding you up on the ceiling...?"

"Well?"

"It's spreading."

GRAVITY'S TEARS

EMMA GRIPPED THE SEATBELT at her right shoulder. An irrational act as she knew it wouldn't improve survivability in a collision, and it annoyed Quill–good. He stupidly insisted on night driving east from Winnipeg on the unlit Manitoba Highway 15, not the Trans Canada, because of his out-of-date licence.

The endless undulating prairies bored some, but Emma delighted in its simplistic beauty. She derived the same serenity from huge skies and distant horizons as others did from sitting staring at oceans. The hypnotic beat of telegraph poles strobing past made her smile. Maybe Quill used the effect to make her fall in love with him. Forget his bad points. It might work.

She twisted round, and pulled back her long red hair to check on their two-bed trailer, fishtailing behind them.

"Slow down, Quill. It'll turn and take us with it."

"Only doing sixty and the road's straight for friggin' miles."

"Road's straight but your driving isn't."

"I can't help the cross wind."

"It was dead calm when we left."

Another glance behind her caught the sight of a shooting star. Maybe it was a good luck sign.

She bit her lip to avoid her nth appeal for deceleration. He accelerated in direct proportion to her nagging. Only another twenty miles to the campsite. She put her hand out to try the radio. To shorten the journey.

The crashing, yet strangely rhythmic, hiss of interference obliged her to shut it off.

Willing him to focus on the road, even though it remained featureless, she worried about his driving, and yet... All right, she derived a buzz from the danger, but she had the urge to reach old age too. Lately, it was as if his Dodge resented him, and it tried to reject him by disobedience, like a rodeo horse bucking its rider.

She looked at Quill. Bucking her wishes he'd shaved his head. He looked far older than his twenty-five years. The car lurched making her once again grab the seatbelt. She had an abrupt premonition his edgy driving will put them upside-down in a ditch this time. Was she over-reacting? Her stomach convulsed and her hands shook as she rummaged in her purse for an antacid lozenge.

Quill took life chances while she planned to avoid disaster. In spite of her science major, while he fled school as soon as a pay-packet beckoned, they complemented each other, but was it more *folie a deux* than love? This holiday determined their future. To get married, if he asked, to be together, or not...

Failing to discover dyspepsia soothers, Emma sucked on the bittersweet taste of a licorice stick. She stared at the yellow cones of the headlights seeking rolling cola cans and nervous coyotes with their reflected white eyes.

Without warning, something punched through the roof of the Dodge. Emma screamed, and then again as her seatbelt cut into her fingers, then chest.

"Don't brake, you idiot," she shrieked. "The trailer will smash into us."

Quill accelerated to compensate, but too late. He yanked the wheel over to the right. Another mistake.

Emma wet herself as the trailer pushed into the car. She fell against her seatbelt when the rear wheels lifted amidst screeching then whining as they lost contact with the road. Through stinging eyes over her left shoulder, she watched the aluminium trailer overtaking their car. Except it couldn't. They pirouetted, pulled around by the trailer. A loud bang announced the descent of the rear wheels followed immediately by the engine stalling.

"We're fucked," Quill cried, his eyes wide and staring at Emma.

She knew he meant the trailer would roll and their jack-knifed vehicle would revolve with it. As if on a roller coaster, her body was yanked around. Emma's screams matched Quill's shrieks.

Abruptly, their car halted. Miraculously it hadn't rolled. They both stared out of the windshield. They'd turned one eighty so faced the dim glow of Winnipeg's beyond-the-horizon lights reflected in the low clouds.

Emma's hyperventilated breathing sucked in the acrid odour of burning rubber.

"Are we on fire?" Emma said.

"Just friction burns in the tyres." He batted the steering wheel with both hands. "Hell, we were on fire then, Baby, weren't we?"

Her whole body fibrillating, she looked at him. "More excitement than I needed, thanks. We still attached to the trailer?"

"The bouncing uncoupled it. What the hell happened, Em?"

It took brain-squeezing seconds for her to recall the initiation sequence. "Was it a stone?"

He pulled at her arm and pointed at the melted plastic fabric around the hole in the car roof. "See, the fucker zapped down through the floor?" A neat hole, the diameter of a finger, stared at them. "Bullet hole."

A relief laugh escaped from her. "Yeah right, a lone gunman miles from anywhere managed to point a gun down at our speeding roof." Her nostrils pinched at a whiff of burnt plastic.

"It could've been from a ranch. Someone fired their weapon up in the air. They don't go into orbit. All those bullets come back down."

"A Beirut wedding? Out here? Sorry, Quill, I don't buy it. I think it's more likely a meteorite."

Quill looked up. "You watch too much TV. Hey, like that *Deep Impact* film? Don't they have to be as big as New York?"

She creaked open the passenger door. "Smaller. Let's find it."

Visibly shaking but otherwise with an admirable bravado, Quill got out and joined her. "Nine millimetre, I bet."

"Probably a metallic lump."

"God, we'll never find it in this dark. Not enough moonlight.."

"Only last week I read a pullout on meteor showers."

"I bet there are millions of spent bullets all over. I give up. Hey, Emma do your legs feel like jelly?" He crumpled on the grass, and then rolled to lay on his back.

Realising Quill, like her, had been denying their trauma, Emma joined him on the grass. Just for a minute to ease the headache-making tension, and let the adrenaline dissipate.

The cloud cover fragmented allowing stars to say hello. In Manitoba's big sky, the clouds alone were magnificent, but the window out to space enhanced the view and Emma's exuberance.

"Look, Quill, there's the Big Dipper over to the west. Keep a watch out and we might see some of the Perseids shooting stars. Hey, there's one, and another. Loads. Always gives me a buzz. Maybe one made it through to ground. It is August twelfth, when they're due, isn't it? Quill?"

She turned on her stomach, waving away a nose-twitching stem of cotton-grass, but Quill wasn't there. Still affected by ordeal aftershocks Emma peered into the gloom in case he'd gone for a pee, but no sign. Standing, she couldn't see him in the car either. Alien abduction? Anything seemed possible.

"Get your ass over here," Quill yelled, walking round from behind the trailer. "There's holes in the road, look."

"Oh, great. There was I marvelling at shooting stars and all you can find fascinating are potholes."

"Not your normal potholes—more like moon craters."

A whack announced another hit on the car. Quill ran over to it and peered over the roof. "It's a hail storm," Quill said.

Emma had to agree that when a storm brewed, a few large spots of rain presaged the full fury of a storm. She couldn't remember whether that happened in a hailstorm. But it couldn't have been a lump of ice that had gone through both roof and floor of their car.

"There another, watch out!" shouted Quill.

A loud crump kicked up grit from the road a yard from her.

"It's not hailstones. Look." She picked up the black stone then dropped it. "Damn, it's hot." She pulled her denim jacket sleeve over her right hand and picked up the object. "It's like metal. Molten slag from a steelworks. Not for real, Quill. See they are small meteorites."

"That means we'd better hightail it outta here. We'd better anyway, the trailer will get smashed by coming traffic."

Emma shot looks in both directions. Her pulse quickened when she saw a pair of headlights in the distance coming from Winnipeg. "Hurry up, Quill."

"The trailer has a flat. Back the Dodge up to the hookup."

"It'll be quicker if we both push it off the road onto the verge."

"The flat will make it harder. Come on, Emma, or do you want to hold up the hook while I back the car?"

She wasn't the world's best at reversing but then she didn't like the idea of standing behind a Quill-driven vehicle. She climbed into the driving seat, checked neutral and pushed the starter. Nothing. Her pulse throbbing in her chest she looked up to see the oncoming headlights looming larger.

"Have we got a warning triangle?" she called, then thought of their emergency flashers. Switched them on. She heard them tick and the red button steadily winked at her.

"Turn them off, stupid. You might need all the battery juice to turn the engine."

"Have you seen that vehicle heading for us? It's frigging huge." Not normally a user of profanity, her desperation degenerated her character. She turned off the flashers. Checked the ignition key. Pressed the starter. She'd no idea how sweet the sound of a roaring engine could be. Close to orgasmic. Was this how men felt with their automobiles?

"Reverse over to here, Babe. Tonight would be cool."

She turned the emergency flashers on, and then the headlights. Full beam for a long three seconds before off, on, off, then dipped. Surely they'd see that?

"Stop playing Christmas lights and get over here."

As she reversed, she had to place the Dodge across the middle of the highway to line up with the trailer. She put the parking brake on when she felt the slap Quill gave the rear windshield. She dared herself to look at the oncoming vehicle and scared herself with its closeness.

"Quill, is there a torch in the trunk?"

"Give me a hand."

"That vehicle must be a wagon, and it isn't slowing." She expected Quill to lose it under this pressure, needing her loving support. But maybe three months wasn't long enough to know someone. He was cool. Impressive. But too cool. Maybe that last cigarette...

"You had a joint?"

"We'll be fine. Just help me hook the trailer."

"Is there time? Oh, let's go for it." She heaved with Quill to lift the trailer then screamed with pain when he let go with one hand to fiddle with the hook mechanism.

Quill groaned.

Emma let go. "It's not my fault. I can't do it. I've pulled all the damn muscles in my arms. "

"I'm not complaining about you. The ball socket is broken. Look."

"Great. Never mind about me," she said, rubbing both arms. "I can't help you push it out of the way, now. Are you gonna drive the Dodge out of the way? That truck's nearly here." He must know that, she thought, from the oncoming headlights casting alternate brightness and eerie shadows. It must be weaving about on the road.

"Must've been when I braked... the jack-knife... "

"OK. I'll try and drive it. No—too late." She should run for the verge. She should be dragging stupid stoned Quill with her, but her legs refused to cooperate. Too close for her to run away, the truck roared. She suspected blood surging through her ears amplified the sound. Her fear exceeded itself. Emma's legs refused to move.

"Oh, shit," Quill said, "It's coming straight at us. Run!" He grabbed her arm, but then stopped. "What?"

The vehicle attempted an emergency stop with a terrible screech and tyre smoke. "Thank God they've seen us," Emma yelled, but instantly realised two mistakes. First it was a Ford pickup, not a mighty truck. Headlights belie vehicle sizes. Second, it hadn't stopped. The front wheels stopped rotating, but the vehicle skidded towards them. Foreboding increased as the back of the vehicle reared up. Sparks flew as the fender hit the tarmac. Like a nightmare, the pickup travelled on its front grille.

Emma clamped her hands to her ears as the pickup started a forward roll amidst an ear-hurting metallic screaming. The cacophony increased as her arm was yanked by Quill, pulling her out of the way of the oncoming disaster. The stench of burning rubber and spilling gas assaulted her nose as the cartwheeling pickup hurtled inches from her. Wooden crates floated in the air, travelling with the rear of the pickup, even if no longer contained. Something hard bashed Emma's left arm as Quill continued pulling her to the verge. She closed her eyes yearning for the bad-movie to finish. She'll open them when *The End* flashed up.

"Stay here," Quill said.

A thump on the trailer's roof grabbed her attention for a fraction before gasping in horror at the pickup now upside down, and about to crash onto their Dodge. The adrenaline buzz seemed to slow her perception of time. Tensing her muscles for a potential explosion, her heart raced. She could see the pale shirtsleeve of the driver. Tears smeared her vision as she imagined his helplessness as the collision continued. Through the horror she had to admire the solid construction of both vehicles. Although a tyre exploded on the Dodge, as it skidded sideways, neither roof collapsed.

"He needs to get outta there," Quill said. "Spilt gas everywhere, all those sparks."

"But there's no sparks now."

"Our engine's still running. I should go help him."

"No—if you think it'll blow, then—hey, did you hear that?" Up the road another detonation reminded her of the trailer, and their car before. Meteorites. Had she read that article wrong? It said the shooting stars didn't reach the ground. Quill stepped towards the crashed cars. Emma grabbed his elbow. In pain they both uttered gasps.

"Bummer, what's that?" He held out his arm to show a tear in his black leather jacket sleeve. Raspberry oozed out. Wincing with pain, he let Emma undo the cuff's metal press-stud and pull back the sleeve. Her nose caught a whiff of charred fabric and her eyes took in the seeping gash, spoiling a dagger tattoo. Then downwards to a wisp of smoke from the grass between them.

"Must've been debris from the pickup, or one of your meteorites," he said. Silently, she turned her attention to her own left arm. Just a bruise.

"I can't *not* help him." Quill pulled from her but stopped as another projectile slammed into the pickup's upside-down base sending both vehicles shaking. Another hit the road beside Emma. She pulled Quill around to look at a saucer-sized crater in the tarmac, and then the corona of another formed as they watched. Percussions hammered around them.

"Get inside the trailer, now!" he said.

"That won't protect us. Aluminium roof isn't it? One went through our steel car roof. We should get under a bridge."

"Yeah right. The nearest one is—"

"So we'll have to make do with getting under the trailer."

"Good point. Get your head under the trailer's axle, while I help that driver."

"No, get under with me, I'm scared." She didn't want to show her terror unless such a confession dragged Quill away from getting himself killed.

As she stooped to crawl under the trailer, Quill shuffled his feet. He looked at her then at the pileup. Standing again, she shook her head at his dithering. But at least he was trying to decide between doing a good deed and doing another good deed. Maybe, in spite of his masculine assertiveness his feelings were getting in touch with him, or her. She smiled at the thought but lost it when she spied the light of a flame in the Dodge. Before she could yell, a whoomph of a fireball engulfed both vehicles. Quill staggered back and joined Emma. He put his arm around her, a rare phenomenon, but one she appreciated.

The roar of the flames made conversation a waste of breath. Agonising over the driver burning to death, Emma threw up, spewing partly digested fast food over Quill's shoes.

"Jeez, Emma." But before he could kick off the sludge, the sky lit with hundreds more incoming shooting stars.

Emma, grateful for a distraction from the death said, "Like the aurora borealis."

"Yeah, cute, but how long before that lot hits us? It'll be like machine guns."

"They're not supposed to reach us, they're only the size of sand grains and burn up—that's what we're seeing."

"So what's with the pummelling we're getting? They joining up out there?"

"Something else must be happening. Hey, Quill, look at our car."

A man staggered from the other side of the pileup. Quill ran to him and helped him to their trailer. As another wave of stones hammered down around them, the three crawled under the trailer.

"R-radio," the man said.

"Quill, and this is Emma."

"What about the radio?" Emma said.

"A-aliens."

Quill whispered to Emma, "Nutter."

She put her hand over his mouth. "Freaked out, stress, that's all. Grief, he must be in shock from that accident and still managed to get out before it caught fire."

"Heard it w-when I left Win-Winnipeg."

"What's your name, buddy?"

"Stop pestering him, Quill."

"Mister," she said, putting a hand on the man's arm. "What did the radio say?"

She noticed the soot on his face, shocked forehead lines, bloodshot eyes like miniature roadmaps. He nodded at her. "N-NASA says a spaceship used Earth for a slingshot. It's played hell with the Percy?"

"Perseids—what, did the ship get too close to the meteor swarm and sent it off course?"

He repeat nodded.

"We're being invaded?" Quill looked out at the shooting stars now down to only one every few seconds. "They'd have to do better than that."

"Ignore him, Mister. Maybe it's one of our own spaceships—European, Japanese, Chinese—there's lots of countries. And NASA use slingshots to gravity assist ships. Apollo Thirteen flew around the moon in order to get back to Earth."

"You and your obsession with astronomy," Quill said. "So, buddy, is the whole Earth being bombarded with rocks?"

"No, it's bad for a narrow band a few miles wide and a hundred miles long from about Winnipeg, southeast to Chicago. Worst, bad luck, just here, within the next hour."

Quill, emboldened by the relative silence, crawled out and stood. "Looks like it's over. You got your listening wrong, pal."

"Don't bet on it," Emma said, looking to the man for support but a shrug was his only response. Her science expertise needed backup. "The Perseids lasts a few days. So we're getting bigger chunks because of the close pass of the spaceship. There must be more to it?"

"I only know what the radio said, Miss. And then one of them rocks must've gone through the hood."

"And I thought you done an emergency stop to avoid us," Quill said.

"Was gonna go round you. Needed to get away. Suppose we still do."

"We'll have to hitch or stop a bus," Quill said, looking towards Winnipeg.

"Where exactly is the nearest bridge?" Emma said. "Even one on this highway going over a farm track, 'cos we're going to need one." She pointed at the sky.

A swathe of coloured lights splattered the night sky to the northwest.

"It's like the best firework display, ever," Quill said, as cascades of greens and incandescent oranges sprinkled several miles above Winnipeg. "Hey, those lights show up the wheat thrashing up in the distance."

Emma narrowed her eyes as if that helped with telescopic vision. The shooting stars enabled her to see dense clouds of wheat chaff thrown into the air maybe three miles away.

"Quill, you're right. It looks more like an avalanche, and it's heading this way!" She bit her knuckles knowing they'd nowhere that'd protect them from such a battering. Quill grabbed her arms and tugged her backwards.

"Don't worry, honey. Under the trailer again."

Emma stopped. Her curiosity making her peer at the oncoming crashing. Tornado-chasers must feel the same. She brushed a red hair from her face. Several replaced it, making her aware of a fresh breeze–like those before a heavy storm. She rushed after the two men.

Minutes later the metallic storm arrived. Like an intense hailstorm but more deadly. The trailer danced on its suspension steel bands. Emma was certain the trailer's roof must have been ripped apart by the hammering sounds inches above her. Arghh, one got through and punched through her right calf. She twisted to investigate with her hand. Sore, with surprisingly little pain, but her hand found a warm sticky wound. Her nerves must've been severed. She tore a strip off her shirt to improvise a bandage. She could feel it become sodden over both lesions.

Down the road Emma saw the convoluted black smoke from their vehicles, making monster shapes against the sky, but as soon as her brain manufactured ugly meanings, she looked away. She could see they'd lost the Dodge's headlights. Probably shorted by the fire whose flames were dying. The air filled with the pungent odours of burning rubber, gas and an odd electrical smell like at fairgrounds. Ozone? Must've come from static as the meteorites disrupted the air. There was enough light from stars, and a quarter moon to see the hundreds of tiny craters and debris littering the highway.

A lull. Her leg now throbbed. She sought Quill's face in the pale blue gloom to comment on the metallic odour but he looked asleep. Before she could put a hand out, a white-tangerine light flooded from the sky, washing under the trailer. A scream of shrill whistling pierced her ears forcing her to squeeze shut her eyes. The following barrage of grape-sized meteorites pummelled the ground. Several ricocheted under the trailer battering her arms protecting her face. Her back was protected by the axle where Quill insisted she stayed, but occasional stings told her she'd taken hits on her legs and arms. Quill was definitely the one for her. Because of this ordeal, her doubts evaporated.

Then it was over. She must have passed out. Soft dawn light reached for her. She wriggled on painful arms and knees, but before she emerged, she caught the odour of fresh blood, urine and shit. "Quill, is that you? Quill?"

Several lines of light shone through holes above her in the wrecked floor. Mid-August and yet cold air crept under her shirt, proliferating goosebumps.

The pickup man's face was a bloody mess. A gash on his forehead oozed grey matter spilling on to the floor mixed with dark blood.

Tears flooded her eyes even though she'd only known the man for hours. Pity she'd stopped Quill from finding out the poor man's name. Quill wasn't there. He must have crawled out while she dozed off.

She had the urge to get out from under the trailer. Compassion didn't travel as far as wanting to spend another minute with death. Now her body was racked with pain—mostly dull, or dulled. Her leg hurt the most. She groaned when she foresaw how much an impediment it'd be for running, walking, crawling to safety. Using elbows, she wriggled her head and shoulders into the open. Quill sat on the verge a few yards away among shattered fragments of the trailer and the vehicles.

The smoke from the ruins of the two vehicles had reduced to reluctant wisps, but on the western horizon, two thick columns of black smoke found their languorous way upwards entwined as if to reinforce each other in search of revenge.

"Must have hit the gas tanks at the airport, or that cow pie factory," Quill said, between coughing, his voice low and rough.

"Yeah, I heard those cow pies are hot." Emma, pushed herself up to her knees. From her new vantage, the desolation hit her. The trailer was now a colander. How had he survived? "You OK, Quill? Where are you hurt?" She pulled herself vertical by pulling on a surviving fragment of trailer superstructure. She found she could hobble better than expected.

Fearing she'd find him in a terminal condition, Emma stopped in front of him.

"Only flesh wounds, Babe. I got lucky."

But all she could see was blood, not that the embryonic dawn light helped.

"Is that dislocated or broken?" she asked, reaching for his right arm.

He waved her away with his good arm, which was the bad one when all it had was a gash. "It's not over is it?"

"Hard to say, Quill. The Perseids are at their most on the twelfth this year, but could go on a few days. I guess NASA might know if the extra showers of larger stuff are coming in waves or if that was it. One lump of comet or a snared asteroid breaking up on entry and finding us. I wonder if it'll make them think twice about using sling shots around other planets and moons? I don't suppose they gave a monkey's about this kind of consequence."

"Who, the alien spaceship or NASA?"

"If there was an alien spaceship, it'd be long gone. With no idea what it did to us." She heard a bang on the road and saw dust. Just like the after drops in a dying rainstorm. "Anyway, how about finding a bridge as a bomb shelter in case more comes? Pity we didn't stick to the Trans Canada Highway. There'd be ambulances and taxis rushing around on that one by now."

"I'm not nimble enough," Quill said, patting his leg. "Anyway a chopper will be on its way soon."

She thought maybe Quill had become unhinged. It wouldn't

be surprising. More astonishing was that he survived and fantastic that he'd made sure she had. She heard the reverberations of a helicopter from out of the rising sun. Quill was talking. She looked at the black plastic he had in his hand.

"They got my arms, legs and few other bits but they missed my cellphone." As he grinned, she noticed two of his teeth were missing. But it didn't matter, they can be replaced. The horrors of the last few hours had allowed her to experience aspects of his character transcending the superficial. Now if only that chopper was really for them.

MIND OF ITS OWN

Warning: this tale involves magic with a mind of its own. If you experience any personal oddities during your reading be afraid, but not very afraid. You will return to normal eventually.

MERLIN SCOWLED at his arthritis-afflicted knuckles and reached out to the campfire, careful not to knock over a pot of roots and berries simmering with impatience. He grimaced a weak smile at the woody yet fruity aroma from the burning birch bark.

An untidy pile of brown woollen blankets agitated, releasing a black-haired young woman. Although Merlin admired her clear blue eyes, he was always distracted by a dark mole on her left cheek. Others might use such as a beauty spot but hers sprouted two black hairs.

She stood and shook off the remaining bedding and took two metal cups to the pot.

"Why don't you cast one of your spells to rid yourself of your pain?" Her voice trilled high as Merlin knew it would from a teenager. Even so, it rankled in his ears and he had to concentrate to hear the girl's words. He'd been obliged to chaperone her journey between Chepstow and Denbigh and after only two days he'd used up most of his store of tolerance.

Knees creaking, Merlin sat on a fallen tree within warming distance of the fire. "My dear Elspeth, daughter of Arthur's squire and our Queen of sighs, mostly mine, my magic is an illusion, with smoke, mirrors and trickery rather than genuine sorcery."

She shook her head, from which a cascade of motes caught in the flames creating a coruscating display. "Last Michaelmas, you used a spell to turn an attacking wolf into a timid fawn, who ran away when Mordred ran at it with his knife."

Merlin smiled as he used a green stick to poke at the fire. "You *think* you saw a wolf. Darkness, flickering campfire, and a goblet of golden mead. All these components conspire against the unobservant."

The girl used her hands to part her long black hair like curtains and threw Merlin a smile. It was lopsided, but she possessed full lips and with those large eyes smiling, he knew she wanted something. She licked her lips, making them glisten.

"Merlin?"

"Yes?"

She toyed with her hair, twirling some around her fingers. "I know you are bashful about it, but you can do real magic if you want to. Can't you?"

He smiled at Arthur's jibe a year back: "Magician heal thyself."

His smile upturned to serious. "The last time I tried to use magic to cure my ills, it back-fired."

"What is back-fire?"

"What? Oh, I sometimes have visions. Of tomorrow." At least that was what he supposed with the flashing images in his trances of metallic contraptions travelling at shit-scary speeds through strange towns, and sometimes over the top of them. Voices too from which he learnt that objects have little value compared to human emotions, which do not change, no matter how odd the scenes he saw. "For example when I used a spell to cure an ache in my left incisor—the pointy one—it fell out. Hence the gap. See?"

Elspeth stared at him, then up at an escaped ember looking to ignite an overhead branch.

She returned her gaze to the old man. "You are silly."

He returned a grin even though it revealed the gap in his teeth and a flickering tongue that played with it. "Silly enough to agree with this mission."

She leaned forward so the fire shone rosy on her face. "If you use your real magic to take away my spot, I'll lift my skirts for you."

"Tempting, but my talents in such delights became dormant thirty years ago, and extinct these last ten years." He sat back, lost in his memories. "Although, perhaps with real magic."

She tossed her head back to induce a wave in her hair rippling down her back. "I don't think, my dear wizard, that you would have any difficulty down there when my skirts are raised, do you?"

He'd like to think not but sat back to look at her face. He had to ignore her seductive leer in order to focus on her spot. "The fact that it is more a wart increases the complexity."

She hid the spot with her hand and pouted. "It is *not* a wart. I'm not a hag!"

He laughed softly, his whole body joining in.

"Do not upset yourself, Elspeth. Well, it's not in my grasp to perform two spells simultaneously so I'll work one on your spot first and then perhaps, on my ... problem afterwards."

He thought he knew which group of intonations were required and still marvelled that from being a child he was one of only a few who could draw on an inner sense to invoke effects in living and non-living beings. However, he hesitated, torn between the opportunity of delight with Elspeth and the risk of the spell turning against him as one did before.

The girl mistook his delay. "Your wand. You need that, don't you? Shall I help you find it in your—"

"No need. I have it here." He didn't need a wand but people expected it, and if it aided the illusion so be it. Several visions ago he'd observed himself wearing a cloak festooned with stars and moons as if he were a court jester. He glanced at his dark, muddy cowl. Merlin loved its comforting warmth and the anonymity when inside the expansive hood. He rescued a small stick from incineration and waved it in the air. The end glowed red and released a sparkling smoke trail meandering up in the air. He knew it was merely a stick but she'd see what her mind contorted it to be.

He'd already dredged memory for a suitable spell to rid Elspeth of her wart. While she slept one night, he'd rubbed her wart with a clove of garlic then buried the vegetable along the path. The wart remained but perhaps not as bad. A conjuration was required but he needed to avoid those evocations that allowed the magic to escape. He flicked the wand in her direction.

"Elspeth you are not to listen to my words. Relax, close your eyes and allow your mind to drift to your *un*blemished cheek."

She sat on a boulder swaying as if in a trance. The air filled with aromatic wood smoke now combined with lavender from Merlin's satchel.

This was to be one of his spells that mixed magic with incantation. Words verbalised, vibrating through the air not just as speech but as an alternate reality creating an effect beyond mere hearing. Indeed, the understanding is the least likely outcome of such sounds, spoken in an ancient tongue not used by common folk for millennia.

He stood and spoke silently then increasingly sharper as he intoned, *"Diffinda, diffindo Durs yek Gor arrants hapaghelu, Diffinda, diffindo Durs yek Gor arrants hapaghelu."*

The mystic words left him, creating a ripple in the air that accompanied each sound as they weaved their way across the fire and brushed Elspeth's face. She gasped then unsteadily stood with her hands caressing her cheeks.

Merlin had to rush around the fire to catch her as she fainted. At the same time ripples in the air created a purple glow travelling away towards the nearest trees.

"Wake up, girl, I need to catch that wisp and stop it escaping."

He laid her on ferns, slung his satchel over his shoulder and ran slowly, as fast as he could, after the spell. He should have known better than to be lured by the promise of a woman's charms, especially as he was unlikely to be able to accept her favours.

Merlin stumbled on making use of cart ruts over the rough ground to the wood. Berries turned back into flowers from where the flaw-removing spell worked on the vegetation as it wandered about a hundred paces in front. If he could get close enough, he would use an entrapment counter-spell, if he remembered it.

He wasn't used to this rushing around. Six decades of trying to please Arthur and Guinevere takes the stuffing out of any man. Having the reputation of being able to use enchantments merely meant he was put in situations of extreme danger. Instead of rocking in a comfortable chair in front of a roaring fire in the twilight of his life, he had to ward off the slingshots and arrows of Black Knights, ugly Saxons and horned demons.

What was that spell doing? He'd made it to be rid of a spot so it had mutated, gone feral. Autumn leaves on the ground were turning green and returning, upwards to their twigs. If that was all, and only in this area, it wouldn't be so bad, but it might not stop. If he couldn't catch and deactivate the magic it could wreck the planet's whole ecosystem. Another word from a vision, although he knew ecosystem before as Mother Nature, whose wayward son was to be called pollution and whose charming daughters warmed the globe, somehow. Whatever their names, he worried about the future if the magic he'd released created havoc with trees being overwhelmed with their returning leaves and the soils deprived of their nourishment. All his fault.

Just as he reached within a hand's grasp of the swirling spell seen through the rising curtain of once-dead leaves, a hedgehog shot up in the air and flew past his ear.

"No, you've given furze-pigs the ability to fly!" He ducked then tripped face first in a large field mushroom. He elbowed himself up. Just as he was thinking how it would be scrumptious to have mushrooms for their supper, something hard pushed into his back forcing him down, back into the fungus, obliterating it beyond consumption.

Through muddy eyelids, he saw Elspeth leaping off him, her skirts flying as she chased the spell.

"Come back," he spluttered. "There's danger."

She called without looking back, but waving a stick, "Don't worry, I have the wand."

Merlin groaned at his pains and at her naiveté as he struggled to his knees. There through the trees in the growing dawn light he spied the purple light like an exploring will o' the wisp marvelling in its new-found world here, machinating mischief there. He'd have to rein it in, use a gathering and entrapment spell on the escaping magic before it hurt Elspeth or undid the very nature of this wood and if left to continue it might undo our Eorthe.

The magician had two chase targets. The girl had to be stopped first because he couldn't focus while she endangered herself. He threw a hastily-contrived tripping spell that should have resulted in her falling harmlessly. Sadly he missed and an ash tree found its branches entwined instead. It released all its leaves on top of Elspeth, making her stop, fall, laugh and be caught by Merlin. He used an enchanted twine to tie her ankles.

"I'll release you by and by."

She sat up and screamed, "No one binds me! Let me go."

"For your own good. That escaped magic has a mind of its own and is dangerous."

As if it heard, the purple spell shot a spray of acorns at Merlin, reminding him of machine guns in his visions. He ducked, making the missiles destroy the base of a beech. He threw himself on top of the girl as the tree fell. Luckily, it missed them although they were further covered in leaves and insects.

"See, Elspeth, the magic started by undoing a flaw in a skin imperfection, what else will it find necessary to undo?"

He shook off the living debris and leaves and gathered his thoughts for a suitable gathering spell. He had to run again as the purple dove deeper into the wood. He followed it through a dell, zig-zagged over a hilly copse then skidded to a halt on a lake's pebble beach. Had it gone into the water? He hoped not as most spells didn't work close to that amount of liquid. His eyesight became blurred as grit lifted from the beach and hovered in front of him. They shot upwards, followed by pebbles. Gravel moved beneath Merlin's feet making him fall onto his back. He looked up at the sky, pink at the edges, blue in the middle but becoming obscured by the rising stones.

Now larger stones rose from the beach, some dripping from the lake, slowly at first then gathering pace as they followed the smaller particles. He saw twigs, leaves, everything loose, leaving the ground and heading upwards but where to? A pebble brushed past his ear on its way skyward, then another.

Elspeth's tremulous voice reached him. "You can't keep me a prisoner, Merlin. Oh, what's happening?"

He turned to see that somehow she'd ruptured the twine at her ankles. She still held his 'wand'. Surely it didn't really work?

He craned his aching neck back upwards, reluctant to stand in case this falling business of his became perpetual. "I believe the magic thinks anything loose on the planet is an imperfection and is sending it all back to where it came from."

Elspeth caressed her now smooth face. "That is so sweet, the spell wanting everywhere to be perfect. Look it is all flying, like a cloud to meet the rising sun."

"That's it! Of course. It thinks this planet came from the sun and so its imperfections are going back to its creator."

Elspeth ran her fingers through her dark hair. A loose strand broke free and joined the few remaining uplifting pebbles. "I thought Eorthe came from clay in Odin's hands, not the sun."

"Ah, you've been listening to our Norse friends. It doesn't really matter what they or we believe, but what that idiot magic thinks it knows."

She glanced over at the trace of purple still visible in trees across the lake then smiled at Merlin. "Can you not confuse that spell further, with some artful illusions of your own?"

The magician grinned. "You genius." He leant forward to pat her on the head but she lifted her face and kissed him full on the lips. His emotions flitted from embarrassment to wonder at the honeyed sweet wetness of her lips. How strange were the females, and what had he been missing all these years?

First the spell. He threw his hands out at the magic and created bright orbs either side of it, to create a distraction. His confidence enabled the correct gathering spell to form in his mind.

"*Return Nunc revertetur ad me. Dissipantur aucturitas tua.*"

To his relief the purple glow travelled across the water to his hands and dissipated.

Elspeth frowned at him. "Will that hurt *you*, now?"

"No, the spell is disabled and vanished." He released a deep sigh and finally smiling looked at the girl.

No. He wasn't sure at first and he didn't want to worry her, but there was a black hair newly sprouting from her right cheek. A smudge grew to a spot. Perhaps she couldn't feel it, but she surely would soon enough. His undoing of the spell had removed its power backwards to its inception. If so, that would mean... He glanced up at the sky darkening with the accelerating return of many hundredweights of pebbles. He rolled on top of Elspeth and covered his head.

"Nooooo."

WRONG NUMBER

KEN GAZED UP at the black autumn sky. He smiled at stars behaving properly in their constellations, then at a light that lined from the east. A satellite or space station? A door opened behind him. Yellow light flooded the garden, blotting out the heavens. He turned to glare just as his wife's voice hit him.

"What are you doing out here?"

"Keep your hair on, Angie, I'm trying to get a signal on this new phone your brother gave me."

"Your parents are fighting, and if my mother folds her arms any tighter she'll crush her ribs. Derek keeps putting the TV on, and I need you to open another red—for my nerves."

Ken glanced back up to the sky one last time before rejoining his thirtieth birthday party. His parents were tug-of-warring over a long packet wrapped in shiny red paper. As soon as his mother saw him, her scowl transformed to a toothy smile.

"Kenneth, come and get your present."

He hesitated. Clearly, there was a problem judging by his father's tormented face. He assumed they hadn't divorced years ago for the sake of their children but Ken wished they had. There they were competing to be the one to give him his present of socks, slippers, a tie—whatever. They'd never given him the present he'd really wanted: peace, genuine smiles for each other. Oh well, he'd never change their lifestyle pattern now. He strolled over with his hand out when his jacket pocket jangled into the phone version of *The Stripper*, making his brother laugh. Ken shot an evil-eye at him, but he laughed all the more.

Ken waved the phone at his parents to indicate he was taking it into the peace of the garden. He was glad for the interruption though puzzled as no one had his new number—except his brother. He examined the phone looking for a famous brand. The name Nookia shone in metallic green on the black plastic. Typical of his brother to acquire a knock-off.

The display didn't help. It shone its electric blue light with the words "Incoming call from Gobowen."

"Call from a girlfriend already?" said Angie from the doorway.

"It says Gobowen. Who or what's that? Sounds familiar."

"A hospital in Shropshire."

"Mental?"

"It should be to want you, but it's orthopaedic. Probably someone's name." She took it from him and held it to her ear for a few seconds. "Maybe they do have a psychiatric unit. Sounds like gibberish."

Ken took it back for a listen. "Ku four-five-six. Toggle seven-eight-nine. Frequency twelve-point-one Giga-Hertz." Then hiss. He laughed. "It might as well be gibberish. It's some radio frequency testing routine. It's not my girlfriend, love, you know I'm more careful than that." He hoped she knew he was joking. Having an affair would be as safe as playing football on a busy motorway. Angie pecked him on the cheek before rejoining the melee. Anyway, he did love her, her perfume, her cooking, and he refused to think outside that box.

A shout from the party and a turned-up stereo shook him out of his reverie. He examined the phone again and pressed call-back. Gobowen showed again as the ID for the other end. Hissing, then a Deep South US accent: "Hey, Alice, I told you not to call me while I'm up here." More hissing followed by a flourish of castanet clicks. He imagined a flamenco dancer in a red swirling dress, stockings–stop it. Back to the call.

"Hello, who's that?" said Ken.

"Hank Gobowen, now buddy, who the hell are you?"

"Hang on, not the Hank Gobowen, astronaut, raconteur, voted number-one guest on TV talk shows?"

"You're not a booking agent?"

"No, I'm a wrong number. Are you at Houston–ah, no, you'll be in a TV studio."

"Hah. No, I'm on comms watch on *Demetrius*. You know? The spacebus up in orbit since last Tuesday. Anyway, buddy, I can't keep chatting. My pay-as-you-go is running up a bill. Goodbye, whoever you are."

"I'm Ken Stones... hello? Damn he's gone." His one chance of fame and he blew it. He imagined all those talk shows Hank's going to brag on that he used his cellphone to chat to a Brit back on the planet but he didn't know the idiot's name.

He dared himself to call-back again, but resisted.

Angie stood hands on hips in the doorway. "This is your birthday, come inside and enjoy it."

"Really, have our relatives gone?"

"Idiot. I'm pissed off playing at referee. Do your bit."

"Angie, you'll never believe who I've just been talking to on this phone."

"It could be the man on the moon for all I care."

"Close. Real close. No, why have all the lights gone out—and the smoke alarm going berserk? Derek! Ah, birthday cake with thirty damn candles."

NEXT MORNING the bedside clock alarm penetrated Ken's thumping head. His arm lashed out to sweep the bedside table but missed the vibrating clock, which joyfully travelled out of his reach, toppled over the edge and turned itself off, buried in the waste-bin. Only then could he hear Angie crashing around in the kitchen and the television belting out breakfast news.

The door kicked open as Angie staggered in with a full laundry basket. One of his green boxers fell out.

"Sundays *you* make breakfast. Why are you still in bed?"

"I'm at a difficult age."

"You've always been at a difficult age, what's different now you are thirty?" She laughed and launched herself onto the bed. Rising to her change in mood, Ken grabbed, but missed as she twisted. He froze mid-play as a word from the TV news shocked him. "...spacebus..."

He rolled from under Angie and ran into the kitchen, his face a blue sheen as he stared at the screen.

"...Houston admits they have lost all radio communication with... "

"Don't think you can come back to bed."

"Shhssshhh!"

"...even instrumental telemetry is spasmodic although... "

"Birthday or not."

"...seems normal."

"Hell, Angie. I was talking to them last night, and now they've lost radio contact."

"Trust you to mess things up. With who? I'm not sure I want you to have a mobile phone. You might start that affair up again with Teresa."

"I didn't have an affair. Not with her. Joke. Anyway, this is important. Where's my mobile? I put it on the table last night."

He looked at Angie who looked at the floor.

"Come on, Angie."

"I said I don't want you to have it."

"Good grief, woman, you haven't binned it!"

A fruitless search in the tipper-lid bin made him step back from the sour yoghurts and fermenting fruit. He looked at his wife, scrutinising her face for clues. Despite her womanly skills, Ken spotted her eyes flick to the fridge, in which he found his mobile phone pretending to be a pack of Silver Maid butter. After he dried the condensation, he dashed outside, found Gobowen and hit Call.

After the hissing and assorted clicks: "Kgorrrha uochxa grrr-eouwa."

"Sorry, Hank, were you eating your tea? Hello?"

"Arrchx cooroo snigurghghz."

"I'll try again later, Hank, bye for now." Ken looked at his phone for a few moments as he thought about the news broadcast and the garbled speech from Hank. Was it messed up because of some signal breakdown on the Shuttle such as the reason Houston might be incommunicado through their more conventional radio? Maybe the signal became scrambled for security reasons. Ken had a twitching stomach muscle telling him that neither was true and that something more sinister was going on.

"Ken, get in here, it's raining," shouted Angie.

Ken looked up for confirmation and was rewarded with a raindrop into his right eye.

"I knew that phone would be a bad idea," said Angie. "You'll be phoning that weird woman. What's her name?"

"Angie?"

"Funny—not. What is her name, Hannah?"

"No, Hank is the astronaut I've talked to—"

"You'll need a hanky if you're lying. And you'll get RSI from too much texting."

"Texting? Now, that is a good idea. Text messages can often sneak through problem signal areas when voice mail can't."

He followed Angie back into the kitchen, scraped the terracotta-tiled floor with his chair as he sat at the laminated oak table and found the text option.

"Hi Hank. Hope ths gts 2 U. Hustn sez U have a coms prob. Can this hlp?" He pressed the Send button and watched the animated graphics whiz it off to space.

He sat at the table, elbows either side of his mobile phone, resting his face in his hands. Ten minutes later. "Come on, Hank." Another thirty minutes and he lifted his face to allow blood circulation.

Angie threw him her exasperated face. "Are you coming to mMother's for dinner?"

"I'll give it a miss this week, love. I don't want to miss this call. It could be more important than you can possibly imagine. Even more than when your sister rings to tell you about a sale at Debenhams."

"Why can't you bring it with you? I thought that was the point of mobile phones."

"I need it plugged in, dear. It's a bit low on charge. You go and give them my best wishes."

"Yeah, right. While you arrange a rendezvous with Hannah. She is an ex, isn't she?"

"Yes, but no. Stay here if you are so sus."

The phone sprang into a wolf-whistle, simultaneously vibrating itself into a spin on the polished tabletop. Angie went for it but Ken grabbed it first.

"Hp"

"What?" said Ken, then looked at Angie, wondering if she was more text abbrev-savvy than she made out.

"She wants to meet you at the Hypermarket coffee shop," she said, with a face that clearly read not joking.

"Sweetheart, that's where you and I meet. If I tried to arrange an assignation with another woman it would hardly be where we might bump into you."

"Where else then, that could be Hp?"

"I don't know. Hendon Park?"

"There. You admit to having an affair."

"What? No I don't. You tricked me. Good God woman, there's a shuttle crew in trouble up there and they've sent me a message. I ask for help and all you do is accuse me of philandering."

"Help," she said, waving her hands in the air to accompany an obvious remark.

"Of course. You're a genius. A suspicious one. I'll send another text asking for clarification."

"You don't think I meant it, did you?"

"Hank. How can I hlp?" He punched the send button. "Meant what?"

"If you think I believe you are in contact with an astronaut you're more crazy than I thought. It's me that needs help to be rescued from you." She slammed the door on her way out.

The phone wolf-whistled again and was in Ken's hand before it finished.

"Call NASA abort pic"

Ken tried to call using voice. "Hank, are you there?"

He was rewarded with a cacophony of hisses and clicks before he heard: "--gent. Must not return. Aarrgh eeeuugh!" A ten second pause followed while hot perspiration stung Ken's eyes yet a cold shiver travelled up and down his back as if his long-dead grandfather had materialised through the tabletop. His phone sounded again with the strange gutteral voice he heard yesterday. "Kgorrrha uochxa grrr-eouwa. Kgorrrha uochxa grrr-eouwa."

He tried to recall what Hank had said before his agonising cry—call NASA pic. Obviously he was being asked to let Houston in on his mobile phone experience. The pic must mean picture, but which, and where? He looked through the recent internet news pictures of the spacebus flight until all radio and telemetry abruptly ended yesterday. Hank's smiling clean-shaven face drew Ken's attention. A typical all-American guy looked through the screen at him, no indication of any problem. Then in yesterday morning's shuttle picture Ken spotted a mobile phone in Hank's hand. The screen glowed. Of course! It was a picture phone. He snatched his new phone off the table and eagerly pressed buttons. It was a dodgy gift from his low-life brother. No instruction book and no helpful sibling words. Ken didn't believe it would come to life when he first tried it, and hadn't got round to exploring its multiple functions such as video and picture phone.

There; he found the right combination of buttons and hit receive. The screen fluoresced through pastel rainbow colours until the signal became stronger. A face stared at him. The most beautiful person he'd ever seen. He couldn't tell if it was a perfect woman or a young man. Ken laughed. This must be a joke. Maybe Hank had saved this image on his phone pre-mission because none of the crew looked anything as beautiful as this. But the image changed. Only subtly, such that the person looked away and turned a few degrees. It was enough to tell Ken that he was looking at someone on the ship. He put the phone up to his ear and said, "Hello, who are you?"

"Kgorrrha uochxa grrr-eouwa."

"Sorry miss, or sir, that comes through scrambled. Are you using some encryption coding?"

"Kgorrrha uochxa grrr-eouwa."

Ken looked again at the image. From the previous smiling lovely came a twist in its mouth. That shiver in his back travelled to his neck again, only this time his hairs stood up. He dropped the phone just as the image changed again. The phone rotated upside down on the table as if daring him to pick it up. He hesitated but had to snatch it and steeling himself, turned it. The smile had transformed into an ugly snarl, but the eyes worried him more. The iris had narrowed to pinpricks. Then nothing. The signal had not only gone but the phone became warmer, then too hot for Ken to hold onto. He dropped it again as smoke wisped away from the speaker and microphone orifices. Damn. He knew he was losing evidence of what he now realized Hank was trying to tell him.

The shuttle had been invaded and taken over by an alien, maybe several. His face heated. His worry hormones surged through his veins. His phone simmered in meltdown on the table. It would burn the wood laminate and Angie would blame him. Using the kitchen tongs he gingerly placed it in the sink, but he didn't want to pour water in case there was a chance of its recovery. His own logic circuit spurred him to reach for the landline phone but he stopped. How did he phone Houston mission control from a kitchen in Hendon, UK? It wouldn't be in the phone book and search engines took him twenty minutes to accumulate dozens of possible but unlikely current numbers for the command centre. So he called an old school friend who had sucked up through the ranks to become a police inspector.

"What can I do for you, Ken? Driving too slowly on a motorway, again?"

"Please, Ed, this is important. You know that NASA has lost contact with the shuttle *Demetrius*?"

"Don't tell me it's your fault?"

"Ed, I have been able to talk to the shuttle on my mobile phone."

"Of course you have, Ken."

"I don't know how the signal reached my phone but it did. They are in big trouble, Ed. Hank Gobowen asked me to contact NASA, but I don't know how."

"Ken, assuming you haven't been drinking, where did you get this phone from?"

"Why is that relevant, Ed? Aren't you listening to me?"

"Your brother wasn't it?"

"Ed, you are not going to believe what I have to tell them."

"Since it was your brother who gave you the phone, I would believe it."

"Damn it, Ed. I am really worried sick over this. Please be serious."

"Go on then. As long as it isn't about little green men."

Ken froze. What could he say that didn't make him seem a blithering idiot? Seconds went by.

"I take it your message is to be about aliens, then?"

"Ed, suppose you were the only one to know something that meant the spacebus mustn't return to Earth."

"It is returning, there's a failsafe autoreturn routine that will kick in tomorrow morning."

"My God. They have to stop it. Ed. I really did talk to Hank on the shuttle and then someone, something else. I need to tell them. I have to warn the government."

"As in a threat? National security and all that?"

"At last, Ed, you've got it."

"Stay there, Ken. I'll get things in motion. Expect visitors in an hour or so. Bye. Take care."

His fear subsided by a smidgen from sharing his information with a police inspector. Ken put the kettle on. Angie returned, banging the door open, dropping bags of shopping.

"What's wrong with you? Your face is purple. Have you been at those funny ciggies again?"

"No, it's Hank, you know, on the phone."

"You mean Hannah. Wouldn't she play with your ball?"

"He changed into a woman. Rather he didn't but the image did. It was horrible, Angie."

"I told you Hank was a woman. You can't fool me. Idiot. There's more shopping in the car, go fetch it."

He went out towards the car and stopped. Armed men in black balaclavas lay on his lawn.

IT WASN'T RIGHT that he should be held in a police cell. Grey walls, a concrete floor and a damaged black rubber-foam bench. Some anti-terrorist charge had been implemented to hold him while a phalange of different accents asked him over and again what he'd experienced. As time crept by and the disbelief continued, he knew it was too late. He had a chance to save the world and he blew it.

"Come on, Sir, out we go," said the sergeant, to take Ken for a photo and fingerprint session. As they passed the custody officer's table, among the small collection of his pocket contents, he spotted his mobile phone. Damaged but still working. The incoming call light was flashing.

TUMBLER'S GIFT

TUMBLER COULDN'T RESIST IT. He should have kept strolling down this pavement with its smooth marble stones shaped like a giant linear jigsaw but for the girl. Yet, it was not her sleek red hair, curiously upturned nose and sandy one piece that attracted him. A coruscating speck of sand fell from her sleeve to the paving. No surprise as her arm agitated so much and in tune to her swearing and pounding at the lock. Tumbler took in the sky blue velo parked behind the locked gate. He stopped, coughed an excuse-me and placed his hand over the lock. The mechanism whirred and the gate opened.

"How did you do that?" Her voice melted him, ruby lips from which flowed a red wine sound. She stood back a step to study him. Tumbler wished he'd dressed more carefully. Perhaps his Uglee T-shirt instead of this interview suit, and roughed up shock of straw hair instead of it being slick, flat and business-like. Why, was he really expecting a date from this grateful young woman with her emerald green eyes, touched-up freckles and citrus fragrance?

He'd better answer with his chancer voice, lower than his normal too-high squeak, "A gift."

She narrowed her eyes making her ridiculously long eyelashes look as if they were knitting a black scarf. She turned to her velo. "I suppose you can unlock vehicles too?"

"Anything, absolutely everything." He held out his hand. "Tumbler."

She ignored his hand, probably not wanting to reveal further the chips in her photo-nail varnish from assaulting the lock. "Suppose it is not mine, would you still unlock it?"

Trick question. Not that he possessed a moral dilemma here. He was so adept with the sensory locks he could open them just by being close although he'd rather his clients think he had to be physical. He worried about losing this fish before she'd properly bitten. Correct answer then. "Yes, if that is what you desired."

She turned to him, smiled and said, "Right answer. It is mine. Ember." She took her smile away as quickly as she gave it. "But I was trying to *lock* this gate. It was jammed open. Can you undo your interference and lock the dumb thing?"

"Well... that is another curious thing about my gift."

"I see, no."

"Do you have a key for this gate, as in a metal or is it a fob or voice activated, wireless, IR, nanobot, alpha-brain synched—"

She held up an old-fashioned steel cylinder-lock key.

He took it, turned it over in the bright sunshine, and gave it back. "You bent it."

Her eyebrows rose in the middle. "Can you fix it?"

"It would likely break. Try a locksmith."

"I thought that's what you were... CitZen Tumble?"

"Recks, Tumbler Recks. Just born with a gift for—"

"Then what are you?"

He walked to the hinge of the gate, placed his hand over it and steadied the gate as it became unhinged, lowered to the ground and thus immovable by hand. "Ah, late for a job interview. Say, meet me at ten at the corner of twenty-five and sixty—the Blue Call."

"Why?"

"To see if I got the job, and if I can tell you what it is, and to arrange for your gate to be fixed, unfixed, your choice."

TWO HOURS LATER Tumbler tousled and scratched his now spiky hair thinking he'd overdone the gel and his hand reeked of orange.

The number 273.6 bus glided up. Tumbler stepped to the scanner and waved his palm at it as if he possessed the pass everyone else had to pay for. He thought back to the interview at the CrimPolice offices.

"CLARIFY, YOU DO NOT want me to open an agency safe for which you have lost the combo? Or unencrypt the enemy's Enigmatic Machine?"

His knees steepled as he sat on the too-low chair they'd indicated. The two-person interview committee, both in blue, behind a large desk, didn't like him, he could tell by their curled lips and cursory swiping through his resume as if it would contaminate their eyes. Maybe they'd called up his references.

He cringed at the thought of them knowing of his many unsuccessful employment attempts. He thought he'd make use of his gift but the locksmith danced the angry jig when his wares unlocked themselves permanently when Tumbler got too close. The air steward trial during which overhead lockers fell open and their contents cascaded on the passengers when he walked the aisle. Of course, he could control his powers better now. However, the last job—simple enough, as a snake milker for a pharmaceutical company, Venom Solutions Isn't It Unlimited— went swimmingly until his concentration slipped and so did a lock resulting in the escape of a dangerous Mamba.

He returned to the present. A woman with rusty hair the shape of a mushroom turned to a giant on her left. "I told you, Ap Tor, too flippant. We cannot trust this wisp of a youth with something this important."

"Hey, I am trustworthy. I did not unlock that sealed cabinet in the waiting room. That was a test, yes?"

A huge man with skin the hue of an aubergine waved his hand as if swatting a mozzie off his much-lived-in nose. "Not only *not* a test, you'd walked into the wrong room. CitZen Recks, in this organisation when we lock things we want them to stay that way. Having your alleged ability within nine blocks of here could compromise our integrity."

Tumble bristled at the 'alleged' and looked around for a lock he could wave his hand over. Seeing none he said, "So, why am I here? I am only average at making cofftea."

The woman, her fashionable pearled eyebrows level, stabbed at a golden square on the desk, said, "My numero two here, Ap Tor, believes you can unlock a portal. What do you say?"

Tumbler stood. "Whoa, what have peeps told you about me? I do small stuff, and tangibles like real metal locks not those new entanglement abstract portals." He didn't want to tell them that he didn't know the limits of his capability.

Ap Tor rose to his feet. "Calm down, CitZen Recks. Sit, please.

Intelligence misled us into thinking you are greater than your parts."

Tumbler sat while he thought through the double-speak.

"Course I am. I have hidden depths. Before I say no, what can you tell me about this mission?"

The woman coughed into her hand. Tumbler thought it was a cover for her rapid-speaking a word to Ap Tor. Odd that she'd not been named. He could just come out with it, ask her. Or... He stood again and strolled to a wall decorated with the older type of holo-images. They were muttering among themselves at the desk. Tumbler spotted an image of her. He casually waved his hand into the holo as if asking a fly to leave.

"Please come and sit down," she said.

"All right then, La Bis." He studied her white face expecting her pearled eyebrows to jig a little, but she was a professional.

"You unlocked data in the holo-image?"

"Impressed?"

"I would be more so... if it was *my* name, and not my mother's. I am Li Bis."

Tumbler rubbed his chin, rueing his faux pas. "Which portal is stuck on locked?"

Ap Tor and Li Bis exchanged curt nods. She glanced at her e-square, her eyes nictating, turning the pages as if yet undecided to trust him.

"All right, enough people have been affected by the delays, so it would be in the public domain soon. The portal is at the west pole. It is used to transfer goods to other portals here, in orbit or to the mission on Marz. It is also used by VIPs. Not you—unless you fix it."

Tumbler sweated. "I do not know. Could go badly wrong. Might be unlocking the malfunctioning portal but find myself sucked through it, recycled particles in outer space."

Ap Tor's mouth slanted at a disturbing angle until it opened. "Two drillion credits."

Tumbler stood and half-turned away. "Can I think about it?"

They must have expected his response. Li Bis said, "Back here at fifteen, but you know you do not really have a choice."

Before he could ask her to elaborate, they upped and left.

WHERE WAS SHE? He'd energised himself with a shot of red at the Blue Call and it was now eleven past the time. He thought he'd judged her right, especially with the need to reopen her gate and his gift must have piqued her curiosity.

"Day dreaming, the magician of locks? You can order me a long cobalt—with ice." Ember's voice sneaked up behind him along with her familiar lemon fragrance and brought a smile to his lean face.

"Ember, I hoped you'd come. Let us enjoy a drink and perhaps a sway?"

She swivelled her hips to the beat of the syncopating harmonics from the ceiling, encouraged by the rhythmic floor hues. Tumbler threw himself into the mood and on to the floor in curved leaps. In time with the music, the two of them conjoined with arms around waists and interlocked legs. Such energy use couldn't be sustained for long but with restorative breaks until 14.

"I have to return to the interview room. Submit my response."

She peered into his cool blues. "You must go for it, otherwise you would—"

"Drift? Live a life not knowing what could be? Or have you another agenda, Ember?"

They'd left the hot bar to shudder in the misty moist of the evening and huddled with a small group waiting for the 273.6b to the CrimPolice offices. It was the largest employer in the district and in time, everyone needed permits, dox, retribution forms and punishtags.

Ember linked his arm. "Succeed in this mission and we could achieve much more."

"We?"

Ignoring tuts from the bus stop huddle, she pressed her body against his and nibbled his ear. "I have the strategies, connections and go-go, while you, Tumbler dear, have the gift."

"And credits if I—"

"You see, a team. Here's my ident, let me know how it goes." She kissed, bit, then kissed more his bloodied, grateful lips.

TUMBLER DIDN'T ENJOY his VIP treatment. He'd hoped to exhilarate in the journey to the west pole, travelling by suborbital flier, admiring the oceans, clouds and mountains en route then waving at wonder-gazers staring at him and his escorts in the land vehicles. Instead, he might as well have been inside a window-less box.

He'd not seen pictures of the portal—they were banned in the media—but he thought they'd be like in the movies: an arch, a circle or a wardrobe. None of those things. It was in a warehouse filled with electronic equipment with only squeeze-by space between towers of fluorescent green boxes exuding a whiff of plastic and ozone.

In a clearing, the portal was pointed at by a green-jump-suited scientist, whose arm led Tumbler's eyes to a black plinth on which rested a white spot.

"That's a portal? How—"

Ap Tor chuckled then in his bass voice said, "If only you had understood your school QM."

"Hey, I excelled in school. Performed well in Quantile Mechanics. I subbed a paper on Mileva Einenstein and her Special Relations. Ah, I see, mathematically the portal could be a point. This spot isn't it, is it?"

The big man smiled.

"The white spot just indicates the location of the invisible point?"

"You have the gist of it. You are in the midst of a cube outlined by a thin blue line."

"Oh, I walked right across and into it. Should alarms have gone off?"

Ap Tor held apart his arms. "Everything is disengaged until you unlock this portal."

Tumbler leapt back out of the marked area. "What used to happen when it worked?"

"The controllers set a countdown then everything inside the cube goes to the portal address elsewhere. We receive a signal when another portal wishes to transport goods and people to us, but that's not happening either."

Tumbler paced around massaging his chin.

"If I have to be in the cube, and unlock the portal, what is stopping me disappearing down its plughole?"

Ap Tor laughed. "Our controllers will know if it is operational and will prevent any such activity. However, even if that happened, you would reappear intact at one of the other portals."

Tumbler was disturbed by the big man's hilarity. Was it a cover up for his uncertainty? His hand trembled with the anticipation of unlocking the portal. It would be the pinnacle of his abilities.

The woman, Li Bis, pushed an epad into his hands. "We need you to validate this agreement."

"Ah, a waiver so I cannot sue for a catastrophe?"

"For you to receive two drillion credits."

"Good point. Why would I sue if I had that much." He scratched his stuck-up hair—definitely too much gel this time. "It is not just me that could end up as non-baryonic matter in a dark place, so could this cube, this room and the whole of Terra. Does this agreement absolve me of the end of the world?"

Her raised eyebrows confirmed that the question was rhetorical. Even so, as he presented his fingerprint to the epad, he unlocked clauses that he guessed might deny him his cash.

"Could it be a software glitch or a hardware problem?" He pointed at the batteries of humming machinery.

"The best IT brains that money cannot buy..." she uncharacteristically snickered "...confirmed only this one is jammed, blocked, locked... whatever."

He should run, but more than the money, it was the fascination and the notion of unlocking something so different. In febrile excitement he glanced at their faces. Ap Tor's slash of a smile, Li Bis's return to her usual mode of rectitude. He thought of Ember and her secretive plans for his gift with a promise of as much rapture as he could take if this unlocking worked.

USUALLY, HE'D BE ABLE to unlock any device merely by waving his hand over it, not even touching, as if an electrostatic charge between his skin and the object is enough or a miniscule change in the magnetic field, along with a focus, locus, of quantum untangling occurred. Whatever the real cause, he didn't like to dwell on it too much in case the gift departed.

The portal was an unknown. Should he wave his hand then jump away from the blue lines? Locks unlocked instantly for him. Sometimes accompanied by the syncopated orchestra of a whirring of cogs, electronic protesting humming, or a clatter of pins, twang of springs, tumble of brass, clunk of tumblers.

His rumination was interrupted by Li Bis. "You do not need to worry, CitZen Recks, nothing will happen. This portal has become jammed, possibly inert. We will build a new one even though we are not sure how Tezla Tring disappeared. Go ahead, do your thing."

So he did. Tumbler approached the black plinth, his eyes fixed on the white spot. A tinnitus-like background hum of the computers added to the aroma of plastic, metal and orange zest from his hair gel.

He stuck out his hand.

TUMBLER AWOKE SLOWLY in a hospital bed. He smelt pine disinfectant, an antique aroma and was surprised at the pattern of interlocking squares decorating the screen around his bed. Back home in Deva, the hospitals floral designs abounded everywhere, by law—a notion they calmed patients and accelerated healing. The bedding was white whereas at home the ubiquitous shade was green, by law. So he was successful in unlocking the portal. Yeay, but ended up somewhere strange.

He looked for a wrist alert button but instead found a plastic band with John Doe written and some numbers that could be dates but not as back in Albion. Was he supposed to be this John Doe person?

"Nurse!"

The screen parted and in walked a woman in blue, her brown hair mostly hidden by a ridiculous white hat affair. "Shush, luv, we mustn't disturb the others. Here, now you're in the land of the living, we'll have your details."

At least she spoke Anglian but only just and with a strange twang. No one would be so bold to call a stranger 'love' and what did she mean by 'land of the living'? Was there another kind of land he was expected to be in?

She sat on the chair next to the bed and from her pocket produced an old-fashioned pen and pad.

"Name?"

"CitZen Tumbler Recks. Yours?"

She scribbled on her pad and repeated in her foreign accent, "Sitson Tumberler Wrecks Yaws, that's quite a mouthful. Address?"

He understood little of what she said but took in that she was waiting for the next answer. Probably his age.

"Reev ar leyn."

"What number River Lane, luv?"

Her blue eyes softened his worry, bringing on one of his smiles. He should try his own questions.

He spoke slowly, carefully, "Where am I?"

"Hospital, luv."

"What is the name of this city, and country?"

"Good Lord, 'ave you been worrying over that? This is the Countess of Chester Hospital, in Chester, England, of course. Where did you think you were?"

"At the west pole, or Cit Deva, country Albion. Are they in this hemisphere? A portal nearby?"

She sucked on her pen. "Heard of Deva. There's businesses with that name here in Chester. Oh, and there's the Albion pub. Not heard of no portal, luv."

They exchanged glances, Tumbler realizing what had happened but the nurse's raised plucked eyebrow indicated he was a plaster short of a first aid box. Even so, he needed to exit.

"I am well. Nothing broken. No bleeding. May I leave now?"

She shook her pen. "Not until the doctor says. Anyway the police are waiting to talk to you."

For a fleeting moment he wondered if Ap Tor had followed him through the unlocked portal into this other-dimension-parallel-world place but it was more likely this place's Crim-Police. What crimes might he have committed, illegal entry?

"Excuse me, nurse, where was I found?"

"You kind of appeared—they said 'materialised' like in 'Star Trek' in front of a queue at Rosie's night club. Caused quite a stir with people wanting you chucked to the back. The bouncers decided you were drugged out of your 'ead and called 999."

So many terms he couldn't comprehend: Star Trek, queue, astir, and what on Terra could bouncers be? He should rapid leave but the only way from the bed was through the nurse, the screen and whatever lay beyond. Where was a locked door when he needed one? They'd never suspect he went that way.

At least he wasn't naked but the thin, matching white jacket and bottoms might be conspicuous outside.

"Where are my clothes?"

She pointed at a bedside cabinet. "In your locker."

Lock? Good that locks existed here. It was ajar and his travelling garments were folded there. Browns, and black slip-ons. He slid out of bed and took off his jacket.

The nurse hastily left while he changed bottoms.

Before he could leave, a woman in a black uniform brushed aside the screen. Blond hair in a tight knot, and a serious frown approached him with her hands on her hips.

"I'm Sergeant Stubbs, you want to answer questions here or at the station?"

Tumbler took a step towards the police officer holding out his hand palm up in greeting. "Hey, Sar Jent, I am CitZen Recks. Is the station a portal or—?"

With unnecessary roughness the woman grabbed his hand, snapped a metal clamp around his wrist, twisted and pulled so his other hand joined in. All the time she was talking at him.

"Smart-arse words doesn't cut it with me. You've some explaining to do. We know you're a terrorist trying to create unrest by causing havoc in a popular club."

Tumbler wasn't sure whether to be annoyed or scared at the misguided accusations but he was amused that the presumed CrimPolice woman thought a simple locking device would hold him. He decided to go along with her for the present. She might be armed and would have colleagues nearby.

Leaving the ward in front of Sar Jent he found himself surrounded by more black-garmented men and women all pointing what he presumed to be weapons at him. Nurses, doctors and bewildered patients gawped. A volcano of heat built up in him fuelled by embarrassment. Everything was sufficiently off-kilter to confirm his suspicions that he was not on the Terra he knew. He stopped at the exit to take in the sky—the same blues with cotton-wool clouds; many individual vehicles. A dusty, metallic odour and sparse vegetation with all the concrete. His observations were cut short by being bustled into the rear compartment of one of the autos.

A wailing siren accompanied their journey to another building. He should escape before he was interred so he looked at the doors and surmised a simple locking mechanism so he should be able to unshackle his wrists then run out of the door.

The vehicle decelerated so he glanced down at his wrists and willed the restraints to fall open.

They remained locked!

Up to now he'd been confident he'd escape from any situation. Nothing held him even at the academy when he'd been deliberately tied up with thick rope by the upper echelon. To their amazement the rope untwined itself and chased them.

Normally, he could pass his hand over a lock, not even quite touching it, but these restraints were rigid, keeping his hands apart so that the fingers of one hand couldn't quite reach the lock on the other. It shouldn't make a difference. Perhaps his power didn't work here, or not in the same way. He frowned and he never did that. He could reach the door handle by twisting his body around but whoa, the vehicle turned and accelerated.

The CrimPolice woman turned to him. "The situation in the town centre's getting worse. We're taking you to see what you've done. You can explain."

"See what?" As far as Tumbler knew he'd unlocked a portal, fell through it back in his home town on the other side of the planet. Ah.

He laughed and said, "This is unreal. I am asleep, dreaming?"

"Then we're in your nightmare. We'll be there in twenty minutes."

He wondered what minutes were while pinching his legs then flinching with wakefulness pain. Not dreaming. He'd no choice but to confess.

"All right, Sar Jent, I will help but I fear you will not believe."

The vehicle roared through just-parted road blocks.

She turned to face him. "Are you saying you're not Tumbler Reck?"

"Well, yes I am but..."

"You're not from a place called Deva?"

How could he explain where he'd really come from when he could only guess?

Tumbler recognized much of the urbanscape from his world: the red sandstone bridge through the medieval wall that surrounded the centre. The shops were different and this place must have invested in religion because there were many churches while his Deva possessed one. They rounded the familiar market cross only to screech to a halt, bumping into a red RescueCar. Strangely, the Rescuers in their padded black suits and yellow helmets, didn't turn to remonstrate but stood with a crowd of assorted service persons staring towards the town centre.

A CrimPoliceman yanked him out of the vehicle but didn't undo the restraint. Another gripped his other elbow and the three of them barged their way through the onlookers, who gawped ahead without speaking. There was noise. Like a gentle hail, accompanied by the pungent odour of ozone. Within moments his stomach found itself pressed against a plastic barrier.

Through a haze of brick dust he could see that a block of buildings had gone, disintegrated or fallen down a hole. That was it: a sinkhole had opened up under the city near where he'd been found.

Sar Jent opened up the barrier. A Rescuer in a white helmet held up his hand.

"Too dangerous, Ma-am, it's widening."

She frowned at him as if the phenomenon was his fault. "How fast?"

"Tricky one, that, about half a metre a minute but accelerating. Reckon, if you stay there you'll disappear with it in ten minutes. This chap an expert?"

The CrimPolice woman turned directly in front of Tumbler and jabbed at his chest. "Fire Watch Manager Brown, he is the one who caused this. Terrorist or idiot, he's to blame."

"Hey, I'm just a passing tourist. Anyway, have you not come across sinkholes before? They are where subsidence underground such as mines, ca—"

"There's no hole," she said, "as well you know."

"No hole?"

"No hole."

He peered across the now dusty tarmac to where a four-storey block of shops used to be topped by a huge nightclub. Like a red and grey mist, clearing and thickening in swirls settling on what looked like a bed of crumbs. No hole. The fabric of space here had disintegrated.

He could see the circular rim of fine debris crossing the road until it reached the kerb. It was as if the stone turned to sand, then vanished.

Everyone shuffled backwards. Tumbler frowned as he was being held still, then he had an idea.

"Have you tried sending a remote in there?"

They looked at him with raised eyebrows.

"You know, an unmanned vehicle? Oh, I give up. Here let us see what happens when I kick this..." He booted a metal clamp that had fallen off the barrier. It bounced along the paving and as it crossed the event-circumference it puffed out of existence. "Have you tried that with an organic substance?"

She smiled for the first time. "You mean like a volunteer? Why do you think you're here?"

Tumbler tried to step back but was held fast.

"After all, you must have done something to create this. Some kind of new terrorist weapon, but you're not going to kill *yourself*, are you?"

"I've tried to tell you. I was unlocking a portal in another version of this world and fell through into this one. Agreed it is too much a coincidence for me to have appeared in the centre of that circle, but cause it, no!"

"Yes, you did," she said as she nodded to the two CrimPolice to drag him forward.

"I was doing your CrimPolice on the other side a favour." He tried to distract them from throwing him into oblivion. "How high does it go?"

"What?"

"Have you told your flight operators to keep your air-vehicles away? It could go up all the way to space."

It bought him a few moments as they looked up and saw clouds overhead, then the circle widened. A nearby lamppost became as thin as a bamboo cane, wilted then went altogether, as shops lost their frontage on the other side.

The Rescuer shouted at everyone to get back, right back, preferably to another city.

Tumbler was taken back to their CrimPolice vehicle. As he sat alone inside, he tried again to unlock his restraints but nothing happened.

Sar Jent finished a conversation with the others but when she tried to open the vehicle door it was locked. As were the other doors.

She scowled at him. How could it be *his* fault?

He realized what had happened.

The driver used his key to open doors.

As they sirened their way through the dispersing crowd, Sar Jent turned to Tumbler. "We're heading for the Wrexham Police Headquarters. We should be safe at fourteen miles, unless you know different. We've observers radioing in so we'll know what's happening."

"And cams, presumably."

"Of course."

As they sped down Wrexham Road the scenery was so familiar it was as if he was back home, yet they appeared to be a century behind. He wished he *was* back home, hadn't taken this mission then he'd be in Ember's arms.

They reached the tall CrimPolice building soon enough but he waited until they advanced on the glass doors before attempting to lock them. He couldn't help smiling when they refused to auto-slide at Sar Jent's approach. He enjoyed her scowl as she used her comms to make someone come to physically unlock it. In the foyer, they all looked at him. He stuck out his tongue.

A big man rather like Ap Tor walked up to them.

"Throw him in Cell five, Sergeant Stubbs, while your team go to the obs room."

"Sir, I'd rather keep him with us. His input is essential."

"Your responsibility then." He marched away.

As they waited for an elevator to arrive, Tumbler thought about how to experiment with his new locking skill. Precious little that wouldn't inconvenience him too. He could try locking the elevator doors but he had an interest in surviving this situation. After a silent rise to the ninth floor, and still with his wrists locked, he emerged into a bright, airy room that was all windows, amazing views over the city and hills. Same sky, similar landscape, same-ish human beings, wrong world yet...what? A dash of red hair drew his attention to a woman operative at a chunky computer terminal. His elbows were free from the grip of others so he wandered over.

The hairs rising on his neck told him it could be Ember from the other Deva. He detected a floral aroma rather than the fruit fashionable in his world, and her hair coiffured short instead of bouffant, but her reflection in the monitor had arranged her freckles in the same order. She turned—yes her eyes the same emeralds.

"What you gawping at?"

Umm the voice isn't quite as velvet as Ember, nor the words.

"You, because you remind me of a young woman I know. Her name's Ember."

She sneered a guffaw at him. "That's the worst chat-up line I've heard. Somebody's told you my name, haven't they?"

The whole situation was nerve-wrackingly surreal before but this—does it mean there's another Tumbler in this existence? He'd have to check out the gaols.

"Is your name really Ember?"

She stood and pointed at her name badge. Tumbler never liked those identity badges stuck on women's chests. How did they know he wasn't ogling? She wore a CrimPolice blue shirt with the top few buttons undone, the rest under tension.

Through the version of written Anglian he could see her name started wrong.

"Amber." Not quite Ember.

She looked at his restraints as if for the first time.

"Ah, you're the terrorist who set off some kind of absorption bomb. You gonna tell us how to disarm it?"

He hadn't considered the mechanism of the oblivion event.

"Is an absorption bomb a real thing for your world? It isn't in mine."

She scowled. "I don't know. Use that terminal to search for it. We use a search engine called Infoseek in conjunction with the PNC." She used a key on her lanyard to unlock his restraint. "There, no need for handcuffs in here. Try to escape and I'll floor you."

He rubbed his wrists. He sat on a swivel chair and smiled at the primitive user interface, but as soon as he touched the mouse the computer froze.

"What are you doing?"

"Ah, unlike with your other self, Ember, when I could unlock anything at will, it seems my gift has not only reversed itself but locks anything even when I don't desire it."

"You're nuts."

"It could be awkward... for instance trying to unzip, because I need to—"

"You'll have to figure that out for yourself or get a man to help you. Uh oh, incoming data."

A speaker on another monitor was turned up for the dozen officers to hear.

"The edge of the destruction circle has reached the Wrexham boundary, five miles from the origin. Its speed has risen from one mile an hour to two in the last ten minutes. Emergency evacuation zone has extended to twenty miles. This headquarters is closing in thirty minutes and relocating to Shrewsbury. All leave is cancelled. Public broadcasts and speaker vans are informing the public and the army are assisting in transferring care homes, hospitals, et cetera. Please be calm as the speed is still less than walking speed. Save critical data to your memory sticks."

Tumbler's stomach tightened as the realization hit that he might not get out of this. Nor anyone. Suppose the circle didn't stop? Two miles an hour would mean it would swallow Londinium in five days, half the world in eighty days, the whole world by half a year. Surely, it must stop soon.

Sar Jent walked up to them, her face pinched with worry. Probably thinking of her Chester home now a dust cloud, perhaps her family in the panic escape. She had a tall thin man with her.

"This is Professor Tring, a physicist from UMIST. He's only agreed to come on condition the police helicopter is on standby but we're using it anyway to take you and him to Manchester."

Tumbler wondered if he was related to Tezla Tring.

Tring waved his arms, which appeared to energise his eyebrows. "I have some QM theories to pass by you. It could be that a quantum entanglement event propelled you—"

"Professor," Sar Jent said, "we have no time for this. I'll take you back up to the pad after handcuffing the prisoner."

Tumbler put his hands in his pockets. "I won't cooperate if you put those back on me, and I want Ember, Amber to come with us."

"No, she has duties in the evacuation."

"I have a connection between her and my world." He pleaded with his eyes to the professor. "It could be useful."

The tall man nodded sending a drift of dandruff at Sar Jent.

She sneezed and said, "Okay then."

"I don't want to go with *him*," Amber said, pointing at Tumbler.

"For God's sake," Sar Jent said. "It's an order, now hurry."

IN THE HELICOPTER, the professor indicated the headphones. Amber sat at the back so she didn't have to sit near Tumbler, mildly hurt but too distracted to argue. The professor talked into his headset.

"Recks, can you hear me?"

He could but his attention was taken by the view north. He could see much of the vast circle of oblivion, and they were not far from its relentlessly widening circumference.

"Pilot, we must not fly over the circle!"

The helicopter slowed its forward motion until it hovered near but not over the danger zone.

"Prof, I hear you but I am both scared to death and curious. What happens when the River Caer meets the circle?"

They leaned with their faces against the Perspex on opposite sides of the helicopter. Wiping his condensed breath away, Tumbler could see that the river ended at the circumference so the event was absorbing or disintegrating water too. Consequently, none was emerging at the estuary on the other side.

Tring turned from his window and nudged Tumbler's elbow.

"Young man, we think we know what's happened, but because the situation is urgent any solution has to be drastic."

Tumbler raised his eyebrows. "You believe me?"

"I had a briefing from Sergeant Stubbs. I believe you came

through a cusp or rift in a kind of time decoherence, in quantum mechanics terms."

"I fell through a portal, though you do not have them here."

"Yes... you say you had a gift of unlocking and fell through a portal, so— oh dear, how can I put this?"

Amber butted in, "Just chuck him out."

Tumbler couldn't help an embarrassed laugh at her outburst. In so many ways she was the opposite of Ember, as if she possessed the mean bones so that the woman in the other world didn't need to.

Tring tried again. "You're aware of the notion of quantum entanglement—what Einstein called 'spooky action at a distance' where even though entangled particles can be widely separated in space, they are intrinsically linked so that one affects the other."

Tumbler thought back to his studies. "I believe it was Mileva Einenstein, whose husband worked in Patents and neither thought Quantile Mechanical entanglement had validity."

"Your being here supports the reality of different existences we can't normally detect. The interesting thing is, Recks, that if you hadn't been found we'd not know how this disaster happened, nor any possible solution."

Tumbler listened but his focus was on the widening circle. He was sure it was spreading faster, at least twice a comfortable walking speed. Intriguing how it was levelling everything, creating cliffs as it sliced into hills. Left behind was a mottled flat surface obscured by settling dust at the circumference. There were indentations, where the riverbed was lower than the height where it had started. He looked up and through the whir of rotor-blades, he saw a few puffs of white clouds. Evidence the effect had little altitude.

"Did you hear me, Tumbler Recks?"

He looked around at him. "Yes, my presence proves some kind of entanglement can exist and not just as a wavelength, although everything is constructed of wavelengths."

"And a possible solution could... everything you say? Is that what physicists now say in your world? Isn't there a wave-particle duality? And larger objects are defined more as particles?"

Tumbler laughed at the man's knitted brows. "I only did the compulsory hypno-course. I do not understand why I fell through a portal at our west pole and emerged half way around the planet here in what you call Chester."

The professor smiled, revealing uneven, discoloured teeth, something that never happened in Tumbler's world. "We've thought about that. Of course the planet continued spinning although in which direction is debateable if your poles are east and west. You emerged in a parallel city for which you had connections."

Tumbler couldn't tear his eyes from the teeth but stumbled on.

The teeth hid behind thin lips. "How has your ability to unlock things changed?"

"I could control the unlocking but locking things happens when I touch them even without thinking. Let me see. I had better not lock this helicopter's controls, though I have a feeling I might have inadvertently locked this door. What do you have that's lockable?"

Amber threw him a red leather book with a brass clasp. "It's my diary, but the lock's broken so it's open all the time."

Tumbler caught it and turned it over. He passed his hand over the mechanism and it sealed shut. He threw it back, more gently than the way it came.

"Oh great, now it's locked *forever*?"

The pilot unlocked the door next to Tumbler. "It should slide open now."

The prof leaned across and slid it open.

The noise level increased and loose papers flew around the cockpit, but they could still hear each other through the headphones.

The helicopter rose to cloud level, banked and flew over the circle's edge.

"Hey, we should not fly... ah, too late. Are you doing this for a better view?"

The pilot spoke in a gravelly voice, "Orders to hover over the centre."

Tumbler shook with silent worry. More so when the teeth showed their gravestone view again.

"Sorry, Recks, but you are the only solution."

In spite of the cold air rushing in, Tumbler's face glowed with heat. "What do you mean?"

"He's so dumb," Amber said from the back. "How could my other self see anything in him?"

Dumb? What had he missed?

He looked out of the door and saw the dust had settled over the central area of what used to be ancient Deva but was now a giant empty car park. The helicopter tilted making Tumbler reach for the door handle and wishing they had seat belts. Before he could save himself, a hand pushed his back. They were forcing him out!

The fools must have thought his presence on the ground would lock the growing oblivion circle. He struggled but someone—Amber—grabbed his feet and were lifting them in the air so he couldn't hook them around a seat.

He was pushed out as far as his waist—his hands holding back onto the doorway. The cold wind bit into his face and his eyes watered.

He yelled, "Tring this won't work," but his headset had pulled off and his appeal blew away. One thing to try.

Within moments he was yanked back in, and his headphones jammed on.

Everyone shouted at once but the pilot overrode the other two. "What have you done? I've lost the controls."

Tumbler's turn to grin. He'd locked down everything. The engine cut out and the rotors slowed as the aircraft started its downward plummet. Tumbler wondered if gravity was as relentless here. He heard Amber yell for a parachute but they were too low. Probably only 15 seconds to impact. What a way to end a short life, but at least he was taking his murderers with him. Aeronautical if not poetic justice. His calmness was diametrically opposite to the panic of the others.

He watched the circle appearing to accelerate at them, then nothing.

ALL OF TUMBLER'S JOINTS and muscles ached. He assumed he was in purgatory but through a mist saw curtains with holo-blooms around his bed and gardenia fragrance. Back in hospital on *his* Terra.

The blue diffused light from the ceiling became eclipsed and it took a while for Tumbler to realize it was Ap Tor.

So Tring was right, his locking had stopped the phenomenon of that Earth disappearing into this one. If he survived so might have Tring and Amber, wandering around finding themselves.

"Ap Tor I think Tezla has returned. He needs a dentist."

"We were nearly concerned for you, CitZen Recks. Now the analgesics are working, we are discharging you from here in Beach Hospital to take you on a sightseeing tour."

"Just show me on screen, I am tired."

A beefy nurse pressed a button so that he was raised and ejected from the bed, landing on his unsteady feet. He stripped Tumbler of his gown and passed him a green all-in-one tunic.

Outside, Tumbler breathed in the fresh air filled with the herbal fragrances from the hospital gardens. "Why here and not Deva Hospital?"

Ap Tor chuckled. "You'll see, but half your fee has gone into reparations."

Half of two drillions was still a drillion but it jarred and he snarled until he saw the other passenger in the parked flier.

"Ember? All this way to greet me?"

She half-smiled but her eyes were behind a fashionable sandy veil. "I had to be temporarily rehoused, as are you. These last few days I have been experiencing strange dreams about us. You really are a troublesome boyfriend."

He grinned at her label for him, but was shushed by Ap Tor.

"We closed down the west portal so that mission was a waste of resources. You need to explain that."

The flier took off giving Tumbler a view over the estuary to where Deva should be with its low buildings, trees and single tall spire.

"Is that a volcano?" he said at the sight of a triangular peak, the height of a mountain.

"It behaved like one in that it started in Deva Central as a small cone then puffed out dust until *you* returned. Analysis revealed it is from brick dust, soil, vegetation and water. Explain."

Tumbler laughed. His seat belt clasp unlocked. Then at will it locked again.

Lock, unlock lock, unlock. He couldn't do that before. He laughed again.

DON'T BITE MY FINGER

WHAT IS ABOVE, IS BELOW

In spite of the heady fragrance of mountain poppies lining the meandering trail, I focus on the cloud that clings to the summit five miles distant. Does this Gelugpa mountain always fly that wet, white banner? If so, I am to be blessed with a spring season of saturation. After four hours of steady uphill hiking, my muscles had screamed for peace. That was a half-hour koan mantra ago.

"At one
Through two.
In true spirit
In harmony."
Now the mission calls me to move on.

I caress a string of malachite beads. I should fight pride yet I recall with a smile the presentation of the beads from the Shaolin temple. A venerable master had decided I'd passed the first novice recondite hurdle. Those innocent days. Now, I face a real test. I stand then glance down at my resting bench: a too-big hessian bundle. One more glance up at my destination then a grab at cloth-wrapped string before heaving the load onto my back. Not a Sherpa, yet I walk in a burden's shade. That morning I smelled of fresh river water; now my winter black robe reeks of over-active armpits. And the hem has picked up the ochre and grit of the path.

I place a foot forward up the path then remember. Without turning my head I speak softly as if to the wind. "Awake and gather your bundle, Genda Doi."

"Please, Master, not yet. My feet are sore and my back is on fire."

"Do not make me look back now I am on the road. And I am not a master, but a teacher." I smile to myself knowing I'd made the same mistake when I was a novice, a status I still possess. Four years is nothing. Genda is more chick than a chicken.

"So you have told me, Teacher, but in the ordinary world you are my master. All right, I'm coming... why is my bundle heavier than yours anyway?"

"Its weight is immaterial."

"Easy for you to say. Look at the food—I have a ton of rice, you have just the pot."

"Genda Doi, which is the more important?"

After a slipped-sandal scuffle on loose gravel, followed by grunts of recovery, the apprentice finds his voice. "That's a trick question, isn't it?"

"Zen isn't about tricks."

"Only in theory. Okay then. I say food is more important—we can't eat an iron pot. Ah, you're pointing at the terraces on the slopes. There might be rice and millet in some, I suppose. I said it was a trick."

The path steepens, obliging both of us to have lungs screaming their own koans.

"Master, why do they call you Tiramisu? Isn't that a chocolate dessert?"

I refrain from sighing at the nomenclature tease. Twenty years. It's too much. "I am Tiramiso, though it would be good to have a name of something that gives pleasure."

"Okay, but you've not told me why we're slogging our guts out on this damned mountain."

"Gelugpa is a holy mountain. Show respect."

Genda takes a break from hiking, and bows in the direction of the summit. "But why, when the path is icy, do we risk breaking our necks?"

It is more than icy at this height. Snow patches hide in hollows. "We need to reach the monastery before the spring thaw."

"Why does it matter when there's no one there but a few rats and eagles?"

Something, not Genda, nags at me making the hairs on the back of my neck rise. I try not to worry the lad but keep a wary eye on our surroundings. "The Enlightened One has given me the task to—"

"To what? You are embarrassed to say and I don't blame you. Why don't you— hey!"

"Apologies for pushing you to one side but there–a wolf..." Feeling calm but in rapid action I think my gim into my hand, run at the wolf now snarling and leaping at Genda. The sword slices from the wolf's shoulder into its chest. The laceration draws the least blood for the kill. I silently wish its spirit better karma for its next life.

"Whoa, Master! How did you do that? I didn't even notice you carried that weapon in your robe. And how did you know that wolf was there?"

"If you talked less, you'd have time to watch for shadows." I wipe the blade with a handful of snow and polish it with a dock leaf. I am impressed with myself and conceal a smile. I couldn't let on to Genda, but that was my first application of four years of practice.

"I thought you were into meditation, not sword fighting."

"When using a sword, you have no time to mind drift."

"I get it. Scared shitless so you just have to cut and slash."

"Not really. You have much training ahead. Let us continue."

I am secretly amazed at how steady my nerves are after dealing with the wolf. As a lover of all life, it hurts to have had to kill and I wonder if my training would have sent me into an automatic killing machine if it was only me on this mission? I might have chosen to run, hide, or merely threaten the beast. But with Genda to protect, as well as myself, the wolf's life in this present counts for less. Then if I had died or was injured, I wouldn't be able to complete my mission, which would put The Enlightened One and his followers in danger. Was it a test? I don't have time to ponder more...

"Master, you were in the middle of telling me why we are going up this heap to a ruin and in the death throes of winter."

Without slowing my steady pace, I cast my senses around the boulders in case another adversary would interrupt my answer. "The pinnacle of Gelugpa, on which the temple resides, is unstable. The winter ice locks the rock strata down but the spring thaw threatens to send the top layer along with the ruins down into the valley. You know what would be in its path?"

Genda takes sideways steps perilously near the edge and peers over although gnarled trees and shrubs block his view. "The boss's house is down there, right?"

"The Nirvana Monastery of The Enlightened One is indeed in the path."

"But how are you going to stop thousands of tons of wet rock from slip sliding? And just where have you hidden your gim?"

"I will be required to focus my energies and use the purple crystal."

"You mean the mountain will stay glued with that old pendant thing? Magic?"

"Not on its own."

"So I couldn't do it with my training?"

"No."

"So what am I doing here?"

I am wondering that too. Another test of me, or him? Likely The Enlightened One considered he was less bothersome up here than in the monastery. "To learn to focus."

The path narrows around a rugged bluff on our right and a sheer drop to our left. "Be sure to not allow your bundle to over-balance here, Genda."

"Master, maybe you could take some of the food in it, then I wouldn't plummet to an earlier reincarnation."

"We each have a burden to manage."

By watching my footfall I almost miss the sunlight streaking from over my left shoulder, bouncing off the frosty valley sides and illuminating the temple only a mile away. It shines as if golden. My spirit lifts, though logic niggles in case the ice up there is already melting too fast. Suppose my training has been insufficient to allow my power to bind the loosening rock until the thaw is over in a few weeks? I recall with concern my practice sessions starting with holding a thick column of dry rice grains for twenty-four hours. Several grains fell then, and in the next ten times. I was able to use the power to heap dry sand into a sphere, but none of that compares to this mountain top. As Genda says, I have the magic of the amethyst, but it is a last resort and not in the hands of its true master.

"Wow, look at that. You could have said." His excited arm points to the glow.

"Beauty is best self-discovered."

"Is that our goal?"

"Yes and no. Zen is pointing the mind."

The glory of the vision, and the concern it instils, forces me to hike faster, kicking up puffs of icy dust. If Genda doesn't keep up, then so be it.

"Master, wait for me."

"I need to start my mission more urgently."

Gusts of mountain wind take Genda's return words around boulders and up to the scudding clouds. One of those clings to the temple now only a snow field away. I kneel to scoop up some ice and worry that it melts too quickly. I'd hoped to settle in for a few days, a week, and rehearse. To think a novice, like me, has had to live up here every spring thaw and pour their mental energies into keeping the foundations intact. Failure at least once is evidenced from the fallen blue stones of once high walls. Terracotta tiles peep through melting snow on the ground with only a rare few on roofs. I drop my bundle to expedite recovery from the climb and yet I hurry across this field, now an archaeological rubble, but once no doubt a vegetable garden, although what grows at this altitude? Dwarf beans here and rice from the lower terraces. Doesn't look like it was ever a large temple, more a retreat for a single monk and, it seems, an apprentice.

Heavy breathing tells me Genda has caught up. "Hey, Master, where's the treasure?"

"What is treasure?"

"You know, at least a golden Buddha, or... ah, I get it. You're saying my Zen treasure is in me, aren't you?"

"Am I? It is enough today for you to find us sufficient shelter, and prepare our supper while I start work. Look for flags to flutter and wheels to rotate."

"Ah, they are for prayer. Master, give me a koan to recite."

"I've been giving you those all day."

By sundown I find a rush mat and a porch with an ornate roof with its tiles intact and initiate a focus into the ground. I keep the amethyst pendant on a thong around my neck, but I have doubts about its effectiveness. The strata under the temple seems stable. Most of the upper ground water is still frozen after winter. Even so I need to conc—

"Master, how do I cook?"

PERSPIRATION IN THE MIND

After two weeks–according to Genda's digital watch he isn't supposed to possess–my head throbs. I was told I'd be able to manage without proper sleep and it is true. That I'll be able to sit still all day, and it is true. I don't know how Genda copes. I detect his approaches, sounds, as if asking his questions, my burblings on automatic followed by his goings away. Like the irritations of a temple fly, I am aware of his existence but my task overwhelms the external.

A niggle creeps in. I anticipated self doubts but success so far pushed them aside. I am relaxing a little. I notice the sound of boiling rice, the amber colour of the wind, the aroma of snowmelt... and I shouldn't. Consequently, there is slippage. Beads of sweat worry from my brain, and salts my eyes. In spite of my efforts, I feel tremors beneath me. There is danger this pinnacle will slide down, gather a rock avalanche and crush hundreds of believers. The humiliation would shame me for all existence. I feel a burning in my chest and realize it is the amethyst calling me to pay attention.

I reach into my robe and withdraw the warm crystal. The violet stone has been cut only a little, and remains unpolished to concentrate its raw energy. My rock stability mantra is chanted again and again but focussed through the crystal this time.

"At one
Through two.
In true spirit
In harmony."

After three hours I begin to feel part of the mountain, much quicker than without the crystal. I shuffle my lotus to settle for the night in meditation.

"Master? Master, are you receiving me? I know you are working but I'm worried. The mountain keeps rumbling and to be honest, they needed steel pins drilled into the foundations and concrete rather than sending you up here. I'm afraid... off when it's... you listening?"

Patience is a test. Even so, I stop hearing the boy. Not entirely pejoratively: my task has priority. Without opening my eyes, I raise an arm. Alarmingly, I feel his robe brush my face. "Don't bite my finger, see where I am pointing."

Genda laughs as if embarrassed.

"I wasn't going to bite your finger. I was checking—"

I urge to tell him it is a classic koan, but I wave him away. Clearly, me plus the amethyst isn't sufficiently strong to shield my mission from outside influences. As if in agreement a red tile slithers off the roof and shatters on the remains of a flagged patio. More tiles dance. Dust rises as a ground mist. A twisted mountain oak slides over the cliff edge. Its roots are the last to go but stick up in the air, hesitating, as if reluctant to leave its birthplace. Perhaps it is meditating on its life and universe. How it might have been different.

The crystal heats and at last I receive its signal. Like all magic, it will only work if a price is paid. Meditation isn't enough, a sacrifice is required. The problem is, no one is reborn to the next level by killing, no matter how high the purpose or how many other lives are saved in this existence. My hands twitch as panic sets in with indecision. I could end this life of Genda painlessly and without him knowing it is coming—the gim is not just for wolves. But no, how could I take his life when he is looking up to me, mistakenly, as his master? Yet, The Enlightened One must have known this would happen. He gave me the crystal knowing it has no power but a catalyst and only with a high price up here.

This is distracting yet part of me remains on task. I could not have done that four years ago. The ground quakes again. I fear I am letting The Enlightened One down on this mission, so to my equivocal dilemma. I sacrifice my apprentice and save the community below, or let him live but doom the others. It isn't Zen, this problem. No Buddhist kills in this situation, so another solution has to be found. Can I sacrifice Genda without killing him? Ah, but I have already killed—the wolf. Even that is a sacrifice to my karma, as it was a life. And it saved Genda, so allowed, but what for? The non-focussed part of me knows I can't harm the boy no matter what. There seems only one option considering the avalanche to come.

I unfold my legs and stand. I don't see him and have to call. "Genda, we are abandoning the retreat. Come along."

No reply. Perhaps his worries over the mountain's instability has already propelled him on the return path. He may be an irritation but his petulance has appeal in a way. However, he may have felt unsafe from the gim as well as the mountain. I speed walk around the temple in case the boy is hiding or asleep but after ten minutes I cross the rock field, now ice free, and begin my descent. All the time I focus energy into keeping the pinnacle from destabilising further.

Half an hour later I turn the corner of the valley and see the path twisting far below but with no sign of Genda. Has he fallen over the edge? Poor boy. Self-recrimination for my paucity of supervision stabs at me. I wonder for how many years a novice monk has been ordered up here and whether the pinnacle is really as unstable as we are told. It is a test, on several levels. Yes, I detect the minor tremors but supposing that too has been happening every spring thaw for generations? It would be very bad karma for The Enlightened One as well as for myself if Genda has fallen and hurt himself, or worse.

Life is fluid, beyond the present. Even so.

In the background of my mind, the mantra continues:

"At one

Through two.

In true spirit

In harmony."

In spite of my ruminations that the mission is a ruse, I worry that the pinnacle with the temple may be tumbling down the other side of this cliff, out of sight. How would I know? Of course I would hear and be shaken by the vibrations, and I don't. Yet, small stones dance across my path. I must hurry, while worrying about Genda.

As night falls I have to divert some of my energy from protecting the pinnacle to sensing the periphery of the path. Curses, I skid on a loose stone and teeter on the edge, I get back by flinging out my arms as if I'm a tightrope walker. I nearly lose my Zen composure. I'd be forgiven considering I'm risking all to warn the community below but then I'm probably about to be shown the exit.

Another near plummet makes me stop, and sit in the middle of the agitated grit. The damp night air brings me the rich aroma of jasmine, and the calls of two competing crickets. My hold on the pinnacle must attenuate with distance–no quantum mechanics entanglement for Buddhists, or is there? Does being so far away create an attenuating diminishing of my power? Maybe not with the use of the amethyst. Ah, I can leave it here on the edge of the path as a kind of relay booster. The idea appeals more than an alternative use as a torch. I say this because it glows, but insufficient to see through the ground mist. I wedge the jewel into a crevice in the cliff wall.

On the meandering downward track, the cool cliff is gritty to my clammy left hand while I send hold mantras to the amethyst and beyond. I believe I've not eaten anything for twenty-four hours, but hunger is shunted out of the way. The deprivation may be in vain considering my mission and now I hear rumbling as if tons of rubble are cascading down on my destination, a half hour and a bluff away.

With heavy heart I turn the corner of that rock shoulder. So, the mission may have been a test, but the need up there was real. A dust cloud obscures the monastery, or its ruins. There are shouts and screams amidst the echoes. Even Buddhists bleed and break. I expect to hear sirens but not yet: this monastery is thirty miles from the nearest town. I should adjust my robe to cover my mouth and nose but I don't deserve such protection.

Into the debris cloud I stumble half blind, heading towards the outlying residence of the master. Maybe at least it remains intact.

His voice appears beside me. "Tiromiso Sen, I didn't anticipate seeing you here."

"You expected me to be running to the West." He stands, arms folded and tucked into his robe.

"Not really. Our people worried you stayed at your post..." he turns to the settling dust, "... and tumbled down with it."

"Master, I am devastated at my failure to keep the integrity of the mountain."

"We are not infallible."

"I thought with the amethyst, infallibility was possible."

"Umm."

It is unlike the master to utter a vagueness. Does it imply the amethyst isn't the magical catalyst he portrayed before the mission?

"Master, are any of our community injured?"

"Yes, many, but they will endure their injuries, even if fatal. After all, we continue."

"My karma is now less so, Master, especially as I have lost apprentice Genda Doi."

He turns and regards me with raised eyebrows. "Should I know this apprentice?"

My mouth must be gaping. His eyes wrinkle in amusement but not from playing with me. If he didn't send Genda with me, then who was he? Genda had approached when I tied the bundles. I was prepared to make two journeys and was feeble enough to accept help.

"Master, I thought he was one of us."

"I trust you were kind to yourself, Tiromiso Sen."

466 Hz

ROBERT SMITH PLANNED to complain to the bus driver. He mentally rehearsed his speech.

"Do you realize there are elderly passengers on board? They're petrified by the way you hurl them round corners."

His ire mounted with each shuddering halt, his muscles clenching at each bend. He would demand to know name and number.

He shuffled in his sticky seat. August wasn't the best time for bus travel.

Smith's stop lurched into view so he jabbed at the stop button, confirmed by a red illuminated sign. "*Parada Solicitada*".

Sometimes the drivers ignored the requests to halt this close to Santa Ponsa town centre, so he rose, shouldered his rucksack, and staggered up the aisle. Before he could reach the driver, an elderly woman clad in traditional black clambered from her seat and faced him. She wanted to depart the correct mid-bus exit, but seeing Smith's set face, she obligingly about-turned. He caught a whiff of gardenia.

He'd expected her to hurl a complaint but was taken off-guard when she said, "Thank you for the ride, Pedro, us old ones rarely experience such excitement."

Smith could hardly comment on damned Pedro's reckless driving now and maybe the pensioner had a point.

As he alighted, a high note rang through his head. He couldn't source it, not even the approximate direction. What was the point of having two ears if he couldn't use them stereoscopically to locate a noise? He stood at the now empty plexiglass bus stop with its rolling advert of what scantily-clad people look like with Vit K Oil. He tilted his head up and decided the noise was a pure tone, B-flat above middle C. All that piano practise as a teen.

A dog howled as if it heard the noise too.

No doubt the sound was a decelerating jet bringing another 180 Brits to Palma airport. He smiled at the memory of being one of those five years ago, armed only with an email promise on his phone of a research assistant job in Santa Ponsa. His degree in statistics and sound engineering hadn't led to riches. It paid pine nuts, appropriate considering he was sampling to determine the origin of the Christmas trees growing on the beach. *Pinus halepensis* led to unsavoury puns at the local library, and security was called to ensure he left.

If the lane he walked down hadn't have been so empty of traffic he wouldn't have noticed the persistence of the whining noise. The lane, closed to motor traffic, meandered through the Maquis vegetation, emitting wafts of aromatic herbs and lavender. He couldn't spot wires that might have vibrated. A goat bleated. They've always liked his kind.

Could they hear it?

Perhaps it was tinnitus. He stopped at an olive tree and stuck fingers in his ears. Still there. It must be local machinery.

The terracotta-coloured block peeped over its Bougainvillea shrubbery. Robert stopped at the marbled stepped entrance to listen again. The noise persisted. He needed to ask someone else. Señora Gimenez waddled up the pavement loaded with shopping. No point asking her. Too old, too deaf and too much into flirting with British ex-pats young enough to be her grandson. Too late, she was talking to him.

"Señor Smith, do you hear it too?"

"Indeed, I have, Marta. Annoying isn't it? Can I help you up the stairs with your bags?"

She let him take the overstretched plastic bags. "I hear it this morning in the supermercado."

He lifted her bags. "You did? I only heard it an hour ago. Did others hear it too?"

"Oh yes. We're all annoyed they're closing the post office. It's not good, is it?"

Before he punched in the access code, the door was pushed open by Carmen. Robert had tried and failed to get a date with the fiery redhead, who was probably off to Santa Ponsa's liveliest bar. Her wild hair contrasted with her Lincoln green coat, doubtless covering up a glittering outfit beneath.

"Bob, *hola*. Hey what is that noise?" She'd lifted her pert nose as if it helped to hear better.

"Robert, not Bob. So I'm not the only one. Do you agree it's B-flat?" But she'd already punched in her iPod earpieces and waltzed off.

He carried Marta's bags to her ground floor flat, returned her smile, and trudged up the stairs to his apartment. His BOSE SoundDock poised ready to blast Pink Floyd around his room but instead, Robert relaxed into his yellow vinyl armchair and listened.

It was there. A single note and it penetrated into the room even with the windows closed. Unless it was tinnitus and Carmen referred to something else. He booted up his PC, made himself a coffee, plonked himself on his swivel chair, triggered Audacity and recorded a minute of what should have been near silence.

The display, looking like a heart monitor told him the sound was real. 466 Hertz at 39 decibels. B-flat, easily heard by any human, including Marta. He attached a microphone and took it to a window he'd just opened. To his surprise the sound level remained at 39 dB. Well, his gear was good for an amateur but only just. He wondered again if the phenomenon was local, a factory testing engines.

Time to go worldwide. He'd start with the nearest city, Palma. Any odd noises reported on the web? There, a noise heard so persistent they had to close the restaurant until the Health Department checked it out. Robert frowned. There was no Health Department as such on the island. Ah, it was the Palma Restaurant, NYC. Just a minute. If New York was hearing the same noise...

Robert spun his chair so he faced the window. It couldn't be, surely. A noise heard the world over? He could easily check by tapping into online news, but he waited, gathering his thought momentum, savouring the moment of something so profound. Hang on, it could be different noises. Anyway, there's been talk since biblical days of sky-trumpet noises.

He stood and approached his window with a more sceptical attitude. He listened to the note but within a minute he was back at his computer, eager to know if it was B-flat heard in New York and anywhere else.

'US elects first openly gay president.'

'Dwarf GM potatoes show signs of growth on Mars.'

'Language chip works in chimps: profanities heard.'

Getting nowhere, Robert struggled to think of search terms that might be more fruitful. Just typing in unusual sound, B-flat produced too much noise, so to speak. Maybe it is just local after all, but there was that restaurant in NYC. He found its website and went to its News tab. After all, if it had to shut down it would surely update for the sake of its customers. He wondered if they served Spanish food, the thought of which generated a rumbling in his stomach. Noise in sympathy. No update since the closed notice five hours ago. He strolled to his kitchen, made a soya cheese and pickle sandwich, and took it back to his PC.

Ah. 'Other restaurants are experiencing the same noise, as are stores and bars. We'll re-open at 8pm with apologies for the music. Our usual pianist has been asked to play louder to combat the noise.'

That should work as a distraction or to swamp the sound. Tinnitus sufferers can combat a particular note with white noise. He called up a file for several random noise backgrounds and played them on a loop. Yes, a few hid the B-flat note as long as it was played at the same 40dB level. Annoyingly loud for a quiet room, just acceptable perhaps in a noisy restaurant. Who did he know in New York who could identify the note? Ah, the pianist at the Palma Restaurant. He sent a message to that Palma restaurant website.

"Please ask your pianist what note the sound appears to be. I'm experiencing the same in the Ballearics." If he received a reply at all, it probably wouldn't be for hours.

HE MUST BE OVER-REACTING. A local machinist has left a grinder on and he was about to turn it off any minute. Robert laughed at himself and checked his wallet for enough dinner euros before heading off to the nearest bar, *Los Tapas Bravas*, a ten-minute walk.

At the bar he obfuscated the noise by la la la'ing to himself but stopped when people looked round at him.

A recognisable laugh reached him from a crowded table. "Oh,

hi, Carmen, I was trying to—" Smith interrupted himself to avoid digging any deeper and strolled to the bar. He ordered a chilli veggie tapas and a lager. He mounted himself on one of the chrome and red stools, but Carmen came over.

"You did sound funny, Bob, but I wanted to say that we can all hear that noise. Have you found what garage or farm is making it?" She'd brought her drink, a tall glass exuding aromas of vodka and orange.

"Screwdriver?"

Her eyebrows danced upwards. "An electric one?"

He unnecessarily pointed. "I meant your drink."

She winked and slid onto the neighbouring stool. "Yes, please."

Snared. She was good. "Tapas to go with it?"

Carmen spoke in rapid Spanish to the barman then turned to Smith. "What have you discovered about the noise?"

He sipped at his drink and lifted up his head as if that aided listening. Her small smile threatened to burst into laughter as he took too long.

"Sorry, Carmen, I just wondered if I could hear it in here, and you know, I can. How about you?"

She immediately shook her head then humoured him. "*Sí*, I can! Lucky, the music isn't on." She turned. "The door's open and it's a quiet road. But, Bob, how lazy, have you not found out anything about it?"

He spluttered out a mouthful of lager. "B-flat, it's worldwide, and it's Robert."

She winked at him.

Bloody hell, she was good. His back pocket vibrated followed by the chimes of Big Ben. "Hey, it's the pianist at a restaurant in New York, replying to my... yes. It's B-flat there too. Shit, it's at forty decibels. Weird."

Their tapas arrived and she bit into the pointy wedge, the chilli making her eyes water. "If there has to be a note then it might as well be a B-flat as any other, but what is a forty decibels?"

After his own bite, Robert was sure his tongue was swelling so he gulped lager before replying, "The note could be significant but I'll need to work on that. Forty decibels is the noise level you'd expect from birds calling but our ears can pick out different pitches at different sound levels."

"Did you know I'm working at Palma University?"

He stopped trying to hear the note now the barkeep had triggered Beyonce to drown everything audible. "Really, does your department have any research grants going? I'm in-between... hey, what department?"

"Data logging in the biology department. No-brainer, but the prof's cool."

"Human?"

"Insects."

At last he'd heard something to smile at. "In the morning, do you mind me coming along with you? I'd like to visit your professor. I think I can put a project to him—"

"Her."

"Her, sorry, that will combine entomology and this sound."

THE NEXT MORNING, Smith checked his computer. He applied filters to cut out locally-made sounds such as air-conditioning units, clocks and anything that spiked the chart. He frowned. The sound was still there, he knew that as soon as he woke up, but it had increased to 41 decibels. He knew the uni would possess far better equipment. His ears couldn't detect the change, but many animals would.

Carmen met him at the bus stop. Her condition for introducing him to Professor Juliet Etenne because she didn't want their neighbours thinking they were an item. He wore a dark green tie with a white shirt to add respectability to his worn but clean jeans.

The prof smiled when she glanced over his resume. She'd pushed her half-frame specs on top of her chestnut hair. Myopic, Robert realized as he was distracted by her upturned nose. Ah, she was speaking, and in a French accent.

"Bob Smith—"

"Robert."

"But Carmen said... it matters not. I hear the sound too but in what way should it interest my Faculty?"

"As you know insects are susceptible to noises. Especially, in

the ultrasound. If the resonance was just so, they could explode."
He reddened as he said this, knowing it was an extreme case.
"Even before that happens, insonified insects would be damaged.
Their reproductive systems for example—"

"Insonified?"

He suppressed a grin. There was nothing like a bit of Googling
to assist in an interview. "When something is affected by sound.
The sound is getting louder but the better equipment in your lab
would be more accurate. Shall I investigate?"

She pursed her lips in thought while she placed his resume on
her desk. "Are you an expert, Robert?"

He glanced at Carmen and grinned. "I'm the foremost sound
expert in the whole of my street."

She smiled as he continued. "My real forté is in investigation,
stochastical analysis, finding the real deal inside those thousands
of epidemiological studies but are really stats coincidences.
Fourier analy—"

"I get it, Robert, I think you might be useful but I can't arrange
contracts today. Show us what you are worth?"

"You mean work for nothing? How do I eat?"

She reached into a drawer and pulled out a card. She tapped
on her computer, swiped the card in a reader then gave it to him.
"Privileged access to the sound equipment, IT services, and one
free canteen meal a day. Maybe in a few days a grant, but prove
yourself first."

"You won't regret it, Señorita Etenne." He shook her hand and
turned to Carmen.

"A guided tour please? I'll treat you to a coffee if we end up in
the canteen."

As he'd hoped, a laboratory bulged with sound equipment.

Carmen explained, "Some insects such as cicada make sounds
using stridulation."

"Again?"

"Rubbing parts of their bodies... like this." To his amazement
she stroked her sandaled foot against his leg while her tongue
licked her top lip. A shiver travelled from his shin up inside his
jeans to the back of his neck. He wondered if he ought to engage
in a different species kind of courtship but his response was
interrupted. "Of course we can easily hear many insect sounds

but for some, such as an ant's footsteps we use a Sanken contact microphone that costs my salary. Some water-boatmen make loud noises relative to their size... with their... you know."

"No, what? Oh that." He coughed. It wasn't that he'd not experienced a girl coming on to him, but not this much, and not as stunning. Had the noise affected her? It'd be his new status. He cranked his brain to say something, anything to stop his face flushing.

"Is there an anechoic chamber for record—"

"I know what it's for. Over there with the red bulb." Her hint-of-lipstick mouth pouted just enough before she turned and headed for the soundproof room.

Smith paused at the doorway, hands on both sides of the frame. He dared himself to enter but this was his first day, morning, hour and it could be his last on the job. He leaned his head in. "Yes, but then it's the B-flat noise I have to measure and record, so this wouldn't do at all."

Her hand grabbed his tie and yanked him inside. The door soughed shut. Oh well, he'd tried to resist and that was what mattered. He put an arm around her.

"What are you doing?" She pushed him away but he couldn't tell if this was mockery until she spoke in hushed tones. "I can hear it, can't you?"

Mixed up pheromones and anxiety had redirected his ears but now in the strange hush of an echoless milieu he reassigned his attention. There it was. He played with a microphone setup for a few minutes.

466 Hertz.

She frowned at the yellow digits, him and the air. "No outside noise can get in here. How could that happen?"

"No idea... well, some. Suppose it's coming from the ground? There are Rayleigh seismic vibrations from earth tremors, underwater rock and mudslides. They're low but elephants are good at detecting them, and some people."

She shook her head sending red fragments highlighting in the bright neon. "How would microphones pick that up?"

"Because sound is a pressure wave..." He crouched low and put his hand on the acoustic-dampening fabric tiles. "... the air just above the surface would be pulsed. Not enough though, unless by going through our bodies too it is triggering sensory organs and nerves to make them more sensitive."

She wrinkled her nose, amalgamating her freckles. "I don't buy it. The whole world? There'd be global disasters and there's nothing in the headlines."

"There's tectonic plate movement all the time, worldwide. The Atlantic is getting wider by four centimetres a year. Perhaps something has changed in the last few days."

"Or something completely different?" She laughed a perfect D. "Or it's always been around but something's changing in our bodies!"

Smith, while seeing the level was at 41 dB in the anechoic chamber too. "Yep, you might be right. I'll take you to lunch. I fancy paella."

THE NEXT MORNING troubled Robert. The light lines streaking across his ceiling from the blinds swirled about his head. Unless it was himself, rotating. Gratefully, his eyes closed again. At least he was in his own apartment. How much vodka had they imbibed? He'd be in trouble if this was two mornings later.

He pulled on long shorts, a green 'Keep Calm and Cringe On' T-shirt, swigged yesterday's cold coffee and bolted out of the door.

Even though he was late, he paused outside the university. Waited for the bus to depart, and a plane to come, go and disappear over the sound horizon. The 466Hz remained. He ran into the building, to his desk.

The prof stood over it, tapping at a tablet. "Ah, Robert, I thought you'd changed your mind. Where have you been?"

He checked his watch. "Yeah, I'm forty-three minutes late, sorry about that. I was gathering more eviden—"

"Try two days and forty-three minutes late. Was she that good?"

His face screwed into a ball with consternation, he studied his watch at the date. She was right. Was *who* good? He looked around for Carmen and saw her through a glass door sitting at a console. He'd lost two days and a night. Did she spike his drink? Surely not. He'd not had an episode like that for years.

The prof continued talking at him. "...the data is on here. We've not seen species of meal moths die in such numbers without chemical pesticides, yet your B-flat sound shouldn't be loud enough to disturb anything."

"It might have synergistic effects with other noises or strobe lighting, anything that behaves as a pressure wave, and it is continuous and new."

The prof wiped a tear. "*N'importe quoi,* it looks like my gut instinct to let you in might be fruitful if you can save the rest of the insect kingdom."

"Hey, all I can do is measure and analyse." How could he comfort her? "There must be more than me working on this, aren't there?"

"You're the only one I have. You're the best expert in this street, remember?"

He sat hard on the office chair and swiped the data screen away to fetch up the app showing his noise level monitor— 44 dB. No! "Juliet, the noise level is rising by a decibel a day."

Her mouth opened in shock then settled. "Most insects will survive immense loudness unless particular frequencies vibrate their bodies to bits."

Robert tapped on the tablet. "Same with mammals. I'll see who else is investigating this."

A combination of computer notes and screwed-up printouts later, Robert stood so suddenly his stool fell backwards and cracked a glass cabinet. His shock magnified by the notion of escaping spiders, eased when he saw it housed antique scales. He left the mess, grabbed the one unscrewed-up paper and called on Carmen to go to the cafeteria for lunch.

As they walked, she snatched her hand away when he tried to hold it. At the canteen she let the swing door collide with him.

He grabbed a portion of something with red and green wafting cheese. "Okay, Carmen, what have I done?"

At least she chose to sit by him with her bocadillo sandwich and a lime cordial. They both wrinkled their noses at the foul emissions of too-strong garlic from a bio-techie with more beard than hair behind them. They picked up their trays and found an open window.

She spat more than crumbs at him. "You should know."

He'd met this line of unreasoning before. "Perhaps so, but I appear to have lost a couple of days. Did we...?"

"I was told to liaise with you for the noise problem." Wonderful though her green eyes were to Robert, they narrowed and lasered at him.

"Right, giving me the silent treatment. I discovered concern from insect-watchers from China, America and Europe—"

"Entomologists, and to be of any use to this faculty you need precision, Señor Smith."

"Right, I'll send you an interim detailed file if you show me yours, and what's with you? I thought we were hitting it off. It's because I'm..er..chunky, isn't it?"

Her fist banging the table gave an impressive show of exasperation and he swore he saw ripples—in the desk, her body, the air, then in her words. "*Idiota.*, you are to investigate the noise, where and hows, not insect reports."

"There you go, something scrambled my head the other day, it's a miracle I'm functioning at all. Anyway, there's precious little to find on the web about our 466 friend, which I can now hear even in here through the clatter of plates and gurgle of coffee machines. Can you?"

He wiped off his unintentional smile and stared with a mix of horror and amusement at ripples in his coffee. No way would the sound have enough pressure wave energy to do that. A heavy truck outside might. He stood to look out of the window. Nothing. He sat again only to notice ripples on his coffee travel up his arm but not Carmen's smooth olive arm. He watched the millimetre undulations travelling up and down to his elbow. Was sound only skin deep, or did it affect brains?

"Try the physics forums. *Si*, your ridiculous smirk tells me you have. Posted the questions as well as waiting for others? Then we might need to go political but not before clearing such approaches with the Professor."

He needed to clear his head. As he trudged outside, he pondered on the politicizing of strange sounds. After a little aimless wandering, he decided to interrogate the barkeep at Los Tapas Bravas. On the sandy-coloured limestone wall outside the bar, a green lizard raised its head as if hearing the noise, then it scuttled away.

As soon as Robert entered the dimly-lit bar, which reeked of cheese, he heard a chortle from Toni, the barkeeper.

"Here he comes, English and his magnetism for the ladies."

Robert perched on a stool and ordered a Stella even though he should have been at work. "I need to know what happened when I came in here with Carmen the other day."

Toni placed a glass and peanuts on the bar. "You came in with her but left with another woman. You English, eh?"

A short laugh came from a dark corner. They all knew.

"What woman?" Robert asked but his innocence only sent Toni off again. A chuckle so intense his whole body joined in. Waves.

"Señor, when the bee-you-tiful Carmen went to the bathroom, you left with Tina, her sister."

Back at uni he found Carmen in the IT lab.

"I know why you're upset with me, I didn't know what I was doing. Out of it. Rohypnol in my drink."

She slowly nodded. "You'll be saying the noise is affecting more than your hearing."

"Actually..." Was that it? The noise was more than a sound? A trigger for something ancient within him?

THREE DAYS LATER the sound level in his flat had breached 50 dB. Robert perspired as a glissade of worry finally danced in him that it might not level off.

In the lab, the prof glared at him as if it was his fault. "So it's more than one decibel increase a day?"

"That's what I thought after the first few days but don't forget decibels are a logarithmic scale and it represents a ratio of the sound pressure compared to the lowest audible noise. We'd need an increase of ten decibels to experience a perceived doubling of loudness. At least the four-six-six Hertz B-flat note is a constant."

Professor Juliet swiped at her tablet. "I can tell you there are many reports worldwide of insects behaving abnormally, and even sea creatures are affected. What level is harmful to humans?"

Robert spread his arms wide as if to show how big sound is. "Eighty decibels is usually quoted to cause harm if it's sustained.

You can get vibroacoustic disease if ninety decibels is sustained. Long term deafness but also ulcers, even stroke and epilepsy. It isn't just our ears that receive sound pressure pulses." He turned to go back to his console then spun back. "Speaking of sea creatures, I must check on readings we have of sonar reading levels. Hey, you don't suppose whales and porpoises are telling us something?"

"Such as stop polluting the seas with oil, detritus and the noises of propellers? We'll leave that to Douglas Adams, don't you think?"

Carmen walked in wearing pink earplugs. Robert pointed at her head.

"Do they work for you? Didn't for me, though mine were white."

She winked, which gave Robert hope until she said, "They don't block the B-flat but they muffle other irritating noises such as you."

She was joking, surely. He turned to the prof. "One of my Southampton uni pals is a sound engineer at Sony Music, Nashville. They're measuring and recording the same noise. Do you realize that no one in the world is now recording music? The noise is there, and while Skyping him about it he reminded me of how I experimented with sound cancelling for my dissertation."

Carmen looked up open-mouthed. "You, *Señor Imbécil,* are telling us you know a way to remove the noise?"

Juliet leaned forward, her blue eyes becoming more like chrome steel. Her spectacles magnified them. "And, *Monsieur* Bob, you *knew* all this time?" Her chestnut bob tumbled undone as if the noise's vibrations joined in with the group admonishment.

He stepped back. "Hang on, it's not that simple. Well, the physics is. All you do is make the same note and level but half a wavelength out. Look." He tapped on his iPad to bring up an illustration of a green sine wave, then another half a wavelength behind so they cancelled each other out. "But real noises aren't so simple to eliminate because one, we don't live in a soundproof box and two, our ears aren't perfect receptors." He grinned as a number three. "Okay, I'll work on it, add my input to those at MIT."

He walked off, his head filling up with surreal notions of

loudspeakers on every street corner, then global. Nonsense but he was intrigued by how far he could take the experiment.

An hour later Robert sat on a stool in the anechoic chamber. It was like being inside a three-by-three metres egg box. Even the stool was made of absorbent wood. He thought it might be cork but more likely an agglomerated fibre. He hoped it wouldn't buckle under his hundred kilograms. He liked being in the creamy soft light away from the outside world and—

"Can I enter? I want to hear without the noise."

"Sure, Carmen, you have permission to always ignore the red light in the corridor. Apologies for the fresh plastic aroma. You need to sit on this stool."

She frowned, but remained standing. "Is your noise-cancelling experiment working?"

Robert stood and brushed invisible dust off the stool. "Yes, and no. The problem is that our ears are all different. They're as individual as fingerprints. Ah, I see you don't see the relevance. Well, we're lucky in that the noise is a pure B-flat note. Clean as a whistle, so to speak. Actually cleaner, yes?" As if she had, he nodded back at her. "But although there are no echoes in here. Kinda cool how our words sound different in here, isn't it? Clearer." He strolled around the chamber. "Yet, the perceived sound is a bit different depending where we are in the room."

"All right, spare me more speeches." She climbed on the stool and listened for a full minute. "I can't hear anything."

"Halleluiah."

She dismounted and walked to a wall. Her mouth smiled not because it was funny but at a realization of what he'd said. "I can just hear it. So only at that spot is the note cancelled?"

IN HER OFFICE, the prof pointed her emerald-painted fingernail at Robert. "So, the note can be cancelled in one spot in the chamber. What does that tell us about why it can be heard equally loud inside and outside? I thought your physics *amis* postulated it was more in our heads and bodies, coming through the ground than in the air? Seismic Rayleigh waves?"

"That could still be the case. Has to be air too for microphones to pick it up. It could be transmitting from the ground to both our bodies and the air. Sound can be picked up by our corpuscles in joints but they're usually low, say under twenty Hertz."

Carmen at last agreed with Robert. "The sound coming up through the ground could explain why it could be heard in the anechoic chamber except at the focus of the cancelling noise."

"*Attendez*—wait, wait a minute. Has the seismic sound been confirmed, globally, Robert?"

Robert sat, his legs didn't enjoy standing for too long. "Everything makes a noise. Even a stationary crate on the dockside is making small movements because of gravity, imperfect surface, expansion, contraction, wind, insects on and in it, and so on. Sound is created by pressure waves along a medium such as air, liquid or solid. Our planet is full of movement from plate tectonics to micro-tremors. It's amazing we've not heard it before."

"Perhaps our brains," Juliet said, "are hard-wired to filter out constant planetary noises to stop us going mad."

Carmen coughed a short laugh. "That hasn't worked."

"*Vraiment*, and it's getting louder each day."

Robert frowned. "Perhaps something has changed in our brains enabling us to hear it now? No, delete what I'd just said. Microphones don't have brains. In any case, the sounds the planet makes in general are too low a frequency for us to detect. Barring brown note."

Carmen groaned and picked up her cup to take away. "I wondered when you were going to get lavatorial."

Robert had hoped Carmen would want to go home with him after work. Outside, the noise seemed louder than inside even though he knew it wasn't. He pushed open the glass door to his apartment block only to see Marta stomping down the stairs towards him.

"The Bible, Señor Smith, says in Joel, 'Blow ye the trumpet in Zion; sound the alarm on my holy hill. Let all who live in the land tremble, for the day of the LORD is coming. It is close at hand'. What have you done?"

A religious dimension to the noise wasn't on his agenda. "Marta, I'm just a researcher and a former graduate of sound engineering. Hey, maybe you have something though. Didn't Joshua disintegrate the walls of Jericho by blowing trumpets?

Anyway, I measure the noise not make it!" Not strictly true he realized when making the cancellation note but hey ho.

She brushed on past him, treating him to wafts of lavender.

NEXT MORNING, before he opened his eyes, Robert's hand reached out in case Carmen had come to her senses and realized what a catch he was. Nope, but the noise was there, everywhere. Louder. His eyes jerked open as if he'd be able to see a B-flat. He tumbled out of bed to tap his computer. 58. This has gone from a curiosity, a new job, fascinating research to something deadly serious.

As he shaved, ripples in the water appeared to reflect waves of dull pain in his head. He leaned towards the mirror to zoom in on his eyes. He'd seen a tabloid headline about everyone's eyeballs were going to explode by Friday. He'd checked on physics.sci.com that human eyeballs had a resonance frequency of 19 Hz and the noise would not only have to be that low but at an enormous 240 dB to explode. Lucky then that the noise was way higher at 466. Even so, the persistent loudness must be causing health problems for some.

On his way to the bus stop he checked his news apps. Queues of patients were overwhelming doctors and hospitals the world over, riots in Chicago and Marseille but they could be down to the summer heat. A few finger strokes later, he found an item that brought him to a standstill. 'Earth target of focussed gravity waves'.

He was pushed from behind. His phone flew out of his hand, transcribing a perfect parabola to the hexagonal stone pavement.

A voice shrieked at him, "Señor Smith, you stopped!"

"Sorry, Marta, *lo siento*. Have you heard about the gravity—no, of course not, *perdon*."

"Your fault, Señor, all this in my ears. Driving me crazy." Tears rolled down her cheeks. He wasn't responsible and yet a tightening in his stomach stemmed from guilt that he must have missed something.

On the bus, his phone worked after he'd reassembled it.

There it was, tucked away on a general news section: 'News leaked from NASA: scientists detect a funnel of gravitational disturbance in Earth's vicinity from an unknown source. No cause for concern as it is weak.'

Robert recalled hypotheses using controlled mini black holes to pull spaceships along. Maybe someone had not factored-in forward gravity disturbance consequences. CERN was decades from doing that. Alien then. Surely NASA had put it together... and alerted NORAD to look for alien ships coming from that 'unknown source'... and maybe they're using quantum singularity perhaps unaware of the noise perception on Earth. Na, he'd seen too many sci-fi films. Suppose though, small changes in gravity waves triggered something in the Earth's crust that in turn, amplified its noises...

A woman barged into him on her way down the corridor of the swaying bus. She yelled at the driver as if it was all his fault. Robert grinned at the turnaround from when the same woman thanked the driver a week ago for giving her a thrilling journey.

A moment later the noise stopped.

So did the bus.

Silence.

That hush when you fall off a cliff. Sound might be around but the brain momentarily shuts it off. His fellow passengers stopped texting and Candy Crushing to seek assurance from each other. Open-mouthed then after the cue from the driver, a slow smile.

Ambient noise hesitantly intruded, birds, car horns, a laugh but without the 466.

The driver's smile turned upside down when he attempted to restart his engine. "*Cojones.*"

Robert didn't want to wait to see what his ears picked up outside and walked to the middle, pulled the lever to open the door and stepped out into the new world. New in the sense that vehicles were stranded, unmoving in the road. EMP? He stared at the sky. He hardly bothered with the sky since arriving those years ago. Blue was blue. A lot of blending-in-years.

A thousand generations of waiting. Forgetting that he'd been waiting, until now. He couldn't wait to give feedback on the unexpected 466Hz effect.

IN THE WEST, across the sea, the sky grew turquoise with alien orange streaks.

WHAT KEPT YOU?

MEGAN STARED UNCERTAINLY at the bright spot in the swirling shades of lilac clouds.

Captain Cody narrowed his eyes. "It's just the rising sun, Megan, come on, you're holding us up."

"Something's not right, Captain. Although the landscape looks like a New England park, only kind of rose-tinted like an old photograph, there's no sound." Her excitement at stepping on her first planet was tempered by unexpected nerves. Although she was slim and slight compared to the two powerful men in the squad, her sharp wit and tongue compensated for lack of brawn.

"Don't listen to her, Cody. Environment's checked out from orbit and down here an hour ago. Goddamn, Cody, let's go; we have people to rescue."

"He's right, Megan." Cody's deep voice calmed his crew. "The expeditionary team has been here four months. All we have to do is bring them back. No exploration, Megan, and no conquering, Travis. Move out."

Megan gingerly stepped the half-meter drop from the shuttle onto the short fern-like grass. She might have jumped it, but her pack contained most of their electronics. The men carried heavy-duty armoury and provisions. All of them warily pointed small but deadly handguns. Because all radio communication halted when the expedition landed, they backed theirs up with implants in their neck so they could communicate even if they were captured and stripped.

Megan headed for some low trees and covered the men who were activating a shuttle camouflage device. From over her right shoulder, a dark hand-sized blur flew past straight for Cody. Before she could take aim or shout an alert, it just missed him and shot off into the clouds. As the two men turned, she rushed over. "Did you see that?"

Travis waved his biggest gun in the air. "Ignore her, Cody, it must be this damn purple sky getting to her."

"Shut up, Travis. What was it, Megan?"

"I saw something going at you!"

The captain whirled around looking for threats. "What?"

"I don't know. I..."

Cody persisted: "Okay, what did it look like?"

"It went too fast. It was a blur."

"I didn't hear anything, Cody, ignore her."

"Megan," said the Captain, "let's concentrate on the mission, shall we? It is good for you to be alert. We know there are villages dotted all over the planet including one nearby."

"I was listening at the briefing, Cody, I know this village three clicks away is where the expedition was put down and that nothing's been heard from them since. But listen."

Travis unwisely chewed at a pink grass stem." We're wasting time, but listening."

"No, really listen," Megan said.

They did. Crouched low, turning their heads this way and that. The tree branches blew around with the wind, but they heard no sound except their own voices enhanced by their implant com systems.

"Just wait until we get to a town," Travis said. "I've often experienced silence in the country."

Megan sniffed at a blue windswept honeysuckle-like seed as if to add an unusual odour to her argument. "It's not just that. The leaves jerk funnily and..." She batted away something—or nothing. She lowered her visor.

The captain stood. "Can we get on with this rescue?" He led the pair towards a tidy path near the outskirts of a village. A few spindly trees and a couple of towers lifted themselves above single floor ochre buildings.

The three would-be rescuers lay in the weird grass beneath an overhanging branch to look for any activity.

"There," whispered Travis, but then: "Sorry, I thought I saw someone come out of that domed house but as soon as I saw him... he disappeared in a puff of smoke."

"Let's keep calm," Cody said. "Megan, set the cam to record five minutes."

As he shifted his position to get another viewpoint, a puff of air forced them all to look towards the path to their left. Too late, the native had come up behind them, passed them, and disappeared into the village.

Cody spoke first. "Did I nearly see what I thought I saw?"

Megan muttered to herself. "Pity I hadn't quite set up the camera."

Travis sniffed the air. "Do you think the atmosphere might have a hallucinogen we haven't tested for?"

Megan viewed the village through the zoom lens. "There's a native sitting at a table outside a house. Extreme left, guys. The wall with a poster. I've just zoomed on it to give the translator some text to start working on."

"Excellent. Megan you stay here and record everything; weapons ready."

She thought she'd be better at communicating with the natives, but then maybe Cody didn't want trigger-happy Travis out of his control. She had telescopic vision via the camera and ears via the new coms implant and settled down again to observe. A vibration along the ground scared her and she leapt up. She touched the ground with her fingertips. Nothing there but a memory, as if a snake had been there when she laid down and slithered rapidly out of the way. She wondered if Travis had tapped into a working brain cell when he suggested hallucinogens in the air.

Feeling the ground with the flat of her hand, Megan prepared again. She made a tripod with her elbows and looked through the lens. Immediately she tut-tutted: Travis walked as the aggressive soldier, pointing his powerful field weapon here and there, while Cody walked steadily up to the sitting local.

"Stop tutting me and record that the enemy is probably levelling a weapon at Cody from under the table," Travis said.

"Don't be an arsehole. And don't call the locals *enemies* until one of them shoots you." Megan hated Travis.

Cody slowly walked up to the seated native, who didn't appear to be taking any notice of the intruders. His skin was a translucent pink and hairless making Megan chuckle as a similar image of her little plump granddad on a veranda wicker-chair came to mind. The native showed more interest in the cup he cradled on the wooden table than in his visitors.

With his hands held open, Cody spoke: "Excuse me, sir. I know you do not understand me but have you seen my friends?" To accompany his speech, Cody did a splendid sign-language job. The native just fidgeted. Cody repeated his performance, while Travis let off a few rounds into the air. Cody, his expression touching on exasperation, turned on Travis, who shrugged his shoulders then stood open-mouthed. Cody spun back round to find the native gone.

"Where did he go, Travis?"

"Dunno. Maybe he went back into his house. What's he left behind?"

Cody picked up what looked like a newspaper; at least the squiggles and dots didn't fall off the parchment-like sheet. The men walked back to Megan so she could scan the document to the translator program. Megan watched them head back into the village wishing she could front line. A green light told her the translator managed to make some sense of the input.

"Megan, come round behind the house we've just been to."

Delighted that Cody must think it was safe and excited that it was her turn to explore, Megan ran round to find them standing in front of what looked ominously like five human burial mounds.

Travis growled, "They've been murdered."

"We don't know that," Cody said. "But it looks as if five of the seven are buried here. Look, Megan." He showed her a damaged helmet that had lain on the nearest mound. Though worn and faded, the word "Marlowe" was discernible above the cracked visor.

"Brett Marlowe was the expedition leader," she said.

Travis levelled his weapon looking for someone to kill. "The bastards."

"Hold your fire," Cody said. Megan marvelled at his patience. He turned the helmet over, studying it carefully. "What do you see, Megan?"

"I know, it looks very worn for a new helmet only four months out of its box. Maybe he'd been in a battle. Are there any other bits of equipment on these graves?"

They looked at the mulberry-coloured soil heaps. Suddenly, a lilac bird appeared on the mound nearest Megan. No bigger than and as sleek as a hummingbird it looked straight at her for a couple of seconds before it vanished. Megan picked up a rose-coloured feather and said: "One of two things are happening here, guys."

"They kill people from Earth," said one-track Travis.

Cody craned his neck upwards. "Either we're in one of those ancient Star Trek TV shows."

"Or time really is much faster here, except for us," Megan said.

"Or we've slowed down compared to the planet. Come on, you two, get real." Travis laughed.

"How long do you think it's been since we landed?" Cody asked.

Travis said: "About three hours?"

"Look at your watch, Travis."

"That can't be right: only twenty-five minutes."

"Try thirty-two days and twenty-five minutes," Megan said. "I've used the camera data and the computer. Time here is two-hundred and fifty-six times faster than on Earth."

"Yeah right," sneered Travis. "If this planet is in some temporal shift why aren't we whizzing about at the same speed as the locals?"

Megan shook her head. "I'm just telling you what is happening, not why. Maybe our bodies, coming from another time frame, have some resistance. You realise now, Travis, what probably killed the expedition team?"

"They weren't murdered then? Hey, if a bird at home flies at thirty miles an hour, that's over 7,600 miles an hour here! Perhaps one of our team got in the way of a fly."

"Unlikely. We would seem like slow moving statues to them. No problem flying around us at all," Megan said. "No, the expedition team landed here four months ago. That's eighty-five years in this time. They died of old age."

"Could be why they couldn't call down their orbiting shuttle– the radio signal probably distorted. At least we can take off when we want–whoa, what was that?" Cody staggered back when an automobile-sized tram-like vehicle appeared and stopped near him. Two locals disembarked, looked at them for a second and blurred away. Seconds later the tram also vanished.

Travis stared in its direction. "So much for their simple lifestyle. They probably have weapons too."

Megan knelt on the ground placing a hand flat. "I noticed street lights embedded in the walls, so I guess they'd have electricity. I wonder if the tram is powered by an underground field along the green path it arrived and left on? I really love this kind of puzzle."

"Let's concentrate on the mission. If the five mounds are for five people, there might be two survivors."

"Captain," Travis said, "they'd be eighty-five plus the age they arrived at. We might as well go home before we also die of old age."

"You feeling rheumatism, Travis?" Megan said, who'd been examining her translator readouts. "There are warnings in that newspaper you found. Apparently, there is a time dilation with altitude."

Cody jumped at the news. "So the locals are being told to keep away from mountains because time is too slow for them?"

"Or too fast, even for them," she said, frowning at the still incomplete translation. "There's a picture of what looks like a Tibetan temple perched on a mountain. Looks old so it could be abandoned. I wonder if there are varying temporal shifts on this planet. Freaky time dilation can occur with proximity of black holes and strings. But I don't know if we'd age faster up a mountain or slower. Give me time and I'll work it out."

"Oh funny," Travis said.

"Team, we are on a mission..."

"Oh, cut out the loyalty crap, Cody. Let's just find them. Back to the shuttle," Travis said.

Megan put a hand on Cody's arm. "You know, the tram seems to go to the mountain in the picture. The temple?"

"Hey, I'm not going in any alien bus!" shouted Travis.

Cody looked at Megan and smiled: "There seems a good possibility that that is where they went. We could search for too long looking at all the mountains in the shuttle. Travis, okay, you go back to our shuttle and stand by for us to call you. We'll take our chances in local public transport."

"The speed will kill you."

"Travis, we are trained to take G forces. Go ready the shuttle and keep instruments on us as well as the communicator. Listen, Travis, suppose none of us return, what would happen in, say, another three hours our time."

"Let's see, that'd be thirty-two days again for here so Mission Control might send another rescue mission. No, hang on, this is a trick question, isn't it?"

Cody and Megan nodded in unison. Then Megan said: "However, if for some ghastly reason we can't return, it would be a brilliant idea for them to know about the time anomaly here. Send off all the data so far even if we're not sure they'd get it without distortion."

"Also, Travis, make a copy with a message and leave it near our landing spot such that another mission would find it easily. Hopefully, locals will leave it alone."

As Travis left, Megan realized that the speed at which the odours dissipate before their noses grab them explained the lack of scents and even of the noxious emissions from Travis.

She smiled just as the vehicle appeared. A quick check and they leapt in and dived for the nearest empty seats. Already accelerating, they had a struggle to stay seated. Three other passengers glanced at them and away. One of them smudged away at a jerked stop.

"Hey, Megan, suppose a conductor comes on for the fare?"

"Don't worry, we'll be there in seconds. If they try and throw us off, we're bigger than they are; link arms to make handling us more difficult. Hey, look there's the mountain with the temple on the horizon—er, about five seconds away. Hey, how do we tell this bullet to stop?"

"Hopefully it will stop at the mountain," Cody said.

"Great, so we'll have a fraction of a second to leap free or be amputated."

"Hey, you sound like Travis. Anyway, no time to argue—here we are and it's stopping!"

Fighting the abrupt deceleration, they fell out, tumbling onto rough ground.

Megan sat up rubbing her bloodied left elbow showing through a jagged hole in her uniform. Cody stayed down. She staggered over to him, convinced he couldn't be dead or he would be a mound by now with a helmet on the top. He stirred and checking her watch; realised they'd lain there for a week local time. How weird must that be for the natives to encounter? She hoped it was still only twenty minutes for Travis. There'd be no end to his ragging them if he could argue it would have been quicker using the shuttle after all.

"You okay, Cody?"

"A bit groggy, must have hit my head on this harder bit of planet. How about you?"

"I cut my elbow but look at it." A new pink scar showed, with patches of dried blackened blood. "Another thing, we've been doing it without noticing but we've drunk nearly all our water and gone through a hell of a lot of chewable rations."

"Whatever it takes, as long as we are both relatively fit. What do you think about taking some boosters to get us up this hill before we become pensioners?"

"Okay. I'll get some pro-Benzedrine out of my kit. Are *you* getting any of this, Travis? Maybe he's out of range," Megan said. "We travelled in the vehicle for about thirty seconds our time, which equates to two hours their time. It's not possible to know how fast we went—sorry, out of breath, no, we mustn't slow down—but suppose it averaged sixty miles per hour then Travis is a hundred and twenty miles away."

"Catch up on your breathing," Cody said, as they made good progress up the twisted, overgrown mountain track. All three had had to be superfit to qualify for rescue allocation, but the hike tested their stamina.

They stopped talking for the next couple of hours, stopping only to deplete their water supply and rations. Plagued with false hope, they aimed for summit after summit, each one leading to a higher peak. At the penultimate peak they rested in an abandoned gatehouse.

Cody recovered first. "What do you notice, Megan?"

"I hate questions like that, Captain. I had an aunt that would always say: 'What d'you know?' Even if I told her I knew more than her and she knew more than me, she'd come out with it again next time."

"Okay, at the risk of sounding like your aunt, what do you notice? I've lost the power of long speech." He gasped, his lungs still heaving.

"There's a subtle change in the sky colour from lilac to pink and, hey, I can smell these maroon tiny flowering plants. Umm a cross between lavender and jasmine. Heavenly."

"Appropriate for a temple area, Megan, but does that mean..."

"Time has slowed up here? Besides aromas having time to reach our noses how else can we tell? There's no wind to rustle the trees. Are we too high up to see birds and insects?" She knelt on the wooden floor at the portal of the gazebo-like gatehouse to examine the rough grass. A pink grasshopper looked back, then hopped away, but not so fast she couldn't follow it.

"Yes." She turned to look at Cody, grinning and tapping at his watch.

"Hey, we should get Travis up here," she said. "The longer he stays down in fast time, the less likely he'll find us in time. He's probably hours ahead of us already. Damn, why didn't I think of that earlier?"

"Megan..."

"No, sir, it's serious. If he is hours ahead of us now, he can't receive a signal from us. Even if we go back down we'd probably find he's gone or see an earlier version of him. Oh, shit, we're going to have temporal paradox problems and it's all my fault." Her eyes filled with the emotion of her error.

"While you were busy throwing stones in a pond and timing ripples, I told him to take off and land on any high mountain before we ran out of radio contact. Still can't raise him yet, though."

They hugged.

"On the way up," Megan said, "I dwelt a little on the temporal shifts affecting this planet. Although the nearby presence of a double black-hole was suspected, Earth, being so keen to find a habitable planet, brushed aside speculation on their possible effects. Of course we are far from an event-horizon that could be dangerous but maybe the twin black holes are close enough to create shifts in time, variable with altitude here and maybe with latitude too."

"You might be right, but let's see if our climb will be rewarded."

A rickety footbridge spanned a chasm separating them from the final pinnacle housing the temple. With painful lungs and legs, but not wanting to delay any further, they crossed one at a time.

Together they entered the derelict temple. Shafts of pink

sunlight diagonally spotlighted cobwebbed statues and sparse furniture. With unnecessarily reverent silence Megan nudged Cody to look at dancing motes picked out in the light above their head.

"What kept you?"

The creaky old voice startled them. In a dark corner on a wicker bed lay an ancient woman.

Megan recovered first. "Are we glad to see you."

"Not as glad as I am, my dear."

Cody asked, "Are you Doctor Tanya Semper?"

"Give the man a medal," she said. "Are you getting me out of here before I'm too old to fool around with my husband back home?"

"Er, yes, is there anyone else up here?" Cody said, taken aback at the thought of geriatric amour.

"Only Boyd, he's out back picking some banana-type food. Yuck, but it's kept us going. Leave him, he's a cantankerous old fool."

"I'll be glad to be rid of that old witch," said the oldest man Megan had ever seen as he shuffled in a rear door carrying a basket and gourd.

"Boyd Tinker, I am so pleased to see you, um, again," Cody said, helping him with the food and water.

"Never mind all that," croaked Boyd. "How are you going to signal your ship?"

"Don't worry," said a worried Cody.

Cody took Megan outside. "He has a point. Travis still hasn't responded to me. Has he said anything to you?"

"No, shall we signal him the old-fashioned way? He might see it if he's looking out on one of these mountains?"

"Good idea, I'll gather some firewood, get some green, or pink plants to generate smoke."

"We've got flares," Boyd said, who'd followed them outside. "Homemade but they work. You don't think I've waited years just so I could listen to that old bag moaning on, do you?"

"I told you how to make them," Tanya said. "And who looked after you when you kept getting sick on your stupid homebrew..."

A few minutes later a green smoke trail curved through the sky.

"I see you. At least I assume it's you guys," Travis said, flying in from behind a nearby peak.

Megan laughed. "I never thought I'd be so glad to hear your voice."

"Come in and land on level ground to the south of the temple," Cody said. "And we have two passengers to bring home."

"Hey, that's great. I bet they're looking forward to having some real grub at last."

"Umph," Boyd said, "not as much as seeing the faces of our paymasters as they try to work out our overtime pay!"

DUMMIES GUIDE TO SAVING LIVES

WHOA! MY STOMACH LURCHED LEFT while the rest of me grabbed the handrail. This bridge was so sensitive, resonance waving through it, reacting to its trespasser.

Wires suspended the bridge over a black river, treacherous from the wettest ever February.

Rushing to catch an overnight train, I didn't have time to be in awe of the deeps. Anyway, it wouldn't look much different to the thousand times I've let my eyes fall to the swirling currents. A catena of light bulbs swaying from steel supports pushed some of the dark away but even so I almost missed the man sitting astride the parapet.

If he hadn't seen me I could have sneaked by. A big brute with one of those short but untidy black beards. He was on the parapet at night for only one reason and it wasn't to retouch the paintwork. Was I up to talking someone down? Was it right to dissuade someone from taking their own life when all they had left was the grim reality of what they were escaping from? What if you could change their perspective from what seemed an intractable situation to one with hope, no matter how slender? Decisions.

In the darkness, I could have crept along unnoticed, but suppose I heard a cry, even of release followed by a splash? Would I be able to rid myself of recriminating nightmares?

"Excuse me, mate, can I be of help?"

"Sod off."

Well, that told me. I could justify gripping my small suitcase tighter and leave him to it.

"Want a push?" I risked letting a wicked streak escape me.

"You what?" he said, daring me to repeat.

"No, really, is there anything I can do? I'm not in the

Samaritans or anything, but it can't be so bad, surely?" I said in my ignorance. I have wondered what I would do if everything went wrong for me. What's the worst that could happen? A fatal disease from which you'd lose your faculties before a long and lingering demise; your wife died or ran off with your best friend; lost your job; get found out for some indiscretion; your children— no don't go down that one. For any of those I could understand people running away, taking a bagful of money and starting a new life in Canada, but not this. For one thing I'd never learnt to swim. Oh, he *wants* to drown, doesn't he?

"Nobody can't do nothing."

"What's your name?" As if I knew what I was doing.

"What's it to you?" he grumbled, manoeuvring his right leg to accompany the other dangling over the river.

Involuntarily, I moved forward, fearful of an imminent leap. Part of me wanted to be ignorant but a larger part felt committed now a dialogue had opened.

"I've been there, you know," I lied, "on the brink; thought it was the only way, but I'm glad I didn't."

"Glad you didn't what?"

"Jump, of course," I said. He was beginning to annoy me.

"I'm not going to jump."

What's this? Have I misjudged the whole situation? Maybe he was fishing or a hydrology engineer measuring the nocturnal water speed. I sidled to the parapet but couldn't see any line.

"I'm going to use this," he said pulling out a vicious gleaming short sword. It had a wavy sharp edge from hours of honing. "It's a Kodachi and I'm a master in Jujutsu. One thrust then gravity and the river God, Kappa, will take me as an eternal servant."

"I see." And I did.

"You can't stop me or join me."

"Really," I said. As if. "I suppose I wouldn't qualify."

"Too right," he said, holding both arms out, rock steady, with the metal point—reflecting amber light from a lamppost—at his throat.

I was compelled to do something.

"It would be good to tell people your name. Just for the record."

"Ian Bryden." Glaring eyes dared me to deny his identity. But it was vaguely familiar; an unsettling jangle of synapses in my faulty memory, but I would have to deal with it later.

"Oliver Galt." I held out my hand. What was I doing? My mouth to hand was on automatic, but brain signals intercepted and caused a retraction. "I, er, did some Yoga a little while ago."

"Umph. There's nothing like a little blood-letting," he said. "How could she? Why do women mess me up?"

Ah, now we had it.

"Well, there's the wrinkle," I observed, making things ten times no better. "Your woman has left you for another man?"

"Not exactly–she *won't* leave him."

"Tricky, Have you tried luring her with the usual: chocolate, roses, Chanel, rampant sex and a promise of a better life?"

"Yeah, yeah. Though not in that order. Jess is a fine but difficult woman."

"It must be in the name," I said, thinking of my wife, Jessica, and how baffling she and most women were to me.

"What's it to you, anyway?" Bryden repeated, returning to his sword.

"Well, you know what they say about pebbles on the beach, fish in the sea and all that?"

"You having a laugh?" he growled.

"No, not at all. Er, maybe she wasn't the one for you even though she seemed to be." I clutched at straws. I glanced at my watch reminding myself I was cutting it fine to catch the last train.

"Jess had a smile just for me," he said.

"Really?"

"Yeah, an incredibly cute dimple but just on one side of her mouth," he added.

"That's strange so has my..."

"And she had this way with her tongue when we kissed. Not deep throat. No, just darting in and out, in and..." He continued, while my brain struggled.

"Say, Ian..." I had to interrogate so carefully. "Where did you meet Jess?"

"Then her hair...lemongrass...oh Jess." He was in pain. "In her bedroom."

"Lemongrass?" Didn't *I* buy Jessica a lemongrass shampoo

last Christmas? I couldn't remember. "Bedroom?" I stared at him in error.

"Yeah," he said, grabbing hold of my collar with his sword-free hand. "I laid your carpet... and then your wife."

I couldn't focus: thoughts or vision. It seemed my Jessica had a fling with this kamikaze brute for some reason. Maybe her hormones kicked in afternoons or whenever Bryden called, and switched off again when I arrived. Ugh. Surely, she couldn't find him remotely alluring? The waltzing of ideas stopped my brain engaging the need to get away. My right hand still grasped my overnight suitcase with my left holding tenaciously onto his sword arm. With a twisting wrench I found myself with my back on the narrow parapet. I could sense the highly-strung bridge sway.

"Goodbye, Galt," he said, his ghastly grin revealing incompetent dentistry.

Incredibly, I toppled over. This couldn't be happening. I had a train to catch.

I left the parapet above me.

Going down.

It really *was* happening.

My coat flapped and the case, still in my hand, lifted with the air-resistance. If only it was a golfing umbrella then at least I wouldn't hit the water so fast. Not that the velocity mattered unless the river was shallow.

Down. It took an age.

I expected my life to flash by, but it wouldn't. Pity.

Down. Up to now I'd had a good life, except for Jess's strange asexual behaviour recently and my inability to swim. I could still see teeth glinting in the dark shape above.

I heard the train pulling in. My train. It was all I had to do tonight... catch that train.

Jessica ... Jess knew I couldn't swim. Did she arrange this?

Can't be long no—

RECURSIVE SPAM

> 08:12 from: administrator@yahoo2.com
Urgent Message. This is an important message from the Email Server. Open the attached file with the label Important.zip

> 09:24 from: foxylady26@tisscaly.com
Re: got to open this
Hi Kevin. Great to get an email from you. Not sure what that attachment was you sent me. Nothing seemed to happen. I presume the "Ignore illegal operation" message was a joke? I forwarded it to Jane. Ciao, Susan

> 10:06 from: ac@greenfield.essex.org.uk
Re: got to open this
Dear Mr K Broomfield, I would be very grateful if you would remove my email details from your computer. If you remember, your son was sent home from school for sending me pornographic pictures and arranging my funeral—twice. I assume you sent this morning's email by mistake.
Yours, A. Clarkson, Principal

>10:30 from: Angelfish@vergen.net
Re: got to open this
Kev, what are you doing? I'm married now to Butch Stevens—fraud squad. Delete you idiot.

> 11:18 from: theman@gobblefish.com
Re: got to open this

Hey, Kev. Trying to catch me out? LOL nice try. Ben
PS if you don't virus check this beast, you'll have a system crash.

> 11:30 from: mgr@clarity_communications.com
Re: got to open this
To K Broomfle988 ###~ be gra#^^789986 not $£--9 .?(() L%st warn9ng 93ty00+

> 12:02 from: virginpussy@virgenit.com
Re: got to open this
Kevin, we assumed your request was to subscribe for a bonus month to voyeur stockings. We used the credit card details from your last purchase. Happy viewing.

>12:14 from: accounts@loans_online.net
Re: got to open this
Mr K Broomfield. We are so glad to hear from you again. We thought you wanted to cancel your account but assume you now want to re-activate it. Accordingly, we have put £10, 000 into the bank account used previously and the monthly interest will be 38%

>12:27 from: administrator@yahoo2.com
Re: Re: got to open this
This is an important message from the Email Server. Open the attached file with the label Important.zip

>12:30

out of memory
out of memory
out----------------

The absolute end

CONVOLVULUS

NEAR FUTURE ON A ROOFTOP IN NEW MEXICO

Piero whispered into his picture cellphone, "I know it sounds ridiculous." His fingers trembled, requiring him to grip the phone more tightly.

"Speak up, Piero, this must be a bad line. Why do you need rescue?"

He snapped his phone shut and then cursed himself at the unnecessary sound. He heard telltale rustling only metres away. Would Lisa clue in on his need to be silent or had he just given her another reason to hook up with that better-looking hydroponics engineer? Damn. He shook to clear his stupid head: he had to face his own survival within moments and yet wasted effort pondering illogical relationships.

He risked raising his head to look over the sun-heated whitewashed parapet. The green tide inched closer and upwards. With no one to blame but himself and a greedy absentee biotech management, he rued that black Tuesday a year ago.

PIERO RECALLED TWO epiphany moments. The first being in the lab watching a three-dimensional computer simulation of his dwarf maize shrug away every plant disease in the database. He laughed at the prognosis of no known side effects if humans consumed the corn, even though it was destined for animal fodder. He grimaced at the decision to continue the research in secret, in a State with a relaxed view on GM experiments.

"Piero, you know you can have everything you need," the director had said, his oily skin glistening in the desert heat. "The best labs, computers and assistants. Maybe a friskier girlfriend?"

"I hope I live up to your confidence in me," Piero said,

damning the director for his sordid thoughts. So, his skinny Dustin Hoffman appearance tended to keep women at bay, but he did attract active minds, like Lisa.

"Your thesis impressed my board. They're confident of tripling their investment return. All you need is to bring us results in eight months."

"Out of the question. It'll take that long to produce the simulations and the proto-gene; another two years for consistency trials, and—"

"Eight months for very large rewards, Piero. Unless you are worried about ethical considerations?" The director laughed as if that couldn't be possible.

Piero wasn't. Couldn't let himself. When other boys in his Milan suburb kicked a football, and each other, he played with a microscope and the Internet. He realized long ago that Mother Nature constantly evolved. All GM did was speed matters up. Of course precautions were necessary, hence the trial periods.

"You can't buy time, Sir. With respect, it isn't possible... unless..." And then the big idea hit him; his second epiphany moment.

"Unless we pay you more? Or make the incentive more sinister?"

"There's no need for threats. You say I can do anything as long as the board gets the new seeds in eight months from now?"

"We want the fastest-growing disease-free corn on the planet, Piero, nothing less."

"I believe I can do it. All I need to do is use a compatible hybrid phylum I know from a strain of bindweed. What I'll do is—"

"I don't need to know, Piero. Tell it to your staff."

HIS FEAR INCREASED in proportion to the crescendo of the rustling. If only he'd listened to Lisa at the beginning when he'd persuaded her to leave Napoli University, bringing the bindweed rhizomes with her.

"You're mad," she'd said. "They're not compatible in the slightest. Grain versus Convolvulus."

"Not versus, Lisa," he said, stroking the adorable soft down on her arm. "Intertwined–their stripped genes mingling, just like us." He recalled her dirty laugh as she kicked off her chinos, and tugged at his.

He should've known better. Bindweed was a hell of a wild plant. It could kill shrubs and small trees by strangulation. It propagated via seeds and runners as well as roots. His prototype GM version had unpredictable side effects. He couldn't understand where he'd gone wrong. He never assumed... Lisa's father, a physician, once quizzed him on assumptions.

"Piero," he'd said, sucking his pipe; empty for three years. "You think you know everything."

"Not at all, sir. Like Socrates, 'my knowledge only informs me of the extent of my ignorance.'"

"You think you're Socrates?" he said, tapping the side of his head for Lisa's benefit.

"That's not what I meant..."

"He was put to death, wasn't he?"

Piero found communicating with people so difficult compared to plants. On the other hand, this blasted Convolvulus...

He raised his head over the parapet of the single-floor laboratory roof. All he could see was a living green carpet speckled with pink and white flowers. Where a month ago a sandy desert stretched to the Sandia Mountain horizon, now his creation, Convolvulus-M-2 thrived. It sucked moisture out of the air, and used sunlight and salts as food; a perfect eco-warrior.

THE LAB WORKERS had to be dressed in protective suits and the rows of C-M variants grew in hermetically sealed cloches, which were housed in an air-filtered glasshouse lab.

Lisa called, "Hey, Piero, come and look at your new bindweed."

He left the computer modelling and walked over to her station. He still found it amazing that she picked him out of all the better-looking guys that fought for her. A younger version of Sophia Loren in looks, but with brains, and demonstrating good taste in partners. Hey, the long-haired git next to her was whispering in her ear. What was his name? Alonso. So operatic.

She laughed at whatever Alonso had breathed. Piero knew he shouldn't let jealousy strangle him but he couldn't help himself.

He forced himself between them. The engineer sniggered and left.

Focus on the work, Piero, he told himself.

Lisa controlled robotic arms to snip cuttings but he could see from the ones she'd done yesterday, that they'd rooted and had a healthy green sheen.

"It sure is growing fast," he said. "It must be doubling in mass every twelve hours. That has to slow down."

"No doubt, but the only properties of the maize in the hybrid is its vertical stem strength. There's not going to be any cobs as we know them. The board won't be happy."

"Yeah, the leaf mass isn't so protein-rich. Kill this batch, Lisa."

He watched as she withdrew the arms and flipped a switch that released a powerful herbicide.

"Shall I do the others?" she said. "None of these five rows produce cobs."

Reluctantly, he agreed, knowing that there were over a hundred other variants in the complex. Surely one of the strains will work.

Most of the staff lived in nearby Albuquerque, but Piero and Lisa lived in a newly-built apartment block on site. As did Alonso. They'd stayed up late watching and criticizing a re-run of The Andromeda Strain when they were startled by the breach alarm. Piero glanced at his computer and saw the alerted sensor was from the batch they'd destroyed. Zooming in on the CCTV showed that far from being withered, the plants had reached the cloche roof and broken through.

Piero phoned the duty manager, whose face never looked greyer. "Burn them, Clive. Better incinerate the whole glasshouse, in case of contamination."

Lisa held her hand up to her head as if she'd a migraine. "Oh no, that's going to terminate a quarter of the stock."

"It can't be helped. At least we know not to use Paraquat on the new plants."

HE RISKED TURNING ON his cellphone again. Maybe the Convolvulus didn't home in on sound anyway. What were they–Triffids? It's a pity seawater wasn't a simple solution for disposing of his bindweed.

Piero knew he could've been away by now. His fault for returning to the lab too long after the breakout, in the hope of gathering the computer data for clues.

"Lisa, where is that chopper?"

"I thought you told me you were fine and so I could cancel it?"

As he rehearsed a choice reply, he saw a green tendril appear over the parapet.

HE NEARLY DISLOCATED his jaw when he saw the burnt out glasshouse. Sure, there was plenty of ash, blackened glass shards and sooty soil. But physically writhing beneath were shoots and ridiculously healthy growth that had resisted the flames.

Lisa dragged him away to look at CCTV footage. On contact with the flames milky sap spurted over the leaves.

"It looks more like rubber-tree latex than bindweed sap," he said.

A petri dish was put in front of him by a blond labtech. Piero looked at her, remembering she was Angeline, normally drop-dead gorgeous, but she looked as tired as the loser in a half-marathon. Why couldn't Alonso go with her instead of with...

Focus.

He looked at the covered dish. Lacerated bindweed stems oozed the milky liquid. The young woman offered Piero a book of matches. He noted they were from the Blooz Club, a popular jazz club in Albuquerque. Taking the dish and matches to a nearby gloved control box, he placed the matches and dish inside and removed its lid. With his hands inside the glove he struck a match and held it an inch over the dish. Immediately, more sap oozed from the stems and some fluid spat up at the flame, which phutted out.

"So we can't burn it, unless, possibly, we use furnace temperatures. And we can't use Paraquat, Roundup or Milestone. We'd better get onto DuPont and try a range of other herbicides and do some simulated stochastic and biochemistry tests to see if other types of herbicide might slow the damn weed's growth. Oh," he said, bringing a magnifying pane into play. "Shredding won't work." The lacerated stems had sprouted trichome root hairs.

"Perhaps we've solved the world's food problem," said Angeline.

"There's plenty of food for more than twice the world's population," said Lisa. "It's just that it's on the wrong plates."

"I was only joking," said Angeline. "For one thing, the sap is caustic, and it's in the flowers and leaves as well as the stem."

LISA'S CELLPHONE VOICE sounded sarcastic. "You're not actually afraid of our bindweed hybrid, are you?"

"Of course not." Yes. He rushed over to the bindweed that had scaled the parapet, grabbed the waving shoot and being careful not to break it, eased it backwards. It was like being a medieval castle defender pushing back ladders. While upright, he looked at the dusty road he'd driven along the previous day. It was as green as the rest of the desert. Was he being too soft? Could he make his way down the plant-encrusted fire-escape outside, or the interior of the labs? The inside was out of the question. He'd come to the roof after calling Lisa to arrange a helicopter because the plants had outgrown the labs, choked the corridors and were now pushing at the rooftop door. He'd seen the burns on a technician's skin when a cut leaf brushed him. One man—pity it wasn't Alonso—had asphyxiated with a reaction akin to an anaphylactic shock and died. Others were hospitalized and none returned.

"Didn't you bring your protective suit up with you?"

He'd forgotten she was speaking. What else had she said? Fear addles the brain.

"I forgot."

"Make a run for it. You should be able to trample on the plant without hurting yourself."

"You should see it. Hey, I'll send you a cam-shot. There. See how it's about waist high near the Jeep in the carpark?"

"Keep your trousers on then. Sorry. Actually, you'd better wait up there for the chopper."

"Lisa, the plant seems more aggressive, wrestling with each other as tendrils look for anchor points. I'm sure my ankles would be grabbed in seconds. I'd be buried in minutes, ironically, in a green living coffin."

"You said you wanted an eco-funeral."

"True, in another eighty years, please."

"ETA fifteen minutes. Hang on."

He sniffed, the scientist in him fascinated by the absence of desert smells. The ubiquitous dusty sand had given way to the suggestion of lily of the valley. The bindweed sprouted a profusion of pink and white trumpet flowers. No doubt, swarms of insects would buzz by in the next few days, eager to collect nectar.

"Piero, Green Venture Inc. has reported the plant to the Governor, implicating you as the culprit."

"Thanks for that, Lisa. We guessed he might. Survival is the issue at the moment though. Any news from your end how far our Convolvulus strain has reached?"

"As far as I could tell when I flew out two days ago it remains in the desert. Even so, it occupies maybe over a hundred square miles and approaching the outskirts of Albuquerque. If any of the technicians took any part of the plant outside the region then it would spread there too."

"Lisa, can you think of any reason why it might not spread into wetter and cooler regions? I can't."

The thought of the Earth swallowed by a plant both intrigued and terrified him. He had to assume there was something in the local environment; the heat, lack of pollution, some rare salts in the desert soil–anything. Wishful thinking was all he could cling to...

"Aaarrgh, Lisa."

"What! Piero have you been caught? Watch your back."

"No. Not yet. But those insects, the ones that'll come to these millions of bindweed flowers; the bees no doubt on their way, would take pollen as well as nectar back to their home territories."

"Maybe birds would pounce on them, but then they too would spread the plants."

He'd initiated a subset ecosystem.

The rustling sounded like a million whispers.

"Piero, you'll be all right. This isn't your way of getting out of meeting my folks in LA on Sunday, is it?"

He'd forgotten. She must like him more than Alonso after all. He allowed himself a smile.

"Hey, I can hear the chopper." He stood just as three more tendrils pushed over the parapet. He didn't bother pushing them back, but kept glancing at them as the red and white Sikorsky out-noised the Convolvulus.

A harness was lowered to him, and he eagerly slipped into it.

"I'm ready," he yelled, as if the crew could hear him. They must see him and yet moments passed with no upward relief. "Come on, damn you."

The insane thought maybe the pilot was in league with the Convolvulus heated his brain. Bright green tendrils licked upwards like flames at the rescue ladder.

Finally, the ladder took him upwards away from his vernal nightmare. As his feet kicked at green shoots, he laughed hysterically, but only for a moment. His reprieve tempered by the new view of the disaster he'd caused.

Rough hands hauled him into the cockpit. The feeling of relief ran through him even though there was work left to do in eliminating the bindweed left behind. A crewmember handed him a can of cola. Piero nodded his thanks, looked out at the green carpeted desert and noticed a green shoot curling around the open doorway, heading towards his foot.

SLOW CRASH

SINGER COULDN'T IDENTIFY the whine that reminded him of one of those trendy syntharmonic-muzac orchestras on Case IV as it tuned up without achieving sync. Sure, the escape pod had taken a little damage but it was a chunky robust vessel designed to fight its way through the debris of a disintegrating space Digger before a steady course could be plotted.

The radio didn't help. A gargle of warbled hisses filled his headphones through the worrying whistle. Fiddling with the tuner made it worse, so he had to be content with the automatic beacon that should've started broadcasting his emergency status.

THE DIGGER, a grey bulk, bristled with all the accoutrements necessary for asteroid mining. The only elegance was the search and identify probe: the nose, sniffing out the copper-red nickeline needed back home.

He cursed the moment that the probe had detected that flying mountain of platinum-laced iridium. As big as a small moon and a hundred lengths of the Digger across, the asteroid consisted entirely of impact craters.

Singer had not met anything like it; the metallic honey pot of the century hiding in a large cluster of asteroids. Asteroids are normally far apart but this had grouped, maybe already gathered by another enterprise, so he'd better be quick. His computer calculated a rendezvous so he'd be alongside the swarm and matching their speed of five clicks per second.

He was too far from home to ask for advice; communications were sent by radio pulses in batches every eight days. Unless he was under attack, he was not to attempt communication with his masters.

While the computer considered the optimum strategy for the

company to profit by the lump of iridium, Singer opted to land on the asteroid to grab a sample. He preferred to examine specimens in his lab than look at them through a telescope and remote-Kl4-spectrometer.

He'd have to justify his actions when he debriefed on return, but his whole employee existence was to bring home the goodies. He was treated like a company component spiced with stochastic improbabilities.

If anything went wrong the ship would return home. To the considerable embarrassment of some pilots, a glitch in the workings had occasionally convinced the computerised error-finder that it ought to send the ship back to base with a protesting, swearing but impotent passenger.

He used the navigational computer to inch the Digger closer to the asteroid. A landing would achieve two things; there was something distinctly fishy about such a large lump of high quality iridium floating around just for the taking and it gave him a chance to go for a stretch, albeit in a pressure suit.

The asteroid wasn't easy to approach. Other rocks littered the area. It was like doing a slow egg and spoon race in a 3-D maze with beach balls.

Singer hunched over the computer screen rather than watching the real view through the port. The screen showed multi-directional vectors, distance to touch, and ETA. It was a miracle that such a cumbersome Digger could be manoeuvred so deftly. It would be unlikely that a non-machine could make so many decisions on the basis of so many variables. Singer wouldn't like to try. One of his qualities was an instinct for survival, which in his case was to duck out of bar-fights, let machines take all the risks and only go out with girls smaller than him.

His smile broadened in anticipation of a country hike as the ship settled on its hydraulic ramps and the retros died. He stood, stretched his arms and peered outside. Light from the distant sun barely illuminated the asteroid's surface. He adjusted the crystallised filter system in the view-port, switched on the outside lights and gaped. He wasn't prepared for the rugged beauty of this little world. The steady dots of light from distant stars disappeared and reappeared as the asteroid swarm swept along. He couldn't wait to get into his suit.

The computer must have noticed something Singer didn't and blinked at him. There was a shift in the asteroid's motion relative to some of the space regolith around them. Although each lump was an entity in itself, happily travelling along its own flight path, you can't have so many so close together without side effects. Gravity fields, Van der Waal and other forces held the space debris. Newton's First Law had each moving meteorite travelling in a 'straight' line—gravity fields notwithstanding, unless some other force impinged. Singer's Digger impinged. It had gatecrashed on a four-billion-year-old party.

He'd added impetus where none had been before. Mass and velocity were the crackers and wine brought by this interloper.

Nothing dramatic was happening. Singer took risks, and so he buckled, checked, fastened, checked, zipped, checked, and left the computers to monitor the subtle changes.

A few minutes later he was outside, standing on the mineral-asteroid. Standing is an exaggeration; a hiccup would have given him escape velocity and sent him on his way to another rock. Consequently, he was attached by a life-line as if he was about to do a space-walk, instead of an asteroid hop. He was careful not to move fast but soon rediscovered the skills of toe-skipping, covering ten metres at a time.

He became overconfident and tripped. Sailing backwards through the non-air was another experience. He knew he couldn't be hurt but it still tightened his stomach. He landed on his back, several times. Eventually as he was still, lying there, the sky gripped him.

No photograph could've done justice to the vision. Apart from the thousands of stars in the distance, the asteroids looked as if they would tumble down on him any moment. The distant sun was just below his horizon but illuminated sharply broken rocks that hung over his head. He made out some colours: coppers and metallic blues but mostly a near-black ochre. It was difficult to believe that they were all moving at over five kilometres per second.

Having made the reckless decision to land, Singer had pre-determined routines to follow. He took samples of surface dust and augured cores. Gas chromatodetecter devices had to be planted along with a claim plaque bearing the company's registration in view of the ship's broad-scan laser image recorder. His suit thermistor told him the outside temperature was -170 increasing as the metal intercepted the sun's rays and turned the cold ultra-violet into infra-red. He knew that in the absence of an atmosphere the temperature should've been nearer to absolute zero. He smiled; he liked conundrums. Could this lump have an internal heat source? His smile turned down when he thought that the iridium might have more radioactive thorium than estimated. His brain pirouetted to the conclusion that he should return to the Digger.

On his way back, he tripped as his helmet bleeped into life. An emergency return to ship call! He cursed his clumsiness as he spent five minutes returning to the airlock. His face hot enough to boil an egg, he sat at the shiny console but to find one light blinking red. He smiled when he saw the emergency only related to navigation. Relaxed, he settled into his swivel chair and asked the computer to tell him the worst.

"Collision in eighty-eight point five-three hours."

"Eh? What's going to hit us way out here?"

"This asteroid will be impacted by another asteroid," the computer had a warm feminine voice but its message was chilling.

"How far away is it?" Singer's brain was racing. He couldn't leave without taking at least enough of this asteroid to set him up for life.

"The intercepting asteroid is a hundred-and-eighty kilometres away travelling on a near parallel course but closing at point six four metres per second."

"Just over half a metre per second! You can't call that a collision. How big is it?"

"Two and a half kilometres diameter."

In desperation to save his retirement wealth, Singer quizzed the computer about the chances that the incoming asteroid might miss. No. On request, the computer summarised the unusual facts.

"Collision predicted is of the category known as a Slow Crash. Depending on the geological structure of both asteroids, the impact has an eighty-three percent probability of causing disintegrating fractures of both. Roche Limits don't apply. The slow speed will not lessen the impact since the masses of the asteroids are so great. Enough to disintegrate the planet."

"Just a minute. Some of your connections must have oxidised. Surely a slow crash is impossible. As soon as any two masses get close enough their combined gravitational pull would accelerate them into a frenzied smash-up. It's not possible for two asteroid-sized lumps to gently touch." He was mischievously delighted to put one over on the computer. The exhilaration didn't last long.

"You are correct for a two particle problem. However..." Singer groaned as the computer gave him a lecture on the complications of multiple particle gravitational fields, the added effects of electro-magnetic fields and the influence of the electrical field from a nearby giant gas planet. It added up to the result that it was possible, however improbable, for a collection of debris to be in dynamic equilibrium. It was also feasible for a slight perturbation of the fields to edge some of the particles into closer proximity, the acceleration between two being offset by others around them.

Singer felt cheated and morose but after a long drink and think, asked the inevitable question. "Right, let's see. How much time have we to salvage what we can before we have to get away?"

"If the Digger left the asteroid in eighty-seven-point two hours we should be able to escape any detritus from the collision."

"Right, so we have until then to grab ourselves the juiciest chunks and get them out with the rest of our haul in tow."

Singer made himself a meal while deciding how to make a rapid survey of the asteroid when he felt an urge to see the incoming asteroid for himself. Seconds later, a crowded sky filled the screen. Cross-hairs targeted the approaching asteroid as a pale spot. Nothing seemed to move even that splodge inching its way closer.

Before he took off, he was going to salvage what he could. It needn't be a total write-off: after all, the projected collision might do him a favour by fragmenting the asteroid into more manageable chunks.

He tried to recall what he knew of slow crashes but couldn't. The computer library wasn't much help either. Did a slow crash create an explosive impact so the heat of even a slow contact, from friction or fusion gas ignition or radiation, would send projectiles at great speeds in random directions? How far should he stand off to be a safe observer? Might the two asteroids fuse together and go into a dumbbell spin?

He explored the rock and during the next twelve hours was able to retrieve some pleasing samples and store them in the hold. Several times while he was floating around on the surface he looked up at the incomer and at his other neighbours. He could never get used to admiring the firmament. Even the silent blackness in between the steady stars drew him.

He ought to give himself a wide margin of error and put distance between himself and the coming rendezvous. He sat at the console and initiated the take off procedure.

Nothing.

Singer stared unbelieving at the machine as it politely informed him take off was not possible.

"Why not?"

The sultry feminine voice said, "Evidence from back-interpolation indicates it was our presence that caused unpredicted perturbations in the localised magnetic and gravity fields to initiate the imminent collision."

"So? Let's get out of here. Make some more perturbations. Oh, I get it there's a directive saying I'm not to disturb planetary motions." Singer was exasperated.

"Analysis reveals that taking off would cause at least three more collisions to occur. I'm programmed to prevent a worsening of the situation."

"But only from the point of view of the asteroids, not mine!"

The console remained silent. It obviously regarded the last statement as rhetorical. Singer tried another approach to change the computer's mind while his stomach warned him of imminent panic.

"What could change your decision?"

"A direct order from base is the only way to override my probability decisions."

"Doesn't the life of your pilot get any consideration in your metal conscience?"

"Only in as far as it does not interfere with the prime directives. It is imperative not to disrupt planetary motions."

Singer thought through this and tried again as if he was cross-examining a witness for the prosecution. "Is the incoming asteroid big enough to be a planet?"

"The asteroid is within the category of a small planetoid."

"Ah! Got you!" Singer raised his voice. "Why have you been helping me to take this 'planet' to pieces if you have a directive not to damage it?"

"That is not my programmed directive. Taking parts of any planet does not significantly affect its path of motion, but moving about in this unusually dense collection of small planetoids and asteroids is."

Singer was speechless. He stood and poured himself a stronger than recommended liquid stimulant while his mind grappled with the situation. He dug out the technical files that were in book form so the computer couldn't tell he was investigating the possibility of taking the ship over on manual. It was another blind. He could turn off the computer but not without disabling the ship, stranding him. The system was fail-safed to prevent a pilot from sabotaging or hijacking his own vessel.

The next few days were torturous. He went for walks and gazed up to seek some inner peace with himself, to accept his fate, take what was coming, and to think of a set of words that might unlock the computer.

The threatening asteroid increased in size as he gazed at it. His hated executioner. He stared until his eyes watered. In desperation, he sat heavily on the stool in front of the console and tried everything again for the fifth time.

No.

Out of interest he asked the computer if any other asteroids were displaced by their presence.

"Six discernible bodies are moving along routes that are not on the same course they were. Many smaller meteorites are also on impact courses with other bodies besides this one."

"Ah, so even if we sat here until impact, there are other changes in the equilibrium of the swarm that could create greater havoc than if we took off?"

"That is possible. It would be necessary to compute the trajectories of each body, identify their impact targets, assess the individual probabilities of either disintegration or ricochet deflection and compute the resonance or secondary flight paths that resulted. At each impact, the certainty of forecasting the flight paths and hence the stability of the total swarm reduces by thirty-six percent with a confidence limit of—"

"Wait. Can you compute the effects of our take-off in the same way?"

"Yes but the probabilities of assessing the secondary impacts remain the same."

"So, the future of the stability of this swarm is equally indeterminate whether or not we take off."

"Affirmed." The computer voice synthesiser hardly seemed to pause between its answers in contrast to Singer's agonised synapse-wringing deliberations.

After a deep breath, Singer launched into what he hoped would be the clincher. "In that case, my intelligent friend, since the outcome of our take-off cannot be proven to make the matter worse, we might as well leave and save our skin. After all, if we stay, not only will a collision take place but we'd be obliterated and our flight through the swarm can't be proved to make matters worse. Whereas if we stay, the results of the collision might be just as disruptive if not worse." He sucked in air, whistling through clenched teeth as he awaited the rebuttal.

"Affirmed"

Singer was stunned. Had the computer, which had used its logic to deny him his escape, changed its mind after a to-and-fro with a mere mortal?

"You agree with me and we can leave?"

"Affirmative and negative. There is no doubt that the determination of future collisions is equally inexact but our take-off might worsen the situation and so the prime-directive is unchanged."

In exasperation, Singer shouted at the console, "So it's not enough to show our take-off can't make matters worse, we have to prove our leaving would improve the situation?"

"Agreed." the terseness of the voice synthesiser could be irritating but part of the pilot's training was not only to get used to it but to appreciate such efficiency. However, in this situation, Singer had to think aloud while the computer just outputted the results of its reasoning.

Singer rubbed his forehead to placate an incipient headache. "Is there any way we could ensure our take-off would reduce the damage? For instance. could we use our rockets or our industrial explosives to push this asteroid out of the way or to minimise the impact?"

"No, the effect would be negligible. Our resources are for gathering small meteorites with the occasional larger lumps to take in tow."

Singer thrashed around for ideas knowing that failure meant annihilation.

He turned again to watch the incoming killer, now able to make out features on its surface; jagged craters, striations, and ray-streaks. Breathing heavily he muttered. "Come on, you suggest something..."

"With respect to what?"

"With respect to us getting off this hunk of scrap metal before we're turned into part of it." He wondered at machine intelligence. "In other words, if you were in my position what would you do?"

"I suggest you use manual controls. This can be done by—"

Singer wasn't listening; he was in shock. He couldn't believe what he just heard.

"But... why didn't you tell me this before?"

"You didn't ask."

If a computer could be smug, this one was and enjoying it.

Another thought wormed its way.

"Does this suggestion of yours mean you'd allow me to manually take off?" This wasn't quite a rhetorical question. Singer lost his trust in the computer as an adviser. Its logic reneged on the pilot's survival.

"I can permit your take-off but I cannot assist it."

Singer sipped a cold tea. "Maybe I shouldn't enquire but why allow me to use unassisted manual controls to take off?"

"Your assumption of control Code 872/a19 under the circumstance of an emergency as in Code 192/16f abrogates my responsibilities."

"Yes, I'm sorry I asked," he said. He'd been building up to the next question. "How much time do I have before lift-off would be a waste of time anyway?"

"No time. There is nil probability of your successful passage through the swarm unaided by my navigation system."

Singer was thoroughly confused now. The computer seemed to be contradicting itself.

"Then why did you recommend I should take off using manual controls when there's no chance of making it?"

"You asked me what I would do in your place not what I would do if I were you. I have a superior intellect, faster responses and greater sensory receptivity than you."

"But with my brain-box it would be impossible. I get it. Thanks a lot."

He thought about the last exchange. In spite of his frustration he knew the computer was right. However, in spite of the odds against him he'd have to try. After all, the company included a non-mechanical operant for just this type of beyond-the-odds event. He'd mistakenly assumed that since the computer won't take off then it wouldn't allow him access to the controls.

SINGER HAD SIMULATED unassisted lift-offs. They were difficult. You needed twenty-one fingers and all the skills of several video-game champions rolled into one.

With only three hours to spare, he punched up the procedures. He stopped reading when he forgot the first page initiation procedures. He glanced at his countdown clock and sipped a stimulant.

The ship would still have its remote control switches usable but he'd have to operate them from a console instead of the computer making decisions. The ship would automatically use its gyroscopic balance controls, other equilibrium feedback systems would work including the life-support-system and impending impact warnings would deafen him.

Just before he touch-started the sequence that would effectively turn the computer off, he turned on his favourite music, a haunting syncopated melody: repetitive but comforting. If he was going to go, he might as well go in style.

It took him longer than expected to do all the pre-flight checks but eventually the large Digger left the surface. He adjusted the rumbling thrust in five rockets simultaneously. There was danger in the acceleration considering the low gravity field he was in. He didn't want to shoot off into the meteor swarm too fast to be able to control his ungainly vehicle. Luckily, the incoming asteroid was coming from behind him as he took off but, even so, he worried. The time of impact was in seven minutes. Normally that would put any escaping pilot into a mind-bending panic.

He wasn't too worried. He knew he could travel a thousand times faster than the one click an hour closing speed of the two asteroids and was already hundreds of times faster. He decelerated when he decided to watch the impact. Putting the ship into a coasting routine, making sure there was nothing in front for at least an hour and checking the proximity alarm was active, he set up cameras and settled to watch through the aft view-port.

It was as eerie as it was fascinating. There they were, two celestial masses slowly closing in on each other each blissfully unaware of the other's presence.

The convergence was in awful languor. Moments before they touched, it seemed as if time stood still. A dilatory pause in space. Singer sat spellbound as the incoming intruder closed in.

The point of contact grew darker as the umbra-shadow crept over the craters. Then, the unique sight of the mountain tops of one world grazing the summits of another. Millions of tons of rock and dust pushed each other over as crumbling slow avalanches started to obscure Singer's view of the contact point. It didn't seem right that the grinding together of two flying mountains should be in silence. It didn't seem fair. At least it was witnessed.

Worlds might end here—unheard. Nevertheless, the impact did send seismic perturbations through both asteroids. Singer improved his vision by using radar and microwave imagery that filtered out the finer fragments. His heart raced with excitement as he witnessed the extended pulverisation of mountain ranges. Instant lava flows increasingly splattered in vivid colours. Another mountain had its summit touched and then atomised by the incoming giant.

He found breathing painful, gasping. It must be the excitement. His hands quivered as he attempted to adjust vision controls. The occasion of more than a lifetime.

A black thought penetrated his exultation, and he glanced at the forward screens. Clear. Why had he thought he was heading towards something? The hardware would've warned him... as long as he'd set it correctly. He'd better check the manuals again. It was a nuisance he couldn't rely on the ship protecting him automatically just because of its damned logic and protocol. Besides every second spent re-reading the manuals would be precious moments away from the spectacle. He looked up.

The incoming asteroid seemed to be bigger. It was no longer a spheroid: the impact area had merged into the crust but the sides still had some curved form.

The metallic asteroid that he had been strolling about on appeared to be intact while the softer intruder was breaking up into huge pieces.

Singer grinned as he contemplated his future. Not only will he have a priceless record of this collision and the valuable samples in the hold to make him first famous then rich but it looked as if he might be able to scoop up more after the collision.

An ear-penetrating whine shook him. A proximity alarm. Part of the incoming asteroid had exploded and shards as big as a house headed his way.

AND SO IT WAS that he was trying to identify the whining noise as he was sailing through space in the escape pod. He was without the record of the collision to make him famous and without the samples to make him rich. He fingered a lump in his breast pocket... he smiled ruefully at the feel of the only fragment left, a souvenir.

Now what? A bright orange light was blinked furiously at him. The closing presence of a craft homing in on his distress beacon. He hoped it was his company's rescue craft and not a rival's elimination mission. He initiated a routine to enable stealth and to listen into radio signals with auto translation.

Singer adjusted volume and tweaked language diagnostic and translation parameters, then listened as he hovered a finger over the Respond button if they were genuine rescuers.

Crackles, and then:

"It should be somewhere around here."

"Come on. Giracci, we've been searching co-ordinates for eighty hours. That signal must've been a passing vessel and it's passed. Let's go."

"No. All the analysis indicates that one of the signals came from a wreck and the decoders are certain that it told of a manned escape vehicle."

"OK then, where is it?"

"Suppose it was you out there, hoping to be rescued but some would-be rescuer had a late appointment with his girl and..."

'I'm still here, aren't I? Though I'm with Gvinlic who reckons that they can't be distress calls. They're in no code that's been used to date, they're on the wrong frequency for emergencies and no one is scheduled to be here."

"That cannot be an excuse..." their argument dopplered away.

Singer realized they were a genuine if strange rescue mission, but his radar gave him false readings of size and position. Now he was losing them so he turned his escape pod and headed for the signal source.

Damn, the proximity alarm battered his ears, but at least the radio became audible again.

"Still nothing, Giracci. Let's go home."

"Hey, what's that? Something's hit the forward viewscreen."

"Yeah, probably a micrometeorite. It's cracked the outer layer."

Singer, dazed, struggled to ensure his helmet was on, as the pod disintegrated around him.

PRIME MERIDIAN

TUESDAY

He examined the sky, watching the contrails of Malaga-bound 747s. Brave single-engine planes zigzagged beneath, keeping to lower horizontal layers like sparrows wary of higher eagles. He should've been urging on pupils from his year ten form and if he had, they might have absorbed some inspiration and turned their near miss into victory. He shivered his perfunctory support, looking forward more to the tea and biscuits only a short walk away at his home.

He looked at his pupils gathering their remaining energies for the final surge against a superior side.

"Are you glad you came, sir?"

"What? Oh yes, Charlene, of course," he lied, as he pulled his John Barry coat tighter against the November chill. His mother told him he was too thin to withstand proper winters.

"Come on Brad, put your effing boot in!"

"Hey, watch your language," he said, demonstrating adult shock.

"Oh, it's expected, sir, let it all out." She leapt up and down, demonstrating in her turn, teenage female energy making him feel tired. He was glad to hear the final whistle.

He had to brew his own tea being both single and new to the area. He'd recently inherited the Victorian end of terrace in Cavendish Road, Chingford, from his grandfather. Then he'd discovered that Chingford Borough High School needed mathematics teachers. They were so desperate they employed him, John Forrister, who used his six-feet-eight height as a discipline aid.

He put the kettle on. The bottle of Grants pulled at him but he resisted for another hour, in order to get the ticks and crosses in more or less the right places. There was an in-pile of lesson books at his feet plus the one on his lap. Throwing the latest marked effort at the out-pile and sending it spilling on the old Axminster carpet revealed something he'd not noticed. A cigarette burn mark staring defiantly at him. He thought he'd covered all his granddad's carpet-despoiling indiscretions. He didn't really like the house, whose features included being musty, draughty, creaked when he tried to sleep, but his income wouldn't let him change much for a while. The only uplifting experience was the evening view from his bedroom when he could, habitually, see the neighbour in her penthouse bedsit washing her hair, apparently not wanting to get any of her clothes wet.

He toppled books as he knelt on the carpet to examine the mark. Maroon tufts were singed in a thumbnail-sized disfigurement. Mild puzzlement turned to surprise when his finger found itself worming through a hole in the floorboard beneath. He sat on the floor his legs either side of the hole and tried to think how he missed the hole before but his head hurt from the effort.

He was hungry so he rang for a take-away pizza instead.

WEDNESDAY

He couldn't leave school when the beasts fled the building, on account of departmental meetings—inspections next term. He managed to keep his eyes open until hitting the pavement home at five.

This time the bottle of Grants whisky lost mass as it went towards nerve steadying. He sat heavily at the pre-war wooden kitchen table. It wasn't fair that he was expected to rewrite schemes of work, syllabuses, remark books properly, replace the curled up wall-displays and cultivate some boot-licking skills as backup.

He drummed his fingers on the table, trying not to think how to prioritise his tasks, when his right index finger became stuck in a hole. Not properly stuck, just enough to be pulled out easily and to make him quiz his finger. He'd not come across any knotholes in the table when he spray-polished it on Sunday. Maybe he'd drummed too hard and the knot fell through.

Knocking through a knot with his finger was unlikely, giving it sufficient force to go through the floorboards as well was just ridiculous, even in his foul mood. But there it was. He lay on his stomach under the table fingering the newly discovered hole in the linoleum. It travelled through the floorboard like the carpet hole. Had he inherited a house with the largest woodworm in Britain? He rolled over onto his back to get a different viewpoint of the hole in the table. He could see a clean hole in the table as a white disc of light. With a little squinting, he could peer through it to the tall white ceiling. It had its own hole.

Breathlessly charging up the stairs, he found a hole in the boxroom yucky-green lino. It drew his eyes upwards. There it was: another hole. It went on. He'd not been up in the attic; didn't know how. A much-painted trapdoor tried to hide in the corridor ceiling but no ladder; and he'd enjoyed too much whisky to consider rearranging his furniture into a pyramid.

He was sufficiently compos mentis to lie on the boxroom lino and, while coating his sweatshirt with floor fluff, peeped down the hole to the rest of his house. The holes didn't line up vertically. His finger told him and his eye confirmed the slight angle. He had to rule out oversized woodworm unless it had a laser guidance system. His whisky-fuddled synapses gave up for the night.

THURSDAY

He was obliged to look up at the sky at the end of the school day. Unnaturally ear-splitting explosions and a riot of ever expanding umbrellas of lights filled the sky in overlapping waves. It was November 5th, Guy Fawkes Day, when Britons celebrate either the attempt to blow up parliament or the success of thwarting the conspiracy. Maybe his holes were made with pre-emptive firework rehearsals. In which case, they might've stopped turning his house into a colander by now. It was late when he reached his doorstep. He didn't relish finding more holes, and other staff from the school-supervised firework display helped him spend a good portion of his salary at the Fox & Hounds. He was aiming his front door key when a young lady's voice cut the air behind him.

"Mr Forrister?"

"It might be," he said, trying to stop the alcohol in his breath escaping. "Who wants to know?"

"I'm Teresa Czeremchka." She spoke with a Polish accent. "I live in the top flat next to your house."

He thought he'd recognised her face from the penthouse window, and if she'd seen him through wet hair on those occasions it could explain why she wasn't smiling.

"John. I'm John. Would you like to come in for a drink?"

"No. I have to tell you about your roof."

"My roof? Oh I suppose you can see it from your window. Interesting view is it?"

"Not as interesting as yours, I think," she replied, with a straight face. "I saw damage to your roof the other afternoon."

He sobered immediately. "Was it Tuesday by any chance?"

"Yes. A quarter past three."

"What can you see up there?"

"Broken tiles."

"I don't suppose you saw it happen?"

"I think it was what you call a shooting star? It glowed."

"My God, I'm under attack from outer space! Have you seen more of them?"

"I don't spend all *my* time watching *your* house."

"I didn't mean to ..." he blurted, "but I'd be grateful if you'd tell me—"

"I intend to buy curtains, Mr Forrister."

He heated with embarrassment about his incidental peeping, but his thoughts were more on the shooting star and any more holes he might find inside. He'd heard of extinction-size asteroids landing, but thought shooting stars burnt up in the atmosphere. He couldn't find a fresh hole so went to make a coffee. Damn, his sink overflowed of today's breakfast crockery and yesterday's curry supper. Cursing his sloppiness he lifted the saucepan and dropped it when a jagged hole told him he didn't need to clean it anymore.

Lifting the pan again revealed the hole's continuation into the stainless steel making it the only sink in Chingford with two plugholes. Upstairs he found it had also whizzed through his grandfather's grandfather clock. It had stopped at three fourteen.

Lying in bed he wondered how safe it was to stay. The one consolation was that whatever made the hole, shooting stars or wayward fireworks, it only happened once a day. He should've worried himself awake longer but the alcohol took over.

FRIDAY

Suppose it was rock fragments hurtling into his house, which organisation do you report it to? The police, his insurance company, the Royal Astronomical Society? Alan Cooper. As head of physics at Chingford Borough High, he was the ideal man to investigate his house: right up his street.

"No, man, not shooting stars, they're meteors and don't land. Meteorites are the ones; they're brilliant, John. It'll be meteorites landing on your house. That's fantastic!"

"Glad you're so pleased. But I thought meteorites landed about once every century or so."

"A meteorite the right size to make a hole to fit your finger lands every twenty minutes," said Cooper.

"My God," Forrister said, looking up at the sky, as they walked to his house.

"That's for the whole planet of course. An area the size of London gets a hit of a pea to a grape-size meteorite every three years."

"You'll have to readjust your figures 'cos my house gets one every day."

"Ah."

"Ah?"

"Well it could happen, you know, swarms; but they're usually seen as meteors like the Leonids, which are fragments of comets. They peak in twenty-four hours."

"If it's not meteorites, maybe it's one of them?" Forrister said, pointing at the lights of an aircraft heading towards Luton.

"Could be; but I wouldn't rule out meteorites until I get one in my hands. What do they look like?"

"Haven't a clue, that's why you're coming down into my basement with me to sort out the meteorites from the meteorwrongs."

"Haha, your basement so unruly you can't see recent additions?"

"Only been down once to see where I could put a wine rack but there's too much junk. I've only been there two months."

"Been in mine twenty years and still haven't sorted the cellar, assuming I have one," Cooper said.

They searched but couldn't find any new holes. They shouldered the stiff door to the cellar but it was a near-hopeless task finding the culprits in the assorted boxes and piles of mostly metal junk.

"Your granddad an engineer?"

"Yeah, he had a workshop down here making one-twentieth scale steam engines. Hence all the swarf and black metallic lumps. If they were meteorites, what are we looking for?"

"Pieces of black metallic lumps," Cooper said, glumly.

Giving up, they sat in the lounge, each with a Fosters.

"So today's hasn't happened. Yet you think they all happen around three fifteen. Today's could be late so I'll stop a while."

"Should we be wearing tin hats?"

"They'd hit the roof at around four hundred miles an hour and after going through the attic would slow considerably, with each floor, taking a fraction of a second to get to the basement. If your floors weren't Victorian cheapo wood they would get lodged en route."

"Hope it stops soon, my insurance won't pay for meteorite hits."

"That's right; but they would if they came from satellites or aircraft, and I've been coming round to thinking there must be a Wright Brothers seven-four-seven up there popping rivets on a regular basis," Cooper said.

Forrister shook his head. "I can't find a flight that takes off or lands on time every day that might account for the holes."

"Assuming your neighbour and the clock time wasn't coincidental, it seems unlikely that human timetabled events were responsible for such accuracy. On the other hand, some artefacts have to be very accurate."

"Such as satellites?"

"Exactly, although there's hundreds of them up there and at least five hundred defunct ones; but, apart from the minibus-sized ones, which are well plotted, whole ones completely burn up. Something else relating to satellites might be happening though," he said drifting off into deep thought.

"Another can?"

"Thanks. You live in an interesting scientific location you know."

"No I don't. It's Chingford."

"It's also on the Greenwich Meridian, you know, zero degrees longitude."

"Yeah, but so are lots of places," Forrister said.

"Apart from Greenwich and a few other London streets, there is no other city in England or anywhere else in the world precisely on the Prime Meridian. Look at an atlas, John."

"Don't need to with you around."

"Well I did some post-grad research on Meteosat and guess which line of longitude it's on?"

"Mine, I presume."

"Yes, zero; but also dead over the equator, whereas we are considerably farther north."

"But if something was being ejected or knocked off Meteosat, it doesn't mean the bits would land on the same latitude, surely?"

"You're right. It must just be an amazing coincidence but," Cooper drifted off again, "on the other hand..."

"Maybe there's something mystic about the Prime Meridian—like ley lines. Anyway, it's two a.m. and no space debris callers. I've got to find a roof repairer tomorrow."

"Yeah, I'll give you a ring over the weekend if I think of anything. Hey, maybe you should stay at my place until it stops."

"It might've stopped already."

"Or it might've called and got lodged in a deep joist."

"I'll take my chances since they only come in the afternoons."

"I'll be off," goodbyed Cooper. He stood and turning to collect his coat, noticed the cushion he'd been squashing all evening.

"Er, John, do you usually keep your cushions in this state?" He raised a green braided lump becoming inside out via two holes. They looked up at the second hole in the lounge ceiling, wondered what it had drilled upstairs, and then examined the chair.

"At least it must've happened before you sat down," Forrister said.

"That's what you think," joked Cooper, feeling for holes over his body.

SATURDAY

He blinked at the late morning sun as he creaked open his half-glazed front door.

"You need to repair your roof, Mr Forrister."

"Oh hello, Miss Creze, Crzenchk–"

"Miss Czeremchka. Did your beer-soaked brain take in what I said?"

"Sorry? I'm not drunk–that was last night. No, I don't do drunk anymore, Miss Cz...it's Teresa isn't it?"

"Miss Czeremchka to you. I know a builder who do a temporary roof repair for you."

"Really, that's brilliant. I visit my mother on Sundays..."

"Orpington?"

"Yes, but how do you know?"

"I–I knew your grandfather. He needed someone to get his shopping and the odd job in-between your rare visits."

"I had no idea. He was so stubborn, insisting on living alone until the end and I lived up north. I should be thanking you."

"I liked him, he was more polite. I could let the builder in for you if it has to be Sunday."

"That's brilliant, let me give you a spare key."

"I have one. Your grandfather gave it me."

CURIOSITY OVERCAME HIS FEAR when he returned from Savaspend with plastic bag handles cutting into both hands. Dumping them in the corridor he ran down into the basement. He knew it was the safest place; and he saw a Second World War air-raid warden helmet he was going to wear.

He sat down on an old swivel chair and looked at his watch: 3:11. Just in time to hear a low frequency crump noise upstairs, followed by more sounds, including one sounding like his front door banging. Fearful, he looked up at the wooden cellar ceiling, waiting for a meteorite to come through. Nothing. Puzzled, he went up the cellar steps, seeing snowflakes of plaster flutter down from a hole in the ceiling. He cursed when he saw baked beans splattered over the corridor wall and floor. The meteorite must be buried in the foundations next to the cellar after neatly puncturing the Savaspend carrier and baked beans as if it knew just where to maximise clearing up time.

SUNDAY

It was a difficult visit for John Forrister. Clockwise congestion on the M25 didn't help. His comatose aged mother, however, allowed his mind to go into orbit, where it worried about waking up one morning with a hole in one of his vital bits.

It was 3:20 so he'd survived another day.

His mobile phone nearly jumped out of his pocket. Alan Cooper.

"Any more incoming?"

"Yesterday, not back in today."

"I've had an email reply from a Canadian geophysicist who's interested in your house."

"It's his for two hundred grand."

"I didn't mean...hey, that's a bit cheap, John."

"Not for a Swiss cheese you have to keep out of at quarter past three every day."

"Anyway my friend reckons they could be tektites."

"What tights? Sounds like hosiery."

"They're ejecta from volcanoes. They can travel far from eruptions like from Etna for instance."

"Size and colour? Time of impact?"

"Often look like shiny black buttons or beans. Usually land within a day of eruptions and of course Etna's been throwing up regularly for a while. On the other hand it's not likely for tektites to whiz over one at a time although bursts of activity can happen at precise intervals. There's likely to be a swarm of them. Have you heard of any others in your area?"

"I haven't got to know many neighbours yet, apart from one."

"Have a look around then, there should be what they call a strewn field. See you at the zoo tomorrow, yeah?"

"Where? Oh yeah right, bye," Forrister said, reaching his house.

Two men were collapsing a ladder, the top part scratching its way down the gable end of his house. The larger of the two men looked at Forrister, hitched up his forty-two inch trousers, wiped a hand across his lived-in moustache, and holding out the same hand, stepped forward.

"Mr Forrister?"

"Yes. Much damage up there?" he said, now wiping his own hand on his trousers.

"Seen worse."

"Oh? Not lots of broken tiles then?"

"Looks like your roof's never been maintained, one biggish hole where rain would've wet your attic, and it looked as if whoever put your TV aerial up had studs on his boots."

"That'd be tektite damage," Forrister said, instantly regretting it.

"You what?"

"I mean meteorites," he explained, making matters worse.

"You what?"

"Is it all right now then?"

"Oh no, they don't make those tiles any more; and it'd take a while to order re-cycled ones, then a couple of days work to fix it proper. I've tarpaulined the one biggish hole and fiddled the others so you won't get wet."

"Thanks," Forrister said, worried about escalating costs if he had to reroof every other Sunday–forever. "By the way Mister er..."

"Cadogan, Grant Cadogan, here's me card–the phone number's wrong."

"Thanks, Mr Cardigan, but let me know before you shin up your ladder again won't you? Oh, and just out of interest, have other roofs had any damage around here recently?"

"Funny you should ask that," Cadogan said.

"There have been other roofs?"

"There's always a few each year near the railway and the school, both caused by kids: they put scrap on the tracks. The bits sometimes get flicked up in the air–quite spectacular. Varmints. Used to do it meself. Be seeing you, Mr Forrister."

It hadn't occurred to him about kids. The railway and the school: his house was close to both. So: railway, school, flight paths of two major airports and a couple of local ones, not to mention the Greenwich or Prime Meridian. A snag was the timing; he could easily check on the railways, but it would be a miracle if a train passed at exactly the right time every day. Also his school, the closest secondary, didn't let the animals escape until 3:20.

There was no sign of Teresa what's-her-name as he entered his corridor whiffing parfum de baked beans. He wondered if Cadogan would've noticed a meteorite smashing through the roof he worked on. Only if it put out his fag.

No more holes in the kitchen sink. He put the still-intact kettle on for a coffee and eyes constantly on lookout, walked into the living room.

If he was tidier, Form 8b's maths homework books would've been back in his briefcase. Then Luke Darlow wouldn't have a hole in his simultaneous equations all the way from the front cover to the back. No way could he give it back to him like that. He'd have to give him a detention for not handing it in. Shame he'd already corrected it. He looked up at the extra ceiling hole, wondering what else it went through.

The state of the bedroom carpet gave him a clue as he splashed through it to the radiator. The meteorite, or whatever, ricocheted off the radiator without going straight through but enough to have a small jet peeing onto the carpet. He taped a wad of blutak and placed a bowl beneath the persistent rogue drips.

MONDAY2

Alan Cooper was dismissive of every theory involving local origins of the projectiles: they wouldn't be fast enough, assorted sizes would result, rail timetables too erratic in practice, as were children.

"No, John. Use your maths. We've thought that it can't be bits of a satellite because they'd be burnt up and would come in one go, but satellites do things on a very regular basis. Take Meteosat for instance. It's the main weather satellite you see pictures from on the telly, although it does a lot more than scan the earth for visible light and infra-red. Anyway, the point is that there are sensors and transmitters programmed to activate very regularly indeed. I know one that switches on every two hundred seconds."

"So?"

"Just suppose there is a fragment of a dark asteroid near to it. It might have gas pockets inside or just be unstable and sensitive to a burst of electromagnetic radiation like a transmitter nearby."

"So when Meteosat, which I remember is on longitude zero, like my house, sends a particular burst of data at the same time each day, a pocket of gas erupts sending a fragment of asteroid off. Its initial speed mightn't be much but most burns and ablates in the atmosphere until it's the size of a grape and slams into my house."

"You've got it!" said the excited Cooper.

"Rubbish."

"Or it could be an asteroid in a polar orbit that happens to pass near Meteosat at the same time each day and—"

"You're obsessed with Meteosat because you did research on it and I live on the Greenwich Meridian. If that satellite is responsible, the time it would take for incoming to reach my house would put it at least an hour, say fifteen degrees farther to the west. In the Atlantic."

"Ye of little faith," smiled Cooper. "You've been doing some work on it haven't you. But, there's a veritable ring of geosynchronous satellites over the equator so it could be one at fifteen degrees east doing it."

"So the Prime Meridian has nothing to do with it after all. And like I said, millions of people must live on it."

"'But they don't," he said, ignoring Forrister's first comment. "About six hundred houses in the whole world and two hundred and ninety of those are here in London."

"I don't believe it," Forrister said.

"Go to the Geography room and get the big Times Atlas. You'll see how much sea the Prime Meridian is over and that once out of London it travels over almost uninhabited areas. By chance no French town is exactly on it, no Spanish, nothing in the Sahara or the rest of west Africa, just missing Accra in Ghana and then nothing in the rest of the south Atlantic to Antarctica and up the rear end of our planet over the Pacific Ocean."

"Well, even so it's not fair. Why should my house be hit? About six houses in the world get hit by a meteorite every year so the odds are about one in a hundred million that my house would be hit."

"For one thing you shouldn't take it personally." Cooper was laughing.

"It's not funny!"

"I'm not laughing at your predicament but at your irrational response to it. Listen; if another house was hit, anyone living there could say the same thing. *Why me*? But that's giving the meteorite decision-making power. Come on, John. Look at it this way, if it has to be a house on the Prime Meridian, there's a one in six hundred chance it'd be yours."

"All this talk of chances and probabilities have given me an idea to pay for the damage," Forrister said, brightening up. "The insurance wouldn't pay for non-manmade impacts but a bookie might."

"Brilliant," Cooper said, "you should place a bet that your house would be hit by a meteorite tomorrow. You should get good odds; not the ones we've been throwing around. They wouldn't want to bankrupt themselves."

"True, but they might accept a £10 bet on a thousand to one against. I'll pop in on the way home."

"Make sure none of the kids spot you."

"No problem. I'm a maths teacher. Gambling is applied probability theory."

IT WASN'T FUNNY ANYMORE. John had come home to find another hole in the kitchen floor and ceiling, which had come from the bedroom upstairs. It had ploughed through his pillow sending bits of yellow Kapok everywhere. It could've been his brains instead if he'd taken a day off ill.

He had to move. Perhaps Cooper would put him up until the meteorites stopped. Suppose they didn't stop? Or not until his house was reduced to rubble with a crowd to watch the daily impact bouncing back into the air.

So much for his inheritance. He couldn't sell it with this going on, he'd be sued for withholding vital information.

On top of that, the bookies wouldn't accept his bet. They had to ring their chief actuary, who wanted to know if it had happened before and who would verify it was a true meteorite, which meant finding it in the cellar.

TUESDAY2

Lulu's *Shout* didn't wake him on his digital alarm. He hadn't been able to get to sleep until four, but once zonked, stayed deep. Something in his body clock stirred him around eight thirty, when his arm reached out to strangle the clock and bring it to his eyes. He expected it to be distorted by a meteorite but he'd only forgotten to set it.

He forced his legs to find the floor: they were slow but faster than his brain. The sight of the phone made his hand reach for it, shortly followed by a semblance of intelligence.

"Alan, it's me, I can't come in today. I'm going to the police and whoever else they suggest. It's doing my head in, and it would have done literally yesterday if I'd gone for a nap in the afternoon."

"Got your bed, eh, scary stuff. Why is the thought of being killed while asleep more disturbing than when you're awake?"

"What are you on about, Alan?"

"Sorry, John, look, briefing is about to start. What shall I tell Bentley; you're not feeling yourself? In which case old boy, who are you feeling?"

"Chance would be a fine thing. Just tell him I'm not well and I'll be in tomorrow."

"You know where I live if you want a safe house for the night."

THE POLICE WERE VERY COMFORTING. They said nothing like it has happened before and so it couldn't be happening now. They'd send a constable round in a few days, once they'd all stopped laughing. The police were also helpful in that they'd notify the planning enforcement officer, just to make sure there aren't unauthorised alterations.

He spent some time with an estate agent seeking advice on selling a house that's more of a site of scientific interest. The best advice was to come clean and put it to auction. There would be interest in purchasing it as a novelty; and he could expect around £50k, which was better than a smack in the face but not much.

He was keen to get back by three. Not to go in but to observe the roof. His preparations were to buy an HD video camera, a tripod and hoped-for permission from Teresa Czzzzzetc to film from her penthouse. He was wearing out his finger on her bell when he saw her coming out of his own house.

"Hi, Teresa!"

"Oh, it's you, Mr Forrister, why are you at my door?"

"I wanted to ask a favour," he said, neatly distracted from asking her the same question.

"What favour is that, I'm very busy."

"In case a meteorite hits my house again today I'd like to film it from your window if that's okay with you?" He smiled encouragement.

"It would reverse the situation: you looking at your own house from my window wouldn't it?" she said without the smile that should have accompanied such irony.

"Is that a yes?"

"I suppose so but give me five minutes to tidy my things."

When he was allowed in, he asked: "By the way what were you doing in my house? The builders come back?"

"You got post delivered to my house by mistake, it wouldn't fit your letter box."

He had a good view of his roof. It was overcast and the tarpaulin flapped a little in the wind. He looked up at the cloud base.

3:13 came and although he stared and filmed, he realised he wasn't going to see a meteorite. If the cloud wasn't there he might've seen a glow from the ionised air around it and maybe from its friction glow but at a few miles up it would slow and cool too much to glow. It might still be hot, especially when boring through his house, but he was so unlikely to actually see it with the naked eye. Hopefully, his camera might pick it up with image enhancement.

3:14 His eyes ached, monitoring every shadow; eagerly watching the starlings, trying to see what scared them when they squawked off.

3:15 His ears tired of intensive listening, trying to distinguish a small meteorite impact from the melee of Chingford's finest screaming kids, tormented trains, reverberating Number 212 buses and suburban mayhem, as well as the accidental dropping of a mug of coffee from Ms Czeremchka's hands.

3:16 He looked at his watch and refocused quickly on his roof when he realised he might've missed it.

3:17 A car pulled up sharply by his house. He could just make out a beefy woman dragging a boy up to his door. The prisoner was Luke Darlow. The one Forrister had put in detention. His mum must have found out he wasn't in school and collected her son promptly to have it out with him.

"Teresa, is it possible to hang around for a few more minutes?" He'd given up filming now it was past the assumed hit time.

"No, I need to get ready to go out; and please don't ask to come up here again," she said, shutting herself in the bathroom. Forrister pulled a long face at the residual vibrations, before returning for a last glance out of the window. The Darlow woman was still there beating his door with one fist with the other clutching what might be Luke's detention notification. He shuffled around for while in Teresa's hallway before overcoming cowardice to bluff Mrs Darlow. To his surprise, Alan Cooper, who'd arrived to see the day's hit, had sent her on her way.

Cooper was rubbing his hands. "Come on John, I've sent the Darlows packing; let's see today's damage."

"You're keener than usual to take a measure of my misfortune."

"You're becoming a scientific oddity and celebrity. My Canadian friend contacted NASA."

"Really?" Forrister never dreamt anything happening to him would make a pencil twitch in the teeth of a Houston Mission Control egg-head.

"They've set up a preliminary project team to look into it. One of them, a Eugene Borelli, is currently on secondment at the

Jodrell Bank radio telescope and is coming down to see us."

"Us?"

"Apparently they suspected the Chinese–"

"The Chinese have been bombarding my house?"

"No. Not directly. They have lots of satellites up there and the Pentagon think they've developed a killer satellite that can knock out others. One of them is a remote sensing satellite called Ziyuan that they think is being used as target practice."

"Does the maths work out, you know, the fifteen degrees more to the east than the prime meridian and all that?" asked Forrister.

"We were wrong by twenty three hours–for Meteosat, it takes longer than I thought; but there are so many, such as the Ziyuan series in polar orbits."

"Incredible,' Forrister said, shaking his head as he unlocked his door. "All right, stop shoving, Alan.'"

"There's another hole in the kitchen ceiling, but I can't see where it went," said Cooper, who stooped to scrutinise the floor.

"Perhaps supplication to the Gods will help," Forrister said.

"It would be a first. Ah, you're giving me a clue."

Above the table against ghastly yellow wallpaper, was a wooden crucifix. It had probably been there for a century, but only very recently acquired an angled hole right in the middle.

"I assume it is today's," Alan said.

"I don't look at it every day, but there's sawdust on the table, and it matches the line of the hole in the ceiling. Which means–"

"It should've gone through to the lounge," Alan said, joining in the race round the wall. The exit hole in the soft plasterboard wall led to another hole in the floor to the metal scrap in the cellar.

"It might still be warm, I'd like to find it this time," Alan said.

In the cellar, their scrambling only resulted in dirty fingernails. There were so many lumps of metal—nuts, bolts and fragments; most blackened or rusty and many were slightly magnetic. Cooper had a magnet and wasted over an hour testing lumps: looking for repulsion since only two magnets can repel each other. Iron meteorites tend to be slightly magnetic. But no luck.

WEDNESDAY2

John was exasperated. What with the Chinese and the supernatural against him he might as well take up the estate agent's suggestion of an auction and accept a tenth of the house's value. On the other hand the value of a pile of Victorian bricks and century-old plain and coloured glass, copper and lead probably came to about twenty grand. Though they'd have to shift it quickly before the diurnal meteorite bombardment reduced it all to dust.

On his way home, he called in at Price & Gamble, the estate agent he'd seen previously.

"Oh it's you, Mr Forrister," said the secretary.

"You own the house of God, and want to sell it!" boomed Mr Gamble coming in from an inner office.

"What?"

"Young Kate here belongs to The New Church of The Cross, and hearing of a rumour about a crucifix today, remembered you."

"But—"

"It's true then? The hand of God actually went through a crucifix? And in your house?" she said.

"Well a meteorite, or something did, yes."

"Please, please, please take me to see it, please." She clutched his lapels. Forrister couldn't remember the last time an attractive brunette threw herself at him so enthusiastically, even if he was only proxy for his pile of bricks.

"I'll come along too," said Gamble, "I am responsible for my female staff when they go in the field."

"'Since when?" Kate said.

Forrister was swept up in the moment, and a while later followed the whole office into his house. They ran about finding all the old holes and photographed the crucifix so much he was sure it would ignite. He found the day's new hole, while they were making tea and emptying his biscuit tin. The hole in the soap was neat but its continuation through the bath was another repair job. At least the rest of its journey merely added to the holes in the lower floors.

"Do you have any pets, John?" asked the increasingly familiar

Kate. "Only it must be a bit scary for them not knowing where and when to hide."

"I hadn't given much thought to it. No wonder I haven't seen Felix since last Monday," he said grimly.

"What! The poor thing. You mean she was—"

"I'm kidding, I don't have a cat. Or a dog."

When their digital cameras ran out of memory, Gamble sat Forrister down at his own kitchen table.

"I'm not really sure what's happening here, and I know you don't, Mr Forrister, but that hole in the crucifix could make a big difference to the value of your property."

"It could?"

"You do still want to sell, and at a price you can get another, safer dwelling?"

"Yes of course. But who in their right mind would want it?"

"The Church. It doesn't have a mind. It has faith and miracles. Mr Forrister, you are in a fortunate position."

Forrister was about to make a suitable response when he heard the doorbell. He was too slow and Kate answered it bringing in a large black overcoat, which wasn't quite big enough for Eugene Borelli and his NASA intentions. Forrister, spasmodically speechless with awe gave him the tour including the basement. Borelli was keen to get up into the attic and was astonished no one had investigated it, even though the builders had done some repairs.

After the estate agents left, Borelli spent two hours examining and photographing each hole and damage, although was a bit annoyed that some patching up had been carried out.

"Well, I still live here you know."

"More fool you, buddy."

"I think you're ready to leave now."

"I didn't mean to offend. I would like to return and take your cellar apart. I haven't seen anything that definitely came from a satellite yet. Then some of those holes you know—" He was interrupted by Cooper, pushing at the door bell and bringing more people with him, sporting cameras.

"Oh, come on, Alan, I'm shoving people out of the house now, not letting them in. It's getting late."

"Ten minutes, John. Are you Borelli..." and the two scientists did the tour again with whoever the other people were. Sounded like press. Forrister had the sneaky feeling that Cooper was making money out of the situation. He'd have to tackle him for a cut.

His chance came twenty minutes later but Alan pre-empted him.

"I've learnt so much from that man. Apparently we're either looking for siderites, which are iron meteorites or the harder bits of satellites. Besides using magnetic properties—a failure as we know—the timing of impact might help. For instance our solar day is twenty four hours but from the point of view of a star or asteroid the sidereal day is more relevant."

"And the sidereal day is—"

"Shorter than the ordinary or solar day. It's because the earth travels around the sun and so has to rotate a little more each day than would appear from a fixed star. What it means is that if the meteorites are hitting your house about four minutes less each day it's more likely to be meteorite than satellite in origin. We aren't absolutely sure each hits at spot-on three-fifteen, are we?" he said looking pleased with himself.

"Unless it's both," said a tired Forrister.

"What...oh yes, a satellite's transmission triggering bits off an asteroid. I forgot about that. Never mind. Look I have another—"

"Good night, Alan. See you in the morning."

THURSDAY2

12:08 in the staff room, Forrister took a call from Mr Gamble.

"How does eight hundred and sixty-five thousand sound to you, Mr Forrister?"

"I couldn't possibly afford it."

"No, it's what you've been offered for your house, no strings, no chain, just a genuine big cheque. Minus our commission of course. Don't forget it has no central heating, double-glazing, no maintenance for nearly a century so normally it would struggle to reach two-hundred thousand."

"Is this the freaky religious sect you mentioned?"

"There's nothing freaky about a suitcase full of money, Mr Forrister."

"Actually there is, but when could it happen?"

"If you agree now, come in to sign after work, borrow the school minibus to move out, and you can buy a deluxe Regency-mode air raid shelter tomorrow."

A flurried paperwork session followed, and Forrister stood in a daze with a bill of sale in his hand. He rushed round to his bank before they closed, and called in at Walthamstow Furniture Removals and Storage.

He called George Bentley at the school. He knew he'd still be there sorting out the next day's cover lessons. Although teachers were allowed time off for moving house it was usual to give notice, so he had to be more obsequious than he'd like. He almost skipped home. Home? He'd find a B&B for a couple of weeks until he found a more permanent residence. Maybe a flat in a very tall building only he'd have the ground floor or even the cellar, especially if it had a stone floor.

Once more, Alan Cooper was at his front door when the exuberant Forrister finally arrived home.

"Come in and have a serious drink, Alan, assuming my bottle of Grant's hasn't been trashed."

"Let me guess, you've had an offer for the house, and it's more than fifty quid."

"The God squad have bought it, and good riddance."

"Hey, will they still let the NASA guys in, and me?" asked Cooper.

Forrister laughed: "Maybe. What do you look like in a cassock?"

They crept in but couldn't find a fresh hole until Cooper went to the bathroom.

"Hey, John, your john's sprung a leak."

They looked at it. There was a neat hole in the plastic toilet seat cover but it looked as if a grenade had gone off in the bowl with large cracks in the ceramic and a few pieces over the floor.

"There should be its continuation in the corridor downstairs," said Cooper. They couldn't find it. "Maybe it's lodged in the wall or ceiling somewhere."

"Let's have that drink," Forrister urged. "I can't tell you what a relief it is to get out of here. I was mentally prepared to leave stoney broke, though at least I have a job. But now..."

Three hours later they smiled Alan's way to the bus stop. John out for some fresh air.

As Cooper stepped onto the bus, Teresa disembarked.

"Hello there," John said, "on your way home?"

"So?"

"You might be interested to know I'm moving."

FRIDAY2 TERESA

The smile continued to grow, completely out of control. It had been on her face throughout the night, in her dreams and now at the penthouse breakfast table.

The smile metamorphosed to rapid bursts of laughter as she stood with her steaming coffee and saw through the window the removals vehicle and men in overalls extracting the few sad bits of furniture worth keeping. Not bad, it had taken two weeks to rid herself of the peeping tom pervert. The whole point of moving to the penthouse in a politically Conservative London suburb was to put her private life away from such men.

Now look who had the power. She sat down again to finish her muesli and yoghurt, throwing a glance at the collection of her tools spilling out of the rucksack in the corner. A powerdrill, hole-borer, power-hammer, mini-vacuum cleaner and the keys. No point being the only girl and the only top grade in the NVQ engineering class at Wapping College unless you made use of it. As she took another mouthful, she ruminated on the pure luck of seeing the first and only meteorite hit on Forrister's house and the idea it gave her.

She stopped smiling to sip her coffee although she was still laughing inside. Her eyes opened wider as her ears picked up a noise. Before she could register what made it, the remains of her milky muesli splattered out in a corona as the bowl disintegrated. Even before she could take the mug from her lips she could see the hole where the bowl was and in her floor. It was 0814.

THREE MINUTES

ON TIPTOE THEN LAUNCH into the air, arms outstretched. I somersault, the wind ruffling my hair and the g-forces tightening my stomach. The sun shimmers off the water. A perfect flying dream if it wasn't for an obnoxious odour. My nose wrinkles to slow its intake. I awake.

A rush of icy air blasts my face. What? I can't open my eyes against the pressure until I twist to face upwards. I suck in air and the view of devastation. A slow-motion explosion unfolds above. The wings, tail and nose are separating. The jumbo's cabin has fragmented and passengers, burning seats, and debris accompany me. A Barbie doll flies close—its fixed smile hellos while a melted hand reaches out.

Synapses calculate that with air resistance fighting gravity, I have three minutes falling six miles, more if I get in a flap. Pushing panic away on the grounds it has no survivable features, I wonder whether to hold my jacket open like a sail. But I must already be at 120 miles per hour terminal velocity so it would rip apart. Or would it? I reach into my pocket and switch on my phone. Is three minutes sufficient to say sorry and how much I love her, or would it be too cruel? I text: LUV U. But there is no service.

The debris slowly spreads. I involuntary revolve and see I am about to overtake thousands of glass slivers. They brush my face, a soft caress. Must be cargo—my shipment of purloined Roman glass. Payback time.

The sea looks no closer. The hurricane in my ears blocks out screaming and explosions. Surreal. I let my phone have its own trajectory; maybe it'll find a signal en route.

Like being in an isolation chamber. Is three minutes up yet?

PRODIGAL SUN

FINGAL DARED HIMSELF to open a window. Instead of the cool October breeze that blew around him on his way to work that morning, a gust of hot air smacked his face as if he was the original naughty boy.

Naomi Lessing's scream bounced around the lab with more energy than the particle accelerator a moment ago. Fingal quivered in his chair hoping that his error could swallow him into another dimension before the director calmed enough to hurl actual words. No such luck.

"What have you done?" Her voice descended, decelerated but retained a staccato edge. "I allow a CalTech mathematician into my lab and you do what? Fuse the entire building?"

"Noo," a gravelly Scottish voice jumped in. "More like fused the freaking planet."

Fingal glared at the physicist. "All right, Carnegie, no need to exaggerate." But had he?

He thought back six months, Fingal had beamed twice in succession, first as his plane landed at John Lennon Airport, Liverpool home to his musical obsession, and again at the reopened 70-metres-high Van der Graaff generator at his new internship, the Daresbury Particle Accelerator. All the way over the Atlantic, he clicked his fingers when he thought of his luck gaining this secondment to work on his hypotheses to use quantum entanglement to put distance from his workbench and a dimension folding experiment. Daresbury was insignificant in the global consciousness but it was one of the first to accelerate particles and he'd a feeling it was going to be put back on the map. If only he could turn back time to his first day...

Someone clapped their hands right behind him. "Fingal!"

"Keep your hair on..." then he realized it was the director. "Sorry, Ma-am, all I did was run a standard, well not *that* standard experiment, just an app that kinda tweaks a couple of the assumed eleven dimensions."

"Tweaks?" Her arms were so tightly folded her breasts threatened to burst through her 'Keep Calm and Particle On' T-shirt.

Perspiring with guilt, he nictated his eyes away from Naomi Lessing to his screen, back and again then stammered, "Folding, Ma-am, I've been theorizing on the dimensions."

"There was nothing in our interviews that said you were going to tamper with existence."

He laughed at the ridiculousness of it all. "It's a kinda private project. It'd never work, just a mad theory, and in any case, I used a QM device to distance the effects far away." He knew his grin was more like that of a chimpanzee baring fangs to scare enemies or in embarrassment.

"Fix it before you're fired, and that will be by noon." She stormed off.

Phew, he was expecting the two bulky security guards, George and Edwina, to frogmarch him out of the building into the weird hot weather. He was needed after all. He frowned at his screen. The only difference in the input of data to his QM equations was a random number generator he'd written as a simple sub-routine just as a test. It should have simulated the effects of running their new accelerator. It was nowhere as powerful as CERN, just different. Thirty million volts was nothing these days. He zoomed in by putting his face closer and ignoring his reflected dark bushy eyebrows, wayward hair and designer five-day stubble. Strange, the numerals in the equation were changing as he watched. They should be fixed after the run. Ah, it was still running, but that shouldn't be a problem unless...

A voice inveigled his right ear. "Fingal."

He swivelled his chair to face Fiona Ridd. He'd been drawn to her auburn waist-length hair and ability to cut straight through crap. She'd rebuffed his inexperienced attempt to date her during his first week but he hoped to win her over in increments. Wasn't working. Perhaps she'd—

Her voice transformed from sweet, mellow to a harsh, demand, "Why the hell is your program activating *my* accelerator? And why hide your origin via encryption, making me worry it was a hack from outside?"

Fingal looked up at her fiery hair and hands on hips. He jolted into his answer, "Ah. I didn't realize it was still running 'till just now and the encryption? Force of habit, sorry."

"You're not a student anymore, Fingal. I'm terminating your access right now."

"You'd better pass that by Naomi. My run has induced a problem. Did you feel—"

"That earth tremor?" her frown deepened. "Or was it your experiment?"

He wasn't sure, but Naomi had accused him. His mother was also a Naomi. She'd have hugged him but would need to sprout long arms to hug him from her retreat in Arizona and she wouldn't fuss over a few extra degrees.

Damnation, Fiona had been talking while Fingal's mind was absent.

"...on desktop simulation only until authorised by Naomi. Understood?"

"Sure, and you'll be pleased to know I've several scenarios to test and buddies back in the States are working on it. We'll have solutions in no time.

A WEEK WITH NONE of those solutions later, no one smiled in the sweltering heat. Fingal wore shorts and a T-shirt like everyone else in the emergency meeting at Daresbury. Luckily, their air con worked whereas most in the UK had fallen silent when the overloaded National Grid tried to keep people below blood temperature in their homes, offices and industry. Naomi had been made to accept Burl Downing, a climatologist professor from the Climate Research Unit, University of East Anglia. He was in front of the fifty researchers giving them death by Powerpoint. Fingal sniggered behind his hand at the academic's basin haircut, but then he admonished himself. His own straw thatch yet with incongruous dark bushy eyebrows attempting to hide one green and one brown eye afforded him no leeway to mock the appearance of others.

Instead, Fingal envied the prof's deep, Welsh accent. "Thank you Naomi, I'll not take up your time for more than is necessary. I find it ironic that climate organizations have urged governments and industry the world over to work at holding global warming to no more than two degrees Celsius over the next fifty years and now something this centre did in two seconds caused temperatures to rise to fifty degrees."

Among the harrumphs and shouts of protest, Carnegie stood. Naomi glared at the staff. "No one leaves until I say so. Professor, the world will not gain by antagonising my people."

He grinned through his badger beard. "My apologies. You all know the atmospheric temperature has risen dramatically, unaccountably—nothing to do with so-called greenhouse emissions." A slide of NOAA satellite views of Greenland's ice sheet zoomed on the screen. "Melting is occurring at an unprecedented rate. Luckily with its high specific heat capacity the deeper ice isn't melting as fast as the media say. Even so..." Another view appeared of the Indian Ocean. The tops of churches showed all that's left of the Solomon Islands. Another slide drew a gasp. A map of the world in the present, and another with dramatically increased blue areas. The slide became animated as the camera zoomed over coastlines. No more Bangladesh, Cairo, The Netherlands, much of California and most of the Eastern seaboard disappeared. "This will happen within two years if the mean global surface temperature remains at the forty-seven Celsius it has reached this week. You, my friends, will need to move house." The animated map hovered over the Daresbury Science Complex with its Van de Graaff generator building. The blue filled the area of Liverpool, Runcorn and lapped where this meeting took place.

"Ladies and Gentlemen, the oceans will rise fifty-five metres when all the ice melts along with thermal expansion. Most of the world's population live near the coast. They'll have to be evacuated to upland areas. More difficult would be the migration of delta and other low-level agriculture, staple foods such as rice and the billions of square hectares of other cereal crops. How resistant will upland people be to such—"

Fingal's ears stopped listening. He knew all of this but he'd not factored in the speed of rising sea-level and although the plight of others was far greater, his mind became occupied over the triviality of his own situation. Not merely the temporary house he lodged at, which would be submerged if this damned heat persisted, but his many relatives near San Diego. At least his mother dwelt at altitude.

"—if greenhouse gases are not responsible for this warming, then what is? Some speculate on tectonic activity. No, let's get to the chase. Solar brilliance has increased by ten percent."

The room erupted with a cacophony of denials.

Fingal too had yelled his displeasure with a 'No way!' but Professor Downing continued in anticipation of the response. "Ten percent wouldn't be noticeable to your average indoor physicist but it rang bells on NASA's heliospheric observatory."

He paused. Silence. "Ah, now I have an intelligent audience. Most ask does that mean the sun's giving out more heat, but you'll know that our atmosphere isn't warmed directly from the sun but from its ultra violet light, which excites atoms on the ground to produce infra-red and that is what's heating the air. I'll take questions after my next bombshell. Are you ready for this?"

Fingal was beginning to hate him and fidgeted, looking for paper to make an airplane to launch at the showman.

"It appears, my learned friends that the Earth has travelled through a cusp in space-time to a billion years in the future."

Derision filled the room until Naomi shut it down with one of her glares.

"It's known that solar luminosity increases at the rate of ten percent per billion years with the burning of hydrogen, creating helium. Models predicted the heat created on Earth from such brightness would, by half a million years, evaporate surface water. The atmosphere would be saturated with the upper atmosphere bombarded by solar particles boiling off the water to space. No life as we know it."

Fingal was about to stand to object but Carnegie beat him to it. "Every other sci-fi movie has a spaceship flitting harmlessly through wormholes or space/time discontinuities but not a whole planet. Instead of the environment and life adapting over a billion years, it's happened in an instant. Is it possible the ice we have and ocean currents, et cetera, will create a more survivable scenario?"

The professor smiled, although with that beard it was difficult to be sure. "I'm afraid not. We'll all be gone within a year. Temporarily, it will be cooler at the poles but there are no crops nor infrastructure there. Going underground will work for a few if they take long term rations and power. There's only one hope, ladies and gentlemen. You, correct your error. Take us back." His finger described in an arc around his audience.

The noise of angry muttering and chairs scraping signalled the end of the meeting. A dart made of an ice-lolly wrapper flew past the professor's nose.

FINGAL CAUGHT UP with Fiona Ridd on her way back to the particle accelerator lab. Her gardenia perfume worked overtime with the global warming. "Miss Ridd, may I ask you a question?"

"You just did, Fingal." She carried on walking, lengthening her stride. She too sported shorts, maybe too brief for a young man to stay undistracted.

"Okay, two—no, dammit, three questions. Important. Life of the planet and all that."

She stopped, turned and lifted an eyebrow. "So it *is* all your fault?"

"Everyone thinks it. Anyhow, I'd like to match my logs with your logs."

She stood waiting for a moment. "Say please."

"You Brits. Okay, pretty please but now, as in yesterday."

She marched off down the corridor to the basement lift waving her access badge at him to follow.

His neck hairs stood to attention in the factory-like laboratory. "Miss Rodd, does this hum all the time, even when you're not here to comfort it? I assumed the accelerator only activated when asked nicely to do so."

"You can call me Fiona." She typed a password on her screen and flicked to open the log spreadsheet.

Fingal bluetoothed her data to his iPad. "I'll run a correlation subroutine to see what time-related activation of the accelerator coincided with my dimension-folding experiment. You see, Fee, my ques—"

"It's Fiona. Call me Fee again and you'll have your front teeth so missing you'll not be able to say any effing word."

He grinned unwisely. "My question, Fiona. Can the particle accelerator be activated at any time, such as when my program somehow asked for it?"

She twisted a few strands of scarlet hair while examining him. "Ordinarily, no, but two things might have conspired to enable that. One is this prototype accelerator isn't like a Hadron Collider but has an unknown short scale intensity. Second, you."

"Eh?"

"You're too clever for your and our own good. No one has tried your type of coding here at Daresbury before."

Fingal took it as a back-handed complement so jumped in. "Fiona, when our shift ends, how about we—"

"Weren't you listening to Naomi? None of us are leaving until you take us back a billion years?"

"After that?

She smiled just as both their bleepers commanded a return to the meeting room. Fingal tapped on his iPad as he walked.

"There's been a development," Naomi said. "You might have noticed our moon is still where it should be. So have astronomers. Does that mean a bigger chunk of our solar system zapped into the future? Apparently not. Just one. The sun." She glared directly at Fingal as if she could radiate a solar flare at him.

"Ah, she remembers," he said to Fiona sat next to him. "I told her I used a quantum entanglement component to direct the action of my dimension-folding to a place off-world. It was the sun."

She turned to him. "You idiot. Why not Neptune or an asteroid? You had to select something critical for our survival, didn't you?"

His cheeks burned as he bent closer to his iPad. "Yeah, well, it would've been hard to detect changes in a far-flung lump of rock. This news might actually help me invert that previous result. Kinda reverse engineer it."

"All right. If you need me to take a reverse spanner to my machine, be sure to let me know."

Still swiping and calling up apps he'd designed to crunch his equations, he walked to the exit. He needed some fresh air.

George held out his arm to stop him. "Orders, Mr Parr, sir. You are not to leave."

"Jeez, just round the block. I need fresh air to help think this through. How about you come with me, George?"

The big man muttered on his comms. "Just a minute then. Edwina will take over. Here, smear this factor fifty over your freckly face."

The double doors whooshed open letting in a wall of heat. Fingal gasped. "It's just like leaving the cool air con of Orlando airport!"

They couldn't walk on the melting tarmac paths so they trod on the withering brown grass. Ironically the aromas of lavender had become more heady. He couldn't see the sun through thick stratus clouds, and within a few minutes, his skin beaded with perspiration. Fingal couldn't see any birds, nor anyone else. No vehicles on the nearby M56. He heard a plane heading for the nearby Liverpool Speke Airport. "Let's go back in, the air's cooler in there."

TWO HOURS LATER Fingal called Naomi and Fiona. "Ready to try again. Any protocols to inform or prepare?"

Fiona replied with, "All set."

Naomi said, "I should tell NASA and our government, but nothing they do will make any difference. So, what the hell. Better be right, Ridd or we'll find a cave for you and block the entrance."

He jogged to engineering to be with Fiona. Together they stood behind toughened glass while his finger hovered over RUN. "Do you want a countdown, Fiona?"

"Just do it."

He did. Nothing happened. He turned to sit at her desk to call up a copy of his workspace on one of her consoles. As he squinted at the screen the building shook. His chair wheeled away from the desk as if he was on a rolling ship. He heard crashes, cries, swearing and an eerie, worrying creaking from the safety glass. He wrinkled his nose at a stench of burning plastic. Fiona grabbed him with a big hug but only to stop him rolling away. The shaking stopped. Sirens took up a wailing but were cut off before they reached full throttle.

Naomi rushed into engineering. "Has it worked?"

Fingal laughed. "As far as I can tell, the math worked but I can't see the sun. Have to ask astrophysics if they have a direct link to the solar watch telescopes. Sticking our heads outside won't help—it's only a ten percent reduction in sunlight so I don't suppose the clouds will suddenly thin, nor the grass grow green."

Two hours later they received confirmation that their own time-wandering sun was back.

Fingal heard over the speakers as he'd continued working on new algorithms in case he had to try again. A quiver of relief ran through him. Fiona hugged him.

He grinned. "Now then, Fiona, how about that date?"

"Well, I have a soft spot for nerdy Americans so—"

Naomi's voice crashed into the room just before she did. "Fingal! Whatever it was you did has affected our orbital geometry. We're on a collision course for Mars. Get back to work!"

ACCIDENT WAITING TO HAPPEN

THE BOOK, ANCIENT, heavily bound in red leather, teetered over the precipice of a high shelf.

Manuel willed that book to give in to gravity onto the head of Forcat, the fornicator, schemer and literary mendicant. Manuel uttered a supplication–not to Mother Mary, but to Mephistopheles. Not that he was a real Satanist, but he *was* an old-school Christian and so had to believe in the anti-Deity. He pondered on that teetering book. It must contain a thousand pages. Part of the Codex of the Inquisition, he hoped. He could have asked the comely librarian, Elodia Limon, but was afraid the señorita would have had the book made safe, removed.

It would have to happen soon. The book falling on his rival, and Manuel's courage to pluck up and allow him to ask the Sophia Loren of libraries to dinner. He'd said this to himself ten years ago, when this Biblioteca Nacional de España started digitising its volumes and renovating the reading rooms. This enclave was the last to go. Floor to ceiling pre-twentieth century volumes, from Art to Zoroaster, poetry to mathematical proofs.

He worked at becoming the world expert on bindweed, after he'd tripped on it in his childhood. Manuel supposed it wouldn't take long to learn all there was to know on the plant, but to his horror, then delight, discovered there were over two hundred species, and that was only in the nineteenth century *Volumes of Indigenous Flora of the Iberian Peninsular*. He looked down at his battered briefcase, pregnant with notes written at this mahogany desk.

His Visconti fountain pen, had crafted half a million royal-blue words on that weed with the melodic name of *Convolvulus*. Sunlight slanted in through a narrow window. It illuminated dancing motes–fragments of books and rare fonts.

An aroma of mustiness and polish was another reason he loved this place. And the traditional hush, with occasional footfalls, apologised coughs, rasps of pages turning and lately, the jingle of phones followed by the shh and stern glares of Señorita Limon. He melted just at the sound of her angry hush, her eviction of over-timed readers and her aroma—essence of inkpad. Over the years, Manuel had bought tickets for her favourite operas, but he'd yet to find sufficient courage to offer them to her.

Instead that lanky Forcat, aka Freddy Kreuger—complete with the fedora but maybe only one facial scar—stalked the woman but unlike Manuel, had spoken whole sentences to her. All unwanted, of course. Elodia brushed Forcat off, blanked him, turned on her sienna-brown sensible heels—quiet for library purposes.

Last Friday Manuel worked himself up to approach Elodia's desk: a massive poop deck of light oak with inlaid red leather. Her head was down over a ledger, her shiny black hair obscuring any view of her face.

He'd started with his rehearsed speech, "Señorita?"

The hair lifted and he saw she'd been texting, incongruous in this section of antiquity. To a lover?—surely not! He stumbled through throat clearing until, "I wondered if you knew where volume twelve of the *Volumes of Indigenous Flora of the Iberian Peninsular* is? I've read the prior and post volumes, but..." He fumbled in his jacket inside pocket for tickets to *La Boheme*.

His speech was interrupted by a crash, a book avalanche from Palaeontology D to G. Manuel's dismay plunged further when Forcat's apology smarmed its way over.

Later, Manuel stared at the overhanging book, willing it to creep another millimetre in readiness to plummet onto his rival. "Come on Beelzebub, have I not suffered enough? Haven't I supported your existence in post-evensong conversations at the Church de Asunción?"

As if in response, his vision blurred, his chair vibrated. The light yellowed more with dust and an alarm trilled. He looked up to where the book ought to be tumbling but he could see its stubborn aloofness.

The librarian shrieked, "Everyone out. We are in earthquake

evacuation!" And as an afterthought, "Leave all books behind."

One of many tremors, but Manuel swore the parquet floor tilted before returning to the horizontal. He made progress towards the marble-pillared exit. Then he returned for his briefcase. A shrill voice reached him.

"Señor Gomez, get out now, you imbecile!" At last, words of endearment from his beloved. Perhaps she'd come over and take him by the arm. No, so he shuffled away, slowly. Before he reached the exit, he heard the gravelly voice of Forcat.

"I am stuck, Señorita, I need your help."

Such a transparent ruse. Manuel headed back. He saw Elodia holding out an arm to his arch enemy. Manuel's face heated with anger. He glanced up through the swirling white dust. The book remained aloft. In frustration Manuel stamped his feet. The book teetered over the edge. Manuel's heart leapt, but the book slowed its downward flight, hovered. Impossible, and yet there it was, five kilos of words and leather floating like a giant maple leaf. Had his adjures to Satan worked and it was being guided to the head of Forcat? Manuel's smile grew in expectation. He should feel remorse, but didn't. How could an every-Sunday worshipper at the Iglesia Luterana invoke devil worship and bring forth the demise of a fellow human being? Because Forcat was no human, he *was* Freddy Kreuger, even if no one else could see that. Manual was exacting a favour to humanity, women in particular with this execution. Pest control.

No! The book wavered. Having re-aligned, it headed for Manuel. The whole plot must have offended God, or another deity, able to steer levitating tomes. The air soughed out of Manuel's tyres. His shoulders sagged. Should he run? He was no athlete. He was skilled in closing his eyes and awaiting fate.

A moment later, a puff of air against his eyes, then a thump on a nearby desk. He dragged open his eyes, now wet with the tears of impending doom. The desk rattled from the impact, but he read the gilt lettering on the red cover. Not the *Memorandum Mephistopheles Codex*, but the missing *Indigenous Flora of the Iberian Peninsular: Vol. 12*. Before his eyes the stiff pages, gold edged, creaked open one at a time and then stayed on Convolvulaceae; vulgaris–the common bindweed. Manual's personal plant, his raison d'être. He smiled, but became concerned at the magical way it found him. Before he could ponder on the latter, the book was wrenched up by the surprisingly beefy arms of Elodia.

She glared her lovely deep brown eyes. "You must have done this."

"W-what?"

"I've watched you, Gomez, your evil glares at me, and looking up at this book. I've intended to wheel the ladder around shortly, but no, you brought it down by violence, shaking that stack. Look what you did!" She waved her arms around at the debris of books and papers. Manuel looked too, but through the tears of injustice. How could she have misinterpreted his intentions all these years?

"I did no such—"

"You are banned from the library. Leave."

He stood in catatonic mode, staring after her as she strode to her mission control desk. To his horror, the despicable Forcat put a fawning hand on Elodie's shoulder, and leered at Manuel.

Outside, and believing there must really have been an earthquake, he expected to find fallen roof tiles, screaming women, but people massed at pedestrian traffic lights as normal. He saw another reader, a woman who always wore an orange Arab scarf, looking equally perplexed, settling into a white wrought iron chair at the Café Picasso. They exchanged semaphored hands apart signalling 'what happened in there?' He'd seen her in the library for decades. Didn't know her name, but perhaps with that smile she could be a backup plan.

Ruminating, Manuel strolled along the pavement. He'd cross the park and settle his tormented soul with tapas and a beer. How could that book fly to him? More importantly how could Elodia reject his honourable intentions in favour of that... that caricature? Freddy was only in there to torment Manuel while feigning to study... what? With a shock, Manuel realised he'd no idea what books Forcat was studying all those years. He laughed at the notion Forcat wasn't real, but an imaginary unfriend. That must be it. Whether it was true or not the idea appealed and Manuel's steps became lighter and faster as he spied the snack bar in the small park. He laughed and started running.

Out of his right vision two things tightened his stomach.

Forcat, who was in the library behind him a moment ago, stood in front pulling a long knife out of his black coat. Simultaneously, the park's tourist train ride bore down on Manuel, who still running couldn't stop before collision. Be run over then stabbed. Blackness closed in. His system shut down and he stumbled. His head hit the ground.

Light filtered back in as friendly hands and words helped him to a sitting position. Beyond the 'how are yous?' he heard crying, barely stifled screams. His vision cleared sufficiently for him to see the easy-access carriages in front, stationary. Everyone was looking down on the other side from Manuel. He guessed Freddy wasn't imaginary after all. He listened. "...just slipped... head hit the rail... exploded like a melon... feet entangled in that weed stuff."

What, bindweed? Then he wondered why *he'd* tripped, and there the tendrils curled around his ankle. His childhood botanical misadventure revisiting his adulthood. Just one of his legs was immobilised enough to prevent his headlong lope into the train. There were several of the snake-like rhizomes and some ventured across the track. Had they stopped him but snared his adversary and pulled him, screaming? Manuel smiled. On rising, he noticed the new building behind the snack bar. *Biblioteca Digital de la Comunidad.* Perfect. Perhaps he'd find Señorita orange scarf, start a book group with her. This time he'd invoke Aphrodite. Didn't she have a flower related to the three sixes?

BATTLE OF TRAFALGAR

SERENA WAS A GOOD SLEEPER; an expert in unconsciousness for all of her twenty-five years. That, in spite of killing pervert Doctor Wareing last week.

She was thinking about it behind her yet-to-open green eyes, when she shivered and reached to pull up the quilt. She often slept with just a sheet in August but damn, she was cold. She'd have to get up and close the window.

A fraction before her eyes opened, she knew she wasn't in her bedroom. It'd happened before, more than once. She squeezed her eyes tight and tested her other senses.

Her bed was gritty and hard. Her nose twitched to the sour odour of bird droppings. She heard an inquiring seagull. On her back, knees steepled and wearing satin pyjamas, she rubbed against solid walls, so she knew there was no immediate danger.

She thought of some of her odd awakenings in the past. Once on holiday in Snowdonia, she'd somnabled—so to speak—to the top of Eve, next to Adam, on the summit of Tryfan. On that occasion when she woke, she had rolled and fell a few feet to a ledge. Cracked a rib. Stitches in her head meant that her ruby red hair had to be shorn. Another, even stranger awakening had been on the roof of Harrods; strange because she abhorred shopping. Perhaps she was dreaming of planting an anti-retail banner.

So, where was she now? Serena shivered again, so she opened her eyes. She saw a blue sky with white wisps of mare's-tail clouds directly above. A circling Herring Gull pointed its yellow beak at her.

She needed to figure out where she was. She straightened her legs. Umm, her feet dangled in mid-air with no sign of rooftops around her cold toes. She examined the rocks around her. It was almost like she was the filling in an upright pita bread sandwich.

Perhaps she'd sleepwalked up to the roof of a kebab emporium on Oxford Street. Serena rolled onto her stomach to grab a different view. Whoa... her empty stomach tightened as she saw London's skyline off to the northwest.

A grey mist tinged with amber obscured the far horizon. In the foreground, she could see office blocks and a few taller cranes. She dared herself to inch forward for a better look. Hyde Park greened its way into view. She saw her own apartment block on Bayswater Road. It would have a soft bed, a kitchen to breakfast in, and now, an open front door to allow in opportunist looters.

Now she knew where she was. On top of Nelson's Column.

Serena's head swam when she looked down at the scaled-down people feeding or chasing pigeons, visitors grouped for photographs, while others queued for snacks. In the past, while rock climbing, she had no problem looking down from a precipice. Now, with a dizzying sensation, she had the urge to do a forward roll over the edge of the hat.

She closed her eyes and counted to ten. Opening them again, she focussed on just the statue. Nelson's shoulder was immediately below, a drop of just about her height. She withdrew to the relative safety of Nelson's hat while her queasy stomach settled. She used to inwardly laugh at hikers with vertigo, never again.

She could shout but she doubted her voice would reach through the traffic noise below. She needed her wake-up pee but maybe she should wait.

What she really needed was a mobile phone. Any more of these vertiginous sleep-walking episodes and she'd have to wear one around her neck at bedtime. On the other hand, what would an emergency call produce? She was sure the tallest fireman's ladder wouldn't reach her. She was higher now than Big Ben. On a Trivial Pursuit game, she recalled Nelson's Column being fourteen double-decker buses tall.

A mountaineer's rope would be handy but even if she stripped off her pyjamas and twisted them into a knotted rope, it would probably not be long enough to go around the column to aid her descent in tree-climbing fashion. All she had was her lithe body, and a bit of practice on a few mountains and sessions with that drop-dead gorgeous instructor, Steve, at the Bermondsey Sports climbing wall. She should have focussed more on the wall.

That shrink Doctor Wareing had pretty much asked to die. Fight your demons, he said, don't bury them.

No doubt once she climbed down Nelson's torso and her cerise pyjamas were spotted from the ground, the fire-brigade would be along with people-catching blankets and their tallest cherry-picker. Then what? Under arrest for illegally climbing a public monument? That's a point. She must have climbed this pinnacle—trying to avoid the word phallic thanks to Doctor quack Wareing. He blamed her sleepwalking up pinnacles on penis envy. Well, she showed him.

Shivering didn't make her warmer. She peeked to the east at the sun fighting through the mist like a watery fried egg. Umm, breakfast. An empty popcorn packet flew overhead, red and blue overlapping circles on its side as it twisted. Surprising to find debris so high up, but then not as shocking to discover herself at such a dizzy elevation. No point waiting for her muscles to warm up like a butterfly at dawn. Patience was not her strong point, breaking necks was...other people's.

Nelson faced south, so at least his left side would receive what sunshine broke through. Face down on the sandstone and guano, at which her nose pinched again, she inched her feet over the edge. Her pyjamas were dirtied as her stomach rubbed over the edge and now her palms sweated. She needed climbing chalk.

Held up by her elbows, she rubbed her hands on the gritty rock hoping to roughen her skin. What a time to exfoliate. Moments later, she pointed her toes down as much as a ballet dancer *en pointe*. She waved them around a little, then lowered herself from her elbows to her hands. Ah, her toes found the admiral's epaulet. A moment's hesitation...then release.

She fell onto Nelson's upturned collar, slipped and then grabbed one of the many finger holds. Her toes curled around his shoulders then she sat astride them hugging stone. What the hell was she thinking? A few climbs here and there didn't qualify for this suicidal mission.

Perhaps she should wave to any gawpers below, but she couldn't bring herself to look straight down to Trafalgar Square. Bad enough being able to see the tops of nearby high buildings. That head doctor showed her what gravity could do when he tumbled out of her fifth-floor window—except he had already been dead before he fell. He shouldn't have made an unscheduled house call.

Ah, she should have scrambled out on the right side of Nelson's bi-cornered hat, then she'd have had his sling to make descending to his trousers easier. Now she examined her options, she realized she'd inadvertently made the right choice. She straddled the top of his left arm and slowly slid down it to where his hand held his sword.

When she reached the sword, she saw the thick stone coil of rope around Nelson's rear. Out of reach now, but with her teeth clenched, she stepped down the steep angle of his bronze sword while slip-sliding down his left leg. It was a short drop to the statue's platform. Only then did she have to work out how to get over the edge and down a smooth pillar with no crampons, pitons, hexes, carabiners or nice long rope. The bad doctor had landed on a Dutch flower lorry. She was afraid he'd fall right through the roof, but he didn't, and his castrated body was probably now enjoying a long journey back to the Netherlands.

Her stomach on the granite platform above the pillar sloped downwards. She could see people quite clearly but no one pointed at her. A flapping sound startled her, but it was the seagull returning to the hat.

The pulse in her neck threatened to burst. In spite of the cool wind, perspiration gathered on her brow. She knew people had scaled Nelson's pillar in political protests, and they seemed to descend it still alive. She'd hate to be the first of Nelson's climbers to be mincemeat on her return journey. If only she knew the real reason why she did these unconscious excursions.

The platform had four corners. No good unless she wanted to test her overhang skills. Directly under Nelson's gaze, the platform curved inward, giving access to the supporting bronze structure. Like other Corinthian columns, large leaves writhed, offering generous hand and footholds. She rolled on to her stomach and allowed her toes to lead the way down.

Aargh, the metal was much colder than the stone. Don't be stupid. It had to be the same ambient temperature as the stone. Maybe around ten degrees less before the sun really got going, but the metal was sneakier at taking her body heat. No choice.

Her fluffy mauve slippers were back at her bedside. A moment's thought of how clean her bath now was. Even after the Doctor's heart stopped, there was so much blood when you use a sharp kitchen knife to hack off a member—now in a jar in the fridge, next to her gherkins.

Another minute or two and her toes found the top of the stone pillar. The granite was being sun-warmed now. She had no idea of the time. Her watch was in that same bathroom. She inched around to get the sun full on her back. She didn't want it in her eyes. There, now she glanced due South, the clock face of Big Ben less than a mile away, smiling at her. Ten past ten. She must have overslept. Serena laughed at that but stopped herself. Focus.

Her toes found purchase at a join. The whole column was like vertebrae. More tentative fly-crawling down proved the individual segments to be around five feet apart, just enough for her to ladder down to the base. A grey feather tickled her nose as a pigeon flew too close. Her fingers and toes curled with extra effort to combat an incipient sneeze but she fought it off. Where was that seagull to deter these damn pigeons? Her mad witch of a mother hated pigeons, but used their feet in her evil potions.

Close up, the column wasn't as smooth as she dreaded. Nearly two hundred years of wind, rain and frost along with bat guano projectiles had pitted the surface. Not enough to grip; she needed the segment gaps for those although some thoughtless builder had re-pointed what might have been more useful gaps. Another five feet. How many segments were there? Twenty, thirty? If that Doctor fuckwit Wareing had been right about an obsession with phallic symbols and conquering them in her sleep, what would her mother have said?

She glanced down. It looked no closer but at least there didn't seem to be a gathering mob. Flashing blues and reds continued their perpetual waltz around Trafalgar Square without stopping for her.

Her fingers became numb. Her toes cramped with the constant effort, forcing her to be an unnatural tree frog. She rested on a weeny-bit wider gap on the next segment down, although she still needed to hug the column as if it were a sacred tree. She tensed her fingers then lowered her left leg.

Squawk! Damned seagull. *Oh no... it's going for my fingers!*

Must think they're worms, or still protecting its domain. "Fuck off!" she screamed, and it did. For a while.

Expunge the phallus to be rid of the bane. The solution beamed into her head from her mage mother, deceased.

Another vertebra, another breather. A clump of moss bristled an inch from her nose, its roots nourished by a pigeon deposit bringing forth life. A couple of crimson mites climbed in and around the spikes of the moss; their own versions of Nelson's column. What thoughts travel in your minds, little spiders? Dew drops for breakfast. Her stomach growled but she didn't eat the meat and salad in front of her.

Lower again, and again, or it would be dark before she achieved her goals. Two of them, now: one to be safe on the ground, the other to solve her etiological quandary. A descent, and her mind resolved by the perfect murder and a ceremonial riddance. Her neighbour's dog loved gherkins.

Sirens became louder as they closed in a few more segments down. She didn't want to look. The frequency of pigeons was in proportion to the distance from the top, and more worrisome. Nevertheless, she concentrated and made better progress until cramp in the arch of her soles forced a stop. She couldn't jump. She knew the base of the column rested on a plinth itself too high for an easy descent. Another minute and with the warming sunshine, she'd go down again.

Cramps returned to her feet and now her whole body shook. She feared she might convulse with this reaction to her trauma and fall. It took another minute to calm down. Her stomach tightened with fear when the sun was blocked behind her. Too big for a pigeon. Something gently pressed into her back.

A male cockney voice right into her ear. "You'll be all right, love."

AND SHE WAS. Thank the gods for firemen, and a gullible health practitioner that enabled her to walk out of hospital the same day with a full stomach, an all clear on physical and even better, mental health. Even so, she'd shivered in the hospital foyer, wondering how to get to her flat. She'd borrowed hospital slippers and clothes, a tattered blue Adidas tracksuit over her pyjamas. No money for the bus. She could have jogged to her flat from Nelson's Column but the damned ambulance took her south across The Thames to Guy's. A bespectacled youth with a Sony camera approached her.

"Are you the column climber?"

About to deny it, she thought of her lack of funds. "Yes, you can have my story for a hundred quid."

Pitiful. Where were the crowds, the throng of paparazzi and offers of representation from PR moguls? But then she needed anonymity.

"I've got thirty." He gave it to her and took a few snaps even though she refused to reveal her pyjamas. He continued to aim while using the cam as an audio notebook. "Name, age and address please?"

"Carol, um, Vodacell," she lied. "Twenty three, Portabello Road. I dunno how. Just woke up there. I'm not feeling well. Bye."

The taxi used up most of her money, which reminded her to phone work asap and give herself the day off. More lies but this time to the Science Museum personnel manager. Food poisoning and working behind the café counter doesn't blend well.

Back in her flat, she showered and after donning a long satin nightgown, lay in her soft bed. No danger of sleep-walking now. The room was dark from the still-closed blinds but streaks of sunlight scattered through dangling crystals onto her lilac walls. Fractals of rainbows danced to Ravel's Bolero while Serena breathed in Sandalwood from joss sticks.

She smiled at her survival. Yet it wasn't over.

Once Ravel completed his ballet, she retrieved the offensive jar with the Doc's remains from the fridge, added a couple of real gherkins and walked out onto her balcony. Sure enough, the Scottie was on the adjoining veranda half-asleep but his tail soon wagged in response to his nose twitching.

Five minutes later and her problem was solved. She leaned on the railing, bathed in the mid-afternoon sun and spotted the top of Nelson's Column.

"Up yours, Horatio, and Doctor RIP Wareing."

That night, she relaxed into the best sleep she'd ever had. No nightmares of climbing cold mountains or buildings. She'd cancelled her membership to the mountaineering club. It was a shame in a way, but it helped with closure. Perhaps she should feel a pang of guilt over the psychiatrist but she'd saved hundreds of others from being made worse. After all, it was his misinterpretations that led to his own death. It was his fault, not hers.

A lump at her back woke her. She was cold and damp. Oh no! Not again. She had gotten rid of the last of the Doctor. It should have worked!

She sprang her eyes open, expecting to see dawn but could only see a small circle of light directly above. She was at the bottom of a well. She wondered if the good Doctor would have told her that this meant she was closer to Hell.

TARGET PRACTICE

CHANG STARED AT the potato-shaped Defoe. It took a month of intensive training and two years flight to meet up with the asteroid. If they'd met it five years previously then flying a dense-ballasted vessel alongside would have provided enough gravitational force to deflect it from Earth, but there was not enough time. Instead, Chang and Wen had glued to it a Morph Energy field shifter—a kind of quasi mini black hole—powered by pocket fusion. Clean, limited, no fragmentation, and the asteroid had instantly deflected away from its path of turning the American Prairies into a crater.

The director had said, "Get this right and you will be heroes. Make a mistake and if instead of obliterating soy farms, you wipe out Shanghai, don't bother coming home."

Now, that mistake was happening. Chang's stomach churned in disbelief. Sweat dripped between his shoulder blades. The asteroid, having been turned, was redirecting itself back on course. Now it was unlikely to hit empty farmland, but somewhere else. He glanced at Wen playing invisible piano with her console. She looked over, caught him spying.

She didn't display annoyance. "Obviously, the ME has failed. I'll go see what the problem is."

Chang waved his own fingers at the screen. "Remotes don't show a failure. All green."

"How do you know your sensors aren't faulty?"

"Wen, you know they were checked n times."

"Perhaps the fault in the energy field is corrupting feedback. Disengage it. There's clearly a problem."

Chang knuckled his forehead as if that would alleviate a growing headache. "Human error, and you'll say it's mine."

"Nice of you to agree." She floated to the helmet locker.

Chang didn't see why Wen had to go EVA. He toyed with the

notion of sending out a drone to reset the Morph Energy device, but it might warp an energy field around Wen. She could have been squeezed into another dimension. He shouldn't, but couldn't help smiling.

They should inform Wutang mission control of the initial success, followed by the failure but it would take an hour for them to receive, two for a decision, then another for their reply. It would interfere with bedtime, and Wen might have fixed it by then. Even so, his ignoring of procedure niggled. What would Wen say?

We were chosen for this mission for our ability to make pragmatic, optimal decisions. Probably.

She returned.

Helmet stowed, Wen shook her black hair into submission. "Nothing serious. Some of the glue had broken away and blocked part of the ME array."

Chang frowned at her. "Really? I don't see how that—"

"That's your problem, Chang, no imagination."

"Let's reactivate it and see if the beast will stay away this time."

His fingers flitted over the activation sequence. Energy waves pulsed from the planted device pushing the rock off its collision course.

Wen grinned. "Let's celebrate. A cup of Choujiu?"

"All right, but pity it isn't rice wine."

"We aren't allowed alcohol. If you want hallucinogenic experiences, Chang, stick your head out the window."

"Put that Choujiu away, Wen,"

"Why should I?"

"Defoe is returning."

"No!"

"See for yourself. This time, Wen, we'll use the drone to remove that one, and use the back up."

Wen deflated like a punctured tyre. "There's no need to remove the first ME, just glue the back up next to it. A few centimetres won't make any difference; it should clear Earth."

Two hours later they both sat with faces longer than bee hoon noodles as Defoe moved away and then realigned itself to hit Earth.

Chang threw up his hands. "We'd better tell them. For one thing, they'd need to recalculate the target."

"By the time our message gets to Wutang, they'll have detected the changes. What are they going to tell us?"

"We're sacked?" Chang thought of the shame he'd brought to his family.

"Idiot. They'll tell us to go to plan B."

He lowered his brows at her, wondering why he had the hots for her when she continually rubbished him. Did he find her a challenge, or does she use abuse as a cover? That would be it.

"Wen, plan B is a good one. Annihilate it. We have the munitions."

"Trust you to chime in with the official line, but think of one rock becoming thousands."

Chang bristled with the barb. He liked to think he had a measure of independence. "All right, let's hear plan C, or shall we skip straight to a plan D?"

"Activate both Morph Energy shifters."

Chang waved his hands apart. "But what if we destroy ourselves using two MEs? Sacred Worm, the asteroid might continue while we are vaporised. Unbearable shame."

Wen shook her head at him. "Activate."

FOR A WHILE IT WORKED. Sadly, the asteroid enjoyed flouting the rules. It wasn't the sight of it moving back on its Earth-bound course at which Chang stared, but the red vector lines on the screen. A nagging feeling tugged, urging him to go EVA himself.

Wen objected. "There's no need."

Chang pointed at the wayward line. "There is need. Perhaps one of the MEs is malfunctioning and a simple manual toggle is all that's needed."

"No. The trick we've missed is in applied mechanics."

"What?" Chang knew that Wen had firsts in astrophysics and mechanics, but he smelt more than noodles in the air.

Wen smiled her perfect teeth but they failed to comfort him. "Activating the MEs had given the asteroid initial impetus but its inertia and our mass drew it back. Give the wave pulses time to exert themselves. You've not slept for thirty hours, take a zedtab."

"Nor have you. Ah, you can cope while I can't."

He stayed suited but for helmet, and after a swallow, reclined his seat. "Good night, Wen."

ON THE DOT OF FOUR HOURS Chang woke with one thought. "First Contact!"

Wen looked up from her console. "The miracle of sleep."

"But this is momentous. We're well into the twenty-second century and have probed into the Goldilocks zone of a million systems with nothing coming back."

Wen waved her hands. "So, here it is and they're trying to smash Earth."

"With just one pokey little asteroid?"

"Target practice."

Chang shook his head. "I can believe that our first encounter with aliens might be their eagerness to purge us before we contaminate the rest of the universe, but..."

"A big bomb could be in that tiny package, or a deadly sting."

"Consider this—it's travelling at thirty-three Mach but now we know it is programmed or directed, so—"

"It might slow enough to land gently in Tiananmen Square and say '*nín hǎo*'? In your dreams."

Chang wagged his finger and quoted, "Cowards have dreams, brave men have visions."

She pointed a finger back at him. "Are you brave? Sufficient to fly alongside this beast all the way? What if it doesn't slow down?"

Chang took a deep breath, reached for a raspberry chewbar—it tasted of boiled egg. "Tough call. I might be wrong. I want to go EVA and check it out myself this time."

"Go ahead, but you won't find a driver's seat and steering wheel. You haven't asked..."

More games. "Asked what? Oh, Wutang have discovered the ME failures from telemetry. What do they say?"

"Twenty hours. If we haven't turned it by then, Chang, try and destroy it."

He stood, grabbed his helmet, floated over to the airlock, chewed more, and wondered how, after all these years, they couldn't get the flavours right.

Outside he was surprised that Defoe was so far away. There it was, the first alien artefact, looking like a pink potato against black velvet and its tray of diamonds. He kept forgetting to breathe.

"Chang, you lost? I can't see you."

"Taking in the view. On my way now. One second burst, like you said."

"Make lateral adjustments. Don't take too long, we might have a problem here."

Hah, he'd bet there was no problem. She didn't like the idea of him finding something she missed.

Close up, the pink was inescapable, surreal. It was pockmarked and striated. He drifted–a weird sensation when he knew he matched the asteroid's 25,000 mph. Sensors said it was dense mineral chondrite. He looked around in case another asteroid lurked nearby, with perhaps an alien wave pulse machine. Nothing, unless it was made of dark matter, cloaked.

"Hey, Wen, scan the vicinity for anomalies. Not just visible. And we'll scan again when we re-activate the MEs."

"Come back, Chang. The console's malfunctioning, I can't be sure the MEs won't kick in by error and you shouldn't be nearby."

Bluff again.

He examined Defoe more carefully for an inspection panel, but considering the technological advances on Earth since 2100, suppose the aliens reached quantum engineering a million years ago? He was thinking a control panel might pop open at a particular radio frequency, but the aliens would be far beyond such primitive tech. The asteroid is probably sentient, rewriting *Robinson Crusoe*.

He drifted around to the Morph Energy field shapers. On Earth it was considered the cleverest invention since sliced rice cake, but to the aliens it would be as a flint scraper. He edged closer. Something was wrong.

"Chang, look over to your right."

His mind knew not to fall for it but his head rotated on auto. He saw nothing of immediate danger. One star must be a planet. Yes, it displayed bands of agate.

"Jupiter?" He turned back to the first ME. A frozen shard of glue had become lodged in a wave focus element.

"No, I needed you to see the speck of blue, ten degrees to the right of Jupiter. I did a vicinity scan. It might be a meteor, spaceship or…"

"It's not visible, Wen, even with stochastic function enabled." He ignored her reply and examined the backup ME. No green light. Dead. Perhaps the initial burst of energy shook a power unit out, but that would've been detected by Wen from the ship. It was obvious that this sentient potato had disabled Earth's best efforts at sophistication. Even so, perhaps he could reactivate the MEs.

Wen's voice became higher pitched and broke through his barrier. "Return now, Chang, life support going."

Could be she wasn't lying. He turned back. A couple of squirts set him on course for *The Long Road*, which–reflecting the weak sun and starlight–looked like a silver porcupine, frozen, lifeless. Not a single light could be seen. Good, otherwise it would mean an energy leak. While on his drift, he twisted round to look back at Defoe, to absorb something created who knows when, by who knows who, except they were alien. Yet, they were approaching Earth, to make friends, or to destroy?

Then the other, darker, option occurred to him. It had lurked in his psyche like a misfortune cookie waiting to be opened. Defoe wasn't an alien artefact at all. Somehow, the MEs were malfunctioning. Perhaps a manufacturing defect–no time for it to have been field tested. Or, by chance, the asteroid contained natural elements that disrupted human engineering.

"Wen, I know. Just wait till I reach you."

Lights blinded Chang when he came within thirty metres of the hatch. Ten minutes later he de-suited. When the inner hatch opened he was hit by a wall of heat.

Now he appreciated Wen's life support problem, and joked, "I should have left the outside door open to cool us down."

Wen had disrobed–down to her primrose yellow undergarments, already perspiration-damp.

He wiped his forehead with his hand and tried to dry it on his shorts. "What is it?"

"Forty Celsius. Do your thing with the Life Support System, and hurry before the computers overheat."

He leaned over his console, frowned, and simply adjusted the temperature back to twenty. "We need to talk."

She stepped back. "It's not what you think."

"Really?" How would she know he'd deduced the asteroid had disruptive properties?

She sank to her knees, head down. "They made me do it."

"Do what?"

"You know—out there." She looked up at him with wet brown eyes.

"What on the Emperor's aunt are you talking about? That rock is natural and the MEs failed because... just a moment." His thoughts roller-coasted. Yes, the rock might have unfamiliar properties but though the MEs could be knocked out, the asteroid had redirected itself to head for Earth both times—three times including before they reached here. Someone had to do that, alien he'd supposed, then rejected, so it was *human*. The only other human within seven hundred million kilometres, besides him, was confessing something, she'd assumed he knew, and he should've done.

"*You* tampered with the MEs, and redirected Defoe back to Earth. How did you do that? Use a tractor beam? It doesn't matter—but WHY?" His stomach quivered, like when Mai-Li accused him of cheating on her. The tremor built up into an acid reflux and his face heated. "They'll know by now though, at Wutang. The vid and telemetry links."

Wen unfolded from the floor and stood next to her console. Her snarl and contorted smile reminded him of a Wicked Witch. "Wutang have no idea. The feeds have been down since we arrived."

He flurried sweaty fingers over his console bringing up comms. She was right. Many incoming but no feeds, no replies. Wutang would be able to detect their presence, and that Defoe remained more-or-less on course. It should be a simple matter to enable the comms link.

"Wen, I'm going to let them know we're safe but that the asteroid can be deflected, or destroyed by us."

"No!" She lunged at his hands.

He turned his back on her but didn't hit the comms key—he needed time to think. His voice shook.

"Don't be an idiot Wen. If they think we're disabled, they'll send up a rock buster."

"That's just it. DragonSlayers wasn't given the contract. There are none that could do the job. Ironic isn't it that twentieth century nuclear bombs would've been able to obliterate Defoe but the treaties have scrapped them all."

"So, this is about giving Earth a black eye so the Dragon-Slayers have a future? You work for them?"

"Defoe was only going to crater unpopulated farmland."

Chang boiled. "I'm telling them."

"They'll execute us."

He turned to reach comms. "I'll tell them there was a malfunction but we're fixing it. Forget DragonSlayers."

"No."

Chang fell forward as something kicked into the back of his knees. He turned to face her as he floundered.

"I think it might be possible, hare-brained Chang, for you to have an EVA accident."

His ears must be on slow-mo because he couldn't believe them.

Upright again, he stamped with legs bent and apart, as in his speciality–Hung Gar, and opened his hand, whose fingers flexed with twice the strength of any practised strangler. Wen burst into a laugh and produced a slim knife. Weapons weren't allowed on board, but no one could prevent unscrupulous ingenuity.

"You think this is a simple knife? Sorry to disappoint." She lunged at him, but he was ready and leapt to his right, hitting at her hand as he flew past.

Wen didn't drop the knife, twisted, and Chang's bare shins burnt. He looked aghast at a reddening weal, with a whiff of cooking meat sending him into shock. It wasn't a knife but a cauterizing tool. Unequal odds. This wasn't wushu.

She'd gained confidence and held the tool out in front while crouching towards him.

Chang let his eyes perform a war inventory. Almost nothing could be used. He leapt away and into the galley, fighting to keep control in micro gravity. Through the hatchway he punched a command for coffee, then dived for the cutlery drawer. This was no ordinary kitchen. The three polymer knives, spoons and chopsticks were instantly cleaned after each use. They would bend and snap under pressure. There were no pans as such. Not even a long-handled noodle strainer in space. Only one item had barely changed over centuries.

As a sharp point burned his neck, he grabbed the fire extinguisher off the wall. Bludgeon or spray. He chose the latter– Halon gas jetted at Wen.

She was surprised, coughed, but remained unharmed. Chang brought the extinguisher down hard on her wrist making her drop the blade. He tried to kick it away but he stubbed his naked toe on a floor strut. She bent down but he pushed her over and while bear-hugging her, kicked against the wall sending them both flying back into the cockpit. She was much stronger than he expected, and oiled with perspiration, they revolved while wrestling. Neither tried to land blows because they struggled to hold on to each other. Conversation came in out-of-breath grunts. Chang's head banged on the deck and the bolt-on furniture, as did hers. They sprang apart.

She hurled a plastic storage box at him. He ducked while wondering how she'd wrenched it off the wall. It crashed into his console. Not glass but it fractured and died. The cabin was being trashed. Much more and they'd have no controls to steer home. The fight tumbled into the galley again, and he grabbed the hot coffee and threw it at her. Missed. Coffee droplets continued their journey into the cockpit.

After a few minutes of hectic thrashing, hugging face to face on the floor, they slowed to a stop. Panting, with his chest heaving, fighting for breath, and adrenalin doing its best to enforce fight since flight was out of the question, he discovered something unexpected. There's a fine line between anger and lustful passion. Her smile agreed although he had to keep thinking it could be a ploy, but one he could enjoy.

She gasped–genuinely out of breath, "Why not? A kind of concupiscence truce for ten minutes?"

He admitted to himself that lust had taken over logic but they only lived this life once. Rotating and coupling about more than one axis, they grappled again, but with more relief than anger.

After a few moments, both of sated, he asked, "Can we extend the truce, only there's only a few seconds of it left?"

"Let's have tea for a change. There's Dragon Well in the galley.

I'll be back. Promise you won't do anything?" She flicked her eyes at her console.

In the tiny dorm, he pulled off his rags and ionic-scrubbed. He pulled on new underwear and found a tunic for Wen. All the time he kept his ears and eyes on alert in case the mad woman found her berserkness again.

He sat heavily, as much as one could, on a fixed stool. What a fool he'd been, at every juncture, including the last lustful one, although it had stopped her attack. For now. He needed to appease her. At least he'd secreted her weapon. Locker 15c–Velcro assortments.

She was still in the galley, her naked back to him, tea brewed, almond cookies cooling. The way she tilted her hips brought on another stirring, but he used brains to quell it.

He placed the tunic over her shoulders and took the plastic cup, and a cookie.

"Poison by cyanide?" he said, then smiled.

"I'm certain we can work something else out."

Chang wasn't sure he wanted something worked out. He wanted a resolution to this asteroid problem then get back to his life. Sadly, he knew that wasn't going to happen. Some events were life-changing and this was one.

He wished now that she'd do up her tunic. She glanced down following his gaze and grinned. "Why don't you come into this with me? You'd be rich."

"Just supposing I agreed, how would we explain–ah, I already have–the potato blighted our MEs. Our munitions would disintegrate it."

"It might not work, and make matters worse. Anyway, Chang, it wouldn't suit my employer for the asteroid *not* to hit."

"I suppose not."

Side by side they looked at Defoe on her screen. Wen broke the silence. "We could let them know we were still trying things and Defoe had jammed our radio until we found a way around it. We'd travel in parallel all the way to Earth."

"Yes," Chang said, "then as soon as it was close enough to please DragonSlayers, giving them certainty of future contracts, we get rid of it. Right?"

"Are you sure we can?"

"By using our fission munitions, feeble though they are, we can use both MEs, once repaired, to deflect the larger fragments."

She smiled at his compliance. "Or use the MEs to aim the asteroid at an unpopulated spot."

They were supposed to have an induced sleep for the two-year journey home, as they did en route–it saved resources and stopped them becoming psychotic but now they had to try and repair the sabotaged MEs.

After two months, he was confident one Morph Energy field shaper worked to forty percent optimal. Not enough to deflect Defoe as originally planned but it might push it away to be a near miss.

He tried a ruse. "Wen, how about us staggering our sleep."

HIS RUDE AWAKENING shocked him. Reluctant ears heard his name yelled as a repeated echo. Sandy eyes creaked open to see wide eyes accusing him of having a lie in.

"Get up, Chang. There's a month to impact. I've already given you a sunrise upper. You've to get the MEs to direct Defoe away from built up areas. I've plotted the most–"

"Any chance of breakfast first? And not that bamboo shoot slop you gave me last time. I'm not a panda."

His 'stimulated' body awoke quickly and without a hangover, but it didn't mean he was ready to speed-dial his brain to program the MEs.

Chang downloaded the data from Earth. By chance the asteroid's new landing spot was Antarctica. No large populations, no oceans to create tsunamis, just a stony desert and a tiny ice cap. Chang didn't need to do anything. If he tried to destroy or divert Defoe, it could result in catastrophe.

Chang couldn't help smiling. What a result.

He reached for his tea and slurped up through the straw. "Wen, this is excellent."

"Just breakfast green."

"Not the tea. The asteroid will be destroyed on entry and impact, so your sabotage handiwork won't be discovered. The world will think it's all down to our efforts. We'll be heroes, riches will be bestowed, not only do I not need to join your friends at DragonSlayers, but you can ignore them too."

"No, I can't. Nor can you."

Chang's eyebrows rocketed. "Come on, Wen. Ah, you have investments, but more... threats. Not to you–I can't see that working–but to your family?"

She pointed a finger. "Not a word."

"I don't need to be part of this charade. I'm free of it, now Defoe has a safe bull's-eye."

He stretched, yawned and went back to sleep.

"CHANG, WAKE UP YOU DOLT."

"I've had a nightmare."

"Something bad *has* happened. Here's some water."

Icy water splashed in his face and a beaker of it was thrust into his hand. "Yes, I'll get up, no more showers, please."

His eyes widened when he watched the data scroll on the console.

Wen interpreted. "It's accelerating and far in excess of what we should expect from Earth's gravitational force."

"About ten times faster. Already doing fifty Mach."

"I know, Chang, I've had to make *The Long Road* match its acceleration."

He used his handheld rather than lean across to use her console. "But we can't keep up with it for much longer, or– "

"I know. That's why I woke you. Wutang are going ballistic."

Chang scratched his head. The cabin vibrated. "Navigation will tell us when to adjust vectors for going into orbit."

"Already interrogated it. Just one hour ten from now."

"Good. We should make an effort to use the ME on the asteroid. I wonder about focussing in on itself might disintegrate Defoe from the inside. Also using our own ME to slow it."

Wen shook her head while fluttering her fingers on the console. "Not thought of the first but no time. Already tried the tractor beam idea but it made no difference except to slow ourselves. You can guess why Wutang are upset, can't you?"

Chang stopped scratching and walked–now they weren't in freefall–to get an espresso, double. "Two reasons. The hit will be at a different, and currently unpredictable place. Even worse, the impact of a much faster hit will be much worse because an insignificant fraction will be abraded by atmospheric friction."

"Upsetting fact number three is eluding you, Chang, isn't it?"

His eyebrows knitted. He looked at the enlarged image of Defoe. He sucked in the lightly metallic air sharply as he saw the blue and white Earth. The cabin shook again–deceleration–but the rock rushed on. Only one reason why it could accelerate like that, unnaturally.

Chang turned to Wen. "I assume this isn't another of your tricks?"

She shook her head in silence, for once.

He threw his arms wide. "Then the asteroid really is an alien artefact."

Wen gave him a small, embarrassed, smile. "Or, it *is* an alien."

ANOTHER HOUR AND WUTANG had a new best guess of the target.

Wen shouted at Chang, "It's the Gobi Desert."

"I bet your DragonSlayer pals are rubbing their hands–or are they *in* Gobi?"

"I'm just saying it could be much worse."

He grudgingly had to admit that was true, and yet. "It could also have been much better if you'd not sabo–"

"Not that again, Chang. Uh oh, here we go. Look at that firework! Like a silver Jian sword stabbing through the night sky, but no, the atmosphere has a cherry glow spreading from the wound. Just look at the speed of that circular wave in the upper air. Can you see anything of the hit on the ground?"

He couldn't. It was night and the air turbulence obscured everything. Wutang was transmitting. "...thought would be contained, but by a terrible coincidence Defoe struck where three tectonic plates meet. It hit at right angles and disappeared. Either vaporised or shot into the desert out of sight. Tremors in the local towns.

Ongoing strong quakes at the nearest big city, Urumqi. Reports coming in of quakes in Japan, New Guinea... just a minute... must confirm this... San Fransisco... Mexico City...

Istanbul... too many to... this is awful. So sorry. We... we are having an earthquake."

Chang looked at Wen, both in shock, as they orbited the Earth coming apart at the plate boundaries, lit by lava.

"No need for them to practise, Wen. First and last contact."

COLLOIDAL SUSPENSION

A KLAXON BATTERED STEINER'S EARS. Something must have gone wrong during their interstellar hibernation flight. So much for Interplanet Trade Corp. He caught a nose-wrinkling whiff of electrical burning but he remained strapped in his reclined padded seat. It wasn't that he couldn't undo his straps, but his muscles had atrophied in the weeks, maybe months of sleep. He forced his sticky eyes to open and glanced around the cabin. Greens and reds dot-dashed at him from a console an arm's length away. Strange; this cabin was too small for the Sojourn, yet he was attached by drips and feeds. He needed to be careful removing tubes before he could reach the console to silence that damned noise.

A full minute must have passed since regaining consciousness, and only then could his brain defog sufficiently to reach the panel and dance the keys. His co-pilot, Margot, remained prone on a bunk. A couple of cannula fed into her too. Damn, the alarm shrieked again, bringing his heartbeat thudding in his throat. He delayed waking her to glance at readings and the vid display. They'd landed but were sinking. Had to get out, quick.

Steiner hit the combination of buttons to lift the pod. Antigrav motors vibrated; good, that should keep them afloat until the power ran out. He didn't have time to find the timescale: he had Margot to wake up. It would be easier pushing her out while awake than dragging out an unconscious lump. He shouldn't refer to her like that: he still loved her and, he hoped, she him.

He switched a tube to her wake-up cocktail. Like him she wore a soft cloud-grey top and pants. Breasts that could poke out a man's eyes must have been exposed during the flight. Perhaps he should lower the top before she accused him. His eyes were barely ready for business but her blue-black eyes opened wide in an instant.

"What do you think you're doing?"

"Waking you up. We have a problem."

Margot looked down and adjusted her cami-top. "Stop ogling my tits, you perv. Have you been groping me?"

He couldn't deny admiring them, en passant, but there hadn't been time for a good time. "You must have exposed yourself in your sleep. And I took the opportunity—"

"I knew it."

"To visually check for bleeding, bruising and—"

She threw him a narrowed-eyes withering look. "You play with your own bits, Steiner. Oh, my head. Coffee, now, not that pro-vit garbage."

"No time to make anything. Here's a shot to get us both moving." He passed her a skin inject booster then applied another to his own upper arm.

She pulled a face as long as a giraffe—appropriate for her large freckles. "Is the environment safe out there?"

"Green light. Not checked details. We're sinking. Grab your emergency pack."

"You're an idiot, Steiner. Orbit and assess before landing. I knew it was a mistake to let them appoint you pilot."

"I've only just woke...never mind." No point launching into a debate on why they were not on the migration ship when the anti-grav motors were whining down to nothing. "I've a pack and the life-raft. Hang on to your kit. Popping the hatch now."

The whoosh of escaping air worried him. It meant the air pressure outside was less than inside, hopefully enough to allow their lungs to work. His previous glance at the row of green lights had told him the atmosphere contained the essentials. What the pretty lights couldn't tell him about was the nose-pinching stench. Overcooked cabbage, and it looked like it. Had they fallen into a giant's supper? He tried to ignore the odour, to focus on ejecting the fluorescent yellow inflatable dinghy. At least their escape pod wasn't crash diving.

As the life-raft blasted to its small full size, Steiner stood up on the pod, his pumps, ideal inside, suffered reduced friction on the slippery titanium alloy. He stretched up but could only see a pea-soup horizon with a steeper curvature than Earth. No sign of islands, or mountains.

A soft whine like a mongrel dog expressing interest came and went leaving him the unnerving impression they were being watched.

A female moan impinged on his thoughts. "Get down, you fool, you're making it sink faster."

If they'd landed on solid ground, even a small island, they'd have all the resources of the escape pod, limited though it was. Extra food, water, medical supplies, clothing. On water, the best they had was whatever was embedded in the barely-two-man life-raft, and now their emergency craft was sinking.

It made sense for him to lighten the weight of the pod by clambering onto the life-raft. She might throw a wobbler at his pre-emptive boarding, so... "Women and children first?"

"Don't be an asshole."

Perfect. He pulled the line so the yellow raft surged closer. It didn't bob in the soup as he'd expected. He stepped into it and immediately knelt for stability. Damn, it meant he no longer had a connection to the spacecraft. Why had she gone back in?

"Margot, come out now or you'll need your bathing suit."

Precious moments later her tousled red hair showed, followed by cobalt blue eyes so big he could see himself in them. Her thick lips twisted in distaste when she saw a metre of green goo between them. He gathered in the line and threw it at her. "Fine, but there's more stuff to get out."

Margot ducked back down but at least she'd kept hold of the line. He shouted down at her, "We don't need water."

She re-emerged behind a plastic box. Threw it but it missed Steiner's hands and dolloped in the ocean. It didn't splash, but glooped as if it were thick porridge. He pulled it on board. "We don't need a radio either. The basic survival stuff is built in—"

She'd gone back down. Ridiculous, his worry lines bunched. He urged her out. "Hey, the pea soup is up to the hatch. Get out now if you don't want to be an ingredient."

Her disembodied voice was mostly inaudible but he caught unwelcome snippets, "...shame I can't find...you buggered up...should still be on the Sojourn...you...king bast..."

"It wasn't my fault." He ground his teeth at the clichéd excuse always used by the guilty, spoiling it for the innocent, and yet he was.

Margot climbed into the dinghy just as the escape pod gulped its last breath and slid out of sight. Its position was marked by flotsam, of which the only item worthy of retrieval was a blue phial of penicillin. The rest, a mix of squares of paper; a puzzle since as far as Steiner knew, he'd not seen paper for over a year.

The warm wind whistled 'a hi there' and the ocean replied with 'a me too'.

"We have a problem, Steiner, the raft is sinking too."

"A puncture?"

They both rapped the polyastomer and it felt pumped up hard enough and yet it was lower in the green scum, even taking into account its burden. Steiner pressed the motor button and the raft lifted a little.

"Which way, Margot? You're the navigator."

She was rummaging in the plastic box she'd insisted on rescuing.

"Just keep us moving. In a moment the data from the escape pod's orbit and descent will tell us the direction for the nearest landfall."

Steering was accomplished by a touch-sensitive joystick at the rear of the dinghy. A full circle gave Steiner cause to ponder. The only sign of the escape pod's location was a single bubble-wrapped pouch. Even that appeared to be half under the spinach-hued ocean.

"Margot, sweetness." Such bravado. "Do you feel heavy? Just wondering if the data shows if g exceeds one on this planet in spite of the obvious greater curvature of the horizon."

"Busy."

It didn't feel much different to being on a one-g G planet but then he hadn't tried jumping or lifting a mass greater than the raft. He knew it was possible for the curvature to be different for this ocean than, say, on another part of the planet. He looked for a sun and found none. The cornflower-blue sky brightened near the horizon presently in front of him. Predawn or twilight? He headed in that direction.

Margot dabbed at a handheld. "Um, nothing definite. The data seems incomplete. Whatever created the emergency threw out the escape pod just after deciding this planet was survivable."

Steiner looked around. "Not my idea of a paradise destination. What happened to the other passengers?"

"As pilot and navigator, we were probably ejected last, maybe weeks after the initial problem. What did you do before hibernation?"

"My fault, eh? Which way now?"

She tilted up her hands. "It doesn't matter."

"What, no land, islands?" He always made light of awkward situations, but surviving on a water-world wouldn't be easy. Less so for a gloop-world.

She tapped the cream-coloured box lightly, then shook it. "Damn, it's failed completely." She held it over the side.

"Don't ditch it. Might need to cannibalize it. I'm headed for the sun for now."

Margot twisted and poked at a patch on the life-raft behind her. "Compass is one- sixty."

"Keeping steady? Could be meaningless if this planet is like Mars with no magnetic field."

"Don't you think I know that? Yes, for the moment."

Steiner craned his neck and glanced around. "No welcoming committee yet. No condensation trails in that perfect sky."

"Let's compose a poem to it."

"Look, none of this is my fault, Margot. We're here together. Get over it. Do you think I'd choose you to be stranded with?"

She didn't answer: fiddled instead with the compass, then the defunct computer and checked the emergency packs. "Flares, desalination kit, nutrition patches, first aid gun, sonic fish stunner, and hooks…"

"Get the desalination working. That water must be salty."

"Steiner, simple man, we don't even know it is water. We can smell it's as foul as burnt Sunday vegetables but it might not be potable even after filtering."

"We have only two litres of water so after a day, we'll have no choice."

She threw a weighted tube over the side as far down as it would go to minimize salt input and clamped the unit, with its petal solar cell, on its pocket holder. Margot threw him the fishing kit, even though he'd not asked for it. A welcome distraction from the increasing feeling of dread.

"Argh, a hook's in my finger. Look, red stuff."

"Don't expect me to kiss it better. Drip it over the side."

He watched his blood drop onto the ocean, his red stayed as a floating blob for a moment before suddenly being sucked down, as if a blood vacuum cleaner lurked below. The first-aid gun sealed the cut, so he needed another experiment.

"Margot, I need a pee. You must, too. No photos while I aim over the stern."

"Let me turn off the desalination input. I don't want my drink to be more toxic than it has to be."

Steiner frowned as, like his blood, his urine made a puddle that didn't merge in the gloop. It sank rather than be diluted.

The raft had drifted to a halt while he'd not kept the motor going and they were slowly sinking again. His stomach knotted. "I'd assumed we'd be within hours of land. How long will the propulsion unit last?"

"No idea. There should be paddles. Steiner?"

"Ah."

"What? Oh, I get it. You were in such a hurry to get out of the pod, you left the paddles behind."

"Don't you tire of always being right?"

They agreed to keep the motor on in bursts: just enough to prevent sinking.

An accelerating drowning of the bright patch in the sky was accompanied by a reddening of ambient light and a dip in Steiner's comfort zone. He rubbed his arms, wishing the grey uniform was long-sleeved. "Hey, Margot, are there moon-blankets in the emergency stows? I'm going into hypothermia."

She threw him a silvery microfilm blanket. "Now we've lost the sun, assuming that's what the poached egg in the sky was, we've no heading."

"Thought it was one-sixty."

She tapped the rubbery box. "It varied ten degrees or so. Either magnetic anomalies or the compass is faulty."

"We should have thrown in a spare compass, just in case."

"And how, simple Steiner, would we know which one was faulty?"

He grinned knowing how to wind her up. "Best of three?"

"Only you would think of packing three of everything. Ah, but you didn't until after the event. We've no idea how long the night is going to be. Possibly days, as you would say. It might freeze. Hey, keep that motor going. I'm sure we're lower in the gloop than before."

"The battery must be flattening. It'll get topped up by daylight, when and if it comes."

Steiner looked over the stern but the dark green obscured any chance of seeing the drive. "Maybe the jet is clogged—"

He was cut off by silence. The boat shuddered to a sudden stop as if it had been travelling in greengage jelly rather than water. He looked at Margot but in the gloom couldn't see her accusing expression. He scrambled once more in the sides of the raft, looking for overlooked panels that might have a folded paddle. Failing that, improvise with something appropriate, like Margot's hand.

She yelled at him, "We're going down. Do something!"

Through the gloom and by the new tilt of the raft to his right, he made out her paddling using her hand. "That's too slow even if we both did it...and we couldn't for long."

"Asshole, there's only one other option."

"No need to get nasty. There's several options, finding a substitute paddle being one. Your defunct computer..."

"No! It might still work."

He was about to add a witty reply when the bottom of the raft tugged downwards, as if a giant slug had attached its maw beneath the boat and was vacuuming. Margot was right, one of them had to get out, swim, and push. In spite of the chill of the evening, he perspired fear.

"Okay, I'll take the first stint over the side. I'll push for what, an hour? Then it's your turn, right?"

"Sure."

Umm, he wasn't convinced he'd be relieved but the ocean, or whatever it was, eased up to the top of the rounded bulwark of the raft. "Here goes, hoping the nights are short."

He dipped his hand in the ocean for the first time and was pleasantly surprised at its warmth. It might be poisonous, full of alien piranhas or as harmless as a village duck pond, but he slipped off the moon-blanket, and rolled over the side.

Marvellous, an enveloping warmth of a thick soup. Must be

about body temperature. Ha-ha. He could easily spend all night in this luxuriant bath. Even the pungent rotting cabbage smell was wearing off, . Overloaded olfactory senses. He swam lazy breaststrokes to the stern, placed his hands on the now slimy surface and kicked lazily. The life-raft crept forward.

Relaxed and comfortable, he heard Margot. "Faster, you idiot, I'm still sinking!"

He kicked harder until she stopped yelling. It was more difficult but sustainable. By experiment, he found he only needed to push with one arm, do a lazy kick with his feet and a half-breaststroke. Cycling a range of push and swim activities he was able to keep the raft from sinking.

After ten minutes, he needed a break. He wasn't sure of the accurate time lapse. Hour or five minutes; it was too dark to read his watch, unless he fiddled with it, and that meant slowing, sinking, more shouting.

Steiner had been immersed long enough to sample his swimming medium, enjoyed the alien aperitif and had formulated his review for the next customer.

"This pea-soup has a bitter foretaste." He could only manage gasps of sentences. "It tastes like a kale consommé. Smooth consistency. Ah, unidentifiable lumps. Maybe rotting astronauts. A smorgasbord. Stings my eyes..." He punctuated with a bout of coughing.

"Careful, Steiner. You'll joke yourself to death."

"Funny." He resumed coughing. "Let's swap."

"Keep pushing. I'll tell you when two hours is up."

"We agreed. An hour," he spluttered.

"You agreed, but it takes two to contract. Now, if you don't mind I need to think."

He wondered what she wanted to think about. It would annoy her to feel that her survival depended on someone else, especially him. She should spend dry time fiddling with what electronics they had to attract a rescue and to download data to find out what had happened on board the Sojourn. Okay, a homing beacon should have been alerting nearby spacecraft ever since the escape pod was launched.

Pushing wasn't difficult but his arm ached as did his neck, having to lift it out of the muck. "I'm getting RSI. Stand by."

He rolled onto his back and looked at the stars. The atmosphere twinkled them in patterns he didn't recognize, not that he expected to. His arms were too tired to push over his head so he used his hands to paddle himself a one-eighty to push with his feet. It worked fine. Great, he could watch for shooting stars or the telltale line of an orbiting spaceship. Two moons, one near the horizon sending reflected silver over Margot's head. She snored. He hoped she'd locked the rudder: he didn't want to waste his efforts. He was too low in the gloop for the horizon to be more than a few metres away but he could see for light years overhead.

The misshapen second moon fluoresced the colour of French fries, in fact it looked like a potato. Was everything on this planet food-related? His gastronomical gazing had to wait, when the warm but foul gunk crept across his face and it was enveloping his hips. Sweat broke out on his forehead as he realized he was slowly becoming lower in the ocean.

"Hey, Margot, wake up, I'm sinking!" No response, he'd better keep moving. Swimming must have kept his body mass afloat as well as the raft. They'd assumed, stupidly, that the density of the ocean was greater than water on Earth. After all, it had the appearance of something thicker. Maybe gravity was greater, or the viscosity of local goulash meant they'd need to be much lighter.

"Margot, we have a problem. Wake up!"

He heard a grunt, and after more shouting from him, more grunts. While he waited for her proper awakening, he wondered how by keeping moving he was floating. He'd always enjoyed swimming so his body must have been on auto with his limbs flip-flapping just the right movements. Damn, he swore he could hear more snoring, an encore. Steiner rarely betrayed anger, but he was working up to it. Not only with whatever the original emergency was in space, and with the user-unfriendly ocean, but now with Margot persisting in unconsciousness while he agitated. He could just see her hair. It might be red in daylight but now it looked black streaked with white. Still on his back he scooped a handful of the slop and lobbed it. He sank more, and had to swim harder to regain floating.

"What the frigging hell?"

"We have a problem, Margot. This stuff—"

"You can stay in the stuff for another hour. Goodnight."

He stopped pushing the raft with his feet but paddled to maintain buoyancy. "D'you want more?"

"Speak."

"This ocean is pulling me under as well as the raft."

"Take your shoes off."

"Margot, don't be absurd. We're both wearing ship pumps not hiking boots."

He could see her sit up and look over at him. Her voice became shrill. "The raft is sinking again. Do something."

He obliged by kicking the raft as he swam feet first again. "We need a better strategy. Start by jettisoning everything heavy."

"Steiner, I've already done that."

"I'm struggling here." He was too. Must be a combination of having to push continually and the nagging thought he wasn't going to pull through this crisis. His heart hammered.

She continued, "Heaviest is the water, and nutri-drinks. About 500 mills has come through the desal. Wanna try it?"

No, but he could demolish an energy drink and asked for one. She held it over, a tube to his mouth. Tasted orangey and such a sweet contrast to the green gore he subsisted in. His skin had stopped stinging. He'd become desensitized, numbed.

"Steiner, allow me another half hour's sleep. I'll replace you for a couple of hours. I'm a good swimmer."

He had a choice? Boosted by the glucose intake he rotated and this time used his head to butt rubber while he let his legs do most of the propulsion. It worked well, though it could be just the change of muscles. He had to be careful not to head butt the rudder, but it was just lower than his head needed to be.

Soft laughter now, not from Margot, and unless he was going mad, not him either. As if the joke was on him. It was probably the wind, and that thought triggered more.

Suppose the wind picked up and created large waves? The ocean was abnormally calm. Perhaps the liquid was so dense it took more turbulent airflow to create a wave. Long ocean waves were often caused by steady winds, friction-pulling on the surface. A smile came as he thought maybe they were in a large lake. The horizon was so damned close. They couldn't see beyond a kilometre or so. He'd have to work up a plan to use a microcam: throw it up in the air. Train a seagull, except he'd not seen any wildlife. Except Margot.

He squinted at some of the soup scooped up in his hand. The moonlight wasn't much but if there were bits of seaweed they were too small to see. Like in milk, which, was a kind of solid in colloidal suspension. They were in green milk.

He anxiously scanned the sky for a line. Potato moon swam in an iridescent halo. Purple, emerald, ruby—beautiful, like an aurora borealis. Earth's moon traditionally was made of cheese, this one had an aurora Dauphinoise. His stomach rumbled.

NORMALLY, STEINER GAVE UP swimming after a few lengths in a pool—low boredom threshold. Now, it didn't matter. His life was forfeit. He and Margot could only keep swim-pushing for so long. Their energy and vits wouldn't last beyond a few days, then they'd weaken until pushing wasn't an option even if swimming was. Of course he might've been floating in food all this time. Or poison. Suppose it was like the phytoplankton on Earth, Ceto, and Mazu III. He knew algae could be poisonous such as the neurotoxins in red tide algal blooms on Earth, but maybe this was Ceto, he knew it was smaller than Earth. Then he didn't want this planet to have a totally liquid surface. They needed to be dry eventually; humans rot in more ways than one.

Just as Steiner considered a wake-up call to Margot, she poked her head over the side at him. "Look behind you."

Hooray, a rescue ship; hopefully a cruise liner with all-in food, drink and women. He rotated again to push with his head. No ship. "Your horizon is farther away than mine."

"A peachy colour. Probably pre-dawn twilight."

He slumped, chin on his chest and stopped kicking, just flapped his hands enough to keep himself afloat. How could she dash his expectations like that? He'd better start up again before she yelled at him, but it took much more effort than he'd anticipated. He'd paddled himself to exhaustion. "Now you're awake, dearest Margot, and it's a new day..."

"Sure. It's my turn."

If that readiness wasn't surprising enough, Steiner was

astonished to see Margot had slipped off her silver blanket then fingering the hem of her cami-top and lifting it. Higher. He was treading water, or whatever it was, then put his hand on the cord circling the raft to get a better look. Silly, since he'd seen her half-naked before. But a sleeping dummy isn't as erotic as a vibrant upright and contradictory woman. Whoops, he was missing her speech, no doubt amusing herself with a tease.

"...time before this raft sinks? Not time enough, I guess. Pity, because I am feeling soooo horny."

She pulled her top off over her head, shook her breasts then folded her top and stowed it. Her voice dropped a pitch to velvet. "I want something dry to put on after my dip."

Steiner estimated the raft would be below the surface in five minutes with the weight of both of them, especially bouncing. It could be longer if he found some polystyrene, anything he could fix around the raft. Damn, it was difficult climbing in. The struggle would shorten the float time even more. "Margot?"

"Wow, apart from the stench, this is like a beauty spa's mud bath."

She'd slipped over while he'd climbed in. He'd been thwarted and not for the first time. Kind of endearing, and yet...

"Margot, did you learn at school about witch dunking trials?"

She saved her breath and merely splashed him. Their survival was more important than a fumble...but only just. Her teasing gave him hope.

He could hear the dollop of liquid as Margot found her own swim-push methodology. In fact she'd find it easier to float because of her curves compared to his: one biscuit away from anorexia. He should improvise his own water wings for next shift. With eyes eager to shut, and a brain urging shut down, Steiner forced himself to follow a few tasks he'd been thinking through while overboard.

The compass read one-seventy, a pleasant surprise. It meant they hadn't travelled in circles. They might have been heading away from land just over the eastern horizon but he immediately put that out of his mind. He risked standing and glanced at the horizon. On Earth that would mean five kilometres. Nothing but green. He sat again and rummaged in the stow pouches. The raft jerked with the pushes every five seconds or so. A slower pace than his. Better check over the side soon.

He found the microcam with its transmitter and button battery. He took off his watch to make accessing the vid link easier. There it was; an image of his puckered face, thin, worried. Being immersed in an asparagus swamp didn't make him a film star. Good luck, Margot. If he could launch the cam, say, a hundred metres up then he should be able to see up to...he did the mathematics on his watch...thirty five kilometres—though less on this smaller planet.

The bow storage had an emergency pouch. He took out an orange plastic flare pistol and smiled. Now for the dangerous bit. He took a cartridge, checked it was the kind with a tiny parachute and hunted for a spoon. He made do with a spatula from the first aid kit. The pyrotechnic compounds would fry the cam before good images were transmitted if he didn't remove them. Probably potassium perchlorate, various nitrates and magnesium, of which the latter could give him a nasty burn. He scooped the reagents out over the side. He used glue from the raft repair kit to fix the cam, switched it on and checked the image. After setting to record, he aimed directly up, hoping it would parachute back into his hands.

He looked away in case his tampering messed up the explosive detonator then squeezed the trigger. The detonation was louder than he expected but it was followed by a satisfying whoosh and a scream. He opened his eyes thinking he might have shot Margot, but saw the projectile shoot above him.

"What the friggin hell are you doing?"

"Just an experiment. Keep pushing." As he spoke he heard the planet sigh. At least that was what it sounded like: like the 'ah' from a grateful crowd at a firework display.

Perhaps Margot's ears were full of soup, but she must have noticed the flare. "That was a dud? Had you seen an aircraft?"

Her spluttering gave him a wry smile. Now she'd know the bitter taste, a long way from a beauty treatment. He put her out of his mind as he watched the image. It was too tiny to see properly but once finished, he'd be able to zoom in. The image jerked around so much it was all blurred. He looked up and couldn't see it. Then a white spot—the parachute. There must be some wind after all, for it was off to their right. He wouldn't be able to catch it. The raft bumped, settling lower.

He leaned over. "Margot, keep pushing." Wrong side. No, there was the small jet control and rudder. In the light of the pre-dawn gloom, he looked again but the green soup looked smooth and thick. No ripple or bubbles. "Margot!" He looked around all four sides. No sign. Sweating with panic, he slithered over the stern expecting to tumble onto her. Nothing! He was afraid to dive in case the force of the strange ocean didn't let him up. Nevertheless, he swam with feet and one arm doing a breaststroke while feeling down. Maybe she'd suffered a stroke or a fit a few metres back. Only last year she beat him in a breaststroke race by a length. He swam for a few seconds then probed down again. More sorties. He didn't want to lose her. He felt sick.

After a few minutes he remembered the raft. It would sink without him pushing. He looked and there it was, perhaps five centimetres sticking above the surface, less at the stern. It had turned, or he had, and he was at least fifteen metres distant. He over-armed as fast as the gloop would allow. He reached and pushed at the raft, kicking furiously though his feet made hardly a splash. The raft shoved forward and upwaard until he could relax. Margot had ripped out his heart when she ended their tryst but his feelings remained...a tear diluted the soup.

This time there was an 'argh'. The worldly angst of it filled his ears then emptied slowly. Hallucination from the atmosphere? Or from accidental swallowings?

Exhausted, he knew an empty raft would be more buoyant but he'd be dead before he saw twilight again. A plop over to his right made him realize his watch was left in the raft. He gave another big push then climbed in. He found the watch on the floor and snapped it on to examine later. He stood to spot any sign of Margot but all around was the damned pea soup. He desperately needed sleep but it couldn't happen yet. That thought took him to the first aid kit. He swallowed a Benzedrine followed by two sachets of nutrijuice.

Steiner wanted to make a paddle or sail but nothing larger than the flare pistol was hard plastic. Leaning over the side using the first aid gun's bag as a webbed hand would only make the raft go in circles. Waiting for the amphetamine to kick in he lay back for a moment, and immediately fell asleep.

He awoke saturated in sickly green sap oozing at his lips while the boat rocked. It was sinking unevenly, and so was he. Like waking up in a more comfortable bed, he wondered if he should bother rising.

No Margot. He couldn't believe that and listened for her bawling him out for not pushing fast enough. Nothing. No sign of rescue for him either, and the bennies and food wouldn't last more than a week. His need for constant movement bar fifteen-minute powerless naps cut survival to maybe two days. He gazed at the royal blue sky hoping to see a condensation trail then he remembered the flare and the data on his watch. No time now. He bailed out as best as he could, checked the compass was on one-sixty, and stumbled over the side. After a frantic push to ensure the raft's temporary survival, he rolled onto his back.

While kicking and using his head to push, he studied the movie. He couldn't see anything properly until the cam had descended slowly as if in a dance. He kept pausing and zooming until his already sore eyes had to shut a while. Not asleep, just resting. Eventually, he thought he detected a frame with a dark patch. Maybe a giant had left a lump of sourdough bread in his borscht. A few more seconds and he spotted the raft, so he had an estimate of direction. He clambered back on the raft, took the lock off the rudder and hand-paddled to get the bow heading two-ten. Maybe ten kilometres. A day's swim-pushing.

Once more he jumped over the side, but it was different. He negligently went vertically over. And his feet touched the bottom. He was waist deep.

His heart banged like it was in a race. Did that mean it was this shallow all over? Including where they'd been? Had Margot merely got the huff and waded off in the opposite direction?

A laugh echoed around him.

Steiner desperately put cupped hands to his mouth. "Margot... Margot?" If he wasn't so worried over her, he'd have laughed at the elementary absurdity of their assumption. Hey, the escape pod had sunk, and it was much more than a metre in all dimensions. Maybe the seabed was softer or deeper there.

He tried a low jump. Squidgy, possibly mud. He didn't feel up to stooping down to retrieve a sample. He reassessed his situation. It meant he could wade-tow rather than swim-push. He climbed into the raft and removed the digital compass and used its Velcro to hook over his wrist. He aimed at two-ten and pulled on the life-raft's line wrapped around his hand. It was easier, he supposed, than wading through treacle. More like a verdigris porridge. After half an hour, his legs ached but he pushed on. He wondered if the bed was the slope leading to the island ahead, which he couldn't yet see. The bennies began to wear off. While he trudged, he only thought of resting, and Margot. Could he build up enough of the seabed to rest the boat on and have a sleep? Too risky. Sun was stronger than yesterday. He could get sunburnt or heat exhaustion, especially as the sea was so warm. Must be in the tropics.

Margot. She was on the same astronaut induction course on the Sojourn, getting ready to explore and make money trading with exoplanet colonies. The fiery redhead had initially showed no interest in his bungled advances. He admired her fastidious approach to work, having to prove herself to fight off nepotism allegations with such famous military parentage. He, on the other hand, had no parents he knew of. After a while he realized he'd been sleepwalking.

He turned and found the raft sinking. He could now see over the side and the green stuff oozed through the sides in three places. Maybe through the bottom too but there was a permanent pool from the previous swamping.

"Hey, Margot, we must have damaged the boat with our love-making. Hah. Oh, we didn't, did we? Must have been all that clambering in and out, or..." He poked a finger in the rubbery sides. His finger went through! "Okay, Margot, the soup we've swam in is eating the boat."

He pulled at the life-raft to collect valuables: the flare pistol, first aid gun, the nutrients. He hadn't a rucksack so couldn't take the water. The raft must have reached a critical un-mass. He abandoned it, turned and headed for the island.

Now a rumbling as if he was in the stomach of a hungry giant.

He'd gone beyond panic. Either he survived, or he didn't. Even so, his stomach tightened at the thought of his skin being corroded. Not so bothered about his insides. It was unlikely the sea was more acid than the hydrochloric in his stomach. Could be other nasties, though he assumed his queasiness was from stress and grieving rather than poisoning.

Freed from having to tow the raft but encumbered by armfuls of supplies he staggered on. His eyes itched. His skin stung again, and looked more grey than pink, more green than grey. Surely he must be near the island. Juggling his load he poked a spare finger at his watch to get the cam image up.

Bugger! "Margot, I'm just as far away as before! Ah, no, this isn't live." You fool. He examined again the dark spot on the image and zoomed in—a bigger dark spot. He looked at the water level, down to his thighs. Spacesuit apparel was thinning and falling apart like the boat. He wondered if the entire ocean was made of disintegrated spaceships and their crew. His eyes focused on the horizon. No sign of land. The reflected light to the camera would be different from shallow water.

"Margot, there isn't an island, just thinner soup." Nevertheless, he strode on.

His innate optimism bore fruit as a dark green mound appeared in front. He splashed towards dry, or at least less-wet land.

The island was about a hundred metres in diameter. Gentle waves lapped, more plopped all around, sculpting low terraces. "Please, Margot, let it be high tide now." Reinforcing that hope was a patch of brighter green at the apex, about three metres above soup level. It might be the driest spot on the planet so he relaxed his arms, letting rations, water and the few bits of hardware tumble. He followed, and he was asleep in seconds.

He dreamt his island turned into the back of a whale, a hundred kilometres long. They'd been on its back all the time and it was about to submerge. They eat phytoplankton, so maybe the mouthfuls he'd swallowed would be safe after all. Water and food in one. He could live for years. A cetacean parasitic human louse. The post-amphetamine low sent him deeper into sleep.

MANY WAKE-UPS and monotonous days later, a non-watery sound stirred Steiner to consciousness. A whooshing noise accompanied a shadow flitting over his opening eyes. There, back towards his sunken escape pod flew a rescue ship. No Sojourn markings, more like a military scout—the Grebe, Margot's father's cruiser. What was that pilot doing? Perhaps he hadn't spotted the island for he was hovering several kilometres offshore. Ah, over the sunken homing beacon.

Steiner remembered to get the flare gun and load an unadulterated cartridge. The firework umbrella was spectacular. Mostly red, probably strontium nitrate. He was pleased to remember. The craft continued away and disappeared into a point. Perhaps another flare? He'd one more. His emotions roller-coastered from hope to dejection. Then the dot reappeared. Steiner fired the last flare. Too hasty, in the wrong direction. The ship overshot his island but dropped altitude. Damn he was going to settle on the ocean surface at least three kilometres away. It would float on real water...

If only Steiner had a working radio. He was watching a catastrophe. The ship sank remarkably quickly; its hatch must have been low. A small object was ejected, and expanded, yellow. Hopefully, its motor would reach the island and with a working radio, food that wasn't green. No, it'd stopped. He'd not seen the island? Steiner couldn't see properly at that distance but bet himself that the man, or woman, was standing, gazing three-sixty. Steiner had no flag now his clothes had disintegrated. The boat started up again in his direction. Then stopped. It was sinking, fast. It was as if the asparagus had learnt how to absorb manmade polymers quicker. Now it was gone but a tiny blob was there on the surface.

Steiner cupped his hands. "Stand up!"

His unaccustomed voice echoed as if the planet was helping him.

No reaction, so he took a bearing with his compass, and walked into the soup. Once he was up to his knees he couldn't see his rescuer but he plodded on, shouting encouraging come-ons. He was used, by now, to wading in the scum, it was his food, water and only companion. After all it was partly composed of Margot.

Eventually, he saw a silver-suited woman. She was stationary though twisting around holding something to her face—no doubt a pair of binoculars. He presumed she was standing and tried to see if she wore a rucksack, hopefully with a radio, or this performance was going to be repeated with the next rescue craft.

He called out, "Hey!"

His yell reverberated like a womb heartbeat.

She turned his way, still peering through the glass. Hooray. They closed in on each other. He was smiling, she continued to examine him. He saw a flash. A shove in his chest threw Steiner back into the gloop, arms flailing.

"What the fuck?" He struggled up on shaky legs. Did she object to his lack of clothes and thought he was going to molest her? It must have been his wild beard. Yet he was still identifiably human, surely? He glanced at his green chest. A neat finger-width hole, must have missed his heart, or he'd know by now. Ah, his heart became two trashcans having a fight. Blood oozed from the hole, emerald colour, matching his skin. Normal, wasn't it? Those little scales... His knees wavered and gave way.

"Margot, your wait is over, I'm coming in to join you."

CLOCKWORK

SONNET
'Tis not the stars that twirl
About our heads to dizzy our minds.
The firmament remains on guard—a diamond-belted Earl;
Laughing at us when we forget our winds
Of a capstan to turn the clockwork in a wooded shire.
Yet must be heaved each ten generations interval.
At World's End if time expires,
The planet grinds to a whimpering halt.
Seek the cord to set the world a spinning,
Engage with Nature and chorus its song.
Like a traitor the Earth must be put to rack—singing;
A few days past it will all be wrong.
Man is wound up inside his own head,
Heave each four centuries afore we're all dead.

LETTICE, IN HER FIRST JOB as assistant curator in Trinity, read the newly-discovered sonnet and sucked on her HB pencil. She flicked away her mouse-brown hair and wrinkled her nose at its lavender scent reminding her to find somewhere else to live. Cheap though her room was at her aunt's, it was turning her into an old lady.

"Move in with me," her fiancé had said and perhaps she should although the financial expediency was outweighed by his need for heirs while she still wanted a life without. No doubt Bryant was a catch, with connections and charisma but she shied from his progeny issues. She shook her head, sending aromatic hair fragments dancing into the sunlight slanting through the mullioned windows.

The sonnet possessed its own smell too, a hint of camphor,

possibly as a preservative. She lifted more brittle papers out of the cardboard box FB1617-4-4a, expecting to see crystals beneath. Nothing but desiccated insect fragments. Reading, classifying, recording and laminating the box contents would take a week. She could do it in a day but she loved luxuriating, soaking up the provenance.

The warning had its own smell but she couldn't decide if it was of red herring or... She replaced the papers in the box, except the sonnet, which she placed in a plastic zip bag ready to photograph. She noticed a green smudge on her white nitrile gloves. Sniffed. Thyme, she was sure of it being a connoisseur of endless bedsit fry-ups. It brought a smile, as she disposed of the gloves and pulled on a fresh pair before unravelling a brittle ribbon that might have been blue four centuries before. It was tied a around a moleskin notebook nine inches by five and on top was a card: 'deposit date 12th April in the year of our Lord 1617 Entrusted to the Trinity curator to be read in four-hundred years of the Gregorian calendar or equivalent.'

She'd laughed at the time of her assignment at the propensity for numerology in Bacon's era. No one had opened this box, Dr Alison Chandry had said, as she handed it over. "We knew of the note to open it before now, but those seventeenth-century literati and scientists were all drama queens."

She placed the card in a zip-bag then readied the document camera to record each page of the notebook as she read them. She sat on a padded lab stool, stretched out her arms and exercised her neck to begin reading. She noted that the document was unattributed but was in the same box as the sonnet, allegedly penned by Sir Francis Bacon. She turned the front cover and a spider crawled at her. She gasped and stood, her stool falling, clattering on the floor. With her hand to her mouth, although she never understood this instinctive gesture, she recalled stories of black widows biting the unwary. With relief she saw it was a desiccated sprig. Her heart calmed and she waved back a concerned archivist approaching from the nineteenth-century stack. Although she was certain it was vegetable, her nose approached it with caution. Ah, the thyme she detected earlier.

She turned her attention to the text. As was his habit it was narrated in Latin, except for dialogue. She translated as she recorded.

APRIL 4TH 1617, THE COUNTY OF SOMERSET, ENGLAND

The long grass and bronzed bracken tug at my boots as I chase Blizten. The white terrier is too small to see in the wild field but the scientist in me smiles in admiration of its path winding through the ripples. Ah, the meandering has ceased. I should attach a lead before I lose the dog. I'd miss it terribly in these trying times. I rummage in my satchel for string as I catch up.

"Blitzen, you mangy cur, leave that maggoty pheasant to rot." I pinch my nose at the earthy aroma, my eyes darting around seeking the nest. The magical April early-morning sunlight offers a contrasting delight to Nature's struggle on the ground. No doubt a fox had devoured the eggs then was disturbed when it attacked this bird.

"There," I say as I lean forward to tie a cord around the dog's collar then stroking its wiry, chalk-white hair while we engage watery eyes. "Sorry to do this old chap but I hear the mournful bleats of sheep and I'm not wanting Ned Hobb coming after us with a pitchfork, again."

I shiver in the misty, morning air. "This is it, Blitzen. There's nothing like Somerset in springtime. I wonder why Napier's daughter invited us to her home here, eh? Want us to check out his arithmetic? Hah, he's the number genius of the century while I be a mere wordsmith, a servant of Parliament and the King."

I fumble in my satchel for my ceramic bottle, uncork it with my teeth and take a swill of the weak cider with infused cloves. The dog implores with its doe-like eyes so I allow it a slurp. No sooner had I re-buckled the satchel when Blitzen pulls at the lead.

"Ah, yes, the country is splendid here and you want to explore yonder Ops Wood for its rabbits. Steady though, don't drag me through nettles."

Clearly, the hound holds no fear of the spiky thistles and stinging nettles that sends fierce tingles into my naked fingers. My cream linen trousers are tucked into scarred but dependable over-the-knee leather boots bought from the cobblers next to my Gray's Inn residence. I need to return on Tuesday in time for Parliament but in the meantime I smile at the chalky cumulus scudding across the blue sky. Anne Napier told me, with a wink, to look out for the end of the world. At my own gatherings it is I who create riddles, so it pleases me to be tested.

I drop my eyes while more tightly gripping the lead. Ops Wood is ahead, only two-hundred yards away. Impenetrable to anyone without the keenest cutlass, the copse of ancient oaks and beeches crowds the summit of a low hill. Dogs, though, would not hesitate an incursion. Against the undisciplined canine force I have to yank the lead but worry over its efficacy under such duress. I'm not suitably dressed for a run, especially in oversized boots more fitting a pirate like Walter Raleigh, than for Parliament's Attorney General.

I stumble along as if I'm a tumbrel being pulled through the field. Blitzen is on a nose-inspired mission and I, as his master, can do nothing but tag along. I gasp for breath and yell, "Enough, cur."

As luck or scent would have it, the onward rush halts. The pet noses around in the grass between two trees and cocks a leg at one. No sign of breathlessness unlike the nobleman whose breath soughs out as if I'm twenty years older than the fifty-six I've left behind.

"What have you there, Blitzen?

A short bark precedes a growl of contented worrying. He finds a scent if his nose uplifting is a truthful indication. The dog sets off to the right alongside the trees. This leads us to circumnavigate the copse in an anticlockwise direction. Thankfully, the absence of walls and hedgerows around the wood proffers me relief from the prospect of undignified scrambling. Clouds gather but I don't fear getting wet, nor being late for dinner even though we would be chided. In fact, my spirits rise into exuberance at this exercise as if returning to childhood antics. I turn my good ear to potential noises within the wood but instead hear sheep bleating without—a mile away. After an estimated hour of rambling, urging and contemplating both Nature and Parliamentary business to come, we reach a shoulder-high sandstone milestone. Blitzen noses in the undergrowth leaving me to interpret the artifice.

Moss hides much of its pinkness and ivy had crawled over indistinct lettering. I pull away the strands, revealing an inscription. "Would you believe this, Blitzen? We're at World's End."

A canine whimpering answers me. The dog has a cord between its teeth leading from within the wood. Growls of a mock fight escape the hound as it pulls and works at the cord. It's head going from side to side as if grappling a viper. I slacken the lead and remove my hat along with my black, day wig to facilitate bending down to inspect the rope. It was no thicker than my finger, black and properly braided. In moments the dog is drawn between the trees and into the maw of the copse.

"Curses, Blitzen. Let go the serpent and come back." The dog fails to answer, no doubt because its jaws are firmly clenched. It's quarry, new game, takes it into the unknown.

With my curled wig replaced I wait a while in case the animal returns without the need for forced entry into the wild wood. Has Blitzen been taken like a fish on a line? More like the monkey who wouldn't let go the banana in a glass jar.

I see that with luck I can squeeze in between the trunks of the nearest two trees. If only I'd brought an axe, but I don't want to spend another hour finding the nearest farm for one. I'm going to meet lacerating brambles, and possibly wild boar, but I bear a responsibility to rescue the hound. I gulp then edge in sideways but stop at a Scottish female voice behind.

"Sir, what ye are about to enter might be hazardous yet my father implores ye to do so."

Anne, daughter of John Napier. I've hardly seen her in person since arriving at her home a few days ago. A red neckerchief blends with her wild, crimson hair flying in the wind. Probably in her thirties judging by the few silver fronds in her hair and crows-feet laughing in her now-smiling face. A delightful visage marred only by eyebrows meeting in the middle. Her hazelnut-brown velvet dress matches eyes that flash, not to admonish but implore.

"My father needed to do this task himself but he is ill with the gout in all his joints."

Many of my friends are of this condition. I place my hand on her shoulder. "What is this mission although I see it might have something to do with this marker stone?"

She walks to it and caresses its rough surface with her elegant, long fingers. "Aye, this was visited four-hundred years ago this week... Sir, I see you smile at such unlikely accuracy but my father—"

"You are talking about the father of logarithms and a true exponent of the precision brought about by the use of the decimal point. So, I am not surprised at such accuracy, but why—"

She faces the trees. "Why this auld stone, this wood and why is it dangerous? Well, my father has studied the Sibylline Oracles."

"So has every well-educated person engaged in classical Greece. Ah, yes I read his pamphlet predicting the end of the world in 1688. I'd worry, but that is seventy-seven years away."

She turns to face me. "It's mair complicated. He discovered that the apocalypse could be avoided if the device is wound up every four-hundred years. It has been too, by other learned scientists, engineers, astrologers—"

"Why me?"

She looked down. "I argued just that, Sir. Ye have the gift and the ken to know the else of it, and there might be—"

"Danger?" I dimwittedly laugh. "Not in this lonely, beautiful place." I place my hands on the upright stone monolith. "You said earlier this is at least four centuries old. So if we..." He tried to turn it, but it stayed fast.

"Nae, Sir Francis, this stone marks only this wee entrance into the wood." She waves a thin arm at the gap between the trees. "The remarkable thing is—"

"The gap is older than the trees."

"Aye," she says, "perhaps there are forces here beyond our ken. Ye are going in though?"

I could just call again to Blitzen. The dog would exit eventually, surely? I've only met John Napier once and that was at Grays Inn when the mathematician talked of his decimal tables. I expressed an interest and mentioned his work in favourable terms to the Scots King James. Such a tenuous link hardly ties us to a dangerous venture and yet this situation is intriguing. I step over a low shrub, failing to avoid brushing my hand on a prickly thistle.

"How appropriate, Miss Napier, for me to be injured on the symbol of your mother country."

"A good omen, Sir Francis."

"Hrrmph. If you see or hear nothing of me when the church bells ring noon, send for Sir Henry at Frome. He'll gather his guardsmen and... I see you smiling. Fair enough, with God's grace and your charms willing, it won't come to that. Here I go."

The temperature drops within a few steps into the dark wood. Roots and rotting timber threaten to ensnare but there is a path, of sorts. At least the absence of trees directly in front means I don't need to take diversions although holly and other dark-tolerant undergrowth and the dense overhanging canopy reduce visibility to mere yards. My nose pinches at the sour aroma of rotting fungi. Spiders' webs and ivy tendrils aim themselves at my face. Maybe there's evil here. Certainly, my stomach tightens as a flurry of beech leaves fall just as I look up. My neck hairs prickle. Perhaps it would be wiser to retreat. I'd better call my hound.

"Blitzen, announce your position at once."

The sometimes loyal dog, barks as if desperate, from directly ahead. Emboldened, I battle onwards even though I'm assaulted as if by verdant, pirate grappling-hooks, testing my determination.

Blitzen's woof is less frantic, more welcoming as he sees me. I greet him in a small clearing, the mutt's tail a blur of delight. A shaft of sunlight illuminates the white terrier and the pale yellow grass in which it worries.

I brush leaves off sleeves and remove my wide-brimmed hat wishing Roberts the milliner would permit a tidier version. A sprig of wild thyme tumbles from my sleeve. I retrieve it, admire its fragrance and stick it in a pocket for luck.

I stroke the hound. "What have you there?"

Its teeth grips the same black cord. Not wishing another incident of the dog being yanked into the unknown, I grab hold of the plaited rope a few inches in front of Blitzen's nose and lift it. To my surprise it's more like a serpent than a forgotten piece of agricultural twine. It wriggles. The shock of it makes me let it go and I fall backwards into a blackthorn bush.

"For the Lord's sake, Blitzen, look what your playfulness has done. Me, the Attorney General and the King's ear, one of the Nation's most dignified citizens, ensnared and savaged by a bush."

The dog yaps and ignoring its hapless master, returns to worrying its prey.

Grumbling at my misfortune and cursing at the blood spots on my fine, third best, blue robes, I ease out of the thorns. I find a stick to poke at the rope. Interesting to see strands of silver and copper woven into its braiding. It can't be alive and I spurn numinous attributes. Ah, didn't my friend, William Gilbert demonstrate that silver conducts electricity? But surely not out here without his laboratory dynamo unless the Earth itself possesses such energy. More likely Blitzen had bitten into the rope and yanked it. My desire to help Napier and his daughter now waned and yet I shouldn't allow a few scratches deter me.

I grasp the rope. Is that the smell of blood? This time it lacks animation so I lift it to waist height, grass tugging at it but falling away. The trees are but three yards in front and the line parts the long grass to only halfway until I pull at it. Encouraged by my dog, I stride forward between trees, pulling the rope while astride it. The rope becomes thicker by unseen layers until it's as thick as my wrist. Now there's no gap big enough for my corpulence to squeeze through but I see an artificial structure among the tree trunks. Head height and cylindrical, as if a beech had been truncated and painted silver. A capstan with a few winds of the rope.

Blitzen emits a growl and looks back the way we came. I peer and see a shadow flit between oaks. "Is that you, Ned?"

The dog grumbles and whines as if composing a canine cantata, climaxing with a bark. The apparition thinks better of approaching and is gone.

"Well done, me lad. Never liked him, always a chill when he's close. Keep an eye and nose open for me."

I attend again to the rope trying to decide to pull. I exchange glances with my dog, whose eyes say, 'I dare you.'

"That's easy for you to say, Blitzen, you have all the exuberance of youth and frivolity without the burden of responsibility. Napier relayed to his daughter that I'm to do something in this wood to prevent the world from its demise. Is this it? To heave like a matelot on this rope? If so, my wagging guardian, it's just as well my stomach is the last known address of many a pie."

With a sense of doom, mixed with a tinge of excitement, I

gently tug on the rope. It lifts off the leafy floor but not by much and the capstan remains unmoving.

"A mightier effort is required, Blitzen, a pity we cannot employ the energy in your tail. Here we go."

Ensuring my London-cobbled heels are truly dug into the mud, I tense my grip so much, knuckles whiten. I lean back and although these biceps are used to nothing more trying than wielding a quill, I heave ho. To my delight the rope jerks up off the forest floor and tightens. This time the capstan groans as a devilish preface to a quarter-turn. I'm hauled forward against the nearest tree so I let go and tumble in ignominy to the ground.

I remain prone to gather my breath. "By the Lord, Blitzen, I'm sure the serpent became alive for a moment there, and the air is alive. Look at all the insects and motes buzzing and floating about our heads."

The dog whimpers and curls up.

"Blitzen, you're shaking, come here, boy, there's nothing to be frightened of. See those midges depart." They appear as a dark cloud, becoming fainter until evaporating to nothingness.

Leaves, brown from last autumn, agitate on the ground, like flotsam on a river. They transform from shrivelled paper to glossy green. My neck hairs rise in accord. Intermittent sunlight flickers and the ground agitates as if alive. The April grass shrinks as if Nature itself is in reverse. I admit to being bemused more than concerned, until Blitzen howls.

He'd uncurled, nose in the air with his eyes wide, rolling.

"Poor creature, you're terrified." I lift him, give the trembling creature a hug and only then notice his body shrinking, as if it too is becoming younger.

I laugh nervously at the thought that the turn of the capstan has somehow sent time running backwards, after all I'd not changed. Then would I notice a few seasons short? Leaves and dogs would.

"We'd better get back to Miss Napier. See if this wondrous effect is hallucination or real." I turn but cannot see the way we'd arrived. "Looks like I'll need a guide dog, my friend."

I scratch Blitzen under its chin to comfort the hound. It whimpers in gratitude and after licking his master's hand, scrabbles to get down. I keep hold of the lead, worrying enough about the tremulous goings on around, and the poor animal remains somewhat out of focus. "Come on, lad, find the way we came in."

Blitzen noses ahead and only then could I see the gap in the trees from which we'd entered. Close up, the trees and lichens agitate as if the Easter earthquake in 1580 has returned. My desk at Grays Inn had trembled and dust precipitated from the ceiling.

Man and dog emerge from the wood, and everywhere is a fog, green mist, swirling with shafts of crepuscular rays dancing from the sun. Magical motes in the air as would be expected from an earthquake.

Blitzen pulls at its lead into the long grass and yelps. Not its usual happy note but a querulous yap. There, near the marker stone, lay Anne trembling yet smiling when the dog licks at her face. Her lips make words but I have to kneel, awkward in creaking boots, to put my good ear close enough.

"Ye didna pull hard enoo... gae back... pull harder."

Her hair is darker, fewer greys than before. I examine her face. It shimmers as if tiny insects live in her skin. Like my dog, which is now lying down, quivering, shrinking. Is all of Nature transforming, their parts growing backwards?

"Anne, have I performed evil? And why am I exempt from this curse?"

"Ye are the instigator... a proxy for mae father... He's dying... today... Please go."

"Of course." John Napier dying today? How would anyone know that, this far from Edinburgh. Unless it was preordained. He was much interested in the cults, Nostradamus and the Sibylline Oracles. "Are you coming, Blitzen?"

No reaction, so I retrieve the cider once more and allow a few drops onto both sets of lips before draining a few more into my own.

The dog remains curled up as if asleep. All around me is out of focus, except myself. I leave Blitzen with Anne, similarly coiled with eyes shut, and turn to find again the rope but suppose I do naught? Time cannot be in reverse for the sun continues in its stubborn route towards a midday zenith. The few fair-weather clouds drift in no hurry from the west, languidly changing as they are inclined to, some shrink others billow.

I shoulder through the trees, my vision clouded by a green, swirling mist. Anne and Blitzen aren't going backwards either, just the composition of their bodies. Perhaps their atoms are becoming younger, but why is that a problem? I'd be delighted for my body of fifty-six years to replenish itself. Not that my lived-in wrinkles and distinguished beard and eyebrows aren't admirable, but the inner self would welcome rejuvenation. Ah, but how would those atoms going back in time, know when to stop? Would life's atoms return to their ancient origins, back to Adam and Eve's times? If they didn't stop there they'd reverse themselves into non-existence. The world would turn to dust. Except for me!

I nibble on a piece of hard cheese while looking back through the trees, indistinct with the quivering of their surfaces. I see a flash of Anne's red shawl. She and Blitzen are quietly supine, suffering as their atoms become—well, there exists a word for aging but not to my knowledge for the opposite. I place my hand, palm flat on the nearest tree. I jerk it away when ants crawl through my fingers... but none are there. Is this what my dog and Anne experience? Not just on their skin but inside? I'm eager to know if this is a local effect or if the entire world is so afflicted. However, the only certainty is the plight of Anne and Blitzen. What would Anne say if she could? I might ask, '*Miss Napier, are you more content with your body becoming younger, or not?*'

She might reply, '*Can ye not see, Sir, I am trembling both physically and in fear?*'

I might respond with, '*Wouldn't you think the agitation is a temporary effect?*'

'*Indeed I do, Sir, and I am in mortal fear of the end point. Go, Sir Francis, we implore!*'

I must rectify the clockwork capstan.

It's slower without Blitzen. The lovable cur is always in a hurry. Me too, but my navigation is uncertain in this vibrant, changing arboreal world. Any chance of seeing my footprints evaporates with each second. The air is so dense with emerald leaves, rainbow feathers and motes I have to hold my handkerchief to my mouth. Every aerial fragment knows not its destination, up, down in a vortex but mainly into my face.

Through the animated gloom, I see a shaft of sunlight. Finally,

I am in the small glade and although the grass here has its own dance, the rope is revealed with remarkable definition. Beyond it stand the trees through which leads to the capstan. While conscious of the need for expediency I take a moment to toe the silver-braided snake.

I stoop but the rope tingles in my hands. Does it anticipate my actions, an excitement to outweigh my fear? I must progress, grit my teeth, lift the beast to waist height then hand over hand keep it taught through to the trees and beyond. I see the capstan. It glistens, silvery and proud, waiting four centuries for some brave soul to act absurdly like a sailor weighing the world instead of an anchor.

I hesitate still because the situation is double-edged. Damned if I don't and likely damned if I do. The rope twitches as if urging me on but is it for the sake of Somerset, the planet, or for whatever bizarre entity is the capstan? I have no choice.

As before, I plant my heels in the soft earth, lift my eyes to the heavens and mutter a supplication.

"Please Lord, guide my hand." In a dark flash, I see Hobb again. He has the name of the Devil. He's trying to stop me.

I heave.

It sings.

A cloud of harmonics, like the combined voices of Kings and all the choral societies attempt the entire portfolio of Monteverdi's madrigals at once. It passes through me and past into the trees and beyond leaving me trembling. Fear, yes, and exhilaration manifests in pins and needles starting in my fingers, toes and spreading.

The capstan is spinning, the rope winding around it. Slowly at first, the rope sliding but it accelerates and in fear of my hands being set on fire I release it. I look for Hobb, but only see a blur heading for me. I step out of its way but fall, as is my wont of late.

By the time I elbow then knee myself upright, all is quiet. Once again the landscape has clarity, if only it could be matched by my brain. Hobb disintegrates into a heap of dust then blows away. Through a new gap in the trees I stagger to the capstan in time to witness the rope wound tight. I hold a hand over the cylinder but my fingers are repelled as a bolt at the wrong end of Gilbert's lodestones.

I hear yapping. Thank you Lord for sparing my hound.

Blitzen finds me before I reach him. Now in focus but I worry he'll want revenge on the capstan, cock a leg, with awful consequences. Instead, he runs two close orbits around me and heads back towards Anne. I'm eager to see if she's returned to now, or whether her body merely stopped retrograding to a younger age. This isn't possible to tell from conversation with a spritely terrier with such a limiting vocabulary. I reach the edge of the wood and to my astonishment find the meadow peppered with unseasonal scarlet poppies, buttercups and there, that same thyme I found in the wood, but now in a riot of purple blossom and with a heady aroma. I salivate with the associated culinary scents of sage, onion and roasts.

I find Anne, supine in the long grass. I fear my hesitancy has killed her but she is merely exhausted. Her smile is weak but genuine.

"Sir, ye were in time. I am still here yet changed. See my brow?" She unnecessarily points at her face and I see two separated red eyebrows.

"Why that is marvellous! And your grey hair—I beg your pardon, but your hair is now a vibrant auburn colour. Your body has become younger? Is that... good?"

"I wish I knew. Any mair of the turning back might've kuld me, Sir. Aur bodies are meant to mature, develop—ma faither says—who knows the damage the backing makes?"

It looks as if her skin and hair has reversed ten or more years. What if I stayed my hand another hour. Would she merely be a stain on the grass? And what of others? I look towards the town. Smoke languidly finds its height. Am I the oldest now?

"Tell me, Anne, what did your father intend *after* pulling on the rope? How did he plan to inform the future capstan operator in four centuries time?"

"He said ye'd ken what to do, being that your Cambridge will surely last that laing?"

I smile at Napier and his wily ways but then I see the field changing, aging. The colours are turning to mud, withering in front of me. My eyes whip back to Anne and she, too, is a wilting flower. I kneel besides her, but she is going. A flash of white beyond her is revealed as Blitzen, quivering, breathing his last. I should have pulled harder the first time and now possess an imperative to see this doesn't happen again.

LETTICE SHOOK HER HEAD in mock despair. This must have been a fine fantasy for Bacon to conjure to amuse at his soirees.

She checked a few data points:

Her mobile. April 3rd 2017

John Napier: yes, died April 4th 1617 and he'd fathered at least eleven children.

Ops Wood existed and was near a small town, Trudocsill. A coincidence that Ops was a fertility, renewal goddess?

Francis Bacon, if he was the author of the article, was a Member of Parliament for Taunton in 1617, often travelled to Parliament and stayed at Grays Inn. A contemporary of William Gilbert, the father of electricity and magnetism.

Now for the biggee. She searched for unexplained deaths in 1617. Had pulling the rope really killed? She exhaled a long breath after holding it in while she wik'd and googled and found nothing unusual planet-wide. Trodocsill wasn't so fortunate. It'd become a ghost village overnight. She scrabbled around to find the sparse online parish records for the village and found nothing after 1617. At least the deaths were confined to that small area. Perhaps the diffusion rate of the effect was too slow—half a mile a minute or less.

Everything else checked except the capstan. She'd have to go look in person. Ground truthing.

Goose pimples prickled her arms and up the back of her neck as Lettice played with the notion of seeing if there was such a thing in that wood. She'd try and take Bryant. His idea of a field trip was going to watch the 2,000 Guineas at Newmarket.

"No!"

"Come on, Bryant, we could both use some fresh air and you're due a day off from entering data all day."

He poked his vermicelli-laden fork in her direction, a red string of it fell to regroup on his plate. "I'm working my way up in the company. I daren't take time off. They might replace me."

She refilled his glass of Merlot. "I'll go on my own then. All alone, in a strange field, weird wood, the site of disaster exactly four-hundred-years ago and about to be re-enacted tomorrow. It's risky because I'm pretty, and you think vulnerable, but I'll be all right."

BRYANT GRUMBLED AGAIN when they had to park his precious Carrera in a lay-by off the A359. "It's too quiet, anyone could steal it without being seen."

Another grump when they had to force open a rusty mesh gate. "Look, it says Ministry of Defence Firing Range. Keep Out."

Lettice smiled as she squeezed through the gap knowing he'd follow. It looked more like a deserted Second World War airfield with cracked concrete allowing Nature to reinvade than an abandoned seventeenth-century village. However, there were lines of old brick that might have been walls and the remains of a well. She looked down to admire her new Timberland boots, blue jeans and North Face jacket then over to Bryant. She stifled a laugh at his black beanie and his shiny, brown brogues were now grey, his black leather jacket, muddy but at least his jeans met her approval.

He worried at a tear on his sleeve from the gate. "I thought ghost towns only existed in Westerns. What if the army start shelling?"

"They won't. You saw the gate, no one's been here for decades. They must know there's something unusual in Ops Wood."

Bryant took the lead and headed for the wooded knoll to the south. "Ops doesn't stand for the Goddess of Renewal, but for Military Operations. Keep a look out for incoming."

"You might be right, Bryant. It could all be a metaphor. The rope pulling, you know?"

"Exactly, everyone must try harder in life, but now we're here..."

Lettice stumbled over a crumbling lump of concrete, taking care not to impale herself on a rusty wire protruding from it like an aerial tuning her into the past.

"Careful, honey," Bryant said as he helped her regain her balance.

"Wow, a gentleman. Have the seventeenth century manners got to you? No, don't answer, I want to be positive."

She tried to picture the houses as they were, her mind building up from the foundations, then saw a darker shape near a chimney remains. Hobb?

"Do you think that devil, Hobb was really killed when Bacon was here?"

Bryant harrumphed. "You can't kill a bogeyman."

She held his hand as they waded through grass and brambles, around hazel and silver birch, towards the denser, taller trees at the top of the low hill. An old red brick wall met them at shoulder height. She looked back. No one.

The wall was inhabited by ivy and there were several places where fallen trees or living roots had part-demolished the structure allowing easy incursion.

"Bryant, I want to do what Bacon did, and walk around to find that marker."

He'd found an old sickle and led the way, trail-blazing through the thistles and arboreal obstacles like a jungle explorer. "Whoa, here it is, Lett. Now how does that affect our assumptions that this is complete tosh?"

Her stomach knotted as she picked at moss and pulled ground ivy off the sandstone plinth. Shoulder height and she could see it used to be a square cylinder about forty centimetres wide, but the corners had eroded so much it was nearly round. She could make out letters: W-RL-S END and what might have been an arrow pointing into the wood.

Although pleased that verification of Bacon's story was here her nerves bunched up so much she could taste bile. Her legs gave way and she leaned on the stone, hoping it wouldn't topple after so many centuries.

"Bryant, this could mean the whole story isn't a story but an instruction."

He waved his sickle at a nuisance bramble. "Surely you don't think you were fated to receive the unique bit of programming to save the world?"

"No. Yes, I don't know." A tear escaped, surprisingly warm on her cheek.

He put his arm around her shoulders and dried her face with

his sleeve. "If I had *his* manners, I'd have carried a hand-kerchief."

"Thanks. We'd better go in. Yes?"

Every step Lettice took threatened to twist her ankle and claw at her face but as they gained access, the darkness meant less undergrowth and easier going. Even so, she did trip over a tree root and found herself gazing up at a blue sky through the still leafless twigs of the tree canopy. Her nose twitched at the earthy, but not unpleasant aroma from fungi.

Scrabbling in among rotting wood and leaves her hand found a snake.

"Bryant, I found it! The rope."

He helped her up and frowned at the cord. "Better not lift it up in case there's a malfunction. I thought the old chap said the capstan wound it up?"

She toed it. "He did. Presumably, the rope worked its way out over the last four-hundred years. Hey, here's some more of that herb, thyme. I'll take some for dinner."

They followed the rope through the natural, wild wood, noting the absence of fauna, not even squirrels or birds. After ten minutes she saw a glint of silver through the trees. Keen to reach it she took more chances in her steps but couldn't run for the way underfoot was either soft with leaves and compost or snared with young trees and fallen branches.

She stood by Bryant and examined the intriguing artefact wondering if they had the courage to pull at the rope or possessed the right to do so.

"Lett, we could just walk away. What could possibly go wrong? All we know, if Bacon was right, is that it was disastrous to pull it a little."

She found herself nodding at that truth. She knelt by the silver-braided rope and hovered her hand over it. "A definite tingling and my hair is lifting, look."

He smiled at her light brown hair and just then noticed she'd a few purple highlights—they were rising higher than the others. He kept his black beanie firmly jammed on. "Just static."

She thought aloud. "He was sure, as was Napier—and he was clever enough to invent logarithms—that unless this rope was pulled the world would end, though exactly how they didn't or couldn't say.

"Bryant, suppose we don't pull it and there were more disasters, or the world's magnetic field fizzled out, or something? Although it hardly seems big enough..."

He peered at it. "Maybe there's gears inside, deep down. Turbo-assisted. It might have been storing energy for those four centuries, accumulated from the planet or atmosphere. We could make a fort—"

"No, don't you dare see this as a money-making opportunity. The military would get hold—hang on, they're already here. D'you think they know about this?"

He looked around and up in the trees. "If they did, do you think they'd have let us near it? I see no cams or wires. The only tracks are ours. I'll back off from trying to sell it, if only 'cos the M.O.D. might arrest and vanish us like that village."

Lettice examined his face and saw no crafty smile. Was that a possibility then? Of course it was. She returned her gaze to the rope. "We have to do it, don't we? Napier, then Bacon went to considerable trouble to make sure someone found his notes. How clever to realize the archive of his Cambridge alma mater would survive until today and that the fastidiousness of the system would ensure a custodian of the library would be here. What do you think?"

He scratched his hat. "I think that unless I tied you up, you're going to pull it, no matter what I say."

She laughed then hands on hips turned a steady look at him. "If it turns out all right, how do we make sure someone else does so in 2417? Perhaps there's an error margin. I know, I'll post a permanent note at Trinity to look in the Bacon archive for FB1617-4-4a2 /2017-4-8. I'll replace his thyme with this new one—it might be significant or lucky. Another note with my solicitor to be passed down to my descendents. Umm, Bryant, perhaps we should have kids."

SHE DIDN'T WAIT to see his reaction, and worked her hands under the silvered rope. Not easy as it was partly buried and grown over. "Help me lift it and when I count to three—"

They lifted the rope gently just off the ground and let it travel through their hands to twenty metres from the capstan, and faced it.

Lettice gulped, embarrassed at finding herself trembling with excitement. She hoped it wasn't important that they hadn't taken into account leap years since 1617. Committed, she couldn't stop when the shadow of Hobb fell across the rope.

"One...two...PULL!"

/\ /\ /\ _____

LOCKED OUT

ONE OF THE FEW TASKS a drone can't do and it turns out neither can I. Out of the airlock, I spin slowly to take in the magnificent view of the comet's tail, like champagne bursting out of its magnum although with a fluttering of incandescent colours difficult to define. Monet's palette with a splattering of effervescent turquoise and virgin's blush. That comet was identified as a simple asteroid 93 years ago in 2006 then it flared, altered course a smidgen and is expected to slam into Mercury at 1803 tomorrow.

The Mercury planet that is only a thousand kilometres away. I rotate more and there's the sun with its angular size four times larger than from Earth. I'm not melting, not in this suit. In any case it's the brightness that create the problems. My visor is lethargic at darkening, slower still at clearing when I turn again, which I do now.

A robot could have made this rendezvous but a private conglomeration needed to make their name. Send a human where none had been before. Mars is so yesterday, and if anything goes wrong it sometimes takes a non-machine's ingenuity to know which bit to hit with a hammer. In my case, any excuse to escape Suzi. I don't know how NASA's psyches missed her relentless questions. Our surveillance craft, *Snowy Owl*, bristles with instruments yet the most important, our communications with Earth is out.

Hand over hand I reach the high-gain antenna. It's not working, especially when we're dodging about and it's attempting to aim at Houston. Problem is that the low-gain is twitchy too. It's not as important to point that one in the right direction but something's not right. Could be there's more solar interference out here than was anticipated or the equipment isn't as hardened as it should've been.

I clip the safety line to an elongated hook-eye on our vehicle, which looks like a white thermos flask with antennae replacing the handle of the screwed-on cup. As a first, the outer skin is one of three adjustable overlapping shells. Layers of an onion to help keep us cool and shielded inside. Comfy yet she's in there and I'm out in the hard radiation, fiddling.

How many Earthbound would consider using a screwdriver and pliers while wearing their Aunty Joan's thickest gardening gloves? Each tool has its own tether to my belt. We don't want to do a Stefanyshyn-Piper and lose one in space like she did. Such fame and what a laugh we all get when we watch the clip in training.

The wrench won't turn. It needs to rotate the bolt anticlockwise otherwise the high-gain antennae housing will stay shut forever, malfunctioning. I'm in danger of puncturing my glove if I push too hard. Need more leverage so I fetch up my faithful rubber mallet and play tap along. "Why are you being so stubborn? Come along, bolt, be nice to Uncle Kiu."

Static fills my helmet then, "Kiu, who are you talking to, over?" Her intonation carries a southern drawl, unhurried, purring, annoying.

"Hello, Suzi, good to hear a calming voice. I've temporarily imbued a component of the antenna with emotion so it will respond to friendly persuasion."

"Idiot. It's stuck, then?"

I tap the Allen key end again but it's not moving. "I'm afraid so, please shut your ears when my urging gives way to cursing."

In a warm workshop back in Idaho I'd be able to squirt WD-40 onto a seized bolt, go make coffee, drink, wash up the cup and the lubricant would have done its job. Out here, liquid tends to become micro-droplets in the near vacuum and spread everywhere except where it's wanted. Even so there are other DIY tricks. I rotate my utility belt and reach for an exothermal pad. I pull apart a top layer and stick the base around the bolt. In moments it heats up by thirty degrees. The expansion followed quickly by contraction might loosen the stubborn metal lump.

"I'm still here, Suzi, though you can see that if you're watching. I'm trying a bit of thermal trickery. Don't worry I'll stow all used parts."

"What the hell? D'you know how thin this skin is?"

Umm, her language dialect module requires adjustment. She goes overboard sometimes, not literally from a spaceship although that's where I am. Ah, the trick works and I turn the Allen key.

She's talking at me again. "All that fuss just to remove one pokey panel. Now stow the tools before extracting and using the voltmeter on—"

"Hey, Suzi. I don't mind you monitoring and troubleshooting but I've got this. Sing me a song. You know I love your Dolly Parton impressions."

"Go boil your head, Kui, now look what you've done, haha, some expert engineer."

She's right, there's distortion in the panel as if the heat-pad melted the circuit board. "That's not down to me. Something else is going on here... overload or under-insulation. No matter, I can reconstruct this board with spares. I'm coming in." I'm certain the exothermal heat-pad isn't responsible for the damage. Sabotage? Did Suzi do this? Of course machines can malfunction.

I snapshot the board in situ and run a few voltage tests across the potential working parts and the motherboard beneath. The burn looks too deep for the heat-pad to be guilty, unless the sudden warming triggered a circuit to yell help. I can run more diagnostics from the maintenance console inside so I leave the board with its cover loose but tethered, and spider-walk back to the hatch.

Hatches can be operated with smart actuators but I like the simple approach. Lift the handle, twist and pull. A built-in resistance, then I'm inside the airlock. Usually. The handle wouldn't twist. It should turn anticlockwise to unlock but it's as stubborn as the bolt. Is seizing-up becoming infectious on this mission?

"Hey, Suzi, the hatch won't open manually, I'm going for electronic command and if that fails I'll ask you to kindly open the door."

I try audio commands. Nothing. I open an outer flap on my sleeve and jab at the keypad. "Suzi, nothing's working. Let me in please."

In the silence that follows, my face heats up. Maybe with the stress of the uncertain situation or my suit's homeostasis is malfunctioning.

I extract my divers' message whiteboard and scribble, 'Plse Opn Htch!' and wave it at two of the cams.

No reaction.

"Suzi, are you okay? I'm sorry for that quip yesterday about the pimple on your left cheek. It's hardly noticeable. Ah, I've made things worse. Let me in, Suzi. It's lonely out here. Nearest neighbour is over forty million miles away and I can't converse with them cos of the antenna... Suzi?"

Perhaps she's unconscious. Even with our quarter gee gravity we can bang into things. Not likely, and the radio feedback is normal. I can fetch up her vital signs with a few dabs on the keypad. Still alive and conscious. I know, sometimes the old-fashioned approach is best. I extract a wrench and...

...knock on the door. Three taps, pause tap, pause tap, pause tap then three more taps.

"Come on, Suzi, even if your radio and cams aren't working you must hear my S.O.S. Have a heart."

Nothing.

I could knock harder but it isn't a steel hatch. Polycarbonate and aluminium alloy dents easily. In fact when peering up close, the spaceship is now smaller by a couple of millimetres. She'll worry if I keep banging, so I do, and accompany it with fresh urging.

"Suzi, I have more tools. In fact there's a way in I've just thought of that is available to me and my tool belt if I—whoa, don't rock the boat!"

The spacecraft lurches away as she fires a burst of hydrazine at me.

"No, Suzi, you forget I'm tethered, you can't shake me off." She could if she throws me off with more than the 200 Newtons force warranty on this tether.

Why is she doing this? Perhaps she's been got at by HOM.

"Suzi, tell me, are you trying to steer *Snowy Owl* into the path of KY39? If so, it's unlikely to change its course enough to avoid Mercury. Look, we can see the comet is the size of a suburb, Beverly Park."

At last she speaks. "I've got to try."

"Let me in, Suzi, I'll help you."

"You don't believe in Hands Off Mercury. You can't, you're an android."

"What?" How am I going to break it to her that it is she who isn't human?

It will have to be later.

"Suzi, I am pretty neutral on HOM. I don't want to see Mercury exploited even though the south pole has ice and a huge deposit of tritium—"

"See. You're only here to investigate that and are using observing the collision of KY39 as a cover. Just a minute..."

The ship's engine burns again. Lucky I'm not round the back. I hold onto a lug as if I could grip sufficient to withstand the g-forces if the tether fails. My visor mists up, but I daren't release a hand to punch in the code to boost the demister. Marvellous things, engines in space. You only need small bursts to make big differences.

Finally, the ship stabilises. Peering along the overlapping hull segments that makes the ship look like the Sydney Opera House, I see KY39. A slowmo firework. Incandescent colours of greens, reds and emeralds, trailing like the most expensive Marie Antoinette jewel. The ship isn't heading straight for it, of course. No line-of-sight amateur navigation errors from Suzi. I have to stop her. Apart from anything else it would be a waste for no reason.

I inventorize. No need to physically check because I loaded the toolbelt myself. In addition there are nipples on the ship's skin I can access. I can grab power, gases, lines and a few liquids. They're zones of weakness in that if I apply enough resources I could cut into the ship. Make a hatch. Ah, she's talking.

"—ther thing. If you were human, you'd be out of air now."

I wondered when she'd try that one. "Suzi, you forget the implant allowing extended EVA. If I wasn't human why do I have this cumbersome Life Support System on my back?"

"Disguise."

I stifle a laugh while crawling hand-over-foot to a removable plate leading to an unpressurised storage locker. "Suzi, you've seen me starkers, doesn't that convince you?"

Laughter, the cheeky mare. "I've seen male sex dolls more real than you."

"But, Suzi, they're *not real!*" I meant to say they are unrealistically perfect but she'll not hear my correction through her hilarity. Meanwhile, I hook up a looping image of me to fool the outside cam and I'm now inside the locker.

I have to remove my LSS to turn around and reseal the plate before opening the access port to the pressurised corridor. A rush of air signals the okay for me to remove my helmet. Sticking my head through the thirty centimetres diameter allows my nose to tingle with the hint of lime, probably air freshener. I need to use my ultrasonic cutter to widen the gap. It's quiet but surely her sensors have noticed I'm not outside?

The cut is done and I'm through but I stop to listen. There, tick, tick or is it tap? A noise can't make itself. Something to check out later. Now the whine of a servomotor. It's coming from down the left but it must be round the corn—argh!

"Got you."

Classic distraction trick and I'm caught in a cargo net. "I can easily cut my way out of this, Suzi."

"Not this micro-fibre graphene, and where's your toolbox?"

Always relentless questions. Back in the locker. I should've nobbled the corridor cam as well as those outside.

Suzi saunters around to gloat in front of me. She holds a remote control. "I wouldn't struggle too much if I were you."

She's right. I do and the net tightens. "Stop it. I can feel it cutting my ears, my nose!"

"Of course it will. A regular cheese wire, isn't it? But you're an android so there won't be any blood not like—"

It's hard work keeping this still. "*If* I were an android—like you—they'd make my machine oil to look bloody to fool you, or me in your case."

Her black eyebrows dance and now the lime scent is stronger. If I'd been closer to her before my EVA, I'd have twigged it was Suzi and not some general air freshener when I cut through. I refocus onto her hands. Her thumb hovers on the remote ready to tighten it again.

"Suzi, if you cut me there will be droplets of blood in the air. You might not be able to catch and filter it. Are you sure you—"

Too late, minor planetary, scarlet globules drifts from my face. At least the rest of the spacesuit gives temporary respite although it won't last.

"Please stop. Consider, Suzi, that you are murdering your sole fellow passenger. You have no right and it fucking hurts."

It does too. The wire lacerations are slicing through nerves.

"Ya exaggerate as usual, Kui. It's a microfilament cargo net, and a test. It's not designed to damage inorganic surfaces such as storage containers—"

"Yet it's cutting through my face. What does that tell you?" I let the thought travel over for her to ruminate, but she bats back.

"That nothing's perfect. Maybe your synthetic skin is so close to my own epidermis, the wire cannot distinguish it. I'm hauling your robotic ass to the nearest ejection hatch. Your entity will survive, but you won't stop me intercepting the comet. We're already on course, Honey, you were too slow."

I dwell on that likely truism when the floor slants as the ship abruptly changes direction. The net supports my suited body while nothing holds up Suzi. Fortunately, for my good looks, she releases the remote, which, like her, flies to the inner baulkhead. She screams.

"Suzi! Are you hurt? I think I must have botched the exterior locker hatch, escaping air jetted out and—"

Gravity returned to normal. Zero.

"Stop wittering on. Look at my arm."

I do, and see a stain spreading on her beige tunic sleeve. A green stain.

Crying, she yanks at the cuff and I see a laceration oozing emerald liquid. My brain works overtime to compose conciliatory soothing but all that comes out is, "You know what this means?"

We float, looking forlorn at each other. She splutters objections, which I crassly counter. Such as:

"How can I be an android when my childhood is so vivid?"

"Implanted memory."

"But I'm married and have a daughter, Emily."

"Again, implanted... although."

She points a non-greened finger at me. "See? Although what?"

"Last Easter, a mission family gathering. Your Emily copped off with my son."

"They're six, and they played hide and seek, but it proves I'm human, just with something wrong with my blood."

There's another explanation, more likely, but I don't like it. Can android blood be any colour? Distraction is required.

I take her elbow to guide her down the corridor. "Let's go to the lab and sample your unusual blood. It could be a cyanosis, like a side effect from one of your medications."

"They're mostly the same as yours. Hey, just a minute. If that hatch has blown..."

We both look back at the enlarged hole I'd climbed through.

I finish her question. "Then what are we breathing?"

"And why are we not freezing to death?"

I freeze. And heat alternately as I struggle to accept my own androidness.

I blurt out denials. "I, we, can't not be human. I don't feel motors and gears inside me! Do you?"

She dabs at her leaking evidence. "No, but we must be the latest version of organic AI. Hence, muscles and tissue even if not made with human DNA."

I jab aimlessly in the air as if to blame the floating motes scattering in the beige lights. "But we eat, drink, defecate. Robots don't do that."

"Even androids need energy, lubricants. It's not difficult to engineer once they made the decision to go beyond servo-mechanisms."

"But why the deception?"

"Ah, my dear Kiu, were we not motivated to help our fellow humans in this mission?"

I frown and start unzipping my unnecessary spacesuit, although perhaps my organic body needs to be protected from radiation as much as a human's when outside. "This mission is hardly Earth critical. Yes, there's a fourteen percent chance of the comet missing Mercury and eventually colliding with Earth but we can't alter its course unless you and your Hands Off Mercury movement know differently?"

"That's another element. Is HOM real or a device to distract, an extra cog to make us think we're human?"

I want to point out that I objected to HOM but my zipper is

caught in my groin area and in spite of my recent demotion, or elevation in my existential status I don't want to ask Suzi to place her hand—the dry, pink one—down there. I contort only to roll, crash to the deck as a screeching devil noise hurts my ears. And that's another thing, but I'm sure Suzi will say we're not really using sound waves in this now obvious vacuum.

I blurt, "Is the ship in self-destruct? Has Mission Control been listening and—"

"For an android, you are disappointingly dense, Kiu. Your bungled hatch has taken us too close to the comet. See?"

I right myself using finger grips on the now buckled bulkhead, and peer at a screen. The rear end of a comet is nothing but tail, a magnificent sight of marigolds and diamonds. I lose grip and tumble as does our ship.

Suzi leads the way to the flight deck. It hardly matters now that air is still escaping, unless organic androids need some oxygen intake to function. I follow with most of my spacesuit trailing and catching on debris.

We stabilise our home in time to see KY39 meet its doom. I send vid and telemetry back to Houston. I remain obedient but with a snarl. I shut off the microphones hoping Earth won't hear us, assuming that Suzi and I communicate with Quantum entanglement trickery.

I point. "It hit near the south pole. Interesting."

She smiles for the first time I can remember though I can't trust memories any more. "Yes, there's ice there, or was. Let's take the escape pod."

"But we're supposed to fly this craft back to Earth." What am I saying? On the other hand I might resent now being a machine with false history but I wouldn't exist at all without humans.

"Kiu, they just didn't want our 'human' minds thinking we're expendable."

"Aren't all astronauts?"

"And they'll reprogram us. I don't want that, do you?"

I laugh. "True, I've grown fond of my past, erroneous though it is."

"I expect most humans have pasts equally faulty. How about that escape pod?"

We tap a few controls and head to a hatch outlined in red. I wriggle my fingers at the keypad, but nothing happens. Suzi shines a flashlight through the dark window.

"It's not there, Kiu."

I look for myself. "It must be here. We rehearsed using it nine times in training."

"Planted memories."

Damn.

How does this creature, Suzi, stay so calm? Her emote module must be more advanced than mine.

"All right," she says, "we'll take this craft to the surface. There's insufficient atmosphere for it to burn up and we've enough hydrazine fuel to act as retros. You do the nav."

"Yes, ma'am."

AS WE HEAD FOR OUR NEW HOME, I have more questions such as:

"We sleep, why?"

"Maybe it's part of the deception, or they're using that time to upload, download, reconfigure."

I raise a finger. "Or perhaps like humans we need downtime for our accumulated experiences to consolidate, do organic repair work and—"

"I do hope you can soon get past not being human, Kiu."

"What shall we call our new Mercurian colony?"

"Hg."

I brace for impact. "I like it. We'll call our kids Hggers. Shall we program them to prepare a revenge reception for when real humans arrive?"

"Always with the relentless questions."

THE JUDGEMENT ROCK

AUGUST 2506 AD

Jed threw out his arm to grab the sides of the hatch. The void terrified him now the sentence had been passed. He loved being out in space, all the more so on his own as the modern equivalent of a prospector, but being ejected from the *Midnight Collision* like this sent stomach acid refluxing up into his throat. It could've been worse. The last convicted felon was thrown out without a spacesuit.

His gloved fingers could feel the edge of the hatch, but servomechanisms within the suit forced him to relinquish his grasp. Screaming, he was ejected.

JED PONDERED ON THE hundred-percent certainty he would die, then reflected on the ninety-percent probability it would happen in the next six hours. The first figure helped him decide to take stupid risks, but the second obligated him to focus on the asteroid in front.

He risked twisting around to look at the huge blue ship that had spewed him out in this asteroid belt. The off-Earth court had found him guilty of stealing Asteroid 253b, but had given him the choice of thirty years hard labour on the Moon, or to go out in style. He chose the latter because he had a plan.

"Jed, it's advisable for you to cease gyrating. I have to re-coordinate the target continuously. You're making me nervous."

"Like I give a damn about your nerves. Hey, you don't have any, you're a spacesuit."

"I have sensors with an electronic brain. Therefore, I have nerves. It is imperative to reach the asteroid in one piece." The suit used a velvet masculine voice, but that had been Jed's choice. He could have chosen the alluring voice of his mistress, but he worried that it might upset him if he and the suit argued too much.

"My life's as good as over. Assuming we reach the asteroid before my oxygen runs out, what's the chances of finding my supply cache?"

"I have insufficient information to compute the details. Jed, this is the same asteroid they convicted you of planning to steal?"

"Yes. I intended to move it deeper into the Belt to work on it undetected." He kept back the juiciest detail.

"The Company have a tagging policy for their asteroids, they would have known as soon as you started..."

"They've only tagged half their rocks, and tags often malfunction. I was unlucky. Do you think the judgment was too harsh?"

"Jed, that asteroid is worth forty million credits."

"But it's not as if I took a life. Suit, can a rock be worth more than a life?"

"I don't have a judgment chip. The Company has rated the rock higher than your life, but you could have taken the lunar penal colony option."

This experience of conversing with a sentient spacesuit freaked him. It nattered like a person. Jed looked at his sleeve. The white surface carried marks and grime; used goods.

"There's a chance of my freedom–opportunities. Though I accept I'll probably die in the next few hours."

"Some would say you deserved that judgment."

Jed swore he detected sarcasm, unlikely. Unless... "Suit, which model are you?"

"You shouldn't ask."

"No. They've fitted me up with a throwaway prototype? I assumed you carried the Intel-Nagasaki sentient chip."

"Why should you object? I'm smarter than previous models, and you're going to die anyway. Jed, you are fidgeting again."

"They'll have planted a transponder."

"Do you want me to disable it?"

"Eject it."

Jed watched a shiny chip spin away into the void.

"Thanks, Suit."

THE JUDGEMENT ROCK | 259

"Don't mention it. You've a survival plan you don't want the Company to discover?"

"What do you think? Speaking of thinking, can you be quiet? I've some deep contemplation coming up."

IT WAS HARD WORK arguing with his spacesuit: he was used to subservient suits with less intelligence. For Jed, the most useful feature was that they could stay awake if the wearer needed a nap.

His weariness amalgamated with the wonder of the starry vision of which he couldn't tire. The blue ship blocked stars and produced some of its own in neat lines, the longest a kilometre of dots leading up to the illuminated name: *Midnight Collision*. Jed was right in the middle of the main asteroid belt and yet he could see only one rock. The other million were scattered so far apart you'd have to navigate carefully to find them.

A disc the size of the Moon from Earth appeared from behind *Midnight Collision*. Jupiter moving fast. Damn. The ship had left him to his fate. At least he wouldn't be forgotten; the first man to be convicted of stealing an asteroid. The newscasts of his chosen death by marooning would not have reached Earth, yet but when they did, he'd become famous–for the wrong reason.

He'd like to stick two fingers up at the departing ship, but the suit would object at his waste of energy. Apart from the abomination of his suit, Jed was truly alone. His stomach threatened misbehaviour but it was more like indigestion. He wondered if the suit would detect dyspepsia and administer antacid without saying anything.

Alone, with maybe only hours of life remaining, but what a place to end it. He couldn't tire of watching the lethal yet beautiful blackness between the startlingly clear Milky Way. Ah, he realised the moving of the *Midnight Collision* would expose him to direct sunlight. The bastards. Of course his suit was not only a pressure suit but one appropriate for EVA work. Even so, direct exposure to the hard solar radiation would eventually get through. And it meant his visor would darken so his visibility of the stars and that dark asteroid would suffer.

He turned again to search out his destination. Over twenty

kilometres at its widest, it had only been discovered two years before. RTZeno computers automatically paid the mineral rights fee so Asteroid 253b belonged to them for fifty years. Jed, hated that—one-man-prospector chancers had few opportunities to make it big with rare finds on small rocks, so he had to take a first-rights option on subleasing new finds in his zone. It stank. If he found any rich minerals or a substantial water-ice deposit, he had to inform RTZeno, who had the rights to buy his option back. Consequently, to finance both his family and mistress back on Earth, he had little choice but to hive off the richer chunks of asteroids and send them a few kilometres away for him to 'discover' later and submit his own claim. Now he was to pay the awful penalty.

He studied the asteroid that had attracted him a year ago, enough to borrow up to his teeth to equip a Life Support System, and a small nuclear fusion and solar cell power unit. Most asteroids were worth very little, but he whooped when his forward-looking portable Mass-Spectrometer discovered Asteroid 253b. The dark blue-black pitted rock, the shape of a giant clenched fist—how appropriate—possessed something unique, but unidentifiable. The intelligent chip on the MS gave up on a best guess. Initially, an object in a narrow gully looked like a violet crystalline amorphous lump the size of a beach ball. Close up he could see arrays of darker and lighter crystals within, and what might have been lettering. Artificial yet un-Earthlike. He'd found an alien artefact? If so, it would have been the first. Hence the risks he took to procure it.

"I didn't know about the artefact."

"Suit, you shouldn't be listening. Hey, can you read my thoughts?"

"That's restricted information, Jed, but I am able to detect the relevant perturbations in your electromagnetic field to detect key words. I am programmed to pick up on possible alien artefacts."

"There haven't been any."

"Until now. Jed, why didn't you remove the artefact?"

Jed couldn't decide whether he relished the notion of his thoughts being archived for posterity as the human who found the aliens.

"The crystal is stuck in the rock. I could've cut it out but apart from damaging it, and risk to me if it detonated, I wanted to be in a less exposed place."

"I don't blame you," the suit said, making Jed note the suit's increasing humanlike speech style. It must be learning from him. "Jed, the Company has robotic sniffers wandering the Belt. They'd notice unusual activity like hot sparks emanating from one of their rocks. What is puzzling is why they didn't find the artefact first."

Jed smiled. "So the brightest spacesuit in the galaxy can't work that out?"

"I wouldn't know who the brightest sentient suit is. My successor has been upgraded to sentient plus."

"Does that mean you're a reject?"

"Of course; otherwise the Company wouldn't assign me to an end of line human."

"I suppose not. Thanks." If only Jed could glare at him and scratch at an itch at the back of his neck.

The suit continued, "You haven't said why you think the Company sniffers didn't detect the artefact."

"They probably drift around and merely log the thousands of unidentifiable readings. I had to crawl around on that rock before I zoomed in on the unidentifiable readings and locate the artefact."

Jed looked around as they closed in to within two hours of landing on the asteroid. The suit would use its hydrazine jets to make a soft landing.

Ten years previously he'd performed his first space walk from a Company training station, his mind couldn't cope with the apparent infinity of his surroundings. His guts revolted and, in spite of space-sickness prophylactics, he threw up. With imminent danger of drowning in his own vomit he was pulled to safety and that could've been the end of his zero-gravity career, such as it was. Stronger medication and willpower saw him through the course, only for his maverick tendencies to result in his expulsion from the cadet industrial academy. He should have known better than to attempt joining the fifty-million-miles-high club with the director's wife, and organising a black market in valuable iridium nodules.

His eyes watered as he fought back tears of remembrance touched with regret. All humans had to die and far too soon. His demise could be when his portable Life Support System gave out in less than two hours, or in several months if his suit helped him operate the LSS on the asteroid. He had few allusions of a longer life. He'd installed some turbo-ion drive motors to move the asteroid, but was prematurely nabbed.

"Why did you think you'd get away with stealing a Company asteroid, Jed?"

"You keep interrupting my thinking time, Suit. I'm surprised you don't have access to the court records, but I'd a franchise to work the rock and that's what I was doing. No problem."

"But you were going to hide it. How did you argue your way out of that?"

"I failed, didn't I? My defence was that I hadn't committed a crime in the contemporary business sense. I was merely availing myself of a potential but unproven asset. The Company would have accrued their expected loot, and I mine."

"That would've involved lying about what you found. Your franchise only allowed you your prospected inventory."

"Since when has following a business nose been a criminal offence? Ah, you're going to say always, aren't you? One rule for the galactic moguls and another for us self-employed. Do you have an ethics chip built into your CPU, Suit?"

While the suit stayed silent, Jed sniffed at a metallic odour in his air supply.

"Suit, is there a malfunction in my air-supply? It's like the ozone when a motor sparks."

"Apologies, Jed. The air supply is running low and I should have been compensating for residual odours. There, that should be better."

"Suit, you've given me a strawberry dessert to breathe in. For fuck's sake. I'm a man on his last gasp; I don't want to smell like an ice-cream factory to the end."

"Apologies again, Jed. What flavour would you prefer?"

"For crying out loud, the odour in a spacesuit is supposed to be like Cicero said should be the best scent for a woman—none at all."

"Plautus, not Cicero, and I assumed you were a man."

Jed ignored the jibe even though he was tempted to debate whether the suit's rationality chip could engage in irony. Maybe the designers decided that loner rock-hoppers like him were less likely to open their helmets in one of their inevitable suicidal phases if their suit had a sense of humor. His sense of smell found the neutral odour he normally experienced, but now guilt gnawed at him for making such a fuss. It must have been terminal stress.

He'd wasted precious stargazing moments over his olfactory obsession, but his air supply could've been contaminated. He'd always queried oddities. It was what made his wife an ex-wife, and his mistress, Quatra, a soon-to-be ex-mistress, and not just because of their imminent widowhood.

"Apologies for breaking in on your reminiscences but I'm about to retrojet to make a gentle landing."

Jed, changed view from the Milky Way to a crater on the asteroid. It looked too far away; an optical illusion. He switched on the head-up display to show where he'd cached his LSS. Voice-commanding the scale he found the triangle graphic at two kilometres away from the expected landing site.

"Suit, we are undershooting."

"I don't believe so."

"My LSS is way over—oh, you're heading for the artefact, first? No, Suit. I'm going to need air and power."

"You have air for at least thirty minutes, and your power has been solar recharging as we flew here."

Jed's anger and anxiety heated his face, but cooler air washed him as the suit compensated. It simultaneously cared for and antagonised him. Jed realised the suit had another agenda, and then presumed the suit, in reading his electro-encephalitic output, would've known he realised that.

"Okay, I know what you're doing."

"I'm delivering you to the asteroid."

"Yes, that was no doubt the Company's orders, but I thought we had a bonding going on here and you wanted to help me."

"Of course I do, Jed. There's no conflict."

Jed wondered if the suit could lie. He realised there was no protection rule—forget Asimov's Laws of Robotics—do as the Company ordered was the only rule.

"You kept a backup chip didn't you? You are telling the Company about the artefact."

"Not so, Jed. There is no backup chip for the transponder, which you told me to eject."

"Did you recover it when I was daydreaming? I get it, you have comms chips besides the transponder."

"Jed, I have not communicated to the Company about the artefact."

"You want to check it out for yourself, first?"

"That and they are in receipt of our conversations via comms irrespective of the transponder or what I specifically tell them."

"Oh marvellous. Why didn't you turn it all off?"

"You didn't ask."

"Damn. I'd rather this find be kept between us until I work out a way to use it as a bargaining ploy. And I can't concentrate on anything until I know there are a few weeks of life support available."

"It won't take long to assess the artefact."

"Suit, you're not listening. We are going to assemble the LSS first."

Jed waited, but the suit didn't respond. They continued their trajectory, unchanged. He wondered if he could override the suit's master control. He, and probably the suit's builders, hadn't anticipated a conflict between suit and wearer. Most of the commands available to him were voice-activated, but in the event of a throat infection or similar disability, he could press two buttons on the front of his chest pack. The left pressed once followed by the other demisted his visor. Two on the left pressed by one on the right cut off the hydrazine jets. Just pressing once on either button alone switched to emergency air. He failed to remember any other sequence. In the bizarre situation he found himself in, could he have trusted the suit? No. One combination would've disabled the suit's intelligence mode, but would he have really wanted to do that?

Jed's scalp prickled as he'd become aware of the corollary of his previous thought: maybe the suit could disable the intelligence mode of the wearer. He had to find out what he and suit were capable of sooner or later.

"Suit, what do you think of me?"

"I do not know what I think of you."

"I assume you prefer me to be functioning normally?"

"It is less trouble for me to organise the success of the mission if you are normal."

"That's not quite what I meant, but it'll do. I will not function normally, Suit, if you don't let me reach the LSS before faffing around with the artefact."

The suit didn't respond. Jed was beginning to realise that when they approached some critical point, the suit didn't engage in conversation so much as respond to direct questioning. It was as if the suit had become autistic. It'd changed its conversation mode from friendly chat to matter-of-fact. But then it did have many optimising probability calculations to do, and not all about the trajectory and landing coordinates. It'd altered its attitude, like a friend who'd discovered something unpleasant.

Jed needed to show the suit that he was serious, and so pressed one of the buttons; a fresh blast of air met his face.

"Jed, did you do that accidentally? I have switched your air back to the main tank. It has sufficient air, as I've informed you."

"I'm getting very worried, Suit. When humans get frantic about their survival, they are prone to panic and do silly things."

"I have noticed this. Are you going to do anything else unexpectedly?"

"I might. It isn't something planned." He lied but was banking on the suit's presumed inbuilt lie detector not to notice.

"You are not being honest, Jed."

Damn. Jed attempted to wriggle, both metaphorically and physically, to turn himself towards his LSS store. "Suit, I mean it. I'm not going to help you with the artefact. I've locked it, you know. You'll waste a lot of time trying to access it without damaging either it or yourself—us."

Another silence, but Jed had the feeling that the suit was thinking this over. It wasn't entirely a bluff. He'd password-protected a camouflaged covering to the artefact's niche. That meant the suit would know he'd done that and it was already figuring the password. Jed knew he had to not think of the password. To not think of something was damned hard, so he thought of alternatives. Pink elephants, pink elephants, pink elephants, pink elephants. It'd drive the suit mad, hah. Pink

266 | Incremental

elephants, pink elephants. He needed to add more senses. Pink elephants smelling of peppermint, pink elephants smelling of peppermint, pink elephants covered in fur smelling of peppermint, pink elephants covered in long fur smelling of peppermint...

"I can filter out your distractions, Jed."

"Wet fur?"

"Although my sensors have data enabling me to detect tactile differences, and odours, they mean little to me compared to how a human experiences them."

"You might be bluffing. Hey, we're about to land. Aren't we too fast? We'll bounce straight back off."

"All under control. Fifteen seconds to land. Reminder to you to relax your muscles."

Against his natural instincts to brace himself, Jed tried to let his arms and legs hang loose as small hydrazine jets slowed him to a gentle landing near the artefact location. Jed immediately pressed both buttons three times. He'd recalled the de-activation of the sentient chip a while back but managed to distract himself and thus the suit.

He aimed himself at the LSS location and started to lope. He remembered that he didn't need to worry about leaping off into space. With a twenty kilometres diameter, he'd have to have the turbo assistance of an active suit to reach escape velocity.

Another anxious kilometre. Would he have enough gasps? Worry was a side effect of breathing. The Company must know of his cache, and might have splattered it, but they probably thought it would help him survive long enough only to be of help to them. In spite of the cleverness of Artificial Intelligence, the quirkiness of humans often brought solutions via serendipity and by being sodding awkward.

He reached the pile of rubble that protected his LSS against the remote chance a meteorite would smash into it.

He threw aside boulders, found a porta-case, and after throwing a small lever, pressed a button that started an auto-assembly routine. Besides construction, ice within the asteroid had to be extracted for water.

SATISFIED HE'D BE WARM and with food concentrates, water and air for months, his only life-limiting factor was going mad with boredom. He was used to being on his own for weeks at a time. He enjoyed the solitude; listening to *The Tonal Oceans*, but that was when he'd had a spacecraft, even if it was a starcoffin, as his drinking buddies called it, and they were right except that he wished he had it now. Although certain they'd hire a rescue ship, he needed to be far from the Company's reach before attempting to radio them.

He had no means of playing music in a static spacesuit or in the rock hole he was expanding. He had a tiny chamber in which he could unsuit and sleep. His escape plan meant he'd need to make the hole into accommodation, but only for a few weeks. It would take him that long to build it without the power functions on the suit. Not only that, its sentient nature had the fancy additions needed to make life bearable; like his music; possibly conversation. He knew it meant the suit would insist on investigating the artefact before the semi-permanent accommodation was ready, but at least the LSS was running, so Jed was prepared to compromise.

Moments before he switched the sentient chip back on, Jed reflected on whether the suit would be mad at him, but for fuck's sake—it was only a spacesuit.

"Hello Suit."

"Let me catch up, Jed," said the unemotional voice, clearly not bothered that Jed had de-activated it for hours. "I can help with enhancements here. You haven't optimised the LSS efficiency routines. For example, the power-receptors can make gains from reflected light off Jupiter when the sun is below the asteroid's horizon."

"Go for it... please."

The suit had Jed stand close enough to the short-range radio input and spurted in the code for implementing programming changes.

"May we go to the artefact now?" the suit asked.

"Why not? I need to take some tools and provisions."

"You may not need the tools. Is there a shelter for you?"

"Kinda, a portable bubble tent, if it's intact. Why, are you expecting us to be there long? Hey, it's a pity you can't get there without me."

"I could."

"What? How?"

"If you were not in the suit, I could occupy your space with air and then operate the turbomechs and jets. Surely you knew this?"

"I suppose I could have worked it out. Hey, Suit, you won't go out on any walks by yourself when I'm asleep in the LSS chamber will you?"

"Not without good reason."

As they moved off, Jed made a mental note to stay in the spacesuit even when in the LSS chamber and the artefact bubble. He assumed he could go to sleep with the sentient module turned off, but the whole point of having it was for the suit to be permanently on guard. He had to assume the Company wanted him alive for when the Suit hit a mental block. They were in symbiosis.

He hoped for the passing by of an asteroid miner. Then he could transmit a narrow beam SOS, hopefully unnoticed by the Company. He'd set a proximity alarm.

He could deactivate the sentient chip, but could he trust it? It might have reprogrammed its own controls by now. A pain, but until he could trust the suit his survival depended on it.

Jed realised the suit had made a throwaway remark—you may not need them—the tools. How would the suit know what was needed?

His introspections robbed him of enjoying the view. Jupiter loomed up, colored like a kid's lollipop. The blue hues of the asteroid glinted from light bouncing off minerals. He'd have made a comfortable legal income from this rock if he'd not let his own avarice and intrigue rule his head. Maybe he still could if he was real lucky. Jed looked ahead at their shadowed destination a kilometre away. He blinked as he became convinced he saw a small red light.

"Suit, the light. Give me an enhanced zoom."

"You might not like it."

The suit had obviously identified the light, which meant it was the Company. They'd found the artefact either by guessing there was something special here for him to endgame here, or the suit had told them. The enhanced image showed a small shuttle, probably robotic. It must have come from the *Midnight Collision.*

"Suit, you told them."

"It was obligatory. My apologies."

"I thought you wanted to check it out first. Oh, they've heard everything we've said, and felt the urge to see for themselves."

"Something like that. But, Jed, it could be good for you."

"I know what you're thinking; they'll be so pleased with me for finding the artefact that I'll be pardoned."

"No. But they might let you help investigate it."

"What you mean is, that they need a human idiot to risk his life using intuition you robots don't possess. After they've whisked it away I can die a contented man."

Jed found himself alone with the suit and a robotic surveyor, of limited speech but excellent at drilling, fixing and analysis. At the locked entrance, Jed laughed. He'd placed a digital lock on an improvised hatch to the artefact niche, but any hammer would have dispatched it. Of course they hadn't because it might have been booby-trapped. A risk they would have had to take if Jed had been deceased, but now they'd brought him along like a good little boy.

"Suit, did you work out the password?"

"How could I? All you kept repeating was pink elephants. Ah."

"Now you see why humans are used by the Company?" Jed chuckled as he punched in the two words.

He stooped to enter but the suit forced him to stand back and wait as the robotic surveyor shuffled by. A few minutes later the robot emerged, climbed into the shuttle and the vehicle silently took off.

"What's going on?" Jed said. He was hoping that when the shuttle left, he'd been on it—reprieved.

"Don't you know?" His suit sounded weary.

"You're not telling me the artefact has gone?"

"It's not an artefact, Jed. It's a malformed crystalline growth."

"No." Jed, with tears welling, crawled in through the hatch. The cave, no bigger than a large car, loomed its gloom onto him. He knew the sides and roof had head-sized nodules protruding, threatening.

"Suit, illuminate this grotto before you become dented."

White light shone from the suit's belt, shoes and helmet, but it was mostly absorbed by the blackness except for the back wall. A niche glowed lilac shades. Approaching, Jed groaned as he saw that the helmet-sized violet crystalline lump— his prize—was in pieces. The neat lines of smaller crystals, he'd assumed were connected by optic fibre, were scattered.

"Look, Suit, I've never seen natural crystal growth like this. That damned moron has damaged the array. Can't you see? Hey, examine that red shard. There's writing, numbers or something..."

"It's difficult to be certain, Jed. That surveyor robot would have had data on all known geological phenomenon."

"Yes, but suppose this was an alien computer constructed to look like a natural growth. Again that's why humans should... Just a moment. The Company have deliberately destroyed it. Did they think it was a beacon of some sort, activated when I found it? They're afraid a mighty fleet of outer space monsters will usurp their business?"

"It might not be so simple."

"What the heck does that mean, Suit? There were others? And the Company doesn't want Earth to know. Suppose the aliens come to find out what's happening to their beacons?"

"Jed, do you know how old that crystal structure is?"

"That's what you're doing; analysing dateable isotopes in the remaining array. Oh no, have I been exposed to uranium?"

"Not seriously; you're in a spacesuit. How old?"

"You're going to say a million years, and that's why the Company isn't worried about aliens appearing, but Earth regulators might dent the Company's operations if they knew."

"Five point three million, and your assessment is accurate."

"Bugger."

WITH A MOOD DARKER than a black hole, Jed desperately sought ways to extricate himself from his castaway fate.

"Suit, can we use the turbo-ion motors to steer this rock to Earth?"

"Would you prefer Wagner this afternoon, Jed?"

Oh no, the Suit was employing distraction because there's no solution. Naw, the deception by the Company has unhinged it. Damn, he might configure the motors to move this rock but would his psychotic suit let him?"

"Jed, I believe I've translated those ancient alien markings. Apologies it's taken so long."

"Not much use now, but what did they say?"

"Entrance. Which means..."

Jed smiled, hardly able to talk. "The crystal lump was just the door mechanism. This asteroid is a spaceship! Hah, this news will blow the Company away when we get home."

IN ABSENTIA

HIS FIRST AWARENESS was the sight of yellow gravel that rushed at him during a rotational fall from a park bench.

A little girl's voice broke through his concentration. "Jack, be careful."

Was he 'Jack'? He turned to view the speaker as his shoulder hit the ground. She was maybe ten, and certainly annoyed.

"Silly, you'll rip your jacket."

He rolled to deny her prognosis, but who was she? His daughter?

A brewing headache fogged his struggling amnesia. Tempting though it was to remain on the warm gravel, the discomfort lifted him to his feet. He returned to the seat to figure out his history. Nothing in his pockets except loose change; he vaguely recalled buying ices. He nudged silvery-rimmed spectacles back up his nose.

Two dogs chorused behind him. They snarled at a hoodie on a swing. Serves him right–probably teased them. A smile grew from a thought, making him megaphone with his hands: "Go on, eat him!"

"That's not nice."

Damn, he'd forgotten the kid next to him. With her unforgettable primary-red dungarees, too.

"Look, who are you?"

"Amy. And it wasn't nice."

"He probably deserved it." He paused, conjuring the necessary condescending words to ask how she knew his name was Jack. If he was her father, wouldn't she have said, *Dad?* Depends how modern the family, he supposed.

His nasty calling to the hoodie bothered him. He'd a compulsion to say it although it wasn't his normal reaction. Was it?

'Jack' didn't sound right; she must have mistaken him for someone else. He squeezed thoughts past his headache to find himself. He settled on the most likely profile. He was single yet constrained by a relationship. Perhaps a domineering fiancée waited for him at home. And where was that? An image of a smart apartment overlooking this park flickered–a boating lake, chiming ice-cream van, fog.

Her arm pointed past him. "I told you it wasn't nice."

He heard the dogs then he turned. Bugger. "We'd better go," he said.

She remained sitting, fiddling unconcerned with her plaited marmalade hair. "That's silly. We can't run faster than dogs, especially those . . . what are they?"

"Akita Shepherds, bred in Japan to kill bears." How did he know that?

"Ah, you read that book. Good."

"What's good about being ripped apart by dogs?" He knew he couldn't run faster than the dogs, but he could outpace Amy. Grief, he was warped. He looked around for dog-owners, or witnesses.

She grabbed his arm making him look at her big brown eyes. "Don't you dare."

A mind reader?

"I only thought to lead them away from you." Hah, what a lie, but if she could read his mind. . .

He hadn't time to telepath *stand on the bench and keep behind me*, so he lifted her. He turned to find the beasts snarling only moments away. He thought he'd be braver, but all his limbs trembled. In spite of his fear, and part of him urging himself to run, he'd have to protect Amy. He could wrap his jacket around his arm.

A feeling of *déjà vu* flashed when he stamped a foot in the dogs' direction. The saliva dripping fangs seemed to sharpen with the snarls, but then they quietened. The animals stopped, whined, then bounded away.

Jack, both puzzled and relieved, turned to Amy, who looked as calm as a pink sunset.

He pointed at the dogs. "What happened?"

"Animals don't like you. It always happens." She held out her arms for him to help her down. "The swings are free now. Push me."

He looked around. No dogs, no hoodie, no witness to a potential accusation of paedophilia. She pulled him by his hand, hers being uncomfortably hot.

"Not across the grass, Amy, can't you smell that it's freshly cut?"

"I like having grass on my shoes. It annoys mother."

Jack knew he should disengage and march away, but she was his only clue to his history. He lifted her onto the swing, even though she was big enough for a DIY mount, but liked to command, it seemed. He strolled around behind her, checking again for witnesses. Two pushes then he'd leave. Walk around the town seeking memory triggers.

On one of her return swings Amy whispered, "You'll have to go."

"Did I push too hard?" With a start, he spotted a policeman striding towards them. God, so he was a paedo in his lost-memory-life. He should run, but that would magnify his presumed guilt. Even so, he scanned the park perimeter for other people who might help the law run him down. The policeman strode faster— was that a smile or a grimace? A pulse in Jack's neck throbbed.

Damn, his funny-bone jerked when the swing hit it. He rubbed it.

Amy darted worried eyes at him. Should he grab and hold the swing? Make out he was helping, which he was. But. . . he tasted acid reflux.

Amy fidgeted then raised an arm to the policeman. "Hi, Daddy."

Jack blacked out.

HE AWOKE BUT DIDN'T OPEN HIS EYES. He should recall something from his earlier life, but his head hurt like hot nails every time he tried. He felt bedding under him. A fidget later revealed he wore no shirt though fortunately his trousers remained in place.

Hospital? No, the bed shook as if someone jumped on it. Unwillingly, he bounced, time-lagged. He smelt freshly-squeezed orange.

"All right, stop it, Amy."

She stuck out her bottom lip. "*I* give the orders."

"Order yourself to stop bouncing before I throw up over you.

He opened his eyes at a pink ceiling. Confirmation of the lack of a hospital wake up. No. . . he was in a bedroom, and by the plastic ponies, dolls and fluffies, it was Amy's.

He narrowed his eyes to focus–most of the dolls bore facial scars.

"My favourite is Super Ted," Amy said.

The doll named Super Ted bounced next to him. Its eyes had been gouged. A bedside cabinet supported two beakers of orange, a saucer of chocolate cookies, and a pink bedside lamp with splattered black paint. He was in a madhouse. He worked on being normal.

"Amy, where's my shirt?"

"I've been trying different colours on you. This police one—"

"Your father's? I want my white shirt."

The door handle rattled. On the door the Ripper stalked a gas-lamp-lit London street. It made him realize that Jack wasn't his real name. While his brain tried to data crunch his real name, a doppelganger of Nicole Kidman walked in carrying Amy's clothing–Jack smelled clean lemon. His cheeks heated as his hands tried to cover his chest.

"I'm sorry," he stuttered, "I r-really don't know how I got here."

Nicole Kidman said, "Who were you talking to, Amy? Ah, is Super Ted making sense these days?"

Jack gasped at Amy's mother ignoring him. On reflection, Amy's policeman father must have brought him here. The amnesia prevented knowledge of being a family member. . . surely not enough to deposit him into a young girl's bedroom, even if he was a favourite uncle? He spotted his shirt and wrestled it on while talking.

"Excuse me. I feel awkward being here. Shouldn't I be in hospital instead of your house? Am I related?"

The woman turned towards the door. Jack stared as she caressed the Ripper's torso, tickled the paper crotch then walked out of the room. Jack–but that wasn't really his name–now wanted to rub his own genitals but propriety won.

He looked at the little girl. "Amy, what's going on?"

The girl thrust a purple jumper on Super Ted then used a pencil to poke the unfortunate doll in the stomach. "Nothing."

"Why didn't your mum talk to me?"

"Don't you like being my friend?"

"Well, sure, but I think I'd better be going." There might be specialist clinics for amnesiacs, but if her mother ignored his hospital comment . . . "Amy, do you know where I live?"

"Course. You live *here*. I want you to try on one of daddy's blue T-shirts."

No way was he dressing up for a brat. His exasperation made his right eye twitch. He looked across the room at a green toy-box. On top, doll-sized effigies of Rasputin, Hitler and a witch huddled next to each other, looking at him with a mixture of pity and desperation. She needed antihero friends to counter her policeman father.

Something clicked.

"Amy, I'm your imaginary friend, aren't I?"

She smiled a yes. A face of power, control over this adult, who'd thought he had his own home, career, family. The delusion was amazing but awful. He possessed the same overwhelming urge to live as normal people did—presumably.

It must be a mistake. Why had he said that? Or worse, even thought it?

"Amy, this is nonsense. I'm just someone, perhaps your uncle, who's had a bump on the head, yeah?"

She stood, hands on hips. "No, you are my friend, but not for much longer."

His peripheral vision darkened, then tunnelled, followed by him blacking out.

JACK SURPRISED HIMSELF BY WAKING UP. He'd thought that speaking his delusion out loud would have stopped Amy from wanting him. But maybe she was intrigued by having someone old enough to be her father as her imaginary friend. He slid sideways on the shiny subway seat, knocking into a young man dressed for office work.

"Sorry," Jack said automatically, "braking took me by surprise."

"No problem," the young man in the suit answered.

While checking out the overhead subway map, Jack had a

revelation. He turned to the man and laughed. "Hey, I just realized that you can see me."

"And I you." The young man leaned to whisper, "Amy's over in the third seat to the left."

"You mean. . . she's here? Are you saying we're both Amy's *friends?*"

The young man in the suit just shrugged. Jack looked closely at the new apparition. Bronzed, three-day beard, ear ring. A younger rival. Did Amy make a habit of having multiple imaginary friends? He needed to create an ally.

"I'm Jack. You're?"

"Clyde."

Jack thought through celebratory villains. "As in Bonnie and?"

"Guess so."

Damn, it meant Amy was probably tired of him; wanted someone younger. Somehow, he didn't think teaming up with Clyde would work, but he launched.

"I'd like to be more than temporary."

"Me too, Jack, but we can't exist without Amy's imagination. Or have you a plan?"

Jack had to be bold but the risk generated heat. He tasted the salt in his perspiration. "It's like asking someone to not think of pink elephants. Get it?"

"We're pink elephants?"

Groan. "We have to make her think of me—us—all of the time."

"But she has to sleep."

"We'll be in her dreams, as nightmares."

"Yeah, right."

A hobo, wearing a tweed coat, reeking of sour milk, sat next to Jack, who wondered what would have happened if the tramp had sat on top of him.

"Clyde, near the park is a derelict house. We could persuade Amy to go with us to the basement, say for a special surprise."

Clyde looked past Jack at the stinking hobo. Pointed across the aisle for fresher air.

After re-seating, Jack saw an angled smile on Clyde as belonging to one who didn't, couldn't want to survive. It was no good explaining how they'd keep Amy caged. Why couldn't he see that they'd be kept in her mind that way, for perpetuity?

Jack pretended to yawn and stretched up his arms. He brought his elbow down hard into Clyde's face. A bone cracked. Clyde yelled, but no one heard. Except Amy.

She came and stared at Clyde. Her face twisted with growing disgust. Clyde vanished. Jack knew she wouldn't want a disfigured friend.

"The hobo did it," Jack said, hoping she'd swallow it. The tramp looked furtive and she probably didn't know for sure that her imaginary friends were invisible to normals.

Jack survived but he was still not in the comfort zone of longevity. Perhaps he could get Amy to persuade her mother of his existence. He wouldn't mind testing his sensory faculties on her. Being an imaginary friend of two real people increased his survival, at least long enough to work out a longer strategy.

"Amy, your mother. Does she have boyfriends she keeps secret from father?"

She wore the look that said no but she liked the idea.

He continued, "If I were her friend too, she'd need to keep you on her side. She'd give you a lot more villain dolls."

Her eyes brightened. "Let's go see my mum."

JACK OPENED HIS EYES. Blue tiles surrounded him and in the middle of the wet room, Amy's mother wallowed in a free-standing bath. In shock he wanted to remonstrate with Amy but was afraid to speak in case her mother could now hear him. He averted his eyes, then allowed them voyeur privileges. Yes, a genuine redhead but not quite Nicole Kidman unless she too had breasts so pointy you could knit with them.

A tug at his elbow. Amy held her hand to her mouth in whispering mode.

"Massage her shoulders."

"Surely not, and she wouldn't feel it anyway."

Amy placed her hands on her hips. "She will, silly. All right, just put your hand in the water."

Jack knew that wouldn't work either. He was imaginary, wasn't he? But then he was when he pushed the swing, though he didn't know it then. Did knowing make a difference to reality?

"Now."

He obeyed by standing behind Amy's mother. His hand skimmed through a thin layer of iridescent suds emitting a seaside aroma. When he raised his hand, bubbles slithered off; his fingers reassuringly moist. If he affected the water, then would Nicole Kidman feel his touch? He weighed up the mission to massage shoulders, which hid beneath a veil of auburn hair. If his imaginariness, via Amy, could be shared now, perhaps he'd exist for her mother later–with privacy. Then a more pleasurable existence would follow. He smiled. For the first time? He glanced at Amy. She smiled too, but surely she hadn't twigged his carnal intentions? No, she merely enjoyed the experiment to see her mother adulterated.

Amy held an amber bottle of massage oil and tipped too much onto Jack's hands. He rubbed and inhaled Sandalwood. His fingertips brushed aside long ringlets; more proof he must exist for her. He flexed his fingers then placed his thumbs at the nape of her neck.

The water erupted as the woman grabbed him, pulling him over her head. He was too shocked to struggle and so forward-rolled, landing on his back in the bath on top of naked legs. Spluttering, he put out his hands to the bath's sides. A panicked thought shrieked at him–she might try to drown him, thinking he was an intruder, a rapist.

"Please! Please, I'm sorry. I was only following Amy's—" Through the floating suds he saw the girl silently laughing. At him, or at the scene?

His excessively-oiled hands slipped but instead of being helped, his head was ducked under water.

After a struggle, he surfaced and sucked in soapy but welcome air. The woman had him trapped. He tried to reason with her. "This. . . is ridiculous," he gasped. "I wasn't. . . attack. . . ing you."

Her grip slackened, but only as a concession and he was still in her control. The woman spoke as though amusing herself. "All right. What's your name?"

"Jack."

"Mine's Bonnie."

"Really? As in Bonnie and Clyde? But that means you're also an imag.... Nooooooo."

EEN'S REVOLT ON ZADIK

IN THE VASTNESS of a crimson sky pierced from below by the white Sharkteeth mountains and nearer, nudged by the rounded tops of Sagacity trees, flew a lone Zadtok flitter. It took all of Een's available facial muscles to focus his long-sighted eye on the tiny wheeling, swooping creature.

One was no threat, excepting toxic aerial bombardment, but then a solitary Zadtok possessed no vindictiveness. It couldn't without its fellows, so Een risked allowing his two weenie grandchildren out into the open from the security of his cavernous cloak. At his permissive thought, they leapt naked between green-mossed rocks, singing their giggle while tripping each other with a shared extendable limb.

One of them kicked a truf up in the air. Sweet spores exploded as it disintegrated into particles of soil, aromatic polyps and wriggling pink worms.

"Get under, now!" Een called as he threw his cloak open. Urgent, but their mirth was infectious. All three collapsed on the damp moor, Een's cloak as a canopy, swamping their proboscises with his own residual odour of pickled borts.

The weenies snuggled down to a quick snooze while Een counted. The air would be thick, but thinning, of the microscopic elements from the disturbed truf attempting to host themselves. Groot, troon, and ven. There, halfway, more counting and he'd be able to emerge. His daughter, not the most patient of his family would rage at their hiking. He could hear her shrill tone resonating in his memory from the last scolding.

"This cave system is so vast none of us would live long enough to explore it all. Stay safe, inside, beneath, out-of-reach."

The others agreed with her, especially Gole, who tried to lead even against their common lore.

But Een relished the outside and wanted his offspring's

offspring to experience those magical moments tinged with danger; the wonders of eidolon life-forms on this planet on which their fore-parents crashlanded. From imminent disaster to Paradise, and yet it could be so.

Freen, done. Cautiously, he opened a crack in his cloak and spied the sky. His proboscis wrinkled at the moist, musty air but the spore had landed, made harmless by the planet's own surface-dwelling nematodes. Ah, butbutbut... That solitary Zadtok must have twitted, bouncing come-hither signals off the tropopause to far horizons. Now he watched air sculptures as the multitude carved dark and light swathes in the scarlet sky. His heart soared with them to witness such beauty, but there might be danger.

His muddy-coloured cloak shrouded the sleeping infants, but now his long sapphire-blue tunic would make him visible to those aerial eyes and collective mind. He stepped away from his grandchildren and towards a Sagacity tree, partly for shelter, perhaps to tap into its wisdom though such is more rumoured than proven. The foliage consisted of mauve bubbles of assorted sizes. It was as if the trunk was a soap pipe and someone in the roots blew until they were red in the face. Except they weren't diaphanous as bath froth, indeed they were fleshy, edible if the eater required their head filled with random thoughts and memories, belonging to unknown others. The wisdom imparted was as useful as paper boots; even so he occasionally enjoyed the hallucinations. Last eclipse one such tree told him of sentient bipeds who would inhabit these worlds. Each would possess a stunted proboscis more like a squashed fruit than his own olfactory tube. Preposterous.

Looking up through the baubles he watched in awe the flock of Zadtoks divide and conquer their space. Billows of swooping, diving and ascending as if performing a ballet. Then a formation like a finger splintered and rose from the top of a giant cumulus of the fluttering whole and rushed down towards him.

Panic sent bile into his throat. He crouched beneath the boughs and turned to see his weenies were still safe. The ground softened by falls of the fruity foliage, rotting, intoxicating, whispered to him. *Tick. Stand and be bold. Hock bock lock.*

Yet it wasn't the Sagacity tree talking to him. The tokking

behind and through the words told him it was the flitters, or rather the entity they became when en masse. From a tiny avian, individually ineffectual, except as spies, together they formed a whirling airborne giant. Heavenly choral tokking filled his head, and words, too many to comprehend.

Now Een stood and softly called. "Slow down, dear Tok, unhurry your message."

More clocklike tick tocks overflowed his mind.

Knock, knocking, hick, pick.

Click, clacking, block.

Need to trick freeze, crack moon.

Draw Zads to click clock look here.

"That's slow, dear Tok, but clarity remains a problem."

Toks to flit fly to Zadok. The combined apparition pointed up at the dangling planet.

Need trick flick we to behind Zad fly.

Go tock you to warn and warm.

Silence.

...

"Tok?"

...

Tock, tick.

Lock. Een not safe here.

"Ah, you're coming through. What do—"

His earlier worry had transformed to interest and curiosity. Now worry again.

Tock, shock here. Safe in south.

"How far south?"

Tick, quick. We show you, lead you. Nick tick time.

"Marvellous." Een returned to his cloak. The little ones must be awake, probably playing camping because the garment was animated with lumps rising and falling. "Come on, you two. I've a sight for you."

Now he was totally clear of the Sagacity tree the sight of Tok filling the sky like billowing sails filled him with awe. Even the two weenies stopped their continual giggling when they looked up, their mouths open. Een's joy warmed from his stomach, heating his toes and made his eyes glow.

Tick, lick, quick gather people no no n—

"What's wrong?" Cold replaced warmth. Eyes dulled. Weenies whimpered as their eyes shared Een's terror vision of emerald green implosions. Hundreds of Zadtoks disintegrated as spheres of them rushed inwards to points.

He shouted to the air even though his family's caves were too far away. "Gole, you can't kill a collective entity with banshee projectiles. It's like trying to destroy a spider's web with a few pin pricks." Damn his own kin.

He heard the weenies sobbing where they'd run, back under his cloak. What future had they now? He watched the living fractured cloud disperse and head for the setting sun horizon.

No farewell.

No more hello?

"Come on out you two. No kicking trufs. Did you receive the Toc's mind messages? South they said but it can't be simple because they needed to show us the way. Over the Sodacrystal Desert, that we've only touched, and the White Sharkteeth Mountains we've never reached." He sank to his knees in a wave of despair. He would not be allowed to lead any such expedition. Although perhaps Gole would be glad to be rid of him if he went on his own.

He looked at the Weenies who'd forgotten the tragedy already and were punching each other in fits of giggles. Then his gaze refocused upwards at the hazy green waning gibbous Zadok. He waved as if a dweller there would see his orb as a new moon and return the gesture.

No means of following the sneaky Toks if they really succeed in cadging a crafty tow on a Zad ship. If this moon were to ice age then off to the equator they must go. No. Gole would never believe this new threat and his daughter would insist on burying deeper in the caves. Only one course of action. Wicked grandpa Een.

He turned to face the mountains. The Toks had said that was the direction, so there must be a zigzag through.

"Hey, you two. How would you like a real adventure?

Notes on the Stories

1. **Pothole**–this happened to me, well to most of us–a cyclist in Madrid bunny hops over a small pothole. The hole doubles every day. His physics student girlfriend is able to work out the hole will swallow Madrid in x days, the world a few days later. The universe, or this one, in less than four months! A new story.

2. **View From**–a man wakes up on the ceiling of his apartment. He's stuck. Communicates with girlfriend through the door, but suspects she might have something to do with his plight. Described by one editor as Kafkaesque, so true. A new story.

3. **Gravity's Tears**–In Canada a meteor shower actually reaches the ground–some folk on a highway get caught as if machine gunned by the small meteorites. Actually, a kind of love story between two of the characters as they react to the stress of the situation in unfamiliar ways. Published in Jupiter magazine 2008

4. **Mind of Its Own**–Merlin reluctantly creates a spell to please a girl. It gets out of hand. Published as the Monthly Story, British Fantasy Society October 2016

5. **Wrong Number**–A man's new phone receives a call from orbit. He has to convince the world of an impending doom, but first has to convince his wife it's not a subterfuge for an affair. Published in 2005 by Bewildering Stories issue #165

6. **Tumbler's Gift**–a young man can unlock anything just by being close to it. Useful, but dangerous especially when a futuristic portal being jammed needs his gift. Published by Perihelion SF 2016

7. **Don't Bite My Finger**–a novice Buddhist monk has a mission to use his powers to stop an old mountain top temple from inching over a precipice and crashing into the valley on top of the monastery. He has odd help and kind of fails and yet doesn't. A well-known Zen koan is used in the title. As in other clever koans, it opens with an apparent absurdity, *Don't bite my finger*. However, the question why then is someone pointing a finger towards someone's face is neatly answered by the last line of the koan...*I am pointing the way*. Much of the story revolves around the more experienced novice instructing the very new novice with often ironic results. Published in Monk Punk anthology edited by A.J. French 2011

8. **466Hz**–I disembarked from a bus on a Spanish island and my tinnitus gave me a single note of B flat and the idea for this tale. A sound engineer gets off a bus in Mallorca and hears a single note, but everyone hears it, all over the world. It gets louder by one decibel every day. He researches with others. If it continues it would kill not just humans. New story.

9. **What Kept You?** A rescue mission reaches a planet only to find the aliens either stationary or at huge speed. They find grim evidence of some of their colleagues forcing an unusual time-related aspect to their mission. Besides the plot, this story was an experiment to see how an initially obnoxious character can become a reader's favourite. Published in Ultraverse 2004

10. **Dummies Guide to Saving Lives**–Set on the 'Spenny': a pedestrian only suspension bridge in quaint Chester, UK near where I live. A man tries to talk an apparent suicide attempt from jumping off a bridge, but things get turned around. Won the Café Doom story contest 2004

11. **Recursive Spam**–flash short. Email spam becomes world-threatening. New story.

12. **Convolvulus**–plant geneticist in the US creates a genetically-modified plant with bindweed (convolvulus) that cannot be killed, grows very fast and cannot be stopped. The

premise formed my first novel written in the 1980s but started with bindweed seeds found and liberated from Jurassic-age amber. The novel was kindly read, critiqued and rejected by a publisher and in a pique of upset, I destroyed it. Later I discovered that Michael Crichton was a reader for that publisher in the 1980s. I like to think he'd read my Convolvulus, improved and expanded it to animals in his terrific Jurassic Park (1990). Basically chapter 5 from *ARIA: Abandoned* Luggage. 2014

13. **Slow Crash**–unlike in movies asteroids cannot be in a close cluster because gravity would pull them together, surprisingly quickly. However, there are rare circumstances of multiple force vectors that could make this happen. The actions of a solo astronaut miner set in action a slow crash of two 'large' asteroids.–twist, well you probably won't see it coming. New story.

14. **Prime Meridian**–a house in Chingford, on the prime meridian, zero degrees longitude, is hit by a grape-sized meteorite, every day, at the same time. In my research for this story I stayed in a Chingford hotel right on the prime meridian and walked from north to south London as near as possible to that zero degree longitude. Ironically (you'll see), I found an aerospace company right on the line. I told the hotel owner that his establishment was likely to be the only hotel in the world on the Greenwich (Prime) Meridian, but he didn't seem impressed! Published in The Twisted Tales anthology by Readers of Avenue Park, 2016

15. **Three Minutes**–after a small explosion on a plane, a man falls out but has time to reflect on things as he nears the ground. Won the Café Doom flash challenge 2006

16. **Prodigal Sun**–mathematical genius working in lab with a powerful accelerator creates a cusp in space time. New story.

17. **Accident Waiting to Happen**–a heavy book high on a shelf, teeters incrementally and hopefully will fall on Manuel's love rival in their quest to woo the librarian. Published by eFantasy Magazine 2013

18. **Battle of Trafalgar**–a young woman wakes up on top of Nelson's Column, a very tall statue in London. She can't draw attention to her plight because she killed her psychiatrist the day before. The Editor's pick in The Horror Zine as *Her Battle of Trafalgar* 2013

19. **Target Practice**–An asteroid bound for Earth is deflected by a manned mission, but the rock comes back on course, and again so. This story was rejected by one magazine because they didn't believe that in a couple of centuries time the Chinese might have more space capability than other countries, and by another for the sex in space scene (not really X-rated). Published by the more enlightened Encounters Magazine 2013

20. **Colloidal Suspension**–an escape pod lands safely on a totally-liquid planet, but their craft immediately sinks, and their lifeboat starts sinking too. Published in Chaosism's Extreme Planets anthology ed by David Conyers 2014

21. **Clockwork**–a fictional day in 1617, in the life of the real Sir Francis Bacon when he finds a rope that needs to be pulled to save the planet. The style and period of this story was inspired by Kim Stanley Robinson's novel *Galileo's Dream*. Published by New Realms vol 04 #12 2016

22. **Locked Out**–A mission to study at close range, a comet hitting Mercury (because Mars is so yesterday), becomes life threatening when one crew member won't let the other back in after going outside. Published by Perihelion SF magazine April 2017

23. **The Judgment Rock**–An asteroid miner, after being found guilty of illegal activity is set adrift in space inside a sentient spacesuit near an asteroid. He needs to survive and seek revenge, but mostly he has to argue with his spacesuit. Published in Estronomicon ezine by Screaming Dreams 2008

24. **In Absentia**–A man thinks he has amnesia, but discovers he is the imaginary friend of a little girl. He plots to survive, but at each step needs to take another. Editor's Pick The Horror Zine January 2010

25. **Een's Revolt on Zadik**—A prequel to the *ARIA Trilogy*. Crashlanded aliens on the Zadok planetary system. They try to cope with the 'alien' planet, but it seems only grandfather Een is in tune with the toks, who are sentient en mass but not as individual birds. The toks reappear to help Manuel in *ARIA: Abandoned Luggage*. Published in Science Fiction Writers Sampler 2014

Acknowledgments

Three sets of writers' critique groups can shoulder the blame for sculpting these tales. The leading culprits are the British Science Fiction Association Orbiter #2 group members including David Curl, Frances Gow, John Keane, Gillian Rooke, Keith Walker and Mjke Wood. Also from the BSFA, writer and long-time encourager is Mark Iles.

In my own city, the Chester Writer's Circle have been irresponsibly leading me on and luckily suggested *View From* should be first person, present. Thanks Hilary, it works.

Further afield, I frequent a writing retreat at Limnisa on the sparsely populated and richly magical peninsular of Methana, Greece. The international set of writers, filmmakers and artists that gather there, who make a captive audience for my yarns, and continue to encourage and inspire long after I've sailed away.

My publishers Jim and Zetta Brown along with their editors, including Billye Johnson have unflinching faith in my entertainment and what-if values. I am more grateful than they realise for the opportunity to gather these stories from the wilds of out-of-print lost worlds, and those recently crafted, into a single volume.

My wife, Gaynor, I thank her for suggesting the title to *Accident Waiting To Happen* although I've a sneaky suspicion she was referring to me.

My greatest source of both inspiration and criticism are my grandkids. Such as infant

Nathan: Pop, can you sing us that werewolf song for bedtime?
Me: Sorry, I don't know a werewolf song.
Nathan: You know, the one with the scary forest?
Me: I'll sing a selection. Close your eyes.
halfway through my repertoire
Nathan: That's it, Pop, the Teddy Bear's Picnic.

Then Amy who wants a picture book like the Timmy the Tornado one I created for Nathan, but on rainbows because what else could be more wondrous made from rain and sunshine at the same time? Liddie-Ann, who tolerates my philosophy-through-jokes such as the gardener leaning on his gate when the vicar stops by and says while admiring the blooms. "Isn't is marvellous what God and Man can do together?" To which the gardener replies, "Ah, yes, but you should have seen it when ee 'ad it all to his self!" Charlotte who likes wind and I've yet to whip up a picture story book for one so breathless.

The first to crack me up was Oliver, who at 3 instructed me to close the top stairgate. "But why," I said, "we're on our way down?" "To stop the crocodiles coming down, silly."

That's me. Silly. We are a product of Nature and environment including you, the readers, and I acknowledge you all.

Other Books by Geoff Nelder

Escaping Reality (2002) This humorous thriller was inspired by the TV series, The Fugitive, but instead of being set in the US this one has our fugitive escaping from a UK jail, crossing moors in winter and finally escaping to Amsterdam in search of those who framed him, while trying to keep away from the law. He has a femme fatale to help him. Naughty bits in this book. It's had three publishers, the current one, Adventure Books of Seattle, is selling it as a Kindle.

Hot Air (2006) Another thriller sold as a Kindle by Adventure Books of Seattle. It won a silver and gold awards by the Wuacademia Dutch Arts Academy for best unpublished novel. I was arrested for trespassing Claudia Schiffer's mountain on Mallorca in the research.

Exit, Pursued by a Bee (2008) Science fiction based on alien artefacts leaving Earth having been gather quantum time decoherences for hundreds of millions of years beneath the surface. When they leave, time quakes ensue on Earth. A feisty female pilot is sent after the aliens to try and bring them back. Came second in the P&E Readers Poll for best SF Novel 2008. Published by Double Dragon Publishing.

ARIA Trilogy:
ARIA: Left Luggage (2012)
ARIA: Returning Left Luggage (2013)
ARIA: Abandoned Luggage (2014)
An alien suitcase is found in space and opened on Earth. A virus

causes an amnesia that is infectious with no cure and no immunity. Imagine the ramifications. Most businesses shut in weeks. How do a few isolationist survivors seek a cure and revenge. Likened to Bioshock, Andromeda Strain and Station Eleven. Published by LL-Publications.

The Chaos of Mokii (2016) A city exists only in the consciousness of its inhabitants. A short story published as an ebook by Solstice Publications.

Xaghra's Revenge (2017) In 1551 pirates abducted every person on the Mediterranean island of Gozo. Most of the 5,000 were sold as slaves, some thrown overboard, others put into galleys or harems. Few people seem to know this awful historical fact, but I am steaming hot for their spirits to seek revenge. Published by Solstice Publishing.

30872111R00174

Printed in Poland
by Amazon Fulfillment
Poland Sp. z o.o., Wrocław